A GRIEVOUS BURDEN

A NOVEL

Other books by Jo-Anne

Yesterday's Shadows

A Walking Shadow

Nets of Gold

Keeping Mum

Taking Stock

The Emperor's Women

Doin' It

The S.O.B.

The Quandary

No Smoke Without Fire

Romany Legacy

Check out the web page at
www.joannesouthernbooks.com

A GRIEVOUS BURDEN

A NOVEL

JO-ANNE SOUTHERN

Primix Publishing
11620 Wilshire Blvd
Suite 900, West Wilshire Center, Los Angeles, CA, 90025
www.primixpublishing.com
Phone: 1-800-538-5788

Published by Primix Publishing   08/19/2021

ISBN: 978-1-955177-33-7(sc)
ISBN: 978-1-955177-34-4(e)

Library of Congress Control Number: 2021917233

CONTENTS

Thou cam'st on earth to make the earth my hell.
A grievous burden was thy birth to me;
Tetchy and wayward was thy infancy;
Thy school days frightful, desperate, wild and furious;
Thy prime of manhood daring, bold and venturous;
Thy age confirm'd, proud, subtle, sly, and bloody,
More mild, but yet more harmful, kind in hatred;
What comfortable hour canst thou name
That ever grac'd me in thy company?

William Shakespeare, Richard 111

ONE

"What's for supper?" Steve asked as he let himself into the tiny cramped apartment.

He grimaced at the messy room, realizing it looked even more cluttered than when he left that morning. Their tiny apartment, a sublet furnished bedsitter, never looked tidy. He sighed irritably.

When they first moved in together Steve never noticed the disorder because they spent most of their time together in bed. Now the thrill was wearing off and, coming from a home where his neat freak mother ruled, he detested the slovenly apartment.

Jenny, did not look up from her work. The room was a shambles as she sewed a dress. Bits of lint, cloth and thread decorated the brown shag carpet and the one upholstered chair, while pieces of paper pattern, the fashion magazines she read, dirty cups, dishes, and cast off clothing littered the table. As he angrily slammed shut the door, she raised her head and her face lit up like a Christmas tree.

"Stevey, baby," she cried, dropping the dress on the floor. "Come here, sugar lips, and give me some of that honey," Draping herself around him, she hugged him hard.

Steve kissed her automatically as she ground herself against him.

From the moment Jenny discovered sex, she became insatiable. A typical teenager, she thought she had discovered something no one else knew about. He glanced around as he held her, tired, hungry and annoyed at finding the place still looking like a garbage dump.

Only this morning his last words to her were, "Please clean this place, Jenny, it looks awful."

"Yah, yah, yah," she had trilled, "another kiss, eh?" Jenny had lunged at him, but he sidestepped so her kiss landed on his cheek. Quickly opening the door and saying: "Sorry, I'm late for work," he'd made his escape.

Now he pushed her away by the shoulders and looked into her face. "Jenny, what's for supper? I'm famished."

She pulled a face and raised her eyes to heaven. "Surely you can make yourself something to eat? You're a big boy now, and I've got to finish this dress for tomorrow. You know it's the election meeting at the tennis club tomorrow afternoon, and I'm running for office. I've told you and told you." Furious and redfaced, she stood, hands on hips. "What do you think I am? I wanted a new dress, but, oh no," she whined, "You said we couldn't afford it, so here am I sewing my own, and you want me to cook your supper?" Her voice rising to a shriek, she burst into tears and flopped down on still open and rumpled bed-chesterfield, sobbing as though her heart would break.

"Aaw, Jenny, I am sorry, love, I'm sorry." Steve, sometimes too soft for his own good, gathered her into his arms and held her closely, patting her back soothingly. "I know what the election means to you and I know you wanted a new dress." He didn't, but it wasn't politic to admit it. "I'm really sorry."

Jenny raised her tearstained face and tried to smile at him, her mouth quivering, a practised enough actress to know how to milk tears for profit.

"Well, you know I can't do everything, Steve," she sniffled and sobbed, but more quietly now. "I'm doing my very best. Surely you can't expect more than that?"

Steve sighed, again she had turned it back on him. "I don't, Jenny, I don't. You get on with your dress and I'll make supper? Okay?"

"Okay," Tears sparkling on her lashes, Jenny smiled at him.

Wait until she told him she was pregnant. She found keeping a secret difficult as normally she spilled the beans immediately, but in this case she decided to wait until she was positive. Jenny meant to time her announcement exactly right because Steve always said he didn't want children until he was thirty-five, or they were married.

The question of marriage constantly presented itself, at Jenny's instigation of course, but Steve refused to consider what he called an outdated ritual. Marriage was merely a legal formality, he said, they were happy as they were and a formal marriage might cause problems. However, a smug Jenny was confidently positive once he knew she was carrying his own child, he might think differently.

Steve rummaged through the cupboards and the fridge looking for something edible. He found a dusty can of tomato soup in the cupboard and half a loaf of bread in the fridge freezer and sighed with annoyance. Undomesticated and childish, Jenny never thought of buying enough food for the week. She never knew what to buy and wandered around the store picking things up and putting them down. Nobody had ever taught her, was her excuse, although he thought she surely had learned the basics, even if it were by osmosis, when shopping with her mother. She couldn't cook worth a damn and much preferred to eat out.

Dirty dishes filled the sink as usual. He opened the can of soup and rinsed out a pot. Jenny never washed up, she left that to him.

"After all, Steve, if I cook the least you can do is wash up," her constant whine.

All well and good, he thought as he stirred the soup. Most of the time he did the cooking plus the dish washing. Her idea of cooking consisted of heating something out of a can or mixing it out of a box. No, Jenny could not cook, nor did she have any intentions of learning, from what he could see.

"Soup's on," he said as he pushed junk to one side of the messy table to make room for the soup bowls.

"Just a minute, just a minute!" Jenny navigated a tricky seam on her machine. "I'll be there in a minute."

The sewing machine belonged to her mother. Jenny took it one day when her parents were at work and so far her mother had not noticed, and if she had, had not said anything. Her mother was a talented seamstress, and from her Jenny had assimilated the knack of sewing. Not that anything Jenny made could compare to her mother's work, although in her own eyes it looked better. Why bother double sewing seams when nobody saw the inside? Why bother with fitted linings, or linings at all if it came to that, and who cared about straight seams if they didn't show?

Steve despondently sipped his soup and ate toast. This must stop. A man couldn't work all day then come home to find no supper waiting. Jenny must learn.

"Well, are you going to eat this or not?" he asked testily.

"In a minute," she said, not raising her head.

"It's going to get cold."

She glared at him. "All right, all right! It's my supper and if it's cold, it's cold. Stop nagging, Steve."

"Not much point in my cooking it then, was there?" he said loudly. Another argument was brewing. "You could have eaten it straight out of the can." Angrily Steve took her bowl and poured the soup back into the pan.

"Don't be such a martyr. I'll be there in a minute." Jenny, not the slightest bit hungry, had eaten two O'Henry's before he arrived home.

Her comments riled the still hungry Steve. "If you don't want it, I'll eat it," he said.

"So eat it! Eat it! Leave me alone." Jenny didn't look up and that made him even angrier. Pushing back his chair and grabbing his coat off the back of the chesterfield, he left, loudly slamming the door behind him. He headed to the local pub to have a few beers.

Jenny's head shot up in surprise when the door slammed, but she felt pleased he had gone. Good. Now she could get on with her dress. Stupid man, thinking she was at his beck and call.

Men were all the same, she thought, recalling how her mother sometimes used to nag to put her father in his place. Steve loved her, she was sure of that, and she loved him, but she was going to steer the ship. After all, she was more intelligent, had more schooling, was smarter than him. In her heart she recognized that Steve was unintelligent, but he was wonderful in bed and that made up for everything. Oh, yes, the sooner she got through to him what his role in the relationship was, the better. She hummed as she turned the dress right way out and held it up to check her handiwork.

The Stevens' cosy bungalow in Alta Vista sat nestled in an acre of land landscaped by Jim Stevens. A small swimming pool at the back sat amid carefully pruned willows and low bushes. Over the years they had added to the house, a wing to one side and a separate garage, turning the original garage into a large family room. It was luxurious in comparison to what it had been when they first moved in, and both were justifiably proud of their accomplishments.

In the family room, Jenny had just dropped her bombshell. Janet and Jim sat in a state of shock. Nobody spoke for a moment.

"Well, I never thought I would hear myself say this, but you are stupid!" Janet Stevens felt so angry she could have hit her daughter. With sudden tears in her eyes, she clamped her hand over her mouth to stop herself saying anything further. Oh, why had she said that? A million things she could have said, a hundred ways of smoothing the way, but no, she had blown her top.

Over the past months she and Jim had discussed Jennifer's relationship with Steve, a man they considered beneath their attractive, intelligent daughter. Now Jenny proved Janet's predictions correct as she triumphantly announced her pregnancy. Jenny, eighteen and completely selfentered, seemed determined to make Steve marry her despite their objections.

Some months earlier Janet had said to Jim, "You know Steve has no intentions of marrying her, don't you? I can tell he's using her. He's not the marrying type."

"Then she'll find that out the hard way, Jan." He was well aware of Janet's upset about this latest relationship also felt the same. "We can't do anything to sway her one way or the other. She's always been stubborn."

"I know that well enough; I ought to. Anyway, mark my words, if she can't get her own way with him, she'll do something stupid."

"What do you mean?" In Jim's eyes, Jenny could do no wrong, so for Janet to even intimate that his princess was less than perfect was fuel for an argument. "She's not stupid, Janet, she's simply a normal teenager and isn't doing anything her friends haven't done or will do."

Janet nodded. "Jenny is intelligent enough when it suits her, but you know she's incapable of thinking straight when she's determined. And she's determined to get Steve, whether he likes it or not. I know her well enough to predict the outcome of this infatuation."

"And what is that?" Jim looked angry and tight lipped.

"She'll get herself pregnant, thinking it will change his mind, but it won't. Steve will never marry her. I don't think he'll ever marry any woman."

Jim's face grew red with anger. She said nothing more, waiting for his temper to take over. "Honestly Janet, to speak in such a way of your own daughter! I'm disappointed in you. That girl has had the best education money can buy. She's had a good commonsense upbringing. She's been schooled in what's right and what's wrong. Even to suggest such a thing is ludicrous. I guarantee she'll never get pregnant to snare him."

"If you say so, Jim, but I think differently."

They argued for nearly an hour. Now two months later Jenny made her announcement. Still, when all was said and done, even if they had known of Jenny's intentions, they were powerless to stop her.

Janet's mind flashed to Steve. Steve Rigby, twenty-four, a well brought up young man, unfortunately lacked personality, brains and ambition. From their meeting in the coffee shop, at the mall where Jenny worked part-time at a gift shop, and a company employed him as a security guard, it had been a whirlwind romance. A romance they had tried to stop with little or no result. Within two months of that date, Jenny started living with Steve in a small furnished bedsitter in the downtown core.

Jim talked to him, needing to know Jenny was safe. At first meeting Steve appeared adult enough to know what he was getting into, but all Jim's words bounced off him. He seemed determined to continue seeing Jenny, despite the Stevens' misgivings.

Steve wanted to become a police officer, however, his love of firearms and a fanatical dedication to strong arm tactics did not endear him to many, particularly the police psychiatrists. Jenny told her parents, with a certain amount of pride, that four different police forces had rejected him. From that and other snippets of information, they realized Steve was a born loser.

According to Jenny it was always because someone else had the inside track, or they already filled the quota, or they were only accepting minorities; anything other than it being Steve's fault. While a fantastic physique and fitness were in his favour, the authorities wanted nothing more to do with him after seeing the results of the psychological tests.

The nature of these rejections worried Jim to the extent that he mentioned to Jenny that Steve might use force on her, but she, madly in love, hormones raging, assured them that he was all talk.

"Steve's a pussy cat," she said, "because he's into body building doesn't mean that he's a bully." She constantly made excuses for his failures.

Janet did not like Steve and did not try to hide it. She could see no good in him, rationalizing this move was Jenny's way of getting out of their control. It was her way of getting to live her own life, though she had no conception of exactly what an unprotected life meant.

Exactly what did she see in Steve, they often asked each other? Both disliked him on sight. His hooded eyes, his hulking body and his shifty manner made them uncomfortable. Knowing Jenny was determined and stubborn when it came to getting what she wanted, would dig in her heels at the slightest suggestion of parental disapproval, they gritted their teeth and said nothing.

Even when Jenny gleefully announced her intention of living with Steve, again they expressed their dismay, but said nothing to persuade her or dissuade her. They had earlier discussed what might happen if this came to pass, as she had been hinting. They fervently hoped the relationship might die a quick death but unfortunately it did not. Starry eyed, Jennifer dreamed of a large wedding, booking the hall and the church before they could stop her. Steve, of course, put a top to her plans.

And now this bombshell.

"You sure called this one, Jan. You were right, I'm sorry to say," Jim said quietly as he looked across at her.

"Right about what?" Jenny asked curiously.

"Nothing." Janet said, looking away.

Jennifer, smirking like the cat who had drunk the cream, sat with her arms around her flat stomach as if protecting her unborn child. Thrilled about the baby, she resented their cold reaction to her fabulous news, but then they were a couple of old fogies and what did they know? Smug, she rejoiced at the expression on their faces, gone were the days when they could order her around or make decisions for her. She had her own life now. Hadn't she already proved that she was an adult?

Jim's mind raced madly, trying to find something to say that might get through to Jenny. He felt inadequate in this moment of crisis, but tried to control his temper. No matter what, he must talk calmly and plainly.

"Jenny, you simply don't use the brains God gave you. You're an intelligent young woman, but you're much too impulsive," he said evenly. "Why didn't you use some common sense? Getting pregnant isn't going to make things any easier. You've hardly finished school, and don't think for one moment that Steve is going to marry you because you're in the family way That does not make him feel any differently than he does now."

Jenny blew. "What the heck do you know, Dad?" Jim winced. "He *is* so going to marry me. Oh, what do you know about anything? This is the 1990's. You are so old fashioned, both of you! Well, I don't live in your Victorian world. I live in today's world. You don't understand, and you never will. Honestly, it's not fair. I can't live by your rules, and I don't have to live like they used to in the dark ages when you were a kid." She knew how to hurt her father, she had always known. "Don't worry, I won't be asking you to dig in your pocket," she spat.

"Jenny! How dare you talk to your father like that?" Janet said, hurt to the quick. How ungrateful could their only child be? Yet they had only themselves to blame for spoiling her rotten, for letting her have her own way in everything. No matter, she saw no need for Jenny to put down her father. She quickly glanced at Jim who looked angry and hurt.

"You too, Mum," Jenny turned on her mother, shaking her finger. "You butt out as well. You always take his side. Both of you are the same. You never think about me, about what I want. I'm an adult, not a five-year-old child. I *know* what I want, and it's not living here with you two old fogies. It's always been what you two want, what *you* think I should do, with you meddling in everything, it's never what *I* want. It's like I'm not allowed to think for myself. I'm sick of your eternal questions and your constant interference in my life."

Standing up, she waved her arms as if to make them understand better. "It's *my* life, you know, not yours. I'm not a baby and I'm tired of you telling me what I should or should not do. Understand? This is *my* life!" She looked at their shocked faces and smiled exultantly. It was time they got the picture, began to understand. "You're both jealous of me because I'm young." She tossed her head, knowing that would upset them. "You think I know nothing, but I know a lot more than you, so stick with your life-in-a-rut and stop interfering in mine."

Subsiding into a sullen lump, she flopped down on the sofa and glared at them, her face a mask of martyred insolence. All they ever did was spoil any fun offered to her, they never let her do anything, and what did they know anyway? They were a pair of oldfashioned old morons, so how could they possibly know what she felt? How could they know what it felt like to love someone as much as she loved Steve?

Janet went to make tea. The chore got her out of the room while she struggled to control her anger. Her mind was in turmoil. Jenny, never easy to deal with, seemed to get worse as a teenager, although they kept telling themselves it was a phase. Her school teachers reinforced this view, talking about the various stages of childhood and pointing out kids soon outgrew them. Yet it seemed Jenny never outgrew her phases. She always was so cocksure, convinced she knew everything, though back then, Janet constantly reminded herself, what teenager didn't have that attitude? Yet, thinking back on her own teen years, she surely had never been so prickly. At Jenny's age, she had been reasonably well adjusted, but then her parents were very demanding as to her conduct, and, of course, it was a different age.

It always came back to the same thing, they had been too permissive with Jenny. Even so, Janet knew she was deluding herself because it was not as simple as Jenny's behaviour as a teenager. Janet's mind flashed back to the years of Jenny's childhood, all the trials and tribulations, all the upsets.

Getting the china cups from the china cabinet in her newly refurbished kitchen, she set a tray. Jenny's vituperation had devastated Jim: she could see how disappointed he was in his little princess.

When they married Janet wanted a child to complete her happiness, but she never conceived. After ten years of trying, they adopted Jenny through an agency, bringing her home when she was only five days old. Yet they had not told Jenny of her adoption because something always seemed to crop up that decided them against it. Gradually it became something rarely remembered and over the years they tended to forget Jenny was not their biological child. Jenny had always been a difficult child and, as she matured, they realized that news of her adoption could turn her against them completely. In her vivid imagination, she would probably think herself of noble birth, or wealthy parents. Thankfully the authorities had sealed the records, so unless Janet or Jim told her, nobody would ever know. Luckily when Jenny began school, they requested her birth certificate before she was enrolled, but never since. Jim kept it in his office safe. However, as was the norm in such cases, it showed them as the parents and did not show the birth mother, and fortunately Jenny was the same blood type as Janet.

Both wanted the best for their daughter. While Jenny was no genius, she could achieve good scholastic standards if she applied herself. Headstrong and strong willed, if she decided she did not like a subject she simply refused to learn. A subject she had known perfectly the day before, she denied any knowledge of the next day, although a month down the road she could recite it word for word.

They had dreamed of her attending university, of getting the education both of them would have given their eye teeth for, but, typical of all children, Jenny could not see any farther into the future than the next five minutes. Capable of far more than she ever accomplished, Jim often became angry when she brought home bad grades.

He was doing well at work so they could afford to pay for extra tutoring. He bought her a set of Encyclopaedia Britannica so she could study at home, and everything was done to make learning easier, but Jenny stubbornly refused to buckle down if it took her away from her social life.

She liked ballet lessons and the glee club, she attended school plays and football games, she went to the movies with friends. Some nights she slept over at a friend's house, experimenting with makeup and hairstyles, anything to get away from studying. They had allowed her demands every time, trying to assure each other she would soon move out of this phase and begin to settle down.

While Jenny got her own way, everything was peachy. The constant arguments and hysterical screaming matches brought on by trying to make her do something she didn't want to do, they alleviated by relenting. Janet nodded, thinking back. Yes, they catered to her every whim, sent her to the best schools, paid for the extra tuition. She went to modelling classes to give her poise; she took dance lessons, music lessons, riding lessons, went to ski school, music camp. They wanted her to have everything they had never had.

Unfortunately Jenny repaid them with peevish complaints. She needed confirmation that she was better than her school chums and, unless her parents were giving her something, or something was done for her, her world was black and depressing. Janet realized it had not taken Jenny long to learn how to make their lives miserable. However, when she got her own way, which became the norm, then the world was all right, everyone basked in her favour and she became a ray of sunshine. For the sake of a quiet life they had let her rule the roost, but now they were paying for it.

Janet sighed as she waited for the kettle to boil. They had envisioned such a bright future for her, dreamed of her marrying a young man with prospects, living in a pleasant house, enjoying a career. Both looked forward to grandchildren, but not like this. As a single mother Jenny could not look after a child properly. At eighteen, she was a child herself.

Look at the place the couple were living! A flea pit, a shabby furnished bedsitter. Yet at home Jenny lived in comparative comfort in their four bedroom Alta Vista bungalow and that alone should have meant Jenny surely had higher standards.

Janet blew out a breath of annoyance as she put the tea pot on the tray. She wiped her eyes and blew her nose before returning to the family room.

"So do you want to have an abortion?" Jim was asking stonily as she entered.

Oh, dear God no, Jim, how could you suggest that, Janet thought, almost dropping the tray.

"No way, Pops." Jenny knew her father hated being called that. "I *want* to have the baby," she said smugly, sure of herself, a cocky smirk on her face. "Oh, don't worry I'm not asking you to have anything to do with it. It'll be my baby, mine and Steve's."

"Jenny!" Janet said, upset. Tears sprang to her eyes and she left the room again before she said something she might regret.

TWO

At his local, the Grape Vine, Steve swivelled on the bar stool, resting his elbows behind him on the bar, as he eyeballed the room. Still early, only a few tables held men on their way home from work. As he turned round on his stool to order another beer, the door opened and one of his work mates sauntered over.

"Yoh, Steve." A hand tapped him on the shoulder, "How's tricks, buddy?"

"Hi, Wayne," he said, as he turned to face his one time partner on the night shift.

"Still with the new chick?" Wayne asked, leering. Wayne thought Jenny a real dish, even if she did look like jail bait.

"Yes." Steve said stiffly, his face closed.

"Oops! Sorry I asked." Wayne turned to look at the other patrons, hoping to spot someone more congenial.

"Want a brew?" Steve asked, not wanting to lose his company.

"Sure," Wayne said, chummy again. He never refused a freebie.

The barman turned on the television and they sat watching a replay golf game, both arm chair experts, although neither of them had ever played.

"Steve! How are you?" At the sound of a familiar voice Steve turned to face Rita, an ex-girl friend.

"Fine 'Ree, and you?"

"I'm great, actually I'm fantastic, but then you know that, eh?" Rita chortled lewdly.

"Oh yeah," Steve laughed, winking. Rita was one of the most sexually inventive females that he knew.

"So what's new? Still with that little girl?" Rita could not help sneering. She didn't like Jenny because Jenny was the reason Steve had broken up with her.

"Sort of."

"What does that mean? Sort of?" The remark sounded promising and Rita claimed the next bar stool as the customer left. "Tell me all about it, Steve." She smelled a break up. The last time she had talked to Steve he had sung Jenny's praises to the high heavens.

"Oh, it's nothing. What do you want to drink?" He put his arm over her shoulders and she smiled.

Rita decided not to push it, at least he was not telling her to get lost this time. "A vodka and orange, please, Stevey." Edging closer, she put her hand on his thigh. "So, do you want to tell me all about it."

By ten-thirty neither of them was feeling any pain. At twelve they left together, and when Steve woke, he was in Rita's bed.

When he got home at two-thirty, Jenny was asleep. Thankfully he got into bed without waking her and sighed as he dropped off, knowing he was in for the third degree in the morning.

"Maybe we should go around to their place," Janet said worriedly. It had been two weeks since Jenny had dropped by and normally she came twice a week to cadge something, or to borrow money - not that she ever repaid it.

Jim sighed irritably. "Now, Jan, you know there's no way that I'd visit that place. She has to invite us and up to now she hasn't done so. Maybe she doesn't want us to see how she lives, have you thought about that? You've seen that building. From the outside it's a dump, and I can well imagine it's twice as bad on the inside. Anyway, she knows how we feel about dropping in on people unannounced. It isn't done."

"But, Jim," Janet argued, "that applies to friends, not family. She's our daughter. She's not a friend or acquaintance, so surely we can go to see her? We don't know whether or not she's all right." She drew in a deeply tremulous breath. "If they had a phone. . ."

Jim put down his paper again and looked at her, grim faced. "Well, they don't, and I want you to promise me, Janet, that you won't go to see her. I don't think she'd want you to drop in unannounced anyway. Remember what we talked about? The girl has to stand on her own two feet, and that's what Jenny wants. I admit she made a tremendous mistake. I know that and you know that, but as much as we love her and want her to be safe, she chose this route, so leave her be. If she needs something, she'll be knocking at the door soon enough. She always is." Jim rustled his paper and disappeared behind it. Discussion over.

Janet felt extremely worried. Her teenage daughter now pregnant, and living with a man neither of them trusted was cause for worry. Suppose Steve became violent and hurt Jenny? He seemed so shifty eyed, and she didn't like the way he could never look anyone in the eye. Suppose Jenny was too sick to leave the apartment? Suppose . . . ?

Sighing with anxiety, she glanced at Jim. Apparently unconcerned, he pored over the sports page. In her heart she knew Jim probably worried as much as she, but from experience knew he would never lower himself to cater to Jenny now. People could only push him so far and no farther. Jenny had disappointed him and Jim might never forgive her.

What to do, what to do? Sighing again, she picked up her library book.

Steve sat pouting sullenly, his mind a million miles away, his eyes glazed, as Jenny laced into him.

". . . and another thing. Don't think you can waltz in and out of this place as though you were a single man. You're not single now, not as far as I'm concerned." She slammed the palm of her hand on the table to get his attention. "I'm your wife, common-law though it may be, and we're going to get married and do things properly and legally. I sent out the invitations to my relatives yesterday, but I suppose it'll be a while before they answer. You'd better get me the names and addresses of your lot and then I can mail them off as well."

Steve heard the last bit. "Just a minute here. What's all this about relatives and invitations? What for and why?" Steve stared at her in consternation.

"The wedding, you stupid idiot, the wedding. You know I booked the hall and the church weeks ago. I made your cummerbund yesterday and one for your best man."

"What fucking wedding?" Steve leapt to his feet, knocking his coffee mug onto the floor. It rolled under the table. Even as he spoke, he wondered how long it would take her to pick it up.

"Our wedding, you moron. What did you think? You thought I'd live in sin for ever? Talk sense." Jenny walked to the kitchen area and noisily started clattering the dirty plates.

Steve seethed with rage and his voice sounded tight. "Wait a cotton picking minute here. I don't remember ever saying I was going to marry you." As the words sank into his consciousness, he felt sick to his stomach.

"Oh, yes, you did," Jenny blazed at him, dropping a plate into the sink so hard that it cracked. "In a moment of passion maybe, but you certainly did. Why did I book the church and the hall and write the invitations? You saw me doing it. You knew what I was doing."

Steve had seen her writing out envelopes and cards, but thought it was something to do with her precious tennis club. He hadn't been much interested, truth be known, and had said nothing, going out to the gym and leaving her to it.

"Do you mean to say you're not going to marry me after all this?" Jenny stared at him aghast, her face tight and pale. "Looks like my parents were right about you, and to think I was so sure of you. How could you do this to me?"

Steve saw her agitation and knew that upsetting Jenny never got anyone anywhere. "Now just a minute, just a minute." He kept his voice calm, "Let's sit and talk about this calmly. You say that I said I'd marry you. I don't remember that and surely it's something a man wouldn't forget. Was I drunk?"

"Thanks a whole lot!" She flounced around and stood with her back to him. "No, you were not drunk. You know how I feel about booze. I'd never have slept with you if you'd been drunk, I can't stand the smell of the stuff. Thanks for the insult, I don't think. You mean you'd have had to be drunk to ask me to marry you?" Whirling around indignant, she threw the dirty dish cloth at him.

Putting up his hand, he caught the cloth. Water ran down his arm and onto his clean shirt. "No, that isn't what I meant at all, and well you know it. I can't remember this proposal you talk about. I don't want to get married."

"Oh, my God!" Jenny wailed, "What am I going to do now? How dare you turn your back on me! You bloody rat. When those RSVPs come in, *you* can answer them. And you call the church *and* the hall *and* the band *and* the caterer." She took and deep breath and screamed. "You can cancel *everything*!"

That stunned Steve as he knew nothing of these arrangements.

"What caterer?" he asked, "What band? Where was I when all this was going on? Who was going to pay for that lot? Not me, I didn't order it." He felt very self-righteous. What a fool he'd been to get involved with a child like Jenny.

She had been so very sweet when he first took her out and he almost, but not quite, fell in love with her when they started to live together, that was when her slovenly habits and her childishness cured him in short order. Steve's brain now actively sought a way out of his dilemma. Maybe he could leave Ottawa, maybe he could get himself a job in another city.

". . .so there you are," she was saying, red faced and angry."You'll have to cancel them. I'm not going to be treated like this, Steve. You said you loved me, you talked me into coming to live with you. I was a virgin when I met you, and as soon as I let you sleep with me, you don't want me," She burst into tears and wailed loudly like a small child wanting her own way.

Steve sighed with exasperation. "Do leave off, Jen. Those tears are all an act. I've seen you do it a hundred times and the act is wearing thin, if you don't mind me saying so. It might work with your parents, but not with me." He stood and reached for his jacket that hung on the doorknob.

"Oh, no, you don't," Jenny said as she rushed to stand in front of the door, arms out, blocking his way. "You're not leaving here until we settle this thing for once and for all. You *have* to marry me. You can't *not* marry me." The tears were gone and her eyes blazed with something akin to hate.

"Come on now, Jenny, move your body." Steve reached for her shoulders to move her away from the door.

"Don't you dare lay a finger on me, Steve Rigby," she warned, "I'll scream so bloody loudly that the neighbours will send for the police."

"Shit, how childish can you be?" Steve slumped into a chair and stared up at her. What a child, and what an idiot he felt for becoming involved.

Suddenly Jenny started to take off her clothes. Steve sat on the arm of the chesterfield and watched. She used sex as a weapon. Strangely enough he felt nothing, only surprise that she resorted to such tactics to win this particular argument.

Dropping her bra on the floor, she stood naked before him. Steve didn't move. Slowly she moved toward him and, opening her legs, dropped onto his lap and leaned toward him, cupping her breasts with her hands, offering them to him.

It didn't take much of this before he became aroused and before he knew it he was pumping into her as she lay on the floor.

"Harder, harder," she moaned and raised her legs over his shoulders. Steve lost his senses completely and rammed into her, not caring if he hurt her. Right then he wanted his own gratification and, in a way, he hoped he hurt her. Look what she was doing to him.

As they lay on the floor gasping for breath, she kissed him gently.

"Don't ever leave me, Steverino," she said softly. "You don't have to marry me. I was wrong, but don't ever leave me."

"All right. I won't leave you, Jenny." Sated, he promised, not meaning a word.

THREE

Jim and Janet sat at the kitchen table, drinking coffee as she told him about their holiday arrangements.

"That's it, all arranged. I have to confirm in two days," Janet said, pleased. She passed back the travel folder.

"Are you sure you want to go to Vegas?" Jim asked as he opened the glossy brochure again.

"Of course I do. Why did I book it if I didn't?" Janet felt annoyed.

Honestly, sometimes Jim treated her like a child, a person unable to make a decision. Janet had always wanted to go to Vegas, and must have mentioned it to him a million times. This tour took them to Las Vegas, then on to Los Angeles. She wanted to see Beverly Hills and Universal Studios, and maybe see a film star.

Jim, however, disliked travelling which was why they rarely went further than two hundred miles from home, and then only by car. Heartily sick and tired of Niagara Falls, Montreal, Quebec City, Nova Scotia and Newfoundland, she thought it about time they went to a destination of her choice.

"How long will we be away?" he asked anxiously as he scanned the coloured pictures of the Caesar's Palace casino and exteriors of the other luxurious hotels.

"Ten days."

"Huh! Look at this, nothing but gambling night and day. Now I know why they call it Sin City." He pointed his pipe stem at the brochure.

Jim wasn't going to annoy her, she decided, not so close to leaving.

"That's right, Jim," she said evenly. "But there's lots of other things to do, you know. Look at all the wonderful shows we could see. When we get to Los Angeles, we'll visit Universal Studios. We can go around Rodeo Drive, and see all those posh stores. We can see the star's homes on a bus tour. There are a million things to do."

"It's complete waste of money if you ask me," he said grumpily.

"But nobody is asking you, Jim," she said, trying to be patient. "It's about time I decided where we went. I work hard all year and I'm entitled to decide where we go after all these years of catering to you. If you don't want to go, say so and I'll ask Betty to go with me." Jim's head shot up. Go away without him? ". . . then you can go wherever you want to for your holidays. As for me, I'm going to Vegas."

He sighed deeply. "As long as you want to go, we'll go, but don't you start complaining when it gets too hot." His voice wasn't exactly full of enthusiasm, Janet thought, but at least he was coming around. "It's much hotter than it is here and you complain enough about our summers. Just you wait, my girl, you've never felt anything like that heat in all your life."

Jim was not going to spoil it for her this time, she thought, smiling.

"Never mind the heat, Jim. They have air conditioning everywhere." So what if it were hot?"

"Gawd. And it's a foreign country. I suppose we have to get our passports renewed."

"Oh golly. Where are they?" Janet became flustered. She had forgotten they needed passports. Two years earlier they had taken them out when the bowling club talked into Jim going to New Orleans. Unfortunately, due to the sudden accidental death of the team skipper and his wife, they did not go and had never used the passports.

Running upstairs, she started checking the drawers in her dressing table.

"What's the occasion?" he asked when he saw Jenny wore her best dress, and even shoes and stockings. He noticed she had set her hair and it rippled in deep waves until it flipped at the end. The same style she wore when he first set eyes on her, he thought. Also, she wore lipstick and eye shadow. What was she up to now?

"What did you say?" Steve shot to his feet and glared at her, eyes popping in shock.

"I'm pregnant. Isn't it wonderful and fantastic?" A beaming Jenny threw her arms around him and snuggled nto his neck.

Steve felt numb. He hadn't bargained for this.

"How did that happen?" he asked, shocked. He looked down at her as she hung around his neck. His hands clenched into fists, not touching her.

"The usual way, about nine weeks ago I'd say," Jenny laughed up at him. "How does it feel to be nearly a daddy?"

Steve pushed her away and she plopped down onto the for once closed up bed-chesterfield with a thud. His eyes flitted around the room, noticing it marvellously tidy. So she must have known what his reaction was going to be, he thought. His mind skittered around, seeking a way out.

"Now look here, Jenny. You said you were going to look after the birth control, didn't you?"

Jenny pouted. She had not expected this reaction, and after she had taken so much care to clean the place and smarten herself as well. She thought he might take her out to supper and they could talk about the wonderful news.

"Yes, I did. I did look after it, this happened . . . " Why was he looking so angry? Why was he not kissing her?

Steve interrupted. "This happened when you forgot to take your pill, that's when this happened," he accused angrily.

"But, Steve," she rushed to assure him, "I never did forget, honest I didn't. It was when the doctor changed my prescription because the other one was making me feel sick all the time, but I did take my pill. Honest to God, I did!" Jenny felt cold inside. This was not the way she had visualized it at all.

The doctor *had* changed her prescription, but warned her to desist from unprotected sex for at least a month while her body adjusted to the new formula. Jenny was smart enough to keep that secret from Steve, although it was not the real reason. Purposely she had not taken any pills for two weeks and sure enough got pregnant. Now he *had* to marry her.

"In that case we'll go to your doctor and ask him how this happened. That man is responsible for your pregnancy, and he'll have to pay for the abortion." Steve glared at her. Stupid little girl. No way was she saddling him with another mouth to feed. Steve felt trapped.

Jenny's mouth dropped open. "What? What do you mean?" she yelled incredulously, "You want to murder your own child? That's terrible. Wait until I tell your mother what you said! She'll beat the daylights out of you when she finds out."

Jenny thought Steve's mother about as understanding as a porcupine, nothing motherly about her in Jenny's eye. Esther Rigby ruled her household with an iron fist. Steve's bus driver father, Frank, a wimp, who all but jumped when his wife spoke, and brothers Steve and brother Shawn learned at an early age who ruled the household. All kissed ass and catered to her. Jenny despised Mrs. Rigby, thinking her crude and uneducated, although in a way Jenny admired her for her strong stand on everything and her superlative housekeeping and cooking.

While Esther could not condone Steve's living in sin with Jenny, she, in turn, openly admired Jenny's manners and education. Jenny knew this from Esther's attitude. Once, in a rare moment of confidence, Esther said that maybe Jenny could turn Steve into a real man, that as parents they knew Steve was not bright, though they never voiced this publicly. Esther said Jenny was a live wire, someone who might get Steve off his backside, someone who might make something of him.

Jenny knew it was also in her favour that she came from a wellheeled family who lived in a classy part of town.

Steve exploded. "What the hell do you think you're talking about? You'll not say anything to my mother! She doesn't need you telling her anything." He thumped the table with his fist.

"You can't stop me!" Jenny blazed. "Who do you think you are, telling me what I can or cannot do? I'll tell her if I want to, and you can't stop me."

Steve raised his hand to her, but even as he did so he knew he could never hit her. She deserved it, God knows she deserved it, but something stayed his hand and he rubbed the back of his head instead. Jenny noticed this reflex and smothered a giggle.

As tough as he talked, Steve knew he was nothing but a wiener like his wimpy father.

"You need a strong-willed woman like your mother and I'm the one. Anyway, now you'll *have* to marry me!"

He hated the look of triumph on her face. "No! I will not have to marry you," he said churlishly, "I asked you to take your pills and you promised you would. I told you that I didn't want children, and you agreed that we should wait until we married. . .*if* we ever married," White faced and angry, his voice became a hoarse whisper. "I won't marry you, Jenny, and nothing on this earth will make me marry you. You say you want this baby, go ahead and have it. But don't expect me to look after the pair of you. This was your decision, Jenny, not mine."

Jenny cried and cried. Steve, stoically looking straight ahead, made no move to comfort her. He noticed her peeping at him through her fingers as she weighed up the situation. When she cried louder, seeking attention, he ignored her. He stared miserably into space, wondering how he could get out of the situation. It was the worst day of his life when he had taken up with Jenny who was nothing but a pampered brat. What had he seen in her, apart from a willing bed partner? Rita, oh Rita, if only I had listened to her, he thought. Rita had adult ideas, behaved like an adult, and he had become tired of babysitting Jenny, the spoiled child.

"Cut out the bloody waterworks, for Christ's sake," he snapped. "You can turn it on and off like a tap. *I* know it, and you know it. It isn't going to work, Jenny, none of these hysterics are going to work. Why don't you go home to your parents?" He touched her on the shoulder, but she shrugged away from his hand.

"No way," she said, gulping back her sobs. "I'm not going back home. Do you think I can walk in and announce I'm back and I'm pregnant? My father would be after you with a shotgun, never mind what my mother might do." Jenny glared up at him through filled eyes and sniffled loudly, childishly wiping her nose on the back of her hand.

"You can't stay here now, Jenny," he spoke softly, not wanting to start her shouting again. "Surely you can see that. You need someone to look after you."

"I want *you* to look after me," she exclaimed, looking bewildered. "You said you'd always look after me. Remember?"

"And *you* said you could look after the birth control. Remember?" He leaned back and put his hands behind his head. Now she seemed calmer, he felt better.

"I did!" she expostulated. "I've told you. It was the new pill the doctor gave me. It isn't my fault that I am pregnant. But I want this baby . . . our baby . . . your baby," She smiled at him, such a sweet smile that Steve felt his heart melt. If she only wasn't so darn beautiful.

The day they bumped into each other at a Rideau Centre coffee shop, he felt thrilled that such an exquisite welldressed girl actually spoke to him. After they shared two coffees, where she hung onto his every word, he felt like a young god. Her looks of adoration turned his head and all afternoon he walked around in a daze. Those deep brown eyes of hers, almond shaped, slightly tilted, they were gorgeous and hypnotized him. He thought her perfect, her auburn hair, her trim figure, her pert way of talking.

The thrill lingered for about two months while he took her out to movies and dances, then they moved in together. At first she had been everything he was looking for in a woman, but now he knew she had only pretended to be the adult person he wanted. The way she had oohed and aahed at his past, the way she had made him feel the most intelligent, the handsomest, the bravest man she had ever met. She convinced him that she could not live without him, convinced him that he could not live without her. All lies and deception. It did not take him long to discover the real Jenny: lazy, untidy, unpunctual, a spendthrift, and a terrible liar.

And she stole. For a while he had thought his memory was playing tricks, until once, when she thought he was sleeping one morning after a late shift, he saw her take money from his wallet. Money had disappeared before, but he thought maybe he had lost it, or spent it. After that, he hid his wallet when he got home. Money didn't vanish any more and it hurt him terribly that she stole from him. Why didn't she ask if she needed money?

Much to his chagrin, she quit her part time job so now his pay was their only income, although he knew she begged money from her parents. Her sloppy housekeeping infuriated him because his mother's house was always spotless. Jenny didn't even wash his clothes, expecting him to do his own washing, saying she wasn't his servant. Thankfully his uniform and shirts went to the laundry for which he got a company allowance. What doubly annoyed him was the fact she took her own clothes home to her mother who washed and ironed them, but never took anything of his.

If their living arrangements were anything like marriage maybe he could have made a go of it, but this arrangement was like living single and looking after an adult child. Steve became tired of cooking, doing his own washing and the food shopping while she lazed around or went down to the tennis club.

That was another thing, the blasted tennis club. Jenny never took him and he guessed she felt ashamed to be seen with him. All those toffee-nosed friends of hers would probably have looked down on him, a lowly security guard. That he did not like her going made no difference, as she went to the club on most fine afternoons, and in the evenings on Saturday and Sunday. It was a good arrangement at first, because at weekends he went carousing with buddies and visited his parents, although soon his mother began asking when he was going to bring Jenny for supper. When he broached the subject, Jenny told him she couldn't make it on Saturday or Sunday because of tournaments, but she could go one night in the week. When Steve argued they did not play tennis at night, she insisted the club had both indoor and outdoor floodlit courts.

Going to visit his parents was not a good arrangement during the week because Steve could not stay out late on a week night. The drive took almost an hour, sometimes more, which did not leave much time for visiting when they had to leave so early. He must get up at five-thirty to get to work before six-thirty.

"So where does this leave us?" Jenny asked tremulously, bringing him back to the present.

She loved him so much, she thought, as she gazed at his pale face. His muscles were well defined even in his uniform. Jenny loved the way he made love to her, no one else could turn her on like Steve. How could she ever find another lover like him, how could she stand to have anyone else's hands on her body? It didn't bear thinking about.

But the baby. What about her baby? No way she could let Steve leave her, and no way she was going to leave him.

"It leaves us where we were ten minutes ago," he said stonily, "With you going back home, me staying here until the lease is up. I can't afford to leave with that hanging over me."

She looked at him with a passion in her eyes that was a wish to have her own way.

"No! Don't ask me to do that, Steve. I love you so much that I'll do anything for you, but I won't leave you to go back home." A lone tear trickled down one perfect cheek as she gazed at him with wide loved filled eyes.

"But you can't stay here, Jenny!" Steve looked at her, steeling his heart against the way she looked and any solutions she may suggest. Jenny was very inventive.

"But, Steve, you said you loved me," Her eyes welled with tears. "You said you'd never leave me," she sobbed.

"But I'm not leaving you. *You* are leaving me."

Jenny was suddenly panic stricken. Surely he didn't mean it. "No! Never! I love you, Steve, please don't turn your back on me. I love you so much. I adore you."

"Stop it, Jenny," Steve said quietly. "Don't say that. Nobody should adore another person, that talk is for prayers. I don't need that responsibility."

She stared at him wide eyed, tears trickling down her cheeks. When Jenny cried, her eyes did not become red.

"What responsibility? Me loving you? Where's the responsibility in that?" She wiped her cheeks with her hands.

He threw his hands out, palm up, trying to make her see. "You're putting pressure on me. You want to make me feel guilty, you want me to marry you, and you want to have the baby. It's all pressure and I don't need it. You know I can't afford it either. You know only too well what I earn." He turned away from her not wanting to see the pain on her face, not wanting to see her tears and the frightened lost look in her eyes.

"But there's no pressure, Steve, I want you to keep loving me like I love you," she begged, pulling him around to look at her. "We don't need much money. We can work things out. Please, Steve, don't push me away, I'll do anything, anything at all so you'll let me stay." Her face crinkled as though she were going to cry again.

Steve sighed deeply. What he wouldn't give for a strong drink right now. "You mean it, Jen? You mean what you say? You'll do *anything* for me?"

"Oh, yes, I do, I do," she said, her eyes shining, beginning to look relaxed, thinking she had won.

He stared at her, his eyes narrow slits. "So have an abortion, then we'll take it from there."

"No! No!" she gasped. "You're a murderer. How can you want to kill your own child?" Horrified, Jenny sprang to her feet and landed a hard blow to the side of Steve's head with her fist. He grabbed her arm as she was swinging it back to strike him again.

"Murderer! Murderer!" she screamed at the top of her lungs as she struggled wildly to free her arm from his grip.

"Stop it, Jen, stop it." He shook her hard trying to bring her to her senses. Completely hysterical, she continued screaming and he didn't know what to do. She went on and on until he became frantic and when he tried to put his hand over her mouth, she bit him and screamed even louder.

"Murderer!"

Someone hammered on the door. Steve looked toward it but could not let go of Jenny who twisted frenziedly in his arms. They knocked again and still she shrieked and screeched.

Then the superintendent, using his passkey, opened the door. A small crowd of neighbours gawped in at them.

"What'sa going on?" he asked. "You gotta trouble?"

Jenny stopped screaming long enough to look at him.

"I fetch police, yes, missus?" he asked.

"No. No police," Steve said letting go of Jenny. "She's very upset about something. Hysterical. We don't want the police."

"You stoppa the noise, eh? The neighbours they complain."

"Sorry about that. We won't be making any more noise, folks," Steve said to the gawking people standing in the doorway, glad for once that it didn't resemble a garbage tip. "The show is over. You can leave now." He automatically spoke in his official security guard voice and they moved away, muttering to each other.

Jenny had the grace to look shamefaced as the superintendent closed the door and left them staring blankly at each other.

Steve sat on the couch. He glanced at her, trying to gauge her mood. "Let's sit and talk about this quietly, Jenny. No more screaming and yelling, only talking."

She sat in the chair, put her hands on her knees and leaned toward him. "Do you want me to leave?" she asked petulantly.

Stone faced, he stared at her. He wasn't going to back down again. "Yes, I do. How many times do I have to tell you?"

"All right, I'll leave, not the way you want me to, but I *will* leave." Grim faced, she went to the closet, and rummaged around on the shelf.

Steve sighed with relief, thinking she was going to pack her clothes, when she turned to him with his revolver in her hands. Her hand shaking with the weight of it, she pointed it at her temple.

Steve leapt to his feet. Had he removed the bullets, or was it still loaded? He hesitated for a split second.

"Goodbye, lover. I love you so very much, Steve. Goodbye," she said, smiling at him through her tears as she tried to pull the trigger, but the gun was too heavy for her. Dropping it to waist height, she gripped it in both hands and raised it to her forehead. As she did so, Steve grabbed it and wrested it away.

Pushing her down onto the chesterfield, he put his face very close to hers. White faced and grim, he was infuriated beyond belief.

"Don't you ever, *do you hear me?* Don't you ever do anything so stupid again."

Her voice was dead sounding. "I don't want to live if I can't have you, Steve. It's no good without you. I'd sooner be dead." She stared at him, her face devoid of emotion. What the hell was she thinking, Steve wondered as he gazed into her blank eyes? Maybe she was deranged. She sure acted that way.

With shaking hands, he checked the gun. It was not loaded, but Jenny could not have known that. God damn it, she was going to kill herself right in front of him. Putting the gun back in the holster, he placed it back on the shelf and shut the closet door.

Jenny lay on the sofa sobbing. "You want to get rid of me and I can't live without you, Steve. I can't live without you."

Sighing with irritation, he sat by her side and put his hand on her arm. "Don't talk so silly, Jenny. Of course you can live without me. What am I, that you should try to kill yourself?"

"You're the love of my life, that's what you are," Jenny said, her voice full of passion, sitting up and looking at him tearfully. "You don't seem to realize how much I feel for you. I've told you and told you how much I love you." Her lip curled peevishly, "But you don't love me, you want to get rid of me. Me, and your baby." She leaned against him and taking his hand, put it on her stomach. "Your baby is feeling abandoned and lonely. His very own father doesn't want him."

Steve snatched his hand back, stood and paced the tiny space. "Do stop it, Jenny. All you have to do is go back home."

"But you said you were going to marry me," she accused.

"I don't ever remember saying that. I'm *not* going to marry you." He picked up his jacket and made for the door.

"Go on. Leave me, you heartless sod," she yelled, "Leave me here, alone and pregnant. You'd better take that gun with you, or you might find me dead when you come back." She smiled grimly, standing hands on hips.

Steve took the gun and holster out of the closet. "Surely you're not that stupid." He paused, his hand on the door knob, and stared at her. "Look at you, a young woman, a beautiful young woman, not even out of her teens, wanting to kill herself," he scoffed, "I thought you had more brains than that, Jen. You keep telling me how intelligent you are, but you're not clever at all. You're stupid, plain damned stupid."

"I am not! How dare you call me stupid? I'm very intelligent and I have a much better education than you."

"Go on! Throw it in my face one more time before I leave. Sure, I didn't have your advantages, but I act like an adult and know what I'm doing. Try using your brain for once. You need to go to a shrink, Jen, to get your head read."

Jenny sat with a thump and stared at him. How had it deteriorated to this? Sniping and arguing about personalities. Where had it gone wrong? Surely it couldn't be her fault.

As she looked at him, it popped into her mind that it was all his fault; he was so selfcentred that he never thought about her, all he wanted was her body. She glowered at him accusingly.

Look at the other night when he stomped off and did not come home until God knows what time. Oh, yes, next day he said he was with his buddies at the pub, but she knew, she could smell the other woman on him. As soon as he got into bed, she knew he'd had sex. The musty smell from his body penetrated her mind as though he had stabbed her.

How could he do that? Wasn't she always more than willing to have sex? Hadn't she attended to his bodily needs as a good wife should?

"You never loved me," she accused vituperatively, "I know about you sleeping with that other woman." She saw him start, so she'd been right after all. "Oh, no, I'm not stupid, Steven, not stupid at all."

Steve felt a prickle of guilt. He knew he shouldn't have slept with Rita. His excuse to himself was that he'd been drunk, and it was all so vague. But how on earth could Jenny have found out?

"What other woman? I never slept with any other woman." Steve hated confrontations and would never admit to any wrong doing or infidelity. Though he was not married to Jenny, he did feel a certain sense of obligation, due to his years of being carefully taught moral responsibility by Esther.

Honestly men were so stupid, Jenny thought. How could a man think his lover couldn't smell another woman on him?

"You *did* sleep with another woman. Don't try and talk your way out of it, Steve. If anyone is stupid, it's you. Did you think that I wouldn't know?" She laughed mirthlessly as she combed her tangled hair with her fingers. "Boy, talk about me being stupid!"

His mind raced frantically trying to figure out how she'd found out, but came up blank.

"So are you going or not?" she asked, proffering the jacket he had thrown onto the chair. "Go on. Get out of here. Leave me to do my own thing. And you do know what that is, don't you, Stevey baby?"

"You're blackmailing me but it won't work, Jenny. It won't work." Grabbing his jacket from her outstretched hand and shrugging into it, he took the gun from the table and left, slamming the door behind him, knocking the calendar off the wall.

Jenny couldn't believe it. He actually went out and left her even though she had threatened to kill herself. For half an hour she stewed over the injustice of it. How could he leave her alone and pregnant? Surely there must be a way to get through to him. This was one fight Jenny was determined to win.

Going into the cramped bathroom, she looked through the tiny rusting medicine cabinet. Apart from toothpaste and deodorant, she found nothing but a bottle of aspirins and an old prescription for pain killers the doctor had given her when she had wrenched a ligament playing tennis. Taking them into the other room, she sat looking at them. She must prove to Steve that he must not leave her.

But might they kill her if she took them? Jenny didn't want to die, only to scare him into staying. Neither of the drugs she held was very powerful, although she bet they'd only put her to sleep. If she lost the baby, so be it.

Jenny, knowing Steve might come in late, planned to take the pills as the bars closed at 1:00 p.m. The sooner he found her the better, but she had to be unconscious. She wondered about simply faking it, then figured her acting skills might not handle that.

Suppose he didn't come home until morning? She shook her head. No way, she told herself. Steve had to be at work early tomorrow and, even though he took his gun with him, his uniform still hung in the closet. One thing about Steve was his work ethic - he was late for work or ever took the day off.

Steve sat in the pub with a couple of pals, drinking beer and telling dirty jokes. While there bodily, his mind was worrying over his problems with Jenny. On one hand he wanted to ask his pals' advice, and on the other didn't want them crowing over his situation. What was he going to do? He mulled over going back to live with his parents, then scrubbed that idea as his mother would be furious. She made no secret of the fact that she liked Jenny. Going home to face her was like getting out of one mess and into another.

"Shit!" he cursed, suddenly remembering that he had to go back to the apartment, he needed his uniform.

Sighing with aggravation, he stood. "Got to go, lads. The old ball and chain gets worried if I'm late." He laughed as he said it, trying to be one of the boys.

"Sure, Steve, pull the other one," Jimmy laughed disdainfully, "That little girl leads you around by the nose by the sound of it." The others joined in with the scoffing as Steve smiled and walked away from their derisive laughter.

He let them think he was taking it all in fun, but one of these days he vowed to get even with that little bastard Jimmy, he promised himself that. Jimmy was always on his case, always telling the boss fibs about him. Him, Steve Rigby, who was so conscientious and reliable, while Jimmy took time off and bragged about stealing from the stores.

Jenny glanced at the clock again. It was nearly one. The time had gone so slowly but was time to take the pills. Filling a glass with water, she began to swallow them. She counted twenty-three aspirins and thought that small amount surely was not harmful. The five pain killers were probably codeine based, but they were old.

When she swallowed the lot, she changed into her best nightdress, combed her hair and dabbed on some makeup so she would look good when he found her. Opening the bed chesterfield, she lay flat on her back with her arms crossed on her chest as though she were dead. She envisaged herself looking like the colour plate lithograph of Ophelia in one of her books, and lay with a small smile on her lips. Strange that she didn't feel anything happening. How long did it take?

It was almost one-thirty when Steve arrived home. The room was dark and he stumbled around trying not to make a sound. It was difficult but thankfully Jenny didn't stir. He heard her slight snoring.

As he sat on the edge of the bed chesterfield, something clattered onto the bare parquet floor. He sat motionless in case it had woken her, but she snored on. About an hour later he woke when turning over and felt Jenny lying heavily on the blanket. She seemed so soundly asleep that she didn't make a sound or even move when he pushed at her, which was unusual.

After asking what was wrong and not getting an answer, he switched on the table lamp and looked down at her. Somehow she didn't look right, she looked pale and still. Then as he was shaking her shoulder to rouse her, the pill bottles winked at him from the floor and, with a sense of dread, he realized she had again tried to kill herself.

Grabbing his pants, he went to hammer on the next apartment's door. God damn it, why didn't they have a telephone? They could have had one installed under her name. Steve opted to forego a phone so his employers couldn't contact him when he wasn't at work; that way he didn't get stuck with extra shifts. Now he rued the day.

His banging finally roused a very grumpy, pyjama clad man who glared at him through halfshut eyes.

"What the hell do you think you are doing? Do you know what time it is?"

Steve said nothing, but, panicking, pushed him aside to pick up the phone from the hall table.

"Emergency, I need an ambulance," he gabbled as he dialled with a shaking hand.

As he waited for someone to answer, the bleary eyed neighbour snorted, "Kill her, did you? I thought you might." Having been privy to the earlier row, he thought Steve had hit her.

Two hours later they let Steve into the ward to see her. White as the sheets, she lay motionless in a narrow bed, an intravenous needle in her arm. The doctors had pumped her stomach.

During the hours of waiting, he racked his mind, trying to reason why he shouldn't walk away from the mess. Jenny was a ticking time bomb. It could happen again, he told himself, she was still too childish to think through the results of her actions.

He felt torn between calling her parents and not doing so. What was the point in worrying them unduly? No, he mustn't call them yet. A nurse told him Jenny was all right, that they had pumped her stomach. She was going to be fine in a few hours and could go home, she told him. Too, Steve knew Jim and Janet did not like him: Jenny told him that often enough.

Getting himself a cup of coffee from the machine, he sat on a cracked plastic chair in the lounge pondering his dilemma and yawning. The earlier beers had worn off and he felt drained, exhausted. In his heart he hoped Jenny might abort the baby; that might be best for everyone.

Suppose he stayed with her? Maybe he could talk to her, talk properly, tell her what he expected. She must act differently if he stayed, no more of this pouncing on him for sex the minute he set foot in the door. Also, she must learn to cook, must wash his clothes and clean the apartment. Yes, he nodded, she must literally clean up her act.

Supposing she had died? He felt the cold chill that came over him when the thought had popped into his mind earlier; that was like committing murder and her being pregnant, like murdering two people. All the neighbours and the super had heard her screaming "Murderer!" at him. They might think he had killed her, not that she had taken pills.

When the police questioned him earlier they took the names of his pals and obviously checked on his whereabouts. Somehow they managed to make him feel like a criminal, and yet he had done nothing to be ashamed of, nothing at all.

Sighing irritably, he strode around the small lounge trying to get the cramp out of his tense legs. Jenny was a problem, a big problem, one he didn't know how to resolve, although for sure he must stick by her until she was over this phase of self-destruction.

Then they told him he could see her.

Looking at her as she lay still and quiet, he experienced a sense of protectiveness. All he wanted to do was hold her and assure her.

Her eyelids fluttered. Her skin was so fine that he could see the tiny veins in her eyelids. More than ever she looked like a child, not a line on her beautiful, but un-lived in face. Steve sat at the side of the bed and waited.

FOUR

"**C**ome on, Jim, do hurry up!" Janet called impatiently, "We're going to be late. They won't hold the plane for us, you know."

Janet checked her purse for the umpteenth time to make sure she had the tickets and the passports. Jim still didn't want to go to Vegas and let her know it in a hundred little ways.

While she waited, she checked the kitchen, making sure all was neat and tidy, unplugged all the appliances. The family room looked tidy, as did the living room. Like her mother before her, Janet spent two days cleaning so she would return to a spotless house. For days she went around after Jim picking up and putting away, trying to keep it immaculate.

Now she smiled with satisfaction as Jim came slowly down the corridor combing his hair. "Where's the taxi?" he asked.

"It'll be here any minute and I don't want you locked in the bathroom while the meter ticks. I don't know what you find to do in there, Jim. It takes you longer to get ready than it does me, and I have to do my hair."

Jim's bathroom habits were a bone of contention. While she knew he took his war story paperbacks in the bathroom to read before bed, she didn't know what he did in there for what seemed like hours when they were getting ready to go out somewhere. That he refused to tell her, either, annoyed her even more.

"Never you mind what I do in there." He started going through the magazine rack. "Where's the morning paper? I have time to check the sports page."

"Take it with you and read it on the plane," Janet said, annoyed, knowing he probably left the bathroom a big mess. She wished he were more pleased about their trip. "They'll probably give you an entire newspaper all to yourself if you ask."

The taxi honked at the front gate and she gathered her coat and purse and picked up her overnight case.

"Get the bags, Jim, come on." Giving a last glance around, one last check to make sure everything was tidy, she opened the front door to wave at the taxi driver.

Jenny smiled at Steve. He arrived at ten, bringing a huge glossy leaved potted plant covered in pink flowers.

"Wow, it's lovely," she said, "Thanks, Steve."

Steve shrugged as if it were nothing, though the plant cost him more than twenty bucks that he borrowed from a friend.

The hospital, Jenny told him, was keeping her in for observation. Steve realized she had lost no time in telling them about her pregnancy. Steve was all for taking her home. Let her lose the baby, he thought, sooner the better as far as he was concerned.

"They sent a psychiatrist to talk to me today," she said, looking at him from under her brows. He could see she felt pleased with herself. "I have to see him twice a week when I get out of here," she announced importantly. Why did she seem so pleased about it, he wondered? Why did she think seeing a shrink was good?

Steve chuckled. "I told you, you needed to see a shrink. What you did wasn't normal, Jenny. They'll soon sort you out, though, no worry about that." He sat on the hard metal chair at the side of the bed and held her hand.

"Do you want me to call your mother?" he asked.

"No way! I don't need her nagging at me right now." She pressed his hand. "I want to go home, with you."

"Well now, I think you ought to go home to your mother until you get your head sorted. This was serious, Jen. The police talked to me and I'm sure they're going to investigate. I mean you living with me and all that. Have they been to see you yet? You caused a lot of trouble for everyone last night."

"Oh Steve, don't be mad at me," Jenny said, hugging his hand to her breast. "I couldn't help it. It wasn't my fault. I can't live without you." She sighed, pleased to be the centre of attention. "Yes, a policeman came and I had to make a statement. I suppose that's why they've got this shrink talking at me. I know it's all my fault, what I did, but you've got to realize how much I love you."

"Okay, Jenny," Steve suddenly impatient, felt he'd heard enough of this love business. "They tell me I have to talk to this doctor of yours, too."

Jenny stared at him, wondering what went on in his mind. "But you're not going to leave me now, Steve, are you?"

"No, Jenny, I won't leave you." It was all he could do to stop himself from heaving a sigh of irritation. Boy, she took the cake.

Lying back on her pillows, she gazed at him. Steve was everything she wanted in a man. His fantastic body and the body building made him stand out among other men. He was tall, dark and handsome and a fantastic lover, not that she had ever made love with anyone else, but she knew. Her body tingled as she thought of their lovemaking.

"I wish I could go home with you right now, Steve," she whispered. "I want to make love."

"Yeah, so do I," He grinned at her. She looked so beautiful. Even in the plain white hospital gown she looked beautiful, and her body turned him on.

Still, who built a relationship on sex and nothing else? If he were honest with himself and ignored her body, he realized he didn't much like her anymore. Yet he was stuck with her, at least until she got her head sorted.

After he left Jenny lay thinking about what she had done. It had made all the difference: look how concerned Steve was, how he promised to stay with her.

Jenny felt delighted that she must see the psychiatrist, it made her special and Dr. Ross was so kind and listened to her every word. He told her she needed therapy, needed counselling. She agreed with him wholeheartedly. At last she was going to get attention and Dr. Ross could maybe help her with Steve's reluctance to marry. Ross seemed so cosmopolitan, so educated, so very warm and giving that she knew he would have all the answers. He didn't ask her many questions that she could recall, but somehow she managed to pour out her tale of woe. She couldn't stop herself, and told him even the most intimate details of her relationship with Steve.

Dr. Ross seemed such a darned good listener, and genuinely interested in what she said. Exactly like Steve had been at first, as though every word from her lips were a diamond. The only thing that niggled at her was that the police had a file on her as an attempted suicide, and she prayed they didn't go to see her parents. She hadn't given their address and hoped Steve hadn't told them.

Oh, what the heck, she tossed on her bed and picked up a glossy magazine a volunteer left, she might as well relax and enjoy her stay. Idly she wondered what was for lunch. She could eat a horse although her throat felt sore.

"Jim! Look, look, it's Wayne Newton!" Janet screamed, punching him in the arm as a long black limo slowly slid past them. She'd been peering into every car they passed hoping to spot a celebrity, and then she spotted Wayne Newton. How exciting.

Jim found it about as stimulating as watching grass grow. He hated Los Vegas: it was too hot, too crowded and much too commercial. Everyone walked around jangling pockets full of silver dollars and stopping to pull the handles of the ever present slot machines. Why, they even had machines in men's toilets and in the airport waiting areas.

A friend of Janet's who had often been to Vegas told her that if she wanted to win on the slots she should try a machine situated close to the spot where people lined up for the hotel show. The ringing of the bells as people won drew the waiting lineup back to the slots when the show was over.

This morning she played ten dollars on a machine near the show lounge and won. After paying out nine-fifty she won twenty-eight dollars, and that to her was a minor miracle. Tonight, she told Jim excitedly, she must play the machine near the doors of the lounge at Circus-Circus for surely that was a winner.

Janet was having a wonderful time. Her excitement was so infectious that Jim soon found pleasure in watching her enjoy herself. It made up for his distaste of any form of gambling, even if it were only a quarter a time. However, the shows were very good, and he enjoyed seeing the show girls in their skimpy, and sometimes none existent, costumes. Some were absolutely gorgeous. He wondered if he would ever recognize any of them during the day time when they wore ordinary clothes.

Since their arrival they had gone on two coach trips, one to Hoover Dam and one to Boulder City. They spent their evenings at a dinner show and later in the casinos and tonight they had booked for the show at Circus-Circus.

"Have you got a pen with you, Jim?" Janet asked as she rummaged through her purse. She wanted to get a postcard off to Jenny. Poor Jenny, she sighed as she wrote the usual platitudes.

"By this time Jenny must be suffering from morning sickness and has no one to talk with about things," she said.

"Serves her right. Don't spoil your holiday worrying about her." Jim sounded annoyed.

In a way, she wished she hadn't come on this trip, or didn't feel so guilty about enjoying it so much, not while Jennifer still lived with that man. Shoving them out of her mind, she looked around the lobby for the mail box, didn't see one and pushed the card back into her purse.

Mrs. Rigby glared at Steve as he stuffed his face with warm pie. Anyone might think he hadn't eaten in a month, she thought, watching him.

"How's Jenny? Why didn't you fetch her with you this time, or should I ask?" Steve was usually ready with an excuse.

"She couldn't come because she's in the hospital," he said around a mouthful of apple and rhubarb. "Good pie, Mum."

"What?" Esther was shocked. "Why didn't you say so when you got here? What's the matter with you, son? No brains at all . . . head full of feathers." Mrs. Rigby sat with her arms crossed over her immense bosom and glared at him. "Right, boy, talk."

His eyes flitted around the cosy kitchen, saw the other pie cooling on the counter top and wondered what it was: pecan maybe. He shrugged. "Oh, it's nothing, Mum. She's in for observation, that's all."

Steve wished he had said nothing now, although his primary thought had been to come and tell his mother everything. He needed to talk about things with somebody who understood. His mother was a good sort and could probably help him, but not having told her immediately had annoyed her.

She looked at him suspiciously. What was he not telling her? "They don't keep people in the hospital for nothing," she said. "Was she sick? Did she have an accident?"

"Well . . .," his brain raced frantically. What should he tell her? "Er, she's had some sort of breakdown."

"What does that mean? Gawd, it's like pulling hen's teeth trying to get you to talk. You were always a mealy-mouthed kid, and you're no different now, Steve. Come on, tell me what's going on."

"All right," he said, wiping his mouth on a paper napkin. "See, it's like this, Mum . . .,"

Later Mrs. Rigby wrote down the hospital room number she had dragged out of Steve, and said she was going to visit Jenny.

"If her parents are away, and I have my doubts about that, my lad, that's all very well, but she's alone in a strange place. She's nothing but a child. And you, you big ox, you've got a lot to answer for. How could you get her into such a state that she'd want to kill herself?"

"I didn't do nothing, Mum. She's not all there." He tapped his temple. "She's mental, and that's why they sent for a psychiatrist. You can't blame me, no matter what she tells you. It was nothing to do with me." Steve slumped in the chair and, pushing it away from the table, started rocking on its back legs.

"Don't do that! How many times do I have to tell you?" she snapped.

Mrs. Rigby knew Steve of old and if he said it wasn't his fault, it usually was. Her instincts told her that this incident was of his doing and she was going to find out exactly what caused Jenny's hospitalization. While Steve was not exactly swift, he was a crafty young beggar, and she doubted Jenny had anything mentally wrong. She was so bright.

By the time his father arrived home from work, Frank was on an afternoon shift, Steve had told his mother everything. While she was not exactly supportive of him, although she still entertained big hopes for their relationship, she told him plainly that he must stay with Jenny, look after her and the baby.

FIVE

anet hit a winning streak on her previously selected slot machine. As Jim stood in the lineup waiting for the lounge doors to open, Janet made a bee line for the machine she had picked out earlier. By the time she noticed the line was moving and joined Jim, she had won so many quarters that they filled both her jumbo size paper cups and her purse.

She grinned ecstatically, but Jim grimly looked at her black fingers and grimaced. "Your hands look like you've just finished work in a coal mine. Go and wash them when we get inside."

"Yes, Jim," she said, still grinning and juggling her money.

They thought the show marvellous. The troupe used a new gimmick in which they played a film on the stage-width screen and suddenly the actors or dancers popped through the screen and carried on with the action. It was spectacular when the horsemen, presumably the three musketeers, materialized, horses and all, and galloped down a ramp and out through the back of the theatre. That even impressed Jim.

Jim and Janet had struck up an acquaintanceship with an English couple over on holiday who had the room next to theirs. After the show they were going to have supper with them at a pseudo Tudor style restaurant.

Ernie and Brenda Thompson came from the north of England and it was their accent that first attracted Janet's attention. Jim and Janet were both born and brought up in Lancashire, emigrating to Canada in the 1950's. Coincidentally it turned out the four had been born within five miles of each other. Janet and Brenda had even attended the same school. To meet someone with whom they had a childhood in common was unusual, and they all got on well.

"What did you two get up to this evening?" Janet asked Brenda as they waited to be seated at the restaurant.

"Tom Jones! We saw Tom Jones," Brenda exclaimed. Brenda loved Tom Jones and had always wanted to see him perform. To her, the cost of the trip was worth having seen Tom in action for two hours.

"Talk about a gigolo!" Ernie snorted. He didn't like Tom Jones, detesting his posturing, swivel hips and the way women threw their underwear at him.

"It was brilliant, Janet, fantastic. We sat close and I could see his long eyelashes and everything. Mind you, I had the binoculars with me," She laughed loudly.

"Tell me all about it." Janet listened with wide eyes as Brenda went into raptures over her idol as Jim and Ernie talked football.

The hostess showed them to a table for four near the entrance.

"Boy, you should have slipped her a ten or something, Jim, this table is almost in the lobby," Ernie laughed as they took their seats.

"I expect she's paid well enough without me giving her money for a table," Jim said firmly. "It's a real pain the way these Maitre d's always have their hands out. I mean, even at the shows they expect money before you get a decent seat. It's a racket if you ask me, and people are stupid enough to pay it and so it's become a habit."

"All right, Jim," Janet patted his hand. If he got started on something like this, he could ruin the entire evening.

"But he's right, you know, Janet," Brenda said, "look at all those empty tables back there yet here we are sitting practically in front of the door."

"I don't mind, Brenda, it's all right, it's the same food no matter where you sit and we aren't going to be here long," Janet said, picking up the huge red leather menu. "Now, what looks good . . ."

The restaurant looked very phoney, they agreed: fake beams, fake velvet chairs where even the wood was fake, fake pewter place plates. The food, the usual overabundant American cuisine, leaned toward barbecue. While they ate their meal, they discussed what they might do later. The women wanted to go to Circus-Circus and play the slots. The men wanted to go to Caesar's Palace and sit in on some sports betting.

As they were gathering themselves to leave and were standing, a couple of men rushed into the restaurant wearing masks and holding guns.

"That must be them," one said as he fired. The other also opened fire. Shots rang out deafening the four and in a split second, before they knew what was happening, even before they had time to duck, Jim and Ernie were lying on the floor bleeding. The men disappeared as quickly, chased by a waiter who got the car licence plate number.

It all happened in a split second. Women began to scream. Waiters rushed toward them. Suddenly all was frantic activity. Brenda grabbed the back of her chair, screamed, then fainted. Janet, struck dumb and stock still with shock, suddenly came to and threw herself on her knees, staring at the front of Jim's white shirt now covered in dark blood. She huddled there, silent and stunned.

Someone yelled orders to call the police, call the ambulance; for everyone to stand back, to stay calm, to sit at the back of the restaurant until the police came. It was like she was in a dream, everything moved so quickly and yet so slowly. She stared at the blood on her hands, on her skirt, on her legs. Jim's blood.

Senior staff applied clean white napkins to wounds to staunch the flow of blood, while others comforted two other diners who had received slight flesh wounds from breaking glass. As a kitchen worker tried to revive a waitress who had fainted, a woman patron screamed hysterically. It was horrible, so horrible that Janet couldn't take it in: it seemed as though she was in a trance or a nightmare.

Suffering from shock and helped by paramedics, the women rode in the police car that followed the ambulance to the hospital. Neither spoke, but clung together mutely. Then they sat in the hospital waiting room trying to comfort each other. Brenda couldn't stop crying while Janet was inarticulate with the horror of it. Two detectives questioned them a short time earlier. Neither wanted to be bothered answering questions, and were very short with the two men who were, after all, only doing their jobs. They didn't know what had happened, both said, it was all in a split second: no, they had seen nothing until it had happened: no, they knew no one in Vegas.

None of the hospital staff told them anything and so they huddled together, worried and frightened. It was a difficult wait. From a vending machine they bought strong, acidic coffee they didn't want and sat sipping it as they tried to reassure each other. Repeating themselves, telling each other that everything was going to be fine.

"Once they remove the bullets, they'll let us see them, I'm sure," Janet assured Brenda for the hundredth time, although not at all certain. Her heart still pounded and she felt terribly frightened. Jim hadn't wanted to come to Vegas and now he was shot. Janet, her heart beating too fast and skipping from nerves, felt sure he was dead and prayed she was wrong. He had been so very still, the blood, so much of it, was such a dark colour, was obviously from an artery. She felt a sense of real guilt on top of the worry. Her mind niggled frantically, trying to think if she had noticed anything at the time of the incident, but her headache steadily got worse. Everything seemed too much of a strain.

"How on earth are we going to pay for the hospital?" Brenda asked for the millionth time. It was all she could think about, other than her husband, as she'd forgotten to take out travel insurance.

"Don't worry about that, Brenda. The restaurant will cover everything, or the state will, don't worry," Janet said for what seemed the thousandth time with a conviction she didn't feel. It was an effort being the level-headed one, trying to appear strong when all she wanted to do was to lie down and cry her eyes out.   Soon a matron came to talk to them. Ernie was in intensive care and they could see him soon. Unfortunately Jim had died on the operating table. A bullet had pierced his lung and heart.

Oh God, and he had not wanted to come here. No, he hadn't, but she had insisted. Janet collapsed in a dead faint.

"There now, are you comfy?"

"Yes, thanks, Mrs. Rigby. This is so nice of you." Jenny snuggled down under an Afghan throw on Mrs. Rigby's overstuffed and cosy couch.

"That's right. You lie there and rest while I start supper. Steve will be home soon." Esther smiled and patted Jenny's shoulder as she passed through on her way to the kitchen. "Holler if you want anything."

Esther Rigby was well pleased with the outcome of her visit to the Civic Hospital. Steve was well and truly back under her thumb again. It was on her insistence that Jenny had come to the house to convalesce in comfort.

"Thank you so much, Mrs. Rigby, I'd love to come to your house," Jenny said immediately Esther made the offer, realizing here was a chance to be waited on hand and foot, and lie around doing nothing. Going back to the apartment meant Steve would go to work, leaving her alone, and she must make his meals.

The Rigby house on the far outskirts of Carleton Place was comfortable, added to which Mrs. Rigby was a fantastic cook. Jenny completely forgot that she hated the fat old frump Steve called Mum. She smiled so winsomely with tears in her eyes that Esther felt a lump in her throat.

Steve, driving his mother's car, had delivered her to his mother's. Still under doctors' care, she must report for therapy twice a week and Esther promised to drive her back and forth. It had all worked out so well, Jenny thought, all she had to do was ask and Esther fetched her things. Unfortunately Esther insisted she cut down on caffeine because of her pregnancy. She was gasping for a Coke.

Lying on the sofa now, soft music playing from the radio, comfortable and secure, she wondered where her parents were. Steve, insisting that she call them, went over to the house when they did not answer the phone. They must have taken a trip somewhere Jenny assumed, saying she'd surely get a card. At the back of her mind she felt pleased. What they didn't know wouldn't worry them.

Steve felt annoyed that his mother had interfered, Jenny recognized that, but she believed she now had a friend in Mrs. Rigby. Esther wanted to see them married, she told Jenny, particularly now the baby was on its way. She actively campaigned to this end, which drove Steve crazy. Steve's father also vigorously requested his son do the right thing by her.

Jenny sat back and carefully watched the family battle of wills. With them on her side, she would get herself the husband of her dreams. She congratulated herself because pretending to commit suicide had done the trick, and she gave herself a mental pat on the back. It had all worked out the way she planned.

While at first she enjoyed having a fuss made of her, after forty-eight hours of enforced idleness everything got on her nerves. Esther, who was as bad as her mother in some ways, insisted Jenny eat vegetables and salad, even though she detested them. She took a mouthful of the broccoli or carrots and chewed them for ages until she had to swallow, at which time she shuddered. Esther, after watching this performance, stopped nagging her.

Even when she wanted to take a stroll around the large garden surrounded by woods, Esther was at her side, hanging onto her arm as though she were on her last legs. Jenny, used to voicing her annoyance at home, soon made Esther's life a misery and her whining complaints rubbed Esther the wrong way.

"I don't know what the problem is, Jenny," Esther said worriedly, "You should be feeling better by now. I think we should take you to see the doctor. Something's very wrong if you're so irritable all the time. You're so prickly that there's no talking to you."

Stupid fat old cow, Jenny thought, always wittering on about something.

"Oh, please," she said witheringly, "give me a break! I want to be left alone, so stop fussing. I don't need to see the doctor. I feel fine. You keep trying to push me around, and I don't like it. If I want to go outside, you don't have to come with me. I'm an adult, not a five-year-old. You're like my mother, always meddling in my life." Sullenly she flounced into the kitchen and started rummaging through the fridge. She could kill for a Coke.

Esther followed her and watched as she looked behind everything on the shelves. She smiled grimly.

"You won't find anything in there that has caffeine in it. I gave it all to my neighbour. You can't drink Coke or coffee anymore, Jenny, it's not good for the baby."

"Shit!" Jenny slammed the fridge door and rounded on Esther. "Who died and put you in charge of me? You can't tell me what to do. I'm going home. You can tell Steve where I am." Pushing past Esther, she picked up the telephone. "I'm calling a taxi and don't try to stop me."

Esther, angrily watched her. "What an ungrateful, spoiled girl, you are, Jenny," she said. "To think I put myself out to help, and is it appreciated? Not in the slightest."

Jenny ignored her and spoke to the dispatcher. Sadly Esther shook her head as she listened to Jenny give the dispatcher directions. Poor Steve, he must be mad to put up with Jenny. Wait until he came home, she must tell him a thing or two.

It had not taken Esther long to discover that Jenny was a sly conniving little bitch. Only two private talks and Esther had her number. Too bad Steve must make a commitment and marry her for the baby's sake. To think she had admired Jenny for her education and charm. Education she may have, but she had very few brains that Esther could see, and very little charm unless things were going her way.

Janet sent a telegram to Jenny telling her of her father's death and asking her to go immediately to the house as she needed to speak to her, instructing her to stay at the house by the phone until she called.

Jenny felt her heart jump with shock when she opened the telegram. Her Dad dead? It had to be some mistake, but no, her mother was not into joke playing. Wanting to talk to someone about it, she went to the

St. Laurent Shopping Centre where she tracked down Steve. He was sitting in the security office questioning a small boy shoplifter.

He took her into the mall after handing over the delinquent to the other guard. "I'm so sorry, Jen," he said, putting his arms around her. Poor girl, having to read a paper that said your father was dead. "Come on now, I'll make arrangements to take the afternoon off, and we'll go over to your house to wait for your mother's call."

Steve liked the Steven's house, an executive home on the outskirts Alta Vista, one of the city's posher districts in the city's west end. It was large rambling home, custom renovated by an architect. Jenny said her parents had lived there since their marriage, adding to it and improving it to its current luxurious condition.

Jenny loved the house, she always had, and making herself comfortable, ordered a pizza. They watched a game show on the thirty-inch colour TV until it arrived. To pay for the pizza, she took twenty dollars out of the little brass jug on the kitchen counter where her mother kept cash in case a tradesman asked for cash payment.

She literally jumped when the phone rang, sounding sounded louder than usual.

"Hello, Mum?" she said tremulously, leaning against the wall, feeling as though she might faint. "What's all this about? Where's Dad? When are you coming home? Was that telegram a joke of some kind? What's going on?"

"Listen to me, Jenny. Your father was shot last night in a restaurant. I have to arrange to have the body shipped home, and I need your help to make arrangements at that end."

Jenny felt a cold chill ran through her body and burst into tears. "Body? Body? You can't mean it, Mum. I can't, I can't do it. Why would you want me to do a thing like that? You'll have to do it yourself." Sobbing wildly, she thrust the phone at Steve who took it and put it to his ear.

"I need your help, Jenny," Janet was saying, "Go to Burnside and Green, the undertakers and tell them to call me at . . .," she gave a bunch of numbers and Steve said: "Steve here, Mrs. Stevens. Jenny is very upset so I took the phone away from her. Let me know what's to be done and I'll do it. Jenny is far too upset right now."

Janet snorted. "Jenny is upset? Not as upset as I am, I'm sure, Steve," she said, feeling the ever present tears starting to well in her eyes. "Be a good lad and go to Burnside and Green, tell them to phone me at . . . oh, have you got a pencil? Good," she gave him the number and said, "Tell them it's very urgent, will you? I can't stand it here and want to come home. Have Jenny stay at the house until I get there. You can stay too, Steve, if needs be."

"Right, Mrs. Stevens, is there anything else I can do?" Steve felt bad about the sudden death, knowing Jim and Janet had been as close as two people could be. How terrified she must feel.

"I think I'd better talk to our lawyer. Look in the phone table drawer. You'll find a small red book. Get me Richard Wyatt's number, please."

Steve, full of curiosity about the death, reckoned he had better wait until Mrs. Stevens came home. Time enough to discover what had happened.

Steve telephoned the funeral director and gave the details to a soft spoken lady who said she could take care of everything. Jenny, having stopped crying, sat sullenly on the sofa eating pizza and watching him. She was angry with her mother, angry with her father for getting himself killed, and angry that Steve was running the show.

"So what the heck is going on? Who shot my Dad?" she asked belligerently as he replaced the receiver. "What is Mum doing in Las Vegas anyway?"

Steve looked at her. Poor Jenny, this was going to disrupt her life and she liked things to run her way or not at all. "Your father got shot when they went out to eat in a restaurant, Jenny, that's all I know so it's no use interrogating me. You'll have to ask your mother. She wants you to stay at the house until she gets back. She said I can stay here as well."

"What am I supposed to do here? All my clothes are at the apartment and so is all my stuff. I'm going back." She stood up and started putting on her coat.

Steve couldn't believe it. "Don't be such a selfish bitch, Jenny," he said incredulously, "Your mother is devastated, and all you can think about is yourself. Honestly, Jen, I don't know what I ever saw in you." He sat on the telephone table chair and stared at her, unable to comprehend what went on in her mind. "Don't you feel anything about your father? What do you think your mother is going through right now?"

Jenny shrugged. "That's nothing to do with me. She'll have to look after it. Dad was never very nice to me that I can remember, and *she* told me I was stupid. They don't care about me at all, so why should I care about them?"

"I don't believe you," Steve felt shaken, "Are you so callous and hardhearted that you're not even upset? I know you were upset when you were asked to be helpful for a change, and you couldn't even talk to her. Some loving daughter you are! You think of nobody but yourself."

She flounced her head and pouted. "Oh, shut up, Steve. What do you know about it, anyway?"

"I know that the minute you're asked to put yourself out, even in a situation like this, you refuse. You always want things to go your way. Bugger everyone else."

Jenny felt hurt. He didn't understand that she was too sensitive to be put under this pressure. "So? Why shouldn't things go my way once in a while?"

"Things always go your way, Jen." His tone was scathing, "You know they do. If you don't get your own way, there's always hell to play."

"Well, pardon me for living," she said sarcastically. "Maybe you got me to the hospital too fast. Maybe it might be better if I were dead and then you'd have to find someone else to boss around."

Steve threw up his hands in despair. "Cut it out, Jenny. Nobody wants you dead and nobody wants to boss you around. The sooner that shrink sorts you out the better. You're paranoiac."

"Piss off, Steve," she tossed her head. "I don't need you, I never did. I love you, but I don't need you." She raised her voice to a shriek, "I don't need you! Can't you get that through your thick head?"

"God in heaven!" Steve slammed the desk top in anger. "What's the matter with you? Have you ever listened to yourself? First of all you can't live without me . . . you even try to off yourself. Now you don't need me? Well, I've had enough, Jenny. I'm going, and you won't be seeing me again. A man can take only so much."

He went to the door and turned to look at her. From standing statue-like, suddenly she came to life and ran toward him, eyes filled with tears.

"Don't leave me, Steve, I didn't mean it," she pleaded. "I need you. You know that I really, really need you. I'm so upset by all this, my Dad being shot, and Mum having to make funeral arrangements, and me getting out of the hospital. It's all too much. Please don't go," she wailed and threw herself into his arms.

Steve held her without much feeling. This was getting to be too much for him. How much longer could he put up with the constant theatrics?

SIX

Richard Wyatt flew down to Vegas on the first available flight after he'd finished talking to Janet. Things must to be set in motion, he told her, a charge must be laid against the restaurant on whose premises Jim had been shot. He figured it could be a very lucrative case.

Janet walked around in a trance, unable to face things. The hotel management took everything out of her hands. The funeral parlour in Ottawa contracted a funeral home in Las Vegas. Arrangements were under way to ship the body back to Canada.

Richard arrived within eight hours, and took over negotiations, with the aid of a local lawyer, in a suit against the restaurant. He was also representing Ernie and Brenda. Janet and Brenda became very close and spent hours commiserating. The one bright spot was that Ernie was well on the way to recovery.

The hotel was not charging either couple for their rooms as a goodwill gesture, and they featured that story on the local television news. Richard said it was because they didn't want any adverse publicity for the city and relied on the gesture to count in their favour. Bad publicity could harm their business.

The police quickly traced the licence plate. The stolen car was found in a parking lot. The trail was dead, but the investigation continued. Not many people actually saw the men, and the fact that they wore masks had not helped. Their general descriptions could have fit a million people. All known gangsters in the vicinity were checked and still nobody had a clue as to the reason for the killing. All Janet heard were apologies and assurances that the murderers might be found soon. Right then she didn't care: she simply wanted to go home.

It was another day before they could fly Jim home. They needed special arrangements to transport a body across a border and a pile of official forms were necessary. It was with a sense of relief that she bid a tearful farewell to Brenda and Ernie and boarded the plane with Richard: the coffin, in a special crate, stowed in the luggage compartment.

When Janet arrived home, Jenny opened the door as the taxi pulled up in front of the house. Running down the walk she threw her arms around Janet crying: "Oh, Mum, Mummy," and Janet burst into tears. The wound was still so raw that she could hardly face walking into the house where she and Jim had been so happy. It was difficult to accept that she had insisted on his going to Vegas, and knew she had caused his death.

With Jenny's arm around her waist, she went into the hall. Steve stood waiting in the living room and had put down a tray with tea things. "Come on and sit down, Mrs. Stevens," he said, taking her hand and leading her to the chesterfield. "Tea's ready. I bet you could murder a cup right now." Why had he said that? It was a common enough expression with English people but how could he have said 'murder'?

Janet heard him, but said nothing. To cover up her feelings, she fussed as she sat on the couch, taking off her small hat and putting her handbag on the floor. She smoothed her skirt and patted the loose cushion. What could she say? What should she say?

"So how did it happen, Mum?" Jenny asked, her voice too shrill and too loud.

"Your father was shot in a restaurant," Even to her own ears, her voice was expressionless, "Two of them, gunmen, you know. Your Dad and Ernie, Brenda's husband, the couple who were with us, was also shot but he's going to be all right. He'll be out of the hospital next week."

"Who did it?" Steve asked, shocked that strangers had murdered someone he knew.

Janet shook her head. "Who knows? They're still investigating. The hotel manager said it was probably a grudge killing, maybe someone had welshed on a bet or something."

"But it wasn't my Dad, so why did they shoot him and this Ernie?" Jenny asked, her voice tended to rise when she was upset and her voice was piercing now. "Did they look like they were gamblers?"

Janet wearily shook her head. "Lower your voice, Jenny, there's no need to shout. I don't know who or what they were. I have to go down to the funeral home now. Will you come with me?"

"No way, Jose! I don't want to go to any creepy funeral home." Jenny stalked out of the room.

Steve sighed. "She's not taking this very well, Mrs. Stevens, but I know it sure isn't easy for you. I'll take you down. Where are the car keys? I'll bring the car around to the front."

"Thanks, Steve, I appreciate everything you've done." Janet put on her coat and picked up her purse, thinking maybe she'd misjudged Steve as Jenny came back into the room. "Are you sure you won't come with me, Jenny?" she asked.

"No. I don't want to," she said like a small sulky child. "You go with Steve. I'll wait here."

She watched them drive away and turned as the phone rang. It was Richard Wyatt.

"Please ask your mother to call me when she gets back, Jenny. If it's late, she can call me at home. I've got some good news for her."

"Oh, is my Dad still alive, then?" Jenny asked sarcastically, making her voice as contemptuous as possible. "That's the only good news we want to hear." She slammed the phone down as hard as she could without asking for his telephone number. Stupid sod of a lawyer. Probably calling to tell her mother how much his bill was. Sod him.

But what could be the good news? Jenny mulled that over that for a few minutes. Good news could only mean they were going to pay her mother compensation. Idly she wondered how much it was, a million dollars maybe? Maybe more. Las Vegas was a very rich place. Wow, that was great. To think her mother soon might have piles of money made her feel cheerful. Her Dad had insurance as well, she knew about it as she overheard them talking one day. She could be a double heiress, for when her old Mum popped off, the money came to her. Humming, she opened another Coke.

Dreary soaking rain fell the day of the funeral. Steve had to force Jenny to attend, making sure she wore something subdued in colour. She stood at her mother's side, dryeyed and belligerent with Steve beside her, hanging onto her arm so that she could not take off as she threatened.

Janet felt numb and clung to Richard Wyatt's arm. This was not the way she had envisioned the end for either of them. How could she face the rest of her life alone? When a sudden break appeared in the clouds the sun shone on them at the grave side, she felt anger that the world went on in the same old way and her Jim was dead. Jim was gone forever.

No more could he see the sun, see the trees and hear the birds. How cruel life seemed. Why was she still alive? Why hadn't the gunman taken her, too? It was so like a nightmare that she couldn't wait for it to end.

She noticed Jenny looking around her with distaste. Everyone's shoes were muddy and the ground was so soggy that heels kept sinking. Jenny stared rudely at the mourners, most of them strangers to her. Janet looked back to the vicar, and clung to Richard's arm.

Looking at her crying mother, it occurred to Jenny to wonder why she personally felt no sorrow. Maybe it was because she hadn't been very close to her father. All he had ever done was tell her off for petty things, things that made no difference to anything. He had been so oldfashioned and stiff, not a nice father, though she could vaguely remember him carrying her around when she was little. He had seemed so jolly in memories of her younger days, a nice dad, a cuddly dad.

The body in the coffin meant nothing to her. She sighed irritably, wondering when they were going to get away from the cemetery and when her mother was going to stop the great bereavement scene. It was getting on her nerves.

She stared as the coffin started on its descent but this so unnerved her mother, that, taking a step forward, Janet cried out and Jenny grimaced with embarrassment.

To Janet the funeral was like living in a kaleidoscope for her; people swam in and out of her vision but didn't register. The faces mournful or complacent meant nothing to her, although the turnout surprised her. How many people had attended the funeral, how many people she had never seen before, strangers, neighbours? Jim had many friends and acquaintances that she did not know, or did not now recognize. For that she was glad, it was a fitting tribute to his life, but why were all these people intruding on her grief?

Jenny, she knew, was acting like a spoiled brat as usual and sniffing her disdain at everything the vicar said. Steve Rigby was more supportive of her, and for that she thanked him, although she still didn't like him much. Yet all of it was so meaningless, and while she wanted people around her, she felt like telling them all to go away. She wanted to be alone to mourn. What was the point in going on? How could she live without Jim?

Janet had looked down at the coffin for the last time and threw a handful of dirt onto its polished top, saying her last farewells to her husband of so many years. She missed him more than she have ever imagined. Jim had been a good husband and a good provider, although over the years they had grown more like brother and sister, than husband and wife. He had become so set in his ways that she often had to bite her tongue, but how she missed him, how she would like to hear him carping about something today.

When they were first married, Janet essentially ruled the roost and Jim seemed glad to let her do so. Over the years, as his progression up the corporate ladder brought him to a position of power, his attitude at home changed and he became bossy and overbearing. She had changed too, she knew that, but then everybody did. Her once passionate love for him had changed subtly into one of a caring and support. She loved him as much, but in a different way.

Jim was an electrical engineer. After his schooling, he was apprenticed to an aircraft manufacturer,then moved into the sales end of things. His expertise and charming manner soon set him on the corporate ladder with the company who had recruited him to come to Canada. Even then, she smiled sadly at the thought, he had come by ocean liner, scared of flying the Atlantic. The job changed him a great deal, although he had never looked back. Neither of them had.

She felt Steve's arm around her shoulders as he steered her away from the grave and led her to the car. Before she got in, she took one last loving look at the grave and whispered: "Goodbye, Jim."

Jenny, she saw, already sat in Richard's car whining about being hungry, and when were they going back to the house? A caterer supplied the funeral meal, and everyone assembled to eat, drink and extend their condolences.

Janet did not look forward to this wake as she detested the hypocritical words that complete strangers mouthed earlier before the church service. All those platitudes, she thought, they didn't mean a word of what they said, they were glad it was not them or their spouse that the gunmen had killed. Maybe, though, it was the mood she was in, for everyone sincerely sympathized. She grudgingly appreciated that.

Janet had no close friends, having never felt a need for a close friend when Jim was alive. Now she would give her eye teeth to have someone to confide in, with whom she could share her grief. Among all those assembled for the funeral meal, she saw not one person to whom she could confidently reveal her feelings. Not even her own daughter who was being so very prickly. It was as if Jenny thought Jim had done it on purpose.

While at the house Richard Wyatt stood by Janet, who was glad of his support, although he said little other than make small talk. Jenny escaped to her old bedroom as soon as possible to watch television.

She hated all the old people who were eating and drinking as though it was a party.

The day after the funeral it actually came home to Jenny that her father was dead. The casket was closed so she never saw him in his coffin. With a jolt it had hit her when she asked her mother for some money to buy a CD player and Janet said: "Ask your father," her normal answer to any request for money.

Stunned, Janet realized what she had said and burst into tears. Jenny stood quite still, not knowing what to do. This outbreak of grief was different from the previous soft weeping. Janet, slumped in the kitchen chair, sobbed, horrible deep gut wrenching sobs, as Jenny stood by uselessly. She did not try to comfort her mother, she didn't know how, but ran to her bedroom to think about things.

Was her mother going to cry for the rest of her life? How often had Janet said to Jenny when she was crying, that tears didn't solve any problem? How often did she tell her not to use tears as a weapon because they didn't work? Maybe at the back of her mind she realized the extent of her mother's grief, however, all she felt now was irritation.

Peevishly she began to pack a few things to take back to the apartment. She and Steve should soon be back to normal, and she had a baby to consider. As she packed, she hummed cheerfully. Let her silly old mother sit and weep, she was young and free and had a life ahead of her . . . and soon all that insurance money.

Steve was still at work when she got back but Jenny recognized the hand of his mother in the appearance of the spotless apartment. She saw no dishes in the sink, no clothes on the floor, and it smelled of Lemon Pledge. Well, let her do it, silly old cow, let her clean and scrub for her precious son. At least it meant that she didn't have to do it.

When Steve arrived home from work, he found an immaculate

apartment with a smiling Jenny dishing up supper. This was more like it, he thought, as he kissed her.

As they ate the takeout chicken and chips she bought with money she removed from the kitchen jug, Jenny chattered on about everything under the sun but the funeral.

"Is your mother all right, Jen?" he asked, wondering why she hadn't said a word about things at home.

She shrugged, uninterested. "Oh, she's okay."

"Why didn't you stay with her for a while? It must be awful for her alone in that house." Steve felt a great deal of compassion for Mrs. Stevens.

"She's okay, I tell you," she said huffily, annoyed at his interest. "Anyway, all that sobbing and sighing got on my nerves. She didn't even think about me, whether I was hungry or not. Well, because she doesn't want to eat doesn't mean that I don't. I had to beg her for money so I could go to McDonald's at lunch time."

"Jenny! All you think about is yourself." Steve stared at her open mouthed. She had reverted to her usual truculent selfish self. "You should have made an effort to get *her* something to eat. How would you feel if you were in her position?"

"Rich, I suppose," Jenny retorted. She had eavesdropped on a conversation between Richard Wyatt and her mother about the settlement Janet was to receive from the restaurant, and it sounded like her mother had struck gold. Yet when Jenny had asked for money for a CD player she did not offer her money, she started crying. To Jenny it seemed that her mother was better off without her stuffy old dad. She could now start to have a wonderful time.

"Your mother has no means of support now, Jenny, think about that. Now she has no one but you. You should help her."

"Come off it! She doesn't need me, Steve. She's got pots of money now and . . ."

"Does that make up for the loss of a husband? Talk sense, Jen. How would you feel if I was shot and killed? No," he flung up his hands, "Don't answer that. Knowing you, you'd probably run out and buy yourself a Porsche with the insurance money and forget me within five minutes."

"Steve! How could you say such a thing?" Tears rolled down her cheeks. "I love you so much that I'd want to die too. I couldn't live without you, you know that."

"And I suppose your mother doesn't feel like that about your father?" Steve asked wondering what went on in her fluffy head.

"Can we please stop talking about my blasted mother? She's all right. She didn't love Dad the way I love you," she scoffed, "I don't suppose she ever did. Let's get on with our own lives, and leave her to it," Her mood changed suddenly and she grinned. "Isn't it great? I should be getting some money soon from Dad's estate. I wonder how much he left me."

Steve stared at her in disbelief. The sooner he removed himself from this relationship the better, and yet he had given his parents his solemn vow to stick by Jenny until the baby was born. He guessed they thought he might change his mind about marrying her once he saw the child. For once he said nothing. What was the use? No matter what he said, he was in the wrong and he was tired of arguing.

Jenny chattered on about buying a house with her inheritance as he sat and stared at his plate. She was so shallow that he could hardly stand it. Pushing back his chair, he took his jacket and gym bag from the floor.

"I'm going to the gym for an hour or so. I won't be late."

Jenny stared at him resentfully. "You mean I have to stay here on my own?" Her voice headed into the whining octave. "What about me? What am I going to do? If we had a television, it might be different."

Steve sighed and turned to look at her. "I always go to the gym on Tuesdays, you know that. If you want a TV, then get a part-time job and buy one."

Jenny flounced her head away from him, a familiar gesture. Sullenly she started to plan how to make him pay for that remark. He was the man of the house, and he should earn enough money to support her. What was going to happen when the baby arrived? How could they manage on his measly pay? Maybe it was as well she had come into money of her own.

All evening she sat brooding on her awful life. When she first moved in with Steve, it was marvellous because things went the way she wanted. Now he was always broke, and she was stuck in this tiny cramped apartment. Petulantly she decided to go to see her mother: at least she could watch television.

Janet, not unusually, found it difficult to adjust to her new life as a widow. She was so used to bouncing everything off Jim, especially since she quit her part time job at a boutique some months ago. Constantly she found herself turning to ask him a question, listening for his key in the door, waking to wonder where he was when she put out a hand and found the bed empty. Her life felt suddenly so barren.

His death was all her fault; that was the hardest part to accept. Guilt made her depressed, made her nervous, and she found herself talking aloud to him, telling him she was sorry. It slowly became easier to accept, after all her guilt was not achieving anything. Nothing would bring him back. Survivors' guilt, they called it, and in her case it was very real. She must make a new life for herself now, look forward to her life alone.

But it was not easy living alone after being so close to Jim for nearly thirty years, not that she'd expected it to be otherwise, but then she supposed that most newly widowed women felt the same. It was all a matter of becoming accustomed to being alone, but now even the word 'alone' sounded frightening to her. The thought of being a single woman with money didn't make it any easier.

It hurt her very much when Jenny walked out. Janet felt very much abandoned, so when Jenny rang the front door bell, Janet felt so very pleased that she welcomed her daughter with open arms.

Jenny, pleased at the change in her mother, never realized how much it hurt Janet to pretend that things were back to normal. They sat watching TV and Jenny talked about Steve and the baby and Mrs. Rigby, everything but her father or the funeral.

"I'm going to start work for Richard Wyatt next week," Janet announced as they drank cocoa later, pleased that Richard had offered her a part-time clerical position in his office. She looked forward to working. Richard, their long time friend, had used his expertise with the profusion of official forms needing processing, handling everything with skill and ease. No wonder he was such a sought after lawyer.

It surprised Janet to discover the settlement amount was for over half a million dollars US and Jim's life insurance, being double indemnity, was for nearly the same amount. She was now a wealthy lady, and while that did not make up for the loss of a husband, it did take the sting out of things. Until she came to terms with everything, the job was the answer to many problems; it would get her out of the house and give her an interest in life.

"What can *you* do in a law office?" Jenny scoffed, amazed. "You've only ever had jobs in stores, and what did you know about the law? You're kidding yourself if you think you could work in an office, especially a law office. Haven't you always said you wished you'd had a good education like me?"

"You'd be surprised what I can do, Jenny," Janet said with a trace of her old spunk. "I know how to type, I can do the filing, I can answer the phone, I can add and subtract. There are a hundred things I can do around an office." Janet felt vexed that Jenny seemed to think her incapable of anything.

"Sorree! Gee, you're so touchy."

"Touchy?" Janet exploded. "I have every right to be touchy. I just lost my husband. What is the matter with you, child? Don't you realize your father is dead?" Janet stared at her daughter, baffled.

Jenny tried not to shrug; that wouldn't be politic. "I do know, Mum, I do know, honest. I just don't get emotional like you. I handle it quietly without any hysterics. You should try it."

"Spoken like a wise old woman, Jenny," Janet laughed mirthlessly. "I should have asked you how I should handle it in the first place."

"There you go again, all hysterical. Cool it, Mum."

"Why don't you go home now, Jenny, before I say something I might regret?" Janet realized she had clenched her hands. She could have hit out, such was her anger. No way Jenny would understand what she felt. She and Jim had done themselves no favours by catering to her for all those years. It was going to be a long time before Jenny grew up enough to think as an adult.

SEVEN

Steve carefully stalked a teenager who had shoplifted a transistor radio from Radio Shack. Skilled in this tactic, he appeared uninterested in the youth because he looked elsewhere every time the boy turned around to see if anyone had spotted him. The teen wandered through the mall, checking out the sidewalk sale displays, working his way to the exit. The minute he stepped outside the door, Steve grabbed him, and demanded he accompany him to the security office.

To get to the office they went through a door to the left of the entrance, and at the side of the supermarket. Most people were unaware of this locked passageway used only by security or maintenance staff. Steve held the boy's arm in a tight grip as the lad desperately sought some way to free himself and escape.

The long passage was of painted cement blocks with no alcoves or side passages. The boy started to panic. If they searched him, they might charge him for sure and he saw no place to dispose of the radio. He struggled to free himself.

Steve became enraged. Young punk, he thought, increasing his grip, and roughly pushing the boy along. Then the lad dug in his heels and lashed out with his brass tipped cowboy boot, hitting Steve on the shin. The radio fell from his pocket to the floor and smashed. They wrestled for a second before Steve slammed the boy against the wall. He viciously started to pummel him in the stomach. In desperation, the lad grabbed at Steve's holster trying to get at his gun. Steve's fury got the better of him. All the rage he'd withheld against Jenny came to the fore and, taking out the gun, he pistol whipped the boy until his head ran with blood as he screamed for help.

Suddenly Steve realized what he had done, and pushed the boy against the wall where he slid down in a whimpering bloody heap. Steve nudged him with his foot.

"Get the hell out of here, punk, and don't let me catch you in the mall again. Go on, scoot."

The boy struggled to his feet and staggered down the passage. As he neared the end he turned and yelled: "You ain't gonna get away with this. I'm going to the police and you'll be charged."

As Steve moved threateningly toward him, he frantically raced away. Steve could have kicked himself. Now he was in big trouble. If anyone found out he had even as much as touched a suspect, they would fire him and he could lose all hope of getting another job in security. He hoped the boy kept his mouth shut. Anyway it was the boy's word against his and he'd always had a clean record.

He went to the security office toilet, washed his hands and cleaned the blood off his gun, straightening his uniform and checking it for blood spots before he sauntered into the mall. The boy was nowhere in sight.

Jenny, cunning enough to smell the money coming to her mother, made sure she went home to visit at least twice a week. It was the least she could do for her old mum, she told herself, her mother being so very alone. Janet, recognizing the ploy, told her not to bother if she had other things to do, that she was fine, but Jenny decided she must stick around until she got her hands on her inheritance. Continually she obliquely referred to the insurance money, Janet, recognizing this, refused to rise to the bait.

Jim had left Jenny forty-thousand dollars in a trust fund, but she would not get it until she was twentyfive, the age Jim had thought she might know how to handle the money. Jenny was a squander bug; money flowed through her fingers like water, so fast her fingers never got wet.

Jenny, who had talked herself into believing that her mother was going to keep the lot, finally came out and asked for the money.

"So when do I get my inheritance?" she asked. "We need that money with the baby on the way."

"Why don't you ask Richard Wyatt?" Janet said quietly, "He's trustee of your father's estate. It's no good asking me about it because I have no control over your trust fund."

"What?" Jenny was red faced and angry. "Why can't I get the money my own father left me? Why do I have to ask that stupid old fool for what's rightfully mine?"

Janet kept her temper, though it was not easy. "Because your father appointed him the trustee, Jenny. Richard has always been our lawyer, you know that. Richard is not stupid, nor is he a fool. Watch your tongue." Janet busied herself in the cupboard not wanting to look at her daughter.

"Do I have to go and see him, or can I telephone?"

"I expect you can call him, but if I were you, I'd make an appointment to see him."

"You do it," Jenny demanded. "You work there. You get me my money."

"It's out of my hands entirely," Janet said firmly. "You have to see Richard yourself."

"What kind of mother are you, anyway?" Jenny flared, "You stand by and let that man have my money? He's probably hoping you won't tell me so he can keep it for himself. It's not fair," Her voice slid into a whining tone and Janet wearily closed her eyes.

"How could you, Mother, how could you? You don't care about me, and you don't like Steve. You've never liked him, and you hate the fact that I'm having his baby. I hate you, I hate you, I hate you! You miserable old cow." Jenny grabbed her shoulder bag and made for the door.

"Jenny! If you don't take that back, I wash my hands of you. How dare you accuse me of not caring? How dare you accuse Richard Wyatt of anything underhanded? How dare you accuse me of being a bad mother, and how could you call me names like that? I've done everything for you, Jenny, everything." Janet angrily turned away and began to wash the kitchen counter.

Jenny paused for a second and realized she was unable to counter argue anything her mother said.

"Oh, all right! I'll go to see old Wyatt," she said shamefaced with very bad grace. "You make the appointment for me. Okay? You work there after all."

Even though she felt hurt and indignant, Janet agreed. "All right, I'll think about it, but I suggest you go home now. I don't want to see you again until I ask you to visit. It's too upsetting."

It was on the tip of Jenny's tongue to say: "See, you always think about number one. Why don't you think about me once in a while?" She thought it, but wise for once, she didn't say it.

EIGHT

Janet was on the switchboard when Jenny called. "Did you make my appointment with Wyatt, Mum?"

"No, I didn't. I'll put you through to his secretary. Make the appointment yourself," Janet said as she quickly transferred the call. It was about time Jenny started to act like the adult she claimed to be.

Jenny felt hurt and angry that her mother had cut her off so abruptly. However, a pleasant voice was saying, "Mr. Wyatt's office," and she had to reply.

The appointment was set for the following week. When Jenny demanded to see him that very day, the woman snippily told her Mr. Wyatt was a very busy man.

"He's in court every day this week and has only one free day for appointments next week." She warned Jenny that she must be on time for her appointment as Mr. Wyatt's next free time was in a further two weeks.

Disgruntled at being spoken to in such a fashion, Jenny slammed down the phone. First her mother acted so cold and strange, and now a jumped up twit of a secretary talked to her as though she were a nobody.

Wait till she got her money, she'd show them! Idly she found herself wondering how long it might be before her mother kicked the bucket.

While this train of thought might have dismayed someone else, it never occurred to Jenny that she was wishing her mother dead. Jenny knew sooner or later her mother must die and she would inherit everything. That's what old people were for, to leave you money, lots of lovely money. She felt no guilt, no unease, considered no remorse at her thoughts, all that mattered was how things affected her. Her father's death made little impression on her, she hadn't much liked him, even if he were her father, and she did not miss him particularly. That he had left her money in his will, that's what was important.

She and Steve presently lived in an uneasy truce. Gone were the carefree days and nights of lovemaking and talking about everything under the sun. He said hello and goodbye, talked about baseball or the gym, asked her how she had spent her day. That was the extent of their present relationship, and she found it unpleasant. Irritated by his coldness, she didn't tell him about her appointment or her inheritance. Once she got her hands on it, she promised herself, she must dump him. What did she need Steve Rigby for when she had money in the bank?

It was just as well she had said nothing because Richard Wyatt explained to her that, under the terms of the will, the estate tied the money up the money until she was twenty-five. No matter how much she had cried and talked about her unborn child and her lack of funds, he refused to advance her a cent.

On the way out of the office suite she glared at her mother and hissed: "You damn well knew about that, didn't you?"

After spending a couple of hours sulking and feeling sorry for herself, she decided staying with Steve was her only means of support. She was carrying his child for heaven's sake. Strange, she always believed that when she found the man of her dreams, her Prince Charming, all her troubles might vanish like smoke in the wind. He would love her and care for her, pamper and treat her like the princess she always longed to be, would never be unkind or unfaithful, never be angry or sullen. Yet the idealized fairy story Prince had never appeared, all she had was Steve.

When Steve arrived home that evening, she made an effort to be nice to him and had cooked dinner. Meat loaf from a mix with instant mashed potatoes, frozen sprouts and gravy out of a can.

Steve, realizing this was a supreme effort on her part, told her how impressed he was with the meal and how she should start to try more recipes, saying he would give her extra housekeeping money.

Jenny crawled over him that evening. She seemed so loving that he almost forgave her everything, although when they made love he did not satisfy her and almost ruptured himself doing it three times.

For days after that he considered things almost idyllic. Jenny seemed so pleasant and happy that Steve forgave the burned offering of steak she put before him one evening, and they even laughed about it later.

Nevertheless, Jenny was biding her time. She had to get back into her mother's good graces to get her hands on money. Surely her mother must give her an advance now that she was so very rich. If not, maybe she could get a bank loan against her expectations.

Looking around the shabby room, she considered what she could do with the money. Buy a house of their own, and furnish it with deep upholstered couches and chairs, a real wood dining room table and chairs, carpets, lace curtains. She wanted parquet floors and oak kitchen cabinets, like her home in Alta Vista. Although maybe, she thought now, she might buy modern stuff, things trendy and fashionable, of glass and chrome, stainless steel and wrought iron and leave the floors uncarpeted.

She donned her coat to go out to read decorating magazines to choose her favourite decoration ideas.

Janet went out to dinner with Richard four or five times. Janet and Jim had always liked Richard, their first lawyer in Canada. Although well into his fifties, with a head of thick white hair, he was tall and imposing and in great shape. They found it easy to talk to each other, and she felt nothing like a client when they met socially, nor did he treat her like a client or employee.

It was a shock to her to realize that she felt warm toward him these days. Of course that was only to be expected, it was common for someone who helped you through such troubled times to become larger than life, to assume the attributes of a more than a professional supporting and sympathetic ear. Janet felt grateful for both his legal expertise and his friendship.

She smiled now, thinking about him. Richard was such a gentleman that he always kissed her hand when he dropped her off, after a date. She found herself wishing he would kiss her lips instead. Janet blushed, although alone, to think she could be so unfaithful to her recently dead husband. He was hardly cold in his grave and already she was looking at another man. How very shocking that seemed.

Richard Wyatt liked Janet. She was what he thought of as his type of woman good looking, good figure, intelligent and personable. His ex-wife had been a beauty, although a stupid woman and not very outgoing, too insecure to talk to people she did not know. It was not a good match for him in the course of business. He felt no surprise when she left him for a Presbyterian minister, and, since she'd had little impact on his life, he did not miss her.

Now much to his surprise, he found himself looking at Janet as a prospective wife. She possessed all the qualities a man in his position required; she was not flighty or flippant, she knew how to dress and could make people feel at ease. Yes, he could do far worse than Janet Stevens. They had known each other for so long, too, and were comfortable with each other. Nevertheless, that he had judged her as a prospect, was that socially correct? That he felt so cold blooded about it? Surely love should hit you like a ton of bricks, and gloss over any character faults the object of your affections may have. Again, maybe he was being too vain, assuming too much. What if she didn't like him in that way? He thought about that once or twice, but pushed it out of his mind as she looked at him in a very flirtatious manner. Still, it might prove embarrassing if he were wrong about her feelings.

Now he thought back to the procession of women who had come

and gone through his life since his divorce. All of them lacked that special something, although God knows many of them had tried to snare him through both fair and foul means; astutely he recognized that for what it was and stopped seeing them. None, however, possessed that indefinable spark that made him think of marriage in the first place.

A letter ordered Steve to appear before the area manager at the downtown office. With a sinking heart he knew it was not for a commendation. The stupid kid must have squealed.

Nervous, he waited in the reception area for someone to escort him to the office, his mind thinking over his planned responses. It took him four days to come up with logical reasons why the kid was lying. Anyway, no one could prove anything against him, he hoped.

An efficient looking young woman escorted him to the office and left him at the door.

"Come in, Steve. Have a seat," Gerry McIntrye said expansively, gesturing to a chair.

Maybe this wasn't what he thought. Gerry seemed very relaxed, not as though he were going to discipline him.

"How are things going, Steve?"

"Fine."

"Any problems at Pinecrest Mall?"

"Nope."

"You have any run-ins with juvenile offenders lately?" Gerry, an ex-policeman and a master at interrogation, noticed the flicker of fear that ran across Steve's face, and knew Steve had indeed beaten up the kid.

"No."

"Think back now, to July twenty-fourth. Did you try to arrest a young man?"

"No sir, I don't think so. Is it in the book?"

"No, there's nothing in the book and that's why I have you here today, to get to the bottom of some very serious charges against you."

Steve's heart skipped a beat. The rotten young sod *had* reported him. "Charges?" he asked, looking puzzled. His hands tightened on the chair arms and Gerry noticed his white knuckles.

"A young man charges that you pistol whipped him, also punched him repeatedly in the stomach. The hospital report states he had internal injuries and needed fifteen stitches to his face and head."

Steve's eyes flickered back and forth but never paused on Gerry's face. "Nothing to do with me, chief. I know nothing about it." He tried to make his voice sound sincere.

"He picked you out from the photos we showed him."

He snorted. "Why pick on me? Anyway, he must have known I was one of the security guards. All the kids know me," he blustered, "This is victimization, if you ask me. It's a set up."

"I doubt that, Steve. Why would anyone want to set you up?" Gerry pulled a photo out from a file. "You recognize this lad?"

Steve took the photo, thankful his hand did not shake. A black and white eight by ten, it showed a severely beaten youth whose face was crisscrossed with stitches, both eyes blackened. God, did I do all that? I must have been as mad as hell, he thought, as he passed it back. "Never saw him in my life," he said firmly, trying to sound nonchalant. "Doesn't look like any of the local kids who hang around the mall. Is this the one accusing me?"

"That's the boyyo." Gerry sat forward in his chair. "Are you sure you never saw him before? He says he has two buddies who saw you take him to security. They were the ones who took him to the emergency room to get him stitched up." Gerry sat back again and looked at Steve intently.

Something about Steve made Gerry feel uncomfortable. His eyes were shifty, and he never looked you in the eye. While Gerry had not entirely trusted Steve, he had hired him for his physique. A wellbuilt security guard could do more with a look than any strong arm tactics, and Steve's performance of his duties had been exemplary, until now.

"No sir. I never saw him before," Steve wondered how much the other kids had seen. They couldn't have seen anything other than him taking the kid to the security corridor. Shrugging he asked: "So what happens now? I never saw him and I certainly didn't beat him up. He's conning you, Gerry."

"Report to work tomorrow at Greenwood and keep your nose clean, Steve. We'll keep you there for a while. There'll have to be a complete investigation of this matter, of course. The kid knows exactly where the Stonecrest security passage is and showed me where he says you beat him. We found blood spots on the wall."

Shit, Steve thought, his stomach contracting, I should have checked the damned wall. I should have seen it when I picked up that broken radio.

"You can argue all you like, but the kid knows what he's talking about. The police must take over now. The lad's father is suing the mall." Gerry closed the file and stood, signalling the end of the interview.

If he hadn't been so short staffed, he could have suspended Steve until the investigation was complete, but Greenwood was a tiny mall and the locals were old age pensioners. Steve could do no harm there. He hoped.

Steve slouched off downtown and went into a sports bar. He sat talking to two of his company's off duty security guards and they discussed the charges against Steve.

"Deny everytin', mon," Don, a tall black man, said, "They'll never be able to pin nuttin' on you. Nobody saw you do nuttin', and even if you was seen takin' the young bugga inta da passage, so what? Who can say what happened den? It happen to me twice awready and you don' have to worry, mon. No one can finger you for nuttin'. It's your word against theirs, and who dey gonna believe?"

"Too true," The other guard said, "I got charged with rape a year back and I even got an apology from the boss." He laughed as if it were a joke. "They couldn't prove anything then, either. Mind you, she wasn't half a nice bit of stuff." He licked his lips and winked.

"You mean you did it?" Steve was amazed. Rape, and he got away with it?

"Nah. I done nothing mate. Whatever gave you that idea?" he said slyly, winking. "Then I got a letter telling me they was sorry about it' 'cos I lost pay and was suspended. I got moved to another project downtown and even got a raise. Now would they do that for someone who was guilty?" Again he winked and smiled.

Steve already felt better. Both of these guys had been guilty as hell, he knew it and they knew it. The old boys' club supported its fraternity members, it seemed.

"You got nuttin' to worry 'bout, Stevey boy. You keep denying it and the boss'll find ways to get you out of it. You can call on us as character witnesses if you like." Again Don winked.

NINE

Jenny schemed how to get around her mother because if she managed to get her hands on five thousand dollars, she could put a down payment on a townhouse in Briarside. Briarside, a small community on the eastern outskirts, was rapidly developing into a bedroom town. Young couples with children moved into the plentiful cheap housing, and already it boasted a large mall and a bus service. Exactly the thing for them and the baby when he arrived, she thought, and a new house too, one in which nobody else had lived. She reread the ad.

Already in her mind's eye she could see the small house, the neat garden, the tree in the front window at Christmas. They could have colonial furniture from The Brick, they could have a dishwasher plus a washer and dryer, Steve could build extra shelves and a garden shed.

Sighing with pleasure, she picked up the latest copy of Better Homes and looked at decorating ideas.

Jenny made many plans, all of them including Steve. While at first she wanted to get rid of him, not wanting him to get at any of her money, a boy needed his father and she knew her unborn child was going to be a boy. How she knew, she had no idea, but she knew.

For days she had plotted and planned, and for days she felt sure of what she must do, but then the ideas melted away from her mind. She started thinking about it again. Strange how one minute she knew her mind, then suddenly she didn't. It was always that way with her. Like when she had listened so attentively at school, and on the way home had planned her homework essay, but the minute she sat to write what she knew, she didn't know it anymore.

She admired a glossy picture for Armstrong Flooring. This was nice, this country kitchen in the full page layout, all those baskets and containers. Yes, she must have a kitchen like this one.

Janet, attending a fund raiser for CHEO, the Children's Hospital of Eastern Ontario, looked forward to meeting the various celebrities. She purchased a new little black dress for the occasion.

Richard bought her a beautiful corsage that she pinned to her black evening purse. Her simple but expensive dress was ornate enough with the addition of her grandmother's diamond starburst brooch at the neck. Janet knew she looked both chic and pampered, having spent an hour at L'Image where she enjoyed a facial and massage, had her hair styled and had a manicure.

She gazed around the ballroom of the Radisson Hotel with pleasure as Richard talked to one of his associates. This was the life for her expensive, tasteful and exciting. Yes, she thought, she could get used to this in a very short time. Every person she met was a 'somebody'. They were all so very well groomed, so educated, so suave and sophisticated. Strangely she realized she felt at home, not at all out of place.

The memory of Jim stayed with her, of course, although now she tended not to superimpose his face on other men. Now she did not feel the same pangs of grief when she heard someone whistle like him, or see a man walk like him. At first she found herself searching for his face everywhere. In crowds on television, in shopping malls, working in the bank, always she looked for him. Now that had stopped almost although the smell of Polo, his usual aftershave caused her stomach to contract.

How very soon it was to be more of her own person, she thought, to have put Jim aside after all the years they were together. Maybe she had not loved him as much as she had thought, because she knew of other widows who never got over the loss of their spouse.

Still, then, of course, she thought, pleased for herself, the widows were not dating a successful wealthy lawyer. Richard had brought her out of her shell, changed her entire outlook and she would always be grateful to him.

"So what's new with you?" Rita asked as she looked him over, admiration in her eyes.

Steve smiled as his eyes feasted on her tight sweater and false eyelashes. Rita, a goodlooking chick, was a tiger in the sack. Her tarty looks didn't bother Steve much, although he might have preferred that she kept the war paint to a minimum.

He smiled warmly. "Not much. I keep seeing you a lot lately."

"Yeah, I guess. You still with that little kid? I thought you said you were going to dump her?" Rita fluttered her eyelashes.

"Yeah well," he admitted ruefully, "I *have* to stay for a while. She's pregnant."

Rita burst out laughing. "You stupid great lummox! You let her do that to you? You've got less in your head than you've got hair on it, I'll say that for you, Steve. Dump the brat and move in with me. You know we're good for each other, and I'll not get pregnant."

He sighed bitterly. "I wish I could, Rita, but my mother made me swear on the Bible."

"So? You think God's going to strike you dead if you leave?" she scoffed, men were sometimes so stupid. "Talk sense, Steve. Get the hell out while you're able."

He groaned. "I can't leave her now, Rita, but that doesn't mean that you and I can't see each other. She's not exactly in any shape for socializing, if you get my drift. Us two could date once in a while."

"Yeah, I suppose so." Rita did not sound too thrilled. "You give me a call sometime. If you do leave her, you come straight to my place. You've always got a bed at my place, anytime."

"Thanks 'Ree, sure you won't have another drink?"

"No thanks, got to rush. See ya," She wiggled her way to the door, turned to waggle her fingers and bat her false eyelashes.

He felt an electric thrill run through his groin and wondered how he could get away from Jenny and still keep his mother off his back.

Jenny again began planning her wedding, this time with the help of Esther Rigby. They told each other it was time for the nuptials - before Jenny showed too much, and way before the baby was born. They had not yet informed Steve. They were keeping it that way for now.

". . .and we can get that place in Carleton Place to do the cooked meats," Esther continued, "They slow cook roasts and things and do ever such a good job of them, so that'll help with the catering. No need to go hog wild, is there? We can do most of the other food ourselves, with the help of a bakery and a couple of neighbours of mine."

Jenny said nothing as she sat pouting. She didn't want a cheap wedding. She wanted a white satin and lace dress with a train, four bridesmaids, a nice stone church with an organist, and a catered reception with a band. Esther was all for a wedding at her house, with home cooking.

"Well? What do you think?" Esther realized she had been chattering away for ages as Jenny said nothing.

"About what?"

"About the wedding, Jenny. Haven't you heard a word I said?"

"Sorree! I was thinking that I'd like a church wedding, white dress and veil and all that."

"It's late for the white dress, deary. That's only for virgins," Esther said a trifle cattily.

"Don't be so silly," Jenny flashed irritably. "Anyone can wear a white dress. It's a bride's prerogative to wear white. You don't *have* to be a virgin. You're so old-fashioned and behind the times, Mrs. Rigby, I *want* a white dress with a train," she said firmly.

"But you can't do that, Jenny. It isn't right, not right at all," Esther said worriedly. She was old fashioned, she realized that, but a pregnant bride dressed in white somehow went against the grain.

"Want to bet? I can do anything I like," Jenny said smugly. "I *want* a white dress, and I shall *have* a white dress." When she conned some money out of her mother, she would buy the wedding dress she had seen at June Brides that cost more than a thousand dollars. After the wedding she would have it cleaned and packed away for her daughter's wedding and start a family tradition. Jenny felt so sure of herself these days and knew it - having money did that for you, she told herself. Yes, having money made all the difference. Then she recalled the problems with her mother.

It didn't seem to matter how pleasant she was to her, Janet wasn't having any of it.

No matter how much she apologized, Jenny's outburst had hurt Janet so badly that she could hardly stand to be civil to her. While Janet realized Jenny's outburst was simply temper, it always was with Jenny, she didn't like it and it offended her. No matter how wheedling and contrite Jenny acted, her mother ignored her blandishments: Janet found it difficult to forgive.

Jim and Janet tried to teach Jenny that you cannot take back a spoken word, no matter how much you apologize. It lingers in the mind forever, always niggling and nagging, and no amount of time or effort could ever erase it. Janet loved Jenny, but Jenny was, as she so often said, her own person and to all intents and purposes had turned her back on her mother. Janet knew full well, though, that as long as she had money in the bank, Jenny would be sniffing around.

Maybe it the genes inherited from her birth parents made her this way, Janet thought now. She and Jim attempted to instill a sense of fair play and pride into Jenny. All her young life they had taught her strong moral and ethical values, or at least thought they had. Apparently Jenny only learned what suited her, not what was correct.

Jenny's birth mother came from Montreal and that was as much as Janet knew, and as much as she wanted to know at the time. So thrilled was she to get a baby, that any inquiries about the background of the parents had been the last thing on her mind. Now she wondered how wise they had been. Could the mother have inherited insanity from her family? Even with all her advantages, Jenny never displayed any of the qualities that education or upbringing should have instilled.

Her childhood brought years of worry, years of upset. Jenny did not learn when she didn't like a subject, and no amount of cajoling or coaching could get the basics into her head. Then suddenly she knew everything, was letter perfect. It was all so upsetting. Janet had twice taken her to the doctor to find out whether it was a physical deficiency of some kind.

Their family GP checked Jenny out and found her perfectly healthy. Saying she was going through a phase, he suggested they not force into something she didn't want to do, but teach her surreptitiously so she didn't realize it was a lesson.

This had worked partially although not perfectly, and Jenny continually brought home notes from the teacher saying she was inattentive and causing trouble in class. She was too impulsive, too quick to raise her hand to someone who was reading a book she wanted, or using paint that she needed. The other children feared her temper. The teachers reported she was above average intelligence, and simply needed to apply herself. She was, they said, uncooperative, stubborn, careless and recalcitrant. They even mentioned ADD, attention deficit disorder, more than once and Janet took Jenny to see the GP again and asked the question.

His tests showed Jenny as perfectly normal. IQ testing showed her to be above average and her IQ 128.9. He suggested that maybe a change of school might be of benefit. Maybe it was the teacher who was the cause of the problem, that was commonplace.

That year they switched Jenny to the all-girl Catholic Grammar School. Here she seemed to improve, though she still brought home notes.

After all these years Jenny had not changed The only reason could be heredity. Her attitude must be a mental defect inherited from her birth parents and Janet found herself wondering now what they had been like.

Whatever happened, she could not allow Jenny to start interfering in her life. No, Jenny must learn to stand on her own two feet, take charge of her own life. Standing aside to watch her make mistakes was difficult, but Jenny needed to learn the hard way. It was the only way she ever did learn.

"Come off it, Steve, Jenny screeched, "You've been with that woman again, haven't you?"

Steve, who had come in the door, threw up his hands in disgust. "I told you twice that I was at work. I did a double shift."

"Bullshit!"

Her language shocked Steve. Jenny rarely resorted to profanity, although lately she had started swearing when things didn't go her way.

"What's the matter with you, Jen? You keep telling me how much education you had, and all the extra classes you took, and yet you sound like a stevedore from the docks. Not very feminine, if you ask me. Swearing isn't ladylike." Steve threw his coat on the table where it landed among the dirty dishes from last night's supper. "What did you have to do that was so important that you couldn't clear the table?"

"Oh, yes, change the subject, eh? Well, it won't wash this time, Steve." She stood with her hands on her hips, confronting him, so sure she was right and he was again in the wrong. "You've been screwing around, haven't you? What about me? Stuck here on my own, pregnant, penniless and forgotten. You don't love me, you never did love me, I know that now. Wait until your mother hears about this, what with the wedding set and all." Her shrill voice became annoying and his hands clenched into fists. A man didn't need this the minute he set foot in the door at night.

He stood clutching the chair back. "God! What's with the wedding bit again? Listen to me and listen carefully to every word." He spoke slowly and clearly, so she would understand. "I will not marry you, and even if they carry me down the aisle kicking and screaming," He raised his voice. "*I am not going to marry you.* I agreed to stay until the baby was born, but I made no other commitment than that."

He looked around the messy room Jenny had ignored for at least two weeks and it looked like a disaster area. He shook his head sadly, knowing she would never change, no matter what she promised.

"But your mother doesn't say that," Jenny shook her fist angrily. "She said you swore on the Bible that you'd never leave me. She says the baby will be a bastard if it hasn't got a legal father, and people will look on me as a fallen woman. She says . . ."

"To blazes with this. Leave my mother out of it. You listen to me, I don't care what my mother says, I don't care what you say, I just don't care. I am *not* marrying you! I wouldn't never want to be tied down to such a childish, foul mouthed, spoiled, selfcentred brat as you, Jenny. Baby or no baby, *I am not going to marry you, ever!*" he shouted angrily. "Discussion over. You made arrangements for a wedding, eh? Well, go find yourself a groom, I won't be attending."

Steve grabbed at his coat and two plates slid to the floor with a loud crash. Slamming out of the apartment, he called over his shoulder: "I won't back this time, Jen. Enough is enough. Get yourself home to your mother's."

Jenny threw the other plates at the door in rage and pondered on her situation. He was as stubborn as she in many ways. Suddenly her mind niggled with doubt at his threat to leave, maybe he *had* left. Well, she couldn't go crawling back to her mother as it would be like admitting she was wrong, and Janet was right.

As she lay in bed thinking things over for the millionth time, she realized no one was going to help her. Miserable, she sobbed wearily, then stopped. It didn't seem worth it, not with nobody around to comfort her. Steve was her reason for living and she must get him back. Tomorrow she must call Esther; Esther always helped her. Funny how someone she could not abide might prove to be her saviour.

TEN

Steve knocked on Rita's apartment door, having managed to get through the outside security door by walking into the lobby with a tenant.

Ready for bed, she warily opened the door on the chain, peering through the gap.

"Steve," she cried delightedly and threw the door open. "Come in, come in."

Steve took her in his arms and kissed her deeply. Knowing she wore nothing under her housecoat, immediately aroused him. It was nearly an hour later before they talked.

"I've left her."

"Good. Are you going to stay with me?" Rita snuggled closer and kissed his chest.

"Can I stay for while? Until I get another place?"

"We could get a larger apartment together, if that's what you'd like," Rita said, already visualizing their life together. She had always fancied Steve, all those muscles.

"Maybe," Steve felt unwilling to commit himself to another relationship so quickly. If he could stay here for a week or so, he thought, he could make a decision. What with the bother at work and the upcoming hearing, he wasn't exactly in the mood for romantic involvement. Still, Rita was a good sort and probably didn't want a commitment either. He knew she had a score of regular dates. After kissing her and hugging her warmly, he rolled onto his back, beginning to snore in less than a minute.

Rita, miffed at his snoring, lay wondering what on earth she saw in him. He was not exactly intelligent, he was a womanizer, he wasn't burning with ambition and, in fact, if she thought about it sensibly, she ought to tell him to get lost. But he was such a hunk, she loved being seen with him, being envied by other women. She adored the way he made love to her, although a voice in the back of her mind told her he was only interested in his own satisfaction. She could do far better than Steve Rigby, but the trouble was that lately nobody else seemed to want her. Look at the way he kept coming back to her. Surely he loved her, surely he wanted to stay with her forever and no other woman had ever brought him back, only herself, Rita Spencer. Yes, she was the one, the only one for Steve, though it was not love but probably lust she felt for him.

Putting her arm across his chest, she sank into sleep.

Janet looked astounded when Richard proposed. While she thought their relationship had progressed, it shocked her when he asked her to marry him so soon. They talked for hours about what it meant to both of them if they took this step.

"I don't want to rush you into anything, Janet," Richard said earnestly. "We should wait a reasonable length of time for the sake of propriety, but I do love you very much and want to be with you twenty-four hours a day."

"And I want to be with you, Richard." Whatever love she felt for Jim suddenly dissipated at hearing these words, and, while she thought of Jim with a great deal of affection, her deep grief was over. It astonished her that she had snapped out of her depression so soon, though suddenly she experienced a real sense of guilt. Yet the deep sense of remorse at leading Jim to his death had dissipated. Let's face it, she told herself, you're a mass of guilt, guilt that Jenny is as she is, guilt on her own insistence that they go to Vegas, now guilt because she even considered marrying another man.

Richard smiled as he looked into her eyes. "Let's face it, Janet, you're very vulnerable right now, and I shouldn't put any pressure on you. Why don't we continue our relationship as it is until we both feel positive that marriage is the right decision?"

"For heaven's sake, Richard," Janet said with laugh, "We're not teenagers." She clung to the lifeline he tossed, knowing marrying him solved so many of her problems. "I do think we know our own minds, but you're right to say we should wait longer. We need to think about it. I know my heart is screaming 'yes', but maybe we *are* rushing it. I wonder if my reaction is because marrying you will give me security." She saw the look that flashed across his face and felt sorry she'd voiced her concern, "Although I doubt that's what I feel, but I do want to be sure, otherwise it's not fair to you."

He kissed her softly and leaned back to gaze at her flushed face. "You're the one and only woman I have ever felt like this about, and it certainly isn't sex."

"And it won't be, not for a while," Janet said, shaking her finger at him, "We don't want to add another pressure."

"Sure, time enough, time enough, but we should at least give it a try," He chuckled, "We might not be compatible."

Janet laughed. "Spoken like a true male. Only one thing on your mind," Giggling like a teenager, she pushed him away. Her body was crying out for his, and the physical attraction she felt was like a pain. She stood. "I'd better make some coffee and get you off to your lonely little cot."

"We could live together for a while before you decide if you want to marry me," he suggested earnestly. Imagine him making such an offer, he thought, him a lawyer and a gentleman. Such a thing would never have entered his mind six months ago.

"Really, Richard," Janet scolded, inordinately pleased that he even considered it. Richard had his reputation to consider, and yet he would sacrifice it to have her with him. Although she should have felt insulted, it hadn't even offended her.

Richard pulled her back into his arms and hugged her close. "You're my type of girl, Janet. I guess in these days of feminism I'm insulting you by calling you a girl, but you know us old dogs, too old to be politically correct in a moment of passion. Will you be my girl?"

She laughed. "I already am, and I don't mind at all being called a girl. I don't go along with all this rubbish about 'persons', mail-persons, chairpersons, and the rest. Why would I want to step down off a pedestal and become a man in drag? I like being treated like a female, I like having doors opened for me, I like being deferred to by a man."

"Good for you," he chuckled. "We think alike on many things. I will always treat you like a lady, my love. Some of the barracudas I meet in business make me want to give them a mouthful, yet to be politically correct I have to bite my tongue and treat them as though I admired their stand. You know what I mean. I think women are equal to men in many ways, however, please leave us poor stags something to paw the ground for." He kissed her and she melted into him, soft and warm. It was difficult for him not to pick her up and carrying her off to the bedroom.

Janet wondered how Richard would like Jenny as a stepfather. He had no children and young adults could prove very trying to someone not familiar with the way their minds worked. Jenny's changes of mood were difficult enough for Janet. To an outsider they must seem very peculiar. Her bad judgement, her utter lack of conscience, her need for constant acceptance, her difficulty at times of separating fantasy from reality. Jenny was not an easy person to like or accept.

Janet already envisioned Jenny's reaction, and mentally shuddered. Richard was well aware of Jenny's situation since seeing her about her trust fund. Although he did not say much, he was always diplomatoc, Janet knew he hadn't much liked Jenny's attitude, but then neither did she.

In view of their engagement, she was not inclined to take Jenny back into the house. For eighteen years she had doted on and lavished her love on a child who was so bristly and antagonistic that it made her feel betrayed. Why had she bestowed so much unappreciated love on Jenny when the girl never reciprocated? Why should she feel any sense of guilt about Jenny's circumstances now? Surely Jenny had brought it all on herself.

It hurt so much that Jenny only thought of her father as a blank cheque. Jenny's very first question after Janet brought him home for burial was that of her inheritance. It had shocked her to realize how mercenary Jenny was, and on top of that, she looked on Janet as another source of revenue. While Janet agreed to pay the rent on the apartment temporarily because Steve had left Jenny, she would never consider taking her back into the house after those unkind, cruel words Yet when she explained that to her, Jenny pulled a face and shrugged as she tossed her peevishly.

In her happiness at finding a future with Richard, she suddenly looked on Jenny through new eyes. Janet still loved her, but it was not an all consuming, protective love. It was like love for favourite relative. Present, but not worth making a fuss over, and that made her feel guilty.

Richard received word from Las Vegas that the police had apprehended the two suspected killers. Paid assassins working for a major gambling club, regularly, and without a pang of conscience, bumped off those gamblers who welshed on their debts. The police arrested them when, stopped by a road check, a search found the guns that killed Jim and injured Ernie.

Not that that was any consolation to the many victims' nearest and dearest, but at least the killers were now in custody. The court slated the case for later in the year. Richard had not told Janet, there may not be much point in returning there for the case. As far as he could tell she had put the incident out of her mind, although he knew she could never completely forget the terrible event.

ELEVEN

No matter how hard she tried, Jenny couldn't find Steve. After she resorted to hanging around the mall coffee shop and chatting to the security guards, she eventually managed to question each of them, but all said they had no idea where Steve was working.

Esther Rigby, both for herself and for Jenny's sake, also tried to locate her son. The office, however, was averse to handing out home addresses. Not that Steve had told them he had moved.

Things were at a stalemate. Jenny felt sure once she could meet Steve face to face, she and he could work things out. Because he had gone out with another woman, she reasoned, was no reason to give up on him. The fact he had slept with another woman only made her more positive that she must win him back. In her mind it made him even more attractive because another woman desired him. Anyway, she must think of the child.

All she had wanted, she fumed, was a loving, handsome husband. She could even settle for a live-in lover, but currently she had nothing, and no one. How disillusioned she felt by the failure of Steve to measure up to her expectations. Her life was nothing like the romance novels promised, she saw no rose-covered cottage or attractive, wealthy husband who would do everything for her. Where had it all gone wrong? Oh well, she must bide her time, she told herself, he had to come back to her, she was far too good a catch for him to walk away. She knew that as a fact, and Steve also knew that. In this she felt supremely confident.

Now she was beginning to show, only to her own eyes of course, she made herself three maternity smocks. It was far too early to wear them, but it made her feel special, made her feel adult. She had always liked people looking at her: once for her good looks and attractive figure, and now for her pregnancy. The pregnancy set her apart since she looked younger than her age and so people might look at her thinking her far too young to be a mother.

That her mother paid the apartment rent was not enough, Jenny suddenly wanted to move back home where her mother could again cater to her. Living alone was not bad, but she detested cooking and cleaning. Of course she refused to listen to Esther Rigby's offer of accommodation, knowing Esther wanted to have her close by because of the grandchild.

Jenny yearned to return to the luxurious home where she belonged, but her mother dug in her heels and refused to take her back. Even as she stewed over this slight, Jenny realized her mother was not stupid, and probably knew full well that Jenny might take advantage of her, as she had always done. Glumly she came to realize that maybe she made her own problems. She was her own worst enemy on the family front.

Every Tuesday and Thursday afternoon Esther came to take her to the doctor's office for her hour session. It was during these drives that they talked about Steve. Esther felt positive he would return to marry her, although, as she pointed out to Jenny, they had to play this very cautiously, not push him too hard. Steve did not like anyone forcing him into anything. Jenny nodded and agreed, but Esther got the impression that Jenny might open her mouth again, and Steve would instantly rebel.

Jenny, she realized, was as bad as Steve in many ways. Always quick to take offence, quick to lie her way out of anything. Both of them were only aware of what they personally wanted, to heck with the consequences their actions had on other people's lives. When she thought about it, Steve and Jenny could never make it as a couple, they were too much alike.

Steve was not very intelligent, she and Frank had always known that, and, as long as he worked hard at school, they accepted his limitations. The Stevens had sent Jenny to the best schools, she'd had the best money could buy, and while she was very intelligent, she often seemed very stupid. She never thought before she spoke, never considered anyone but herself, was so egotistical that she thought everyone had only *her* interests at heart. She never seemed able to work things out in her mind. That Esther found disturbing. Jenny always wanted someone else to decide things, to take a problem off her shoulders.

So Jenny spent her days looking for Steve and sulking over the injustice of her situation. She became nasty to Esther when Esther asked about her welfare, and she was pissed off at her mother for saying she could not move back home. Furious at the inequity of everything, she walked around looking a picture of misery.

Then she got an idea.

Though her mother was giving her cash to pay the rent, she swallowed her pride and went to the welfare people posing as an abandoned common-law wife. Before the week was up, they had made her an allowance and were paying her rent direct to the landlord. Jenny had no intentions of telling her mother of these arrangements and smirked. Nobody could say that she did not use her head. With her brains she could accomplish anything.

Social services told her she soon could take the lease on a rent controlled townhouse. A bedsitter was no place to raise a child, they said, suggesting she looked at the townhouses in the west end subdivision, Westhaven, in which they housed their welfare cases. The houses included basic furniture and appliances.

Jenny felt proud of herself for having such foresight. She had always been so sure that she could stand on her own feet, and this was proof. Seeing how easily she got herself onto welfare was somehow not a disgrace in her eyes, it showed good planning. Then she reasoned that she could never let her mother know what she had done because Janet would be furious. It would be a matter of starving to death, she told herself, before she would ask her mother for anything more than the rent, and that cash could now be spent any way she saw fit. The welfare people would never know.

However, the shoddy row houses in Westhaven, did not impress her. Expecting smart townhouses with cultivated gardens, she looked aghast at the sight of so many run down row houses with patches of dirt in front of them. Screaming kids of all colours raced around the one-way street. Harassed looking, shabby women called for children to come home, hung washing or sat talking on the rickety steps.

The superintendent showed her around a recently vacated house saying it was already spoken for, but that her name was on his list for one of the next available units. The townhouse was compact but comfortable, having two bedrooms and a large bathroom upstairs, while downstairs was a living room/dining room and a small kitchen. The furniture, strictly utilitarian, looked adequate. The stove and fridge were almost new and the cheap carpeting seemed clean.

Most of the occupants of Westhaven were abandoned women, those whose husbands were wife beaters or welfare cases. The super told her his job was to keep things running smoothly for the tenants. All the units had a bell in the front hall that, when pushed, brought him running. Apparently he often functioned as a security guard when irate husbands showed up looking for their children.

Jenny thought about Westhaven as she sat on the bus. All the women she saw looked so hopeless. Was this what she wanted from her life? She didn't think so. Darn it all, if she could only return home. Too bad that her mother had no sense of humour. Why make a big fuss over one little remark? She had become far too crotchety, but then it crossed her mind that perhaps it was because of her father's sudden death. No matter, it still rankled when Janet refused to take her back to her good address, pleasant home and a comfortable life.

Even considering she would soon have an entire house for herself, she did not much relish being on her own. For years she had dreamed about getting out from un der her parent's control and had thought Steve Rigby was the answer. Too bad he turned out to be such a fink, although she would take him back in a flash if she could find him. She heaved a sigh of desperation and shivered.

Three weeks later she began to feel ill. With nobody watching her diet, she subsisted on chocolate bars and soft drinks. After two days of feeling so sick she could hardly stand, she knew must see the doctor. Not having a phone meant she must go down to the pay phone in the lobby to make an appointment. With perspiration streaming down her face, she tried to dial the number, and, leaning against the wall for support, fainted.

When she came to her senses, she was in the hospital where a doctor told her she was suffering from malnutrition and anaemia. In her purse they had found her mother's telephone number and a pale and worried Janet rushed to see her.

The words woke her from her drowsing. "How are you feeling, Jenny?"

Jenny's lip curled nastily. "All right, I guess. Nice of you to worry about me."

"There's no need to be sarcastic. Of course I worry about you." Janet struggled to stay calm, knowing the situation would be everybody's fault but Jenny's.

"Huh! Seems like it. You didn't want me to move back home, but you offered to pay my rent. Some mother you are," she said scathingly.

"Jenny! I see no need for all this sniping. I *can't* have you move back home. You said far too much for me to forgive so easily. Time might change that, but for now you're not moving back home."

Jenny pulled a face. "Gee, thanks a lot. So you came to tell me that you've disinherited me. Is that it? Huh! Just what I needed, Mum." Tossing her head, she looked out the dust spattered, grimy window.

Janet sighed. If only Jenny would listen, would try to understand."I didn't say that, Jenny. It's simply that we need some time apart. I find it hard to forgive things you said, but I still love you. I'll always love you. I'll pay your rent and make sure you lack for nothing, but I do not want you in the house. We'll spend more time fighting than anything else. You know it and I know it."

As hard as it was to accept, Jenny knew she was right and nodded.

They had always been at odds. "I suppose," she admitted peevishly, "But if I were at home I wouldn't be like this, that's all."

"No. If you were sensible and made sure you ate properly, you wouldn't be like this," Janet said, determined that Jenny wasn't going to lay a guilt trip on her this time.

Jenny stuck out her bottom lip, like she did when she was four or so, Janet thought, wondering why she had reverted to childhood.

"You don't care about me," she said sullenly, "No matter what you say, you don't care. Anyway, keep your money." Even as she spoke out of spite, she could have bitten her tongue. "I don't need it. I went to welfare and they're looking after me so I don't want anything from you, you miserable old cow." Jenny stuck out her tongue like a small child. Where had that come from, why had she said it? Oh well, she had and that was that.

Janet felt an icy spike pierce her heart. What was the matter with the girl?

"I can see that I'm not helping things much," she said tremulously. "I hope you feel better soon. Call me if you need anything."

"When hell freezes over, Mum, that's when I'll call you." Turning her face to the window, she waited for Janet to leave.

As the door closed, she burst into tears. Why had she done that? Why was she so nasty to her mother, who was only trying to help? Now she would not have twice the money coming in. What an idiot she was. Her joy for life was escaping her, everything seemed suddenly so black, all her dreams had vanished and she felt cheated.

Janet called Esther Rigby to let her know they had hospitalized Jenny and asked if Esther had heard from Steve.

"Not a word, Janet. I've been looking for him all over. The other day I saw him with a woman on Queen Street, but by the time I found somewhere to park, they'd disappeared. I walked up and down for nearly an hour, but I couldn't find him."

"I think he should know about this latest situation," Janet said seriously. "It looks serious. Jenny says she is now on welfare and told me she doesn't want my money or help. I'm very upset about things, Esther."

Esther sighed. She knew what Janet meant. "So am I. That son of mine has a lot to answer for. I thought Jenny might help make a man of him. Now she's going to have a child, Frank and I thought he'd marry her, but Jenny tells me that he's refused again. As a matter of fact, Jenny and I were making wedding plans. That's when he balked and did a runner."

A surge of anger rushed through Janet, she felt furious, her free hand formed into a fist and she found herself holding her breath. Jenny was making wedding plans with Esther yet she hadn't said a word to her, her own mother?

Biting back her rage, she kept her voice even. "I'm sorry it was a waste of time, Esther, but let's face it Steve always did say he would never marry her. I don't suppose a baby made much difference to the situation. It's the child I feel sorry for, truth be known."

Esther nodded. "Yes, poor little mite. Well, I suppose we'll have to make sure between us that things run smoothly until she has the baby. I offered to have her stay here, Janet, but she won't even consider it. She tells me you refused to take her in," Janet gasped. What on earth had Jenny been saying about her behind her back? "Mind you," Esther continued. "I imagine what she tells me and the truth, are two different things. Sounds as though you have your hands full with that girl."

Tears welled in her eyes, Jenny was so unfeeling, talking about her to Esther, and heaven's only knew what she had said. She cleared her throat and tried to speak normally. "I loved and nourished that child and catered to her, both Jim and I did. It hurts that she told me I was a bad parent and didn't care about her. She said some very hateful things and, to be honest, I'm finding it hard to forgive her." She wiped her face with her free hand, making her voice stronger. "I'm sure with time I'll get over it, but for now I can't have her in the house. It's too soon after losing her father and my nerves are shot. I told her today that we would only fight constantly and that would not be good for her, or the baby. I think Jenny appreciates that."

"Yes," said Esther, "I agree with you. Jenny can have a very cutting tongue. She's not exactly known for her diplomacy. I know exactly what you mean and think you're very wise not to let her back home. Maybe she'll grow up."

"I only hope so," Janet said with a sigh, "It's about time she did."

"I'll pop over to the hospital tonight to see her. I'll let you know what she said."

As she hung up Esther smiled grimly thinking of Steve and his new lady. That blasted son of hers must pay for this state of affairs, and soon.

Six weeks later Jenny moved into her new house. Esther went over to the apartment to help her pack, and expressed her shock at the state of the place. Cast off clothing lay against the baseboard where Jenny had tossed it, the kitchen area was filthy. Dirty dishes, cutlery, opened cans and empty pizza boxes littered the counter.

"Oh my," she gasped as she looked around. "Not much of a housekeeper, are you?" The remark immediately put Jenny in a rage.

"So? What concern is that of yours?" Jenny blazed. "This is my place and I like it this way. You come here to help or to pick on me?"

"Sorry. I didn't think any female liked to live in a pigsty like this," Esther said quietly as she started to pick up the soiled clothing.

"It suits me and that's all that matters," Jenny said putting dirty dishes into a cardboard box.

Esther saw what she was doing and sighed. "Don't do that, Jenny. Look, you sit down and read or something. I'll wash those things before we pack them."

Jenny smirked as she sat at the table. Esther was such a fuss budget that Jenny knew full well anything not done properly would be taken out of her hands and done by the house-proud and excessively neat Esther. It hadn't taken long to figure that out, not when she had stayed with them and seen Esther in action. Oh yes, she was very bright, she was, chuffed that she could sit and watch Esther work, pleased to know she could always figure out a way to sit idle. And Steve called her stupid?

Esther washed, cleaned and packed as Jenny sat watching, leafing through a magazine. It was super. She had always wanted a maid.

Once they arrived at the townhouse, Esther cleaned the already clean cupboards and put away Jenny's few dishes. Then she went to a nearby Laundromat and washed the dirty clothes. When she returned, fetching supper from Kentucky Fried Chicken, Jenny felt very happy. All in all, Jenny concluded Esther had probably had a wonderful time organizing everything.

"You know my mother should have been doing this, Mrs. Rigby," Jenny said as she ate the last of her chips, dipping them in gravy.

"You won't let her, even if she offered, from what she tells me," Esther said, her lips tight with disapproval.

Jenny leaned forward, she must tell old Esther which end was up in her relationship with her stupid mother.

"She didn't offer to help, you know, in fact she offered me money to stay away, like the remittance men they had back in the old days." Her voice was expressionless.

"Now, Jenny, don't tell lies," Esther warned, "Your mother thinks the world of you, and you know it. Let's face it, you weren't very nice to her, and right after she had lost her husband. Grief is a terrible thing, Jenny."

"Come off it, Mrs. Rigby!" Jenny scoffed. "I lost a father. Doesn't that count?"

Esther shook her head sadly. Jenny couldn't see it. "Of course it does, but she was much closer to her husband than you were to your father. It's a different type of love, no matter which way you look at it, a woman's love for a husband is very deep."

Jenny flounced her head. "Huh! Some excuse for tossing me out like that, I don't think."

Esther stared at her. What was the matter with the girl? She acted like a five-year-old at times.

"Now, Jenny, don't go into one of your flights of fancy. *You* left the house. Your mother never tossed you out. She simply wouldn't take you back after you said what you did, and I can't say I blame her. You're a very ungrateful girl, Jenny. Sometimes I don't know what my Steve sees in you."

Jenny snorted. "Not much apparently, since he walked out and left me pregnant and penniless. He's not much of a man, is he?"

Esther might have agreed with Jenny's sentiments but she was not about to admit it.

"Now don't you start on my Steve. He told me you were taking care of birth control, and you certainly did, didn't you? And where did it get you? Look at you now." She gazed out the window, thinking aloud, "I knew what could happen if he took up with you, you being such a child and all, and I made sure it was understood that you'd take precautions. From what he told me you didn't, and it's your own fault that you're pregnant."

Jenny tossed down her paper napkin. "All right, all right, you might as well lay into me as well. Your whole generation is dead set against any of my generation having any life at all. You're all senile, stay at home, live in a rut grumps, grouses and old fogies. I don't need this, Mrs. Rigby. I don't need you, I don't need my mother, I never needed my father, and I don't certainly need your precious son. I'll manage on my own."

Ether stared at her, appalled that such an innocent looking girl could be so deprecating. "Be sure you mean what you say, Jenny. You've upset your mother enough, you've upset Steve with your childish ways, and now you've upset me. It isn't good to keep alienating people this way."

Jenny lost her temper. She'd heard enough people preaching, telling her how stupid she was. "Oh, go home, why don't you! I've had enough of the lecture, thank you very much. I'll manage on my own." Slumping in her chair, she sipped her milk.

"You call me if you need anything, you hear me, Jenny?" Esther said as she put on her coat.

"I won't be calling you, I'll never call you," Jenny said scathingly.

"In that case, I'll be calling you," Esther said coldly, "I'm thinking about my grandchild, not you, missy. Anyway, I'll still be taking you to see Dr. Ross. I promised him I'd make sure you saw him and from the way you're acting, it's just as well a professional is concerned about your mental condition."

Jenny shoved her chair back and went to the front door, which she stood holding open as if to shoo Esther out faster. Esther picked up her cleaning gear and her bag of polishes and cleansers and left without a backward glance.

She never even thanked me for helping her, Esther thought resentfully, or for buying supper. A small 'thank you' might have been nice. What a selfish person, and to think she had thought her to be good for Steve. Maybe Steve was wise to take off like he had, maybe he wasn't as stupid as they thought.

Jenny went upstairs to bed. Esther had made the bed and it looked welcoming with the eiderdown she had brought from her house. It sat in rosy splendour on top of the blanket.

To complete her home Jenny wanted a television and, as she got ready for bed, decided to call the social services first thing tomorrow to see what they could do for her. Overall she was pleased with the way things had gone. Here she was in her own little house, all furnished and newly painted. All she lacked was a TV and a dishwasher, and she had heard welfare could supply them. All this and a regular cheque coming in every month, things couldn't be better, she told herself.

Well, maybe they could, she thought as she dozed. If she could get Steve back she would be completely happy.

TWELVE

Apprehensive, Jenny listened to the social worker explaining the new situation.

"The rules have changed, Jenny. The province now insists that welfare recipients attempt to find work. We can offer you a cashier's job at the local supermarket."

"What?" A shocked Jenny sat mouth open.

While they could not insist, the social worker said (she didn't put it in so many words), the inference was that unless Jenny took it, they could make it difficult for someone of her obvious youth and energy to collect a cheque. However, she had a choice of going back to school or working.

Feeling very disgruntled and put on, she took the cashier's job that was only twenty hours a week and in the afternoon. Jenny did not want to go back to school. To have to write exams again was not on her agenda and she already knew everything she needed to know.

Janet, from talking to Esther, found out about Jenny's job and went to the supermarket to talk to her. It was like a slap in the face, Janet thought, as she tearfully drove home. When Jenny, stacking shelves, spotted her, she rushed off into the staff area where Janet could not enter.

After rationalizing that it was maybe the very nature of the low paying job that made Jenny ashamed of her fall from grace, Janet promised herself she must make one more attempt.

Two days later she went to the store and Jenny again ran away and into the back. Heartsick and upset, she vowed never to attempt to talk to Jenny again as the obvious rejection was too hard on her nerves. What had she done that the child on whom she lavished love and affection for all those years, had turned against her? It had to be in Jenny's genes. After all, who knew what sickness, mental or physical, was in her biological family?

Janet thoughts dwelt on it for hours afterwards. When they had first heard about the baby coming up for adoption, the agency told them the mother was a teenager from Montreal. Neither Janet nor Jim cared, all they wanted was a baby of their own. Now as Jenny angered her repeatedly, she was not so sure they had made a good choice. Maybe they should have investigated the family, for surely it was this background that had resulted in the way Jenny had turned out, and surely not their lack of parental guidance. In no way could Jenny be a product of her environment.

She talked it over with Richard who suggested he should make some enquiries for her. With his connections he could discover more about the birth mother's family and their background through Parent Finders and other sources.

When, her conscience getting the better of her, she went back to the store to try again to speak to her daughter, they said Jenny had left.

"I am sorry, Mrs. Stevens, but we made many allowances for Jenny after social services told us about her circumstances. The staff put themselves out to be kind to her. Unfortunately, she did not try to get along, or be a team player. She talked back to customers, was extremely rude to her fellow workers. I got all kinds of complaints. When I moved her onto a cash register, she regularly checked out short and when someone caught her with the money she had stolen, she just shrugged. What could I do? I had to fire her."

"Now I'm sorry that she caused so many problems. How much did she take? I'd like to pay it back."

"According to our head cashier, it was somewhere between two and three hundred. I can have her work it out for you but to save time, why don't we call it $150.00?"

Janet wrote a cheque and handed it to him, her heart heavy with disappointment in her daughter. Jenny, so sublimely sure of herself, had not thought anyone would notice her theft. She could not confront her with this knowledge or it would start another fight.

"Thank you, Mrs. Stevens. I hope your daughter learns some sense and manages to get another job. She didn't argue with me when I told her to pick up her cheque and leave, so I'm sure she knows what she did was wrong."

"I hope so," Janet said as she picked up her purse.

Now sitting at home, having had time to think about her firing, Jenny seethed over the injustice of it. To think that they fired her, a person with her academic qualifications, from a lowly cashier's job in a two-bit supermarket. Shamefaced, she told her social worker lies about the management, saying they did not want pregnant females.

She sat silent and sulky as the worker, who had contacted the store manager and knew the truth, explained to her that it was a case of work, or get no welfare. Jenny still had the option of going back to school, the worker said, where she could take up typing or bookkeeping.

Jenny refused to consider returning to school. Why would she want to go back to that, she asked herself, what could they teach her at her age? Anyway, soon she soon might be a married woman with a child, that is if she could find Steve. Working wasn't her thing, staying at home and playing with her lovely baby was what she wanted more than anything. In her mind it was akin to owning a live Barbie Doll.

A week later the doctor hospitalized Janet. What had begun as a summer cold rapidly developed into bronchitis, and, with the residual stress of losing her husband and the strain of Jenny's attitude, it escalated into pneumonia.

Richard, very supportive, visited the hospital, where he sat with her for hours in the evening. He insisted on a private room where they pampered and catered to her. Janet could relax, he said, forget the world outside and concentrate on getting better. She loved him even more for his caring attitude.

As she lay watching TV or reading a book, her mind flipped to Jenny, wondering how she could get her child back, how they could ever become friends again.

Esther, who constantly called her with reports, faithfully took Jenny to the doctor and saw more of Jenny these days than herself. Esther was shocked to find Jenny had reverted to her old ways. The house was filthy and when Esther bluntly said so, Jenny laid into her with a mouthful of swear words. An angry Esther simply stared at her and marched out. When she got home, she immediately called the law office to tell Janet how Jenny was living.

On discovering Janet was in the hospital, Esther rushed over with a gift basket of fruit and the latest fashion magazines. When she described the manner in which Jenny lived, Janet became upset but tried not to show it, although Esther saw right through her. It was not right for Janet to be alone, she thought, and Esther did not know who Janet's friends were, or if anyone else had been to see her.

On the way home she stopped off at Jenny's and marched around the side and into the weed-choked back garden. Jenny lay on an old blanket wearing a pair of shorts and a halter top, sunbathing, reading a comic.

"So this is where you are."

"Who the fuck invited you?" Jenny said nastily as she sat up.

"I thought I'd better let you know that your mother is in the hospital," Esther said, trying to keep her temper.

"So?" Jenny glowered at Esther. What the heck did Esther think she was going to do, burst into tears? What was her mother to her these days?

"Don't you think you should go to see her?"

"What for?" Jenny cracked her gum.

Esther stood with her hands on her hips, dying to slap the girl into acting normally. "Common courtesy, if nothing else. Your own mother, and you turn your back on her like this? She told me you refused to talk to her at the store. And while I am on the subject of work, why aren't you there today?"

"I told them where to shove it." Jenny tossed her head and smirked. "I'm starting work next week at Welbourn Papers."

Welbourn Papers took her on as a packer. She was to take small boxes of tissues and put them into the larger shipping carton. It was boring, mindless work, she immediately saw that when they showed her where she was going to be working, but at least it got the welfare people off her back. It irked her that she was now on shift work and had to work twenty-four hours a week at the company's discretion. They told her that in her condition it could be either morning or afternoons, never evenings. Actually all she wanted to do was laze around and wait for her baby.

Esther looked down at Jenny. If only she could say what she thought, but better not. "Hmm. I think you should go to see your mother, Jenny. She's the only mother you'll ever have and I hate to see you fighting with her over nothing."

"Yeah, yeah, so much for what you hate. I *hate* her! And it's not over nothing. She'd sooner see me live on welfare, starving to death, than take me back into my own home. She's got all that room now that Dad is dead but, oh no, she doesn't want me there. After she threw me ou. . .,"

Esther saw red. "She did *not* throw you out, Jenny. Don't ever say that again! You left home to live with Steve. I know your parents were against that move, as were we, but they thought you'd come to your senses and go back home."

The next door neighbour came out to hang some washing and stood listening to the exchange.

Putting down her comic, she stood and confronted Esther. "Seems as though you all were dead wrong, doesn't it? I'm an adult now. I wish you'd all stop treating me as though I were a baby."

Esther kept her voice low. "You are a child to us, Jenny. You'll always be a child to us, and after the way you have displayed your maturity so far, I guess you're not as grown up as you seem to think. The very least you could do is go and visit your mother when she needs you. Leave it too late, and she won't be there any more," she warned.

Even though Esther was only trying to make a point, it got through to Jenny who picked up on her mother not being there anymore. She eyed Esther, thinking it over. Did this mean Janet was dying? Visions of untold wealth popped into her head and swiftly made up her mind.

Picking up her blanket and comic, she said: "I suppose I'd better go then. You're going to drive me there, aren't you?"

Janet looked thrilled to see Jenny, who stood inside the door, peering around at the room. It was not the usual hospital room, even Jenny could see that. She noticed a comfortable arm chair near the window and a small table on which sat a large floral arrangement. Colourful drapes hung at a picture window and an alcove held a tiny sink, a hot plate, and an electric kettle. The large colour television Janet was watching dominated a credenza at the end of the room. She took off the headphones and smiled a welcome.

Jenny saw nothing wrong with her mother. She looked pale but wore lipstick and her hair was neat and tidy.

"So?" Jenny said, annoyed that she was not visibly sick, her hopes of sudden riches dashed.

"Do sit down, Jenny. It's wonderful to see you. How did you know I was here?"

"Nosy old Esther came and fetched me. That woman is a pain in the ass. Always sticking her nose in where it isn't wanted," Jenny said sulkily.

Janet smiled, she would not let Jenny rile her this time. "I'm grateful to Esther for bringing you. I felt upset when you slighted me the last two times I tried to talk to you. What have I ever done to turn you against me, Jenny?" She saw the stubborn look come onto Jenny's face and changed tack. "Oh, no, no. Don't get upset, it isn't important. All that matters is that you are here now. Now tell me, how are you keeping?"

Jenny shrugged. "All right."

"I must admit you look very well. I hear you now have a townhouse. That must be nice for you," Janet tried to keep her voice light, not wanting to precipitate another row.

After Esther gave her Jenny's address, Janet drove past the row houses, dismayed at the evident poverty. That day it had been difficult for her not to knock on Jenny's door and beg her to come home. Upset, she talked it over with Richard, who said she must give Jenny some breathing space as Jenny was not the type to appreciate the offer even if she accepted. Janet needed to put things in perspective.

Jenny shrugged "S'all right."

This conversation was tough going, Janet thought, already tiring, though she smiled as though things were normal. Jenny answered all her questions in one or two words.

After ten minutes she found it hard to find a topic of conversation and Jenny did not offer anything.

"How is the job? Are you still there?" Better not to let Jenny know that she knew of her dismissal.

"Okay. I start at Welbourn's on Monday."

"Welbourn's? In the office?" Janet asked hopefully.

"No. Packing boxes in the warehouse," Jenny felt delighted and grinned when she saw Janet's look of dismay.

"Why don't you look around for an office job, Jenny?" Janet asked quietly. "Why do you take these menial positions? You're capable of much more than a factory job. I'm sure you could get a clerical position in a nice place. I don't like to think of you working in a factory."

"Yeah. Like someone is going to hire me, pregnant? Come off it, Mum, join the human race. Too many people are out of work right now for them to hire someone who's going to be quitting in a couple of months."

"You could go to Office Overload. I'm sure they could find you something."

"You could get me a job at the office, if it comes to that, now couldn't you?" Jenny said spitefully.

Janet nodded, but no way was she having Jenny at the office. "I suppose. I could talk to Mrs. Roberts first. She's the personnel manager."

"Huh! If I'd bet on that one, I'd have won," Jenny scoffed. "I knew you wouldn't. You could get me a job without trying, so don't start telling me you have nothing to do with who gets hired. You're dating Richard Wyatt, aren't you?"

Janet closed her eyes realizing she didn't know how to talk to Jenny, how to get through to her. Childish as ever, she never saw anything other than what she wanted to see.

Jenny glared at her and saw her closed eyes. She picked up the card on the table and started to read it. "All my love, Richard." Well, well, maybe things were heating up between the two old fogies, maybe her mother was on the road to romance these days. She replaced the card as Janet opened her eyes.

"I'd like to move back home, Mum. Please let me move back in." Jenny made her face angelic and her voice sweet. She wanted to go home, to have her mother look after her, cook her meals, do her washing. Mind you, she must live by her mother's rules and those were strict.

Her heart sank as she heard her mother say: "I'll have to think about that, Jenny. First of all I have to get well, then I'll think about it."

"You can tell me now. What's to decide?" she said impatiently. "Either you let me come home, or you don't. I could make the welfare people force you to let me back home, but I'd sooner you let me move back."

"It's not as easy as that, Jenny. Too many words have passed between us. I'm still terribly upset about your calling me a bad mother when I did everything I could to make you happy."

"So? You know me. All talk," Jenny smiled, happy that it was only something she had said. That was soon mended.

Janet smiled wryly. "Yes, I do know you. However, I don't know whether I could go through that again. You haven't changed much, Jenny, you're still as thoughtless and selfcentred as ever. I don't know if I want to live with you anymore. Give me some time."

Jenny flounced her head, and looked at the large television. "You've had all the time you need, Mum. It seems to me that you don't want me around while you're messing around with old Wyatt. Talk about a fit mother! My Dad is hardly cold in his grave and you're playing kissy-face with my Dad's lawyer. I bet he's watching you do it, too." She pointed to heaven, "Huh!"

"Jenny! That's not true," Janet said, her eyes full of sudden tears.

"Oh, no? What's this then?" Jenny brandished the getwell card, "A figment of my imagination?"

"It's a getwell card, and that's all it is."

"Sure! All my love, Richard," she read with a voice filled with scorn. "Some mother you are. I bet you two have been sleeping together for years, eh? I suppose the next thing I know you'll be getting married. Well, don't invite me to the wedding. I already had a Dad, I don't want another that you've chosen."

Janet felt her head start to swim. "Jenny, please leave now. My blood pressure is very high and I mustn't get upset like this."

Grabbing her carry-all, she clattered the chair back as she stood. "Why don't you pop off, Mum? That'll solve all my troubles."

Janet sank back on her pillows, white and exhausted. Now she was being told to drop dead. The tears streamed down her cheeks and she felt very ill. As she heard the door shut, she rang for the nurse.

Esther was in the waiting room as Jenny came out. "How is she today?" she asked.

Jenny did not stop walking. "All right. Come on, come on, let's get out of here. I'm hungry."

"But I wanted to go and see her," Esther said perplexed, walking quickly to catch up with her.

"So? See her some other time. The nurse is with her right now. Come on, let's go."

"Look at that," Esther said as they passed a bronze Jaguar in the parking lot. "What a beautiful car." She paused to admire it and touch the gold jaguar gracing the radiator. "Why, I think it belongs to your mother's lawyer, Richard Wyatt," she said as she noticed the personalized licence plate.

"It does?" Jenny immediately took notice. It was a very expensive car, she recognized that immediately. Jenny was very conscious of the monetary value of things like cars and jewellery. It must have cost at least a hundred thousand, she thought, admiring the beige leather interior. If Wyatt could afford to drive a car as classy as this, then he must be very wealthy. A smile lifted her lips. Maybe her mother could do worse than marry him, she thought with pursed up eyes, maybe she should encourage her mother to marry him. Imagine all the money she might get when he died, and what was so good was that they were both already so old.

That evening as she ate two O'Henry chocolate bars for supper and drank a bottle of Coke, she thought about how to get back into her mother's good books. First she must start acting nicely and not give any lip, perhaps take some flowers and some chocolates to the hospital, and not use swear words. Yes, it could be easy if she set her mind to it. She had always prided herself on her acting.

THIRTEEN

"**C**ome on, lazy bones," Rita said trying to jolly Steve into getting off the couch where he lay watching a television football game. She wanted him in the kitchen where supper was already on the table.

"All right," he grumbled as he stood. He pulled the TV over to the right so he could watch the action while he ate.

Rita sighed deeply. Things were not right between them lately. Steve had become so miserable and grumpy that she hardly dared open her mouth. Before she broached their difficulties, she must wait until he was in a good mood.

Every day he came home and ate supper before going down to the gym where he worked every evening on his body building. He was in great shape, that she had to admit. Constant exercise had sharply defined his upper body muscles and he looked as good as Arnold Schwarzenneger. Why this sudden complete dedication to his physique, she did not know, but she recognized he was troubled about something. She hated to think it might be their relationship.

The small apartment was that, small, and the two of them seemed to be continually under each other's feet. While that was a plus at first, she found it now got on her nerves, especially as Steve treated her like a servant, never picking up or putting anything away.

When she was alone, the place appeared spacious in that she didn't own much furniture, only the basics. Now with Steve messing it up and lounging around on the couch, it was too confining, too claustrophobic. That he did not contribute anything to the rent and never even offered, also annoyed her. Under the circumstances she couldn't even think of finding them a bigger apartment.

"I thought we could wallpaper the living room this weekend," she said as a commercial started blaring.

"Go ahead. Don't let me stop you," Steve said as he filled his mouth with meat loaf.

"I thought we could do it together."

"All the same, you women, always nest building. Now listen carefully. Watch my lips," he said viciously. "I don't know *how* to wallpaper, I don't *want* to wallpaper, and I *won't* wallpaper."

Rita said nothing more, but she felt hurt. He was starting to talk to her as if she were an idiot. She sensed the relationship was nearly over. He was randy enough to shove it to her every chance he got, but not man enough to do the right thing and marry her. His vehemence when she once mentioned getting married scared her, and, although he said it was because Jenny had tried to blackmail him into marriage, Rita perceived it as something more than that. Personally she thought Steve hated marriage.

This weekend, she decided, was the point at which she must let him know how she felt. She watched as he got his gym gear and rummaged through the closet for his wind cheater. She saw no future in their relationship and she wasn't getting any younger. Rita wanted to marry, felt the need for the security of a family as her thirty-first birthday neared.

As Steve came out of the gym, he literally bumped into his mother. His appearance, as she headed back to her car, both startled and astonished Esther. When last she saw him, she had been near this place and it never occurred to her that he had joined the Weiland Health club as since his schools days he always patronized the more utilitarian and older Cavanagh Gym. It was first place she visited when she started to look for him. Obviously he knew that and changed his venue.

"Steve! Where have you been?" Esther grabbed his sleeve to ensure he didn't run away.

"Oh about. You know," Trapped, his face reddened, he hadn't realized he could still blush.

Esther was grim faced. "No. I don't know. Your father and I have been very worried about you. What about Jenny?" She pulled him over to the wall out of the way of pedestrians.

"Butt out, Mum. What happened between Jenny and me is our affair. Let's say we agreed to call it off."

"Steve! I never thought you could be so callous. I might not like Jenny very much, but you do owe her something. She's having your child. Doesn't that mean anything to you?"

Steve stared into space. He wouldn't look at his mother. "Of course it does, but she's also determined to make me marry her and I can't do that."

"Come along," Esther said, pulling him along to where she had parked her car. "You're coming home with me and we're going to talk this through. Your father was frantic and even called the hospitals when you disappeared. We tried everything to find you."

Putting the car in gear, she drove off rapidly, keeping up a flow of talk as she drove. Steve looked out the side window, letting it wash over him. Once his mother got it out of her system she would soon realize that he had done the only thing he could.

By ten-thirty, Steve was fed up with the constant nagging. Even his Dad, who rarely got to put two words in, was insisting Steve do the right thing.

"All right! All right!" Steve threw up his hands in surrender. "Please let me make up my own mind. All right, so I agree I should be supporting Jenny right now, but from what you've told me she's making out okay. She's got a house and a job."

"But welfare, Steve," Esther couldn't believe that this was her son talking. So hard hearted, so stubborn, so intractable. "The girl is on *welfare* when you should be looking after her. She has to work in a factory packing boxes, and she's carrying your child, for heaven's sake."

"We've been going around in circles for hours it seems and I still won't marry her, and that's what you're angling for. I know you, Mum, you're like a dog with a bone when it comes to getting your own way. But this time I'm not being railroaded into anything."

He stood prior to leaving, glancing at his watch. Rita would be furious if he got back late. She hated having her beauty sleep interrupted.

Esther, grimly glared at Frank, stupid sod, sitting there saying nothing. What use was he? "You're not leaving, Steve?" she said, "Nothing is sorted out yet."

"So? I have to be up early in the morning and you have to run me back to town. It wasn't my idea, coming all this way, you know."

"All right, we can talk in the car. Get your coat, Frank, we're going out." Frank Rigby wanted nothing more than to go to bed, but never dared contradict his wife. Wearily, he went to get his coat.

By the time they were nearing the outskirts of the city Steve had more or less agreed to return to Jenny until the baby arrived. In a way he was glad they had taken the decision off his hands. The lust he had felt for Rita had worn off and he had begun to find her boring, knowing they had little in common. Not that Jenny appealed to him much either, but at least she was easier to deceive.

Steve insisted they drop him at the health club, saying he had to go back inside to get something from his locker because he didn't want them to know where he was living. Calling in unannounced tomorrow evening would be just like his mother, and he did not want them to see Rita, who looked like the tart she was.

As they drove away, he came back out of the lobby and headed home. Too bad that he was so late. Tomorrow was the hearing on the kid he had beaten up and he wanted to get a good night's sleep. He needed his wits about him.

Janet, wearing the pink satin housecoat, a present from Richard, was sitting in the armchair when he arrived. Kissing her, he gave her the library books he had fetched and appraised her appearance. Tonight she wore some makeup and someone had washed and set her hair. At last she had begun to look more like her old self.

"You look a lot better today, Janet. You have more colour in your face."

She smiled happily. "I feel wonderful today. The doctor says if I keep it up I can go home this weekend. I can hardly wait to get out of here, although I must admit I loved the coddling."

"You concentrate on getting better. We'll get you a home help for a week when you go home. That'll take off the strain." He smiled, taking her hand and caressing it with his thumb.

Janet, thrilled at the thought of this extra pampering, realized he was doing too much. "Richard, that's wonderful, but I don't think it'll be necessary. I can look after myself."

"Nevertheless, <u>I</u> think it will be necessary and *I* insist. I want you fit and well enough to marry me. This illness of yours made me realize how much you mean to me. Please marry me soon, Janet."

"I will, Richard, but I have to solve my problems with Jenny first. Let's face it, she doesn't like you."

He smiled grimly. "To tell you the truth I don't much care for her. That girl is taking far too much out of you. I thought the psychiatrist might help her come to terms with things."

"So did I. Dr. Ross isn't doing much good as far as I can see, not that therapy is a rapid cure: it sometimes takes years. I went to see him myself to find out how I could help her. He says she has to make up her own mind and it will take him a while to get transference from her, whatever that means. I felt really guilty by the time I left his office. Apparently, according to him, some of the blame is mine, mine and Jim's. Somehow we are to blame for her confusion. We didn't do her any favours by loving her so much, then expecting her to live up to our expectations."

Richard patted her hand. "I can see nothing different in your actions than in any other parents. But I for one tend to side with you, Janet,

I think it's a simple matter of her ancestry. You did everything for the girl, and I never did hear that loving a child led only to rebellion or delinquency."

"Thanks, Richard. Maybe I should have told him about us adopting her."

"I thought you had," Richard said, taken aback. From his enquiries he learned that Jenny's birth mother came from a lower class neighbourhood where she and her family still lived in poverty. The man she married was an alcoholic so she returned to prostitution. Then, deserting her six children, she left with another man. Not a very nice background for anyone.

Janet shook her head. She felt guilty about not saying anything to Dr. Ross. "I was going to, but something told me it might make Jenny more confused than ever if she thought that a mother she never knew had given her away. You know what I mean?"

"Yes, but I think once the therapy starts to help her come to grips with life, that is the time to tell her the facts. You shouldn't be blaming yourself for any of this, Janet. You gave her a good home, all the creature comforts and a comfortable life. If she chose to throw it all away, why should you take the blame?" He laughed, "Would you listen to me. Here am I, a man who never had a child of my own, telling you, who raised one from an infant, how you should have run your life."

"However, I know you're right, Richard. I should tell Dr. Ross, although I shudder to think that the news should come from him. That's my job. Anyway, even after all she has done and said, I still love her, you know. She'll never be the girl I want her to be, but I do love her." She wondered if she did, or was it lip service so Richard wouldn't think badly of her. "I devoted myself to making everything so nice for her for all those years." Janet smiled sadly, thinking back to when they had first bought her home. "She couldn't have had better parents, even if I do say so myself."

Richard kissed the top of her head. "Jenny should consider herself lucky to have you as a mother. After what she put you through, she should be glad you even try to speak to her, never mind still love her."

"I always wanted so much for her, you know? I wonder why she can't see that?" Janet sighed deeply, "Jenny always rebelled against anything we wanted for her. Right from the time she could talk she always demanded things her own way." Tears came to her eyes. "She didn't appreciate anything. What a waste of love and time."

Richard, noticing how upset Janet looked, leaned over to kiss her. "Janet, you can't change her. She's become the person she is, and nothing will ever change that. Stop feeling so guilty and let her get on with her own life. Now let's talk about something more cheerful.

She smiled. "When do you think we should get married?"

FOURTEEN

When she arrived home from work on Tuesday, Jenny spotted Steve's panel truck in front of the house. She recognized the licence plate. Curious, she looked up and down the street and into the cab. It was definitely his truck.

Then she saw him come out of the Mac's Milk on the corner carrying two bags. Earlier in the afternoon he and Rita had had a knock down fight, and after he gave her a black eye and a split lip, he packed his stuff into garbage bags and left.

The hearing had resulted in his dismissal from the security force, so he was now unemployed. Once he told her about his job loss, Rita ordered him out and that's when he hit her. She was not going to support him, she told him, not a man who beat up a kid.

Steve could never go home and tell his mother what had happened so he took the only other option. He decided to go back to Jenny. His mother had told him where she lived in Westboro and he headed for the town houses.

"Steve," Jenny rushed at him and he put down his shopping bags to take her in his arms. She kissed him all over his face. "You've come back? Please say you've come back."

"Yes, I'm back, if you'll have me."

Jenny felt jubilant. "If I'll have you? Stupid question, Steverino. Come on, let me show you our new home." Her face alight with joy, she led him to the front door of her house.

Jenny felt proud of her accomplishments. Steve must agree she wasn't stupid and realize she was capable of looking after herself. He must never know how hard she had looked for him, not unless it was to her benefit, anyway.

It wasn't half bad, Steve thought, looking around the messy kitchen, the slovenly living room tastefully decorated with empty soft drink cans and chocolate bar wrappers. Jenny, he saw, had not changed one bit.

As she made them instant coffee, Steve watched her. She had put on a lot of weight, looked chunky, though her pregnancy didn't show much under a loose top.

"You still seeing that shrink, Jen?" he asked.

"Oh sure, your mother makes sure I go. She comes to pick me up every Tuesday and Thursday and drives me to his office. It's a waste of time if you ask me, but I suppose he's making money out of it. I know I don't feel any different. He always wants me to talk about my parents for some reason. I thought he was supposed to be helping *me*."

Steve relaxed, feeling better. At least she was trying to sort herself out. "He is. He's trying to put you in touch with your true feelings toward them."

"Who died and made you my shrink then?" Jenny laughed at him, delighted to have him back. She went over and sat on his knee, cuddling close to him. "I love you, Steve, I honestly love you. Our baby loves you too." She put his hand on her plump stomach. "Wait until he starts to move. You'll be able to feel him then."

He drew back to look into her face. "He? Is it a boy? Did you have that ultra sound thing?"

"No. I know he's a boy," Jenny smiled maternally as she pictured her very own little baby. She mentally pictured caring for her own child like playing dolls, did not envisage the dirty diapers, the constant tending, the sleepless nights, the total commitment. Her baby would be perfect, sleep all night, always be smiling and cheerful, always be clean and well dressed.

"When can I quit work?" she asked him, "I don't want to go back to that awful factory again." She told him about Welbourn Papers.

Steve shook his head. "I hate to tell you this, Jen, but you'll have stay at work. I got laid off today and until I get a job, we'll have to rely on your welfare cheque. Anyway, if I'm working, you won't get welfare."

Jenny stared at him, aghast. This was not good news at all, but then he was back where he belonged. That was all that mattered.

". . .but I've got my eye on a truck driving job," he continued, "They'll pay me under the table and you can stay on welfare. As long as they don't find out I'm bringing in money, that's the main thing."

Jenny stared at him. "That's illegal, isn't it?" Somehow she didn't like to think that she was party to a crime, even if it were only ripping off the government, though when she was gypping welfare herself that was different.

"Look, Jen, we have to play this cool. Nobody must know that I live here full time. You'll have to tell any nosy neighbours that I am a relative of yours and that I'm on welfare, too."

Jenny did not feel so sure of him now. It didn't sound right, but she wasn't about to start making waves if he were talking about staying.

She kissed him. "Forget the coffee. Let's go to bed, eh?"

They released Janet from the hospital on the Friday, and Richard planned to look after her until the day nurse started work on Monday. He slept in the guest room and strangely she didn't care what the neighbours might think.

The more she saw of him, the more she thought she loved him, but realized only time would tell. How could she compare Richard and her dead husband? They were as different as chalk and cheese.

Richard was a warm outgoing man. He was personable, confident, well educated, self-made and proud of it, whereas Jim Stevens had slowly worked his way up through the ranks. That being so, he had never become comfortable with any new position in the hierarchy. His demeanor was always one of subservience, no matter what his station: that she knew from watching him at company dances. However, the deferential attitude did not apply when he was at home where he was king of the castle, stern and demanding.

Yes, she would marry Richard. When she did not know, but she *would* marry him. The problem was, after thinking about it long and hard, weighing up the pros and cons, she realized marriage to him would give her financial security and social standing in the community. It occurred to her to wonder again if she wanted to marry him primarily for that reason. Yet, surely with the insurance money and the compensation from the restaurant, she was wealthy in her own right. Day by day she felt herself falling more in love with him and sometimes felt like a teenager. Yes, she kept telling herself, she loved him and she would marry him. But not yet.

If she could solve her problems with Jenny, she would feel more confident, although she was beginning to weaken in that regard. The more she thought about it, the more she realized Richard was right. She should start to think about herself for a change, because Jenny had never given a thought to her parents. Jenny thought only about Jenny. The only thing she wants from me is my money, Janet decided, with a pang of angry sorrow, and giving Jenny money was never the answer. Janet knew that only too well.

Too, the adoption weighed heavily on her. Should she tell Jenny or push it out of her mind as usual? It did not seem to make much sense to alienate Jenny even further, and giving her the details would probably create more problems all round. Maybe she should discuss it with Dr. Ross as Richard suggested. He was a professional. Still, first she must talk it over with Richard.

Having someone to talk to was pleasant. She liked to talk seriously about things that affected her life and Richard was a fantastic conversationalist. They talked for hours, whereas Jim Stevens had been a very taciturn man, and she could hardly remember when they had sat and had a decent conversation. Of course they must have done so, but she was finding his memory blurring more and now Richard's face came into her mind when she felt troubled.

Steve, much to his chagrin, found it impossible to get another job. He never imagined he would ever have the problem at his age, but it was one closed door after another. None of the local security firms would take him on after they discovered his record for assault. The record for assault on file with his ex-employer meant the local Police Forces would not even talk to him, never mind grant him an interview. The lead someone gave him about hiring on as a driver for Forward Lines fell through because a man who had the "D" class licence which Steve did not possess got the job. He had reached a dead end.

Not having anything better to do, he sat the exam and took the driving test for his "D" class, which he got with very little trouble. Now he spent his time visiting the local trucking companies looking for work.

Two weeks later he struck it lucky. Forward Lines, whose offices he visited often, asked him if he could cover for one of their men who was sick. It meant driving to Buffalo, on to Plattsburgh and back through Montreal. Steve was overjoyed. At last, a job.

Full of joy and with a spring in his step he went home to tell Jenny.

"You said what?" Jenny screeched.

"I said I'd take the job." His smile dropped. "What is it with you anyway?"

"Like hell you will," she yelled. "You go right back there and tell them you can't. I'm pregnant and anything might happen. You can't go and that's that."

Steve tried to be reasonable. "Do we or do we not need the money?"

Jenny was already sulking. He sighed, knowing that look.

"Yes," she whined, "We do, but not if you're going to be leaving me alone for days at a time."

"Look, Jenny, use some common sense. If I do this job and help them out I have a good chance of being taken on permanent staff." He threw out his hands in supplication.

"No way, Steverino," Jenny, grim faced, held her hands over her stomach. "You can't take a job that keeps you away from the house. Find yourself a job locally. Apply to the police forces like you keep saying."

"Jenny. Don't you ever listen? I've got a record now and," he blew out an exasperated breath. " . . . no company will hire me, not even as a security guard. I can't even get an interview with any of the local police forces because of it."

"So?" She wasn't interested in his record. "Serves you right for beating up some poor kid. God only knows what you've got in your head, you don't have enough brains to make a flea's garter," she said scathingly.

"You know, Jen, I'd like to thank you for being so very supportive," he said sarcastically. "You're everything a man would want in a woman, I don't think. I *am* taking this job and I *am* going on the road. You can either like it or lump it."

Grabbing his coat from the back of the chair, he left in a foul mood. Angrily Jenny glared after him and threw her can of Pepsi against the wall. It splattered all over the new paint work but she didn't care and made no effort to wipe it clean. Esther would fix it when she came.

Esther was forever cleaning when she came to pick Jenny up for her appointments and, because of that, Jenny let the place get into a mess. Anyway, she didn't see it herself most of the time and didn't think it important. If Esther was a compulsive cleaner, good for her.

The town house wasn't bad, though the furniture was old and decrepit after countless helpless women and children had used it. Esther advised her to rent a steam cleaner and clean the couch and chairs, but that sounded like hard work to Jenny who lived with their odour and dirty appearance. It was enough that she was comfortable.

When he got home later, the worse for wear and smelling of rum, Jenny sat waiting for him. Tossing his coat onto the couch, he slumped down beside it.

His face sullen and closed, he said, "Let's have it then." Might as well get the argument over with right away, he thought.

"Have what?" Jenny smiled and acted mystified. "Did you have a good evening?"

"I guess." Again she surprised him. He had expected fireworks. "What've you been doing?"

"Not much. I watched TV and made a couple of little nighties for the baby. Want to see them?"

Steve looked at her closely. What was she up to this time? She was being far too amicable.

Social Services had managed to find her a second hand TV set which, although battered and missing a knob, worked well enough. Jenny watched it for hours.

She came back with two tiny nightgowns. Both were in pale blue flannelette and had a bluebird pattern.

"Nice, eh?" she said, holding one up for his inspection.

He took it and saw the rough stitching, the uneven hems. Exactly what he would have expected. "Great." He handed it back, still wary of her mood swing.

"So when do you go on this drive around?" she asked, her voice changed subtly, but he heard the underlying nastiness waiting to emerge.

"Tomorrow night. I'll be back Friday morning. It takes time delivering and then loading at these places." He spoke as if he had done it often, though he knew from talking to the other drivers that loading and unloading took time.

"I wondered if you could bring me back a microwave. They're cheaper in the States and you can bring it in under the load."

So that was it. If she saw something in it for her, then everything was all right. He sighed, wondering if it could be done, because if he agreed and did not deliver, his life would not be worth living. "I don't know if I can. Have you got some money to pay one? I'm broke."

"Sure, I'll get your mother to lend me some until my cheque comes."

Steve felt the hair on his nape rise. "You will not! Don't you dare ask my mother for money." God, here we go again, he thought. It seemed like all they did was fight. "Ask *your* mother, you keep telling me how much she has, what with the insurance and compensation."

Instead of yelling at him, she said amiably: "Good idea. I'll call her tomorrow and get some. I'll ask her for some extra so I can buy some microwave dishes as well."

FIFTEEN

anet stared at Jenny. Continually she came begging and that she expected, but what was unusual was her demeanor. She was being so pleasant. She even asked about Richard, remarking that her mother could do worse.

"He's good looking and he drives a terrific car, Mum," she chattered happily, smiling a lot. "I bet he's got a huge house and everything."

Knowing that her mother was particular about the way she dressed, she had made an effort and wore one of her maternity tops, clean jeans and a pair of reasonably clean Reboks.

"No. He lives in a high rise condo," Janet said trying to keep her voice even. The little minx was already counting his money as well, she thought. How could they have raised such an avaricious daughter? Her every thought was of money or possessions. It was her measuring stick for everyone and everything.

"So are you going to marry him?" Jenny asked, looking up under her brows.

"I might. What do you have to say about that?"

Jenny clapped her hands like child. "Goody! He's a catch, Mum. Will you live with him in his condo? Or will you both live here at the house?"

Janet wondered what went on in her devious little mind. "Good gracious. We're not at that stage yet, Jenny. I have to wait until he asks me and *then* we'll talk about where we're going to live." Janet was not about to tell Jenny that the wedding was fixed for December 4. That was their business. She didn't want Jenny making a mess of their plans, and she surely would, given half a chance.

"Oh." Jenny looked disappointed and started picking at her chipped nail polish.

Janet looked at her. Jenny had something in mind but she wouldn't come straight out and say it. They would go all around the houses as usual before what she was thinking would come out.

"How was your last checkup?" Janet asked.

"All right, I guess. I'm putting on too much weight, but I can't help it. I'm so hungry all the time."

Janet could not help saying: "Yes, and you also eat too much junk food and candy."

"Don't start, Mum," Jenny warned, "Steve is bad enough and his mother is a real pain about what I eat and drink."

"It's only that everyone is thinking about your health and that of the baby," Janet said shaking her head. "All that chocolate and Coca-Cola are not doing either of you any good. Too much caffeine is bad for you."

"Oh, all right, Mum!" Jenny snapped. "So everyone tells me. I've had enough lectures about what I should and should not eat. Now, are you going to sell the house if you marry him?" Jenny glanced around the large, superbly appointed kitchen where they were drinking tea.

"Why this sudden interest?" Janet asked suspiciously.

"Well," narrowing her eyes, Jenny looked at Janet very hard, "I thought you should keep this house and let me and Steve live in it. You can go and live in Richard's condo. Dad would have wanted you to do that," she said smugly. "It's a brilliant idea, one that would solve all my problems until I get my inheritance."

Janet looked at her, her eyes wide with shock. What on earth went on this child's mind? "Jenny! Do you think I can afford to simply give this house away?"

"Golly, you wouldn't be giving it away," Jenny argued, "it would still be in the family. I mean, it would be an investment. When you die it would come to me anyway."

"I have no intention of dying, not for a very long time." Janet felt hurt to the quick. Was her inheritance all Jenny ever thought about? Does she look on me strictly as a meal ticket? she wondered, knowing the answer was probably 'yes.' "I'll talk this over with Richard when the time comes. He knows more about these things than I do. Personally I don't think it's a very good idea. We might decide that we want to live here."

Obviously without thinking, Jenny said: "Then he can give me his condo. You won't want that as well."

That flabbergasted Janet. "What is the matter with you, Jenny? Why would Richard give you his condo?"

Jenny smiled smugly. "Because he'll be my new father and I'll be his responsibility," she announced with a great deal of satisfaction.

Janet laughed, she couldn't help it as she thought what a mentally backward child Jenny made herself appear. She felt sorry for her as she said, "No. He will not be your father, or even your stepfather. I can recall you telling me in no uncertain terms that your father was dead. Listen to me, Jenny, you're now over eighteen. That means in law you're an adult, as you constantly remind me, and not a child. Richard has no responsibility for you and neither do I, unless I choose it, of course."

Jenny's face was a picture as she struggled to find a way through the legal ramifications. "Then you'd better let me have the house. How is it going to look? Mr. Richard Wyatt, famous rich lawyer, whose stepdaughter is living on welfare and who has no home?" Jenny started sulking.

Janet sighed. "I'll talk to Richard, as I told you. Not yet though because you're not exactly number one in his books after all the aggravation you've caused." Janet filled the kettle. Another cup of tea would be the thing right now, it would help smooth things over.

"Thanks, Mum," Jenny smiled thinking she had won.

Janet watched her as she went to the powder room, noticing she opened the french doors and looked around the cosy living room. Bet's she's admiring furniture, she thought, seeing herself living here again.

How foolish she was to have left it, and she had probably come to realize it, but Janet felt dead set against letting her back into the house.

Janet's mother passed away suddenly, and, unfortunately, left money to her granddaughter. A lawyer's letter arrived from England enclosing a copy of the will and with some dismay Janet read the enclosed letter.

Lillian Holmes, a middle class widow, whose astute investments made her golden years comfortable, left a considerable estate. Janet was her only child and Jenny her only grandchild. The youthful Jenny who went on holiday to England with her parents when she was ten left a lasting impression on Lillian.

Because Jenny had auburn hair like her grandmother, it caused neighbours to remark to Lillian that her grandchild was the spitting image of her. This pleased Lillian excessively, and although she knew they had adopted Jenny, she fell in love with the sweet youngster. Of course she didn't realize Jenny was kissing up, simply accepted the grovelling as a granddaughter's aim to please her grandmother, with, in Jenny's case, an eye to the main chance.

Except for much property that she left to Janet, the residue of the liquid estate came to Jenny. After Janet paid taxes and death duties, this amounted to more than twenty-five thousand dollars.

Janet mourned her mother. However, she had been away in Canada for so long and had seen little of her in recent years. They were not a close knit family and few letters had passed between them. Still and all, it was her mother and the occasion of her death was sad. Even so, she was not best pleased at this latest turn of events with the will, and wondered if the knowledge was best kept from Jenny until she was twenty-one, the date on which she would get the money.

Richard advised her to show Jenny the letter and when she did Jenny's thrilled face that 'the horrible old hag', as she called her grandmother, had left her so much, said it all. Janet felt another jolt of anger.

"It goes to show you," Jenny said gleefully, "what can happen if you are nice to old people who have money."

Jenny congratulated herself. Yes, she must be nice to old Wyatt, she told herself, he must have piles of money if his car was anything to go by, plus his ritzy penthouse condo. Didn't people say that those who had money could make more money? If she were left part of Richard's estate and her mother's estate, she could finish up a rich woman.

Her mind turned to what she would do when she came into possession of all this wealth. She dreamed of cars, yachts, Monte Carlo, Rome and Paris, large houses, fine furs and designer clothes. Soon they would all fall into her lap. She was so lucky. Now if she could sort out Steve,things would be really peachy.

Jenny, excited and piercingly loud, showed Steve a copy of the letter when he arrived home, without her microwave. She forgot that. Excitedly she showed him how much money she was going to have soon.

It was his suggestion that she go to the bank to borrow against her legacy. After trying four banks and getting nowhere, she visited a credit agency and found them more than willing to advance her funds. It did not occur to her that she had to make monthly payments, or that they charged 23% interest on the advance. It was enough that they gave her a cheque for two thousand. She signed.

Within a week, she squandered the lot. Apart from buying a microwave, she wasted most of it on rubbish, although she did put a down payment on a second hand car. Things looked wonderful and she could always get more money when she needed it.

SIXTEEN

Janet and Richard went to Montreal for a weekend, and while away made more definite plans for their wedding. The ceremony would be a quiet one at the City Hall. Then to celebrate, they would throw a large party for friends in the evening at The Radisson Hotel.

With dismay Janet realized most of the guests would be Richard's business associates and friends as she and Jim had not had many close friends and no relatives in Canada. Somehow that made her feel unworthy of Richard. He laughed away her fears and soon, lying in the king-size bed, Janet felt at long last she had found the man of her dreams.

Richard was a marvellous lover. Jim had not been a very physical man and love making to him was simply a biological act. He never reached her because he never displayed any real passion. With Richard she bloomed, their lovemaking was the most satisfying thing she had ever experienced and now she couldn't wait to marry him. All those wasted years, she told herself, and I never knew that passion like this existed. It was like she was now complete.

"I wish I'd met you thirty years ago, Richard," she said as they lay in each other's arms.

"If we had met then I wouldn't have liked you and you surely wouldn't have liked me. We're the product of all the years we didn't know each other."

"I suppose we are. Still, I can't imagine my life without you now."

"Me too."

Jenny wondered what the large expensively embossed envelope could be when she took it from the mail box.

When she opened it, she felt both shocked and thrilled to read that her silly old mother was going to marry old Wyatt after all. Thinking smugly that she would be very wealthy one of these days, she called Janet. She would tell her categorically of her annoyance that the invitation did not include the actual ceremony, but only some celebratory party at a hotel.

"Hi, Mum," she was sharp. "Got your invitation. How come you're not getting married in a church, and why can't I be there?"

Janet held her tongue. "Having a church wedding at our age isn't necessary. We've both been married before. A civil ceremony is as binding as a church ceremony. We don't want a lot of fuss."

"How come I don't get to go to the wedding?" Jenny whined. "I'm very upset about it. My own mother getting married and you didn't invite me to be present?" The fact they had sent her an invitation to The Radisson only made her indignant. Where was she going to find the money to buy something nice to wear? Too, Steve didn't own anything decent apart from a security guard's uniform that he had never returned.

Janet sighed. "I told you, Jenny, it's a private ceremony. Why should you attend?"

Jenny sniggered. "I bet you're not marrying him at all. You're going to live in sin like me. Talk about stupid, Mum. Who the hell cares if you're shacking up? I don't."

"Jenny! We would never do such a thing. If it is that important for you to be there, all right. If you wear something appropriate. I don't want you showing up in old jeans or that horrible baggy sweater you like so much."

"You could lend me some money and I could buy something spiffy," Jenny suggested. This was more like it. "Anyway, if I'm coming to your party I'll need to look nice. It wouldn't look good for Richard to have a ragged stepdaughter, now would it?"

Janet sighed. Money, that was all that this was about. She would give Jenny money and she would waste it and turn up in something totally unsuitable.

"We'll go shopping next week, you and I," she decided suddenly. "I'll buy you an outfit."

"Can't you give me a couple of hundred and let me buy my own stuff? Anyone would think I was a child, the way you treat me."

Oh, yes, Jenny was at it again. Over the last two months Janet had given her almost a thousand dollars. It was certain that Jenny had nothing to show for her expenditures.

"No! I suggest you and I go shopping, Jenny. I want to make sure you buy something good. Cheap clothes are not the answer, nor are outlandish styles. You need a decent pair of shoes. I don't think I want to see you in those old running shoes at a wedding."

"I suppose," Jenny sighed as if it were a great imposition to have someone buy her good shoes. "Those sneakers are so comfortable and anyway my feet are swelling these days. Leather shoes would only cripple me."

"We'll see, but properly fitted expensive shoes don't hurt. So when do you want to go shopping? Monday, Wednesday, when is it convenient?" She asked knowing Jenny's therapy sessions were Tuesday and Thursday, also knowing every day was convenient now since Jenny quit at Welbourns.

Janet decided to let Jenny keep some of her pride and did not say anything about her being unemployed. Esther had told her Steve was working as a truck driver and apparently making enough money that Jenny was no longer on welfare. At least, that's what he told Esther. He seemed to have settled down at long last.

"Wednesday, I guess," Jenny said already planning how to con her mother out of hard cash.

"You should join the army, laddie. Make a man of you, it would, and look at the pension you'd get at the end," Frank said to his son, "You'd see the world and they'd train you in computers or some such. Yes indeed, you could come out of it with a pension and a career. And the longer you stay in, the more your pension you'll collect. Then if you get promoted, you get even an even better pension, indexed too." Frank sucked his unlit pipe and stared at Steve who sat gazing into space, his eyes glazed.

Steve and Shawn had come home for supper as they did every year on Esther's birthday. Right now she was busy in the kitchen slaughtering the fatted calf for her boys while they sat talking to Frank.

"Look at young Shawn now," Frank nodded at Shawn who was reading the sports page, "He got himself into the Civil Service and he's doing all right, aren't you, Shawn?"

Shawn nodded although he didn't hear the question. His father was such a witterer, neither of them listened to anything he had to say.

"Shawn'll have a nice pension, indexed too, when he retires. You could do far worse than join the army, Steve."

Steve turned on the television. This was all he needed, his Dad going on about pensions when he was hardly thirty. All the old man thought about these days was retiring.

Esther came in with a loaded tray that she set down on the coffee table. "Here we are, something to be going on with. Supper won't be until seven."

"Why don't you sit down, Mum?" Shawn said, cutting a hunk of cheese and taking some crackers. "It's your birthday, for heaven's sake. Stop dashing around and catering to us for a while."

Esther smiled lovingly. Shawn was such a good boy.

"Now, Shawn," she said, "You know I like doing it. Anyway, my birthday was yesterday. It's too bad that neither of you could get off work and come for supper. Your Dad sent out for Chinese, though, didn't you, Frank?"

Frank nodded and stared at the TV.

That evening Steve ate and drank beer and talked about the game with Shawn as Frank dozed in his chair. Esther sat for an hour or so and then started on Steve about joining the army. Obviously she and Frank had talked about it at length, so Steve soon realized where the idea started. His mother, whom they all knew used devious means to achieve her own ends, had probably given his father his orders.

"Look here, Mum. I don't *want* to join the army. It's no life for an army wife. I mean, all that moving. Jenny wouldn't like it."

Esther felt overjoyed to hear that. "So when are you getting married?" she asked, face wreathed in smiles.

"I didn't say that, Mum," he said, dashing her hopes. "I'm not marrying Jenny. We talked about this before."

"Nevertheless, you said it's not a nice life for an army wife and that Jenny wouldn't like it."

"True enough. Don't take things so literally, Mum. I'm not marrying Jenny and I never will. I'll stick by her until the baby is born. I promised you that, but I'm not marrying her."

Esther glared at him, the young sod! Still, at least he was still with Jenny and she was sure he would change his mind once he held the child in his arms.

"So," she said now, "You planning on driving trucks for ever?"

"It's a good living. I could do far worse," he said, shrugging. "I like being on my own, nobody breathing down my neck. If I want to drive all night and make a fast trip, I can always claim it took me longer. There's nobody harassing me. In fact, I'm my own boss."

A frisson of fear ran through Esther. That didn't sound right at all.

"I thought the transport people checked your log book at all those stops. How can you drive for longer than the limit they set? Surely that's illegal."

Steve chuckled. "I don't fill it in until I get to a check point, and I know where they all are. You can take back roads and miss them altogether. Of course, when you cross the border, that's different."

Steve did not tell her that he could also cook the books on that as well. Esther was a very moral person and what he was doing was illegal and dangerous. The crooked company he presently drove for had two log books for each truck. One was completed when the truck arrived back at the garage and showed actual pick up and delivery points, another was used on the road. Since they paid road taxes on mileage recorded in these log books, drivers for the less reputable companies cooked their books, the actual mileage being recorded in one book, the fixed in another. The garage mechanics turned speedometers back to reflect the log book figure. Most transport companies were honest, as were their drivers. Nevertheless, some smaller companies did everything they could to make a profit.

Steve had a sideline when he did a run stateside, because under his return cargo he hid cases of booze, small appliances or leather goods. These he sold to a fence in lower town Ottawa and made a healthy profit.

Esther eyed him speculatively. "How's Jenny? Why didn't she come with you this time? I mean the truth, not that bunch of lies you told me earlier, Steve." She glared at him, watching his face for signs of lying.

"It's the truth, Mum, she's busy sewing for the wedding. I told you her mother was marrying that lawyer."

That didn't convince Esther. "What's she sewing? Surely her mother would have bought her something to wear to the reception."

Steve laughed. "She did, but you know Jenny. She copied the maternity top, took it back and pocketed the money. Now she's making an identical one."

"That girl is crackers," Esther said, "Imagine her thinking her mother wouldn't know. I've seen her dressmaking handiwork and it's slipshod at best. Janet isn't going to be pleased, I can tell you that much."

With a sinking heart Steve knew he had blown it, and after he'd promised Jenny he would never mention it to anyone. Esther would get on the telephone to Janet and tell her what Jenny had done. He could have kicked himself.

"Look, Mum, promise me you won't tell Mrs. Stevens," he heard himself begging. "Jenny'll kill me if she finds out I told on her. We needed the money to buy things for the baby."

Esther waved away rhetoric. "That's nothing but an excuse. I've told you time and time again that I'll buy whatever you need for the child. Anyway, what about all the money you're making driving a truck? From what you said it sounded as if you were rolling in it." Esther was grim faced now. Steve wasn't a good liar, he always tripped himself up.

Steve's mind quickly flipped through possible explanations and struck on one he thought was plausible. "Like I said, I *do* make good money but we wanted to save as much as we could to get a new place to live. You know those houses are cramped and the neighbourhood isn't very nice. We want to put a down payment on a townhouse in Barhaven."

"Hmm," Esther eyed Steve as he spoke and noticed his eyes looked everywhere but at her. It was another pack of lies. "How much do you need?"

"At least ten thousand," he said, wondering whether he'd given too small or too large an amount.

"Exactly how much have you got right now?" Esther asked shrewdly, knowing that he lied.

He shrugged. "I don't know. About four thousand. I guess."

Esther smiled grimly. "My word, truck driving must be very lucrative," she said sarcastically, "But if you have four thousand, why did Jenny take that maternity top back, then go out and buy material to make another? It sounds like a waste of time and effort to me."

"I don't know, Mum," he sighed wearily. "Jenny does what Jenny wants to do. You know that. Can we drop it?"

"Hmm. I think I'll call Jenny and have a talk with her."

"God, Mum! Don't you dare. If you mention any of this, she'll kill me." They anguished Steve's face, as was his voice.

Esther smiled. It looked as though Jenny was at long last bringing Steve to heel. Good for her. They would have a wedding soon. She knew it.

SEVENTEEN

Jenny sewed, unpicked and sewed again. She had bought a cheap material in almost the same colour as the outfit she returned, and while the pattern was not difficult, she had problems because the material was too thin, had hardly any sizing and was difficult to handle. The seams kept puckering and, try as she would, she couldn't keep the slippery material straight. Sighing with annoyance, she started to unpick it yet again. Maybe taking the other one back was not such a good idea after all. Her mother had forked out more than five hundred dollars for the outfit and all it represented to Jenny was money wasted. Returning it and spending twenty-five dollars on material had seemed like such a good idea at the time. Now she wondered.

If she only knew more about adjusting the tension and the different grades of thread and needles. She dared not call to ask her mother for advice. Suppose she wanted to know what Jenny was sewing and what type of material?

Tossing the mess on the floor, she went to get herself a Coke. Two hours later she had to admit that she couldn't do it. After calling in one of her neighbours who did alterations but couldn't help, she gave it up as a bad job. Even the neighbour could find no way to fix after all her unpicking and resewing.

What was she going to do, she wondered? Maybe she could go back to the shop and buy back the outfit. Yet how could she pay for it? The finance company! That was the answer. She would ask them for five hundred against her inheritance. Problem solved.

The next day she again signed on the dotted line but when she got to the shop and looked for her outfit, it had been sold. After checking out the remaining stock, she bought a similar outfit in a different colour, a cheap knock-off of the same pattern, that was only fifty dollars. She figured she could always tell her mother that beige made her sallow so she had exchanged it because navy blue looked better. Too bad that the shoes were beige, as was the purse. At least the small flowered hat looked all right. With a sigh of relief she took her package home.

As they came down the stairs to the lobby at City Hall Janet felt a surge of aggravation as she saw Jenny with Steve. What on earth was Jenny wearing? Not the very expensive maternity outfit she had bought. This was navy blue and with sparkles of metallic thread. Smiling at Richard, and unwilling to spoil their day, she decided to say nothing to Jenny until they were alone.

Steve wore a suit. Not a good suit, but a suit nonetheless. It belonged to his brother Shawn. He even wore regular shoes instead of running shoes. Janet smiled at him and, taking his hand, kissed his cheek.

"Hello, Steve."

"Congratulations, Mrs. Stevens," Steve said, "I mean Mrs. Wyatt. I hope you'll be very happy."

"Thank you, Steve," Janet turned to Jenny who seemed unusually quiet. "How are you, Jenny? I'm glad you could come, though I had thought you were coming to the reception since you didn't show up for the ceremony."

Jenny's tension drained away. Her mother didn't even notice the outfit was different. Old people had bad memories, she knew, and now she could relax and enjoy herself.

"I'm fine. I wanted to come here, you know that, you're my mother. I forgot the time and we got here late. So you've done the deed, eh?"

Richard came back up the marble stairs from the cloakroom and headed toward them. He looked swish in his new suit. Jenny always noticed everything. Gee, he was handsome, was her new dad.

She threw her arms around his neck and smiled up at him. "Hello, my new daddy," she gushed.

Richard did not know what to do. He smiled with embarrassment and said nothing.

Janet was livid. The gesture was so blatantly phoney that she felt like pulling Jenny away and slapping her face. Instead she stood smiling stonily until Jenny took her arms down and stood simpering and practically flirting with Richard.

The reception was delightful and Janet found it thoroughly enjoyable. The food was superb, the staff courteous and eager to please, the surroundings plush and comfortable, and the small string ensemble was fabulous. Jenny and Steve were somewhere in the crowd and she completely pushed them out of her mind. She forgot to talk to Jenny about the outfit. She forgot everything but her handsome new husband.

Jenny sat sulking. The reception was groovy, but here she was looking like a blimp and Steve didn't dance very well. After she had stuffed her face at the buffet and talked to a few people, she became bored to tears. Steve was talking to some guy who had his own trucking company. Suddenly she wanted to go home, now!

Pulling at Steve's arm, she whined in an undertone that she felt sick.

Glaring at her, he said, "One moment, please, Jenny. I happen to be talking. You look perfectly all right to me. Go to the ladies' room and wash your face. We'll leave in about half an hour."

She pouted and postured as she hung onto his arm, but neither man looked at her. Petulantly she flounced off to the washroom and sat on one of the chaises in the outer lounge.

"Jenny. What are you doing in here?" Janet asked as she came into the lounge, her voice full of concern.

"Well, well, if it isn't the new Mrs. Richard Wyatt," Jenny said sarcastically. "I'm fine. I'm resting my feet. I told you my feet swelled and these shoes are killing me." She lifted one leg. The shoes were the most comfortable she had ever worn and her ankles looked trim and perfect, worst luck.

"Where is the outfit I bought you, Jenny?" Janet asked quietly.

"What's it to you? I like this one. It suits me better than that old beige thing."

"That 'old beige thing' cost me almost five hundred dollars." Jenny always made her angry these days. "It was a designer original and would have lasted you for years. They designed it so you could have it taken in."

"Well, I didn't like it. I liked this one better and anyway I had to wear it, not you," Jenny retorted.

That it was not exactly suitable and did not suit Jenny was beside the point. Janet had no intention of arguing with her daughter, not today. She would be wasting her breath, anyway.

"I'm glad you like it, then," Janet said, smiling a smile both mirthless and loveless. Jenny didn't notice. She adjusted her hair in the lighted mirror, pink tinted, she noticed, it made her look young and fresh.

"So when are you leaving for your honeymoon?" Jenny asked, "I bet he's taking you somewhere fantastic."

"We're not going away yet. We're going to take a while to sort out our domestic arrangements. Richard has a hefty law case on his hands at the moment. We thought we'd go to the Caribbean for Christmas."

Jenny sat up straight. "Could I come with you? I need to get away. Especially after having the baby. We could both come."

"Of course you can't!" Janet was shocked. What was the matter with the girl? To even to think about asking if she could accompany someone on their honeymoon. "It would be my honeymoon."

"So what? You already had one with Dad so this shouldn't be

anything more than a holiday," Jenny scoffed, "I bet Daddy Richard would let me come along if I asked him."

"Don't even think about it," Janet shuddered. This girl of hers was trouble personified. The way Jenny dressed had not impressed Richard and, though he said nothing, Janet saw the way he looked at Jenny when he thought Janet didn't see.

"I'll go and ask him right now, should I?" Jenny said as she stood. She was halfway out the room before Janet managed to grab her arm.

"Don't you dare, Jenny," She heard the tears in her voice and knew Jenny had heard them. The tears flooded her eyes at the thought of Jenny's spoiling her wedding day.

"Oh, all right, Mum," Jenny said, pleased to have upset her mother. "Don't get so hysterical. I won't talk to him yet. Let him get used to living with you first, eh?" As they left the lounge and parted ways, she smiled and walked over to where Steve stood talking to the trucker.

In late December Jenny's labour pains started. Steve was away in Montreal and didn't get back until after she'd given birth. She would never forgive him for that, but she forgot everything when she saw her son. Jenny had already picked the name Christian for him. Christian Rigby sounded nice to her ears.

Esther and Frank arrived bearing a teddy bear and a new receiving blanket. Frank said nothing, but she could tell he was pleased when he held the baby. She had to laugh at the funny faces and baby noises he made.

Her mother and Richard arrived with a complete layette and a brochure on the new pram they bought. Richard also presented the baby with a silver spoon and an engraved christening mug.

It was wonderful. She had a new son, her family was gathering around to admire the baby and everything in the garden was lovely.

Until Steve arrived.

"Hello, Jenny," she felt him shaking her shoulder. She had fallen asleep after feeding the baby.

"Steve," Her face full of joy, she showed him his son. "Isn't he wonderful? Here," she thrust the baby at him, "You can hold him."

Steve backed away as though she had offered him something horrible. "No thanks. Sorry I was late, but the traffic in Montreal was terrible. I got back as fast as I could. Was it bad?"

Steve thought she looked fine, but what did he know about having a baby?

He was going to suffer for not being here, she was going to make sure of that. "Yes. It was absolutely terrible. I had to have stitches. I told you to stay home but, oh no, you had to make one more trip." Her lip trembled as she remembered the agony.

"Sorry," he said, uninterested. "Anyway it's over with now and you look okay. When do you get out of here?" Steve felt uncomfortable in the maternity ward.

"I don't know. I only had the baby last night. In a couple of days, I guess. Your mother will know. She said she'll stay with us for a week until I get over the birth."

Steve sighed with annoyance. Not what he needed for sure, his mother living with them. "Guess he'll only get one lot of presents, though," he said, indicating the baby with a flip of his hand.

Steve showed very little interest in his child, Jenny thought, and surely that was not normal. "What do you mean?"

"Well, I mean since he's been born so close to Christmas he won't get two lots of presents. You know, one lot for his birthday and the other lot for Christmas. Poor little kid."

"Don't be silly. Of course he'll get two lots of presents. Won't you, my little Christian?"

Steve looked at her hard. "What did you call him?"

Jenny smiled. "Christian. That's his name. Christian Rigby."

Suddenly Steve's natural masculine pride surged to the fore. "No way is *my* son going to get stuck with a name like that. They'll call him 'Chrissy the sissy.' He's got to have a nice manly name. Something nobody can make fun of."

Jenny's expression blackened. "I'm telling you his name is Christian. I already told everyone and they all said it was such a nice name. I suppose you want him called Steve like you, or Shawn, or Frank after your dad."

"Anything but a wimpy name like Christian. Anyway, who said his name was Rigby? I thought he had to be Stevens since we're not married."

Jenny, he could see, was livid. "You're his father. He should have your surname. I registered in as Jenny Rigby and that's how they registered him." Jenny cuddled her son and kissed his downy head, ignoring Steve.

He stared at her. Look at her all broody and maternal. Well, it didn't change a thing as far as he was concerned. "I'm not going to marry you, Jenny, if that's what you think. That's out of the question. I said I would stay until the kid was born, and now he is and now I'm leaving."

"Oh, Steve. What does that mean? After all I've been through for you?" Jenny began to cry. Was he going to desert her after she had given birth to his son? She had been in agony for hours, had screamed for painkillers, but the nurses had refused her. The doctor was as bad, telling her that hundreds of women had babies every day and she was no different. All she had to do was breath properly, relax between contractions. How would they know, they'd probably never given birth themselves, and here was Steve, not wanting to know what she had gone through to give him a son.

He started to pace, fed up to the back teeth with her demands. "All right," God, he hated all these tears. "All right! I'll stay until my mother goes back home, but I can't promise more than that," he said with very bad grace. When he went to register the birth, he'd fix it, he would tell them the name was Stevens. That would fix her little game, all right.

He had seen Rita twice in the last month and slept with her both times. She was still hot for his body and had apparently forgiven him. Now she had begun begging him to move back in with her, and he desperately wanted to take her up on the offer.

Jenny looked down at the baby, Steve forgotten. A real live baby boy of her very own, how marvellous. She felt happy and could hardly wait to go home so she could have him all to herself. The way the nurses kept taking him back to the nursery got on her nerves. They refused to let her keep him to cuddle even when he was asleep. She bet that they let him cry and cry back there with all the other babies.

"Well, I'm going. You need anything? I can fetch it when I come in tomorrow." Steve was already half out the door.

"Yes! I need a lot of things," Jenny said scathingly, angry because he was leaving so soon and before he had even held the baby. "Still, don't let me keep you." Sarcasm was her only weapon although she knew full well that Steve never recognized it as such. "I'm sure you have far more important things to do than see your new son."

"Make a list and give it to my Mum when she comes," Steve said casually, sure that his mother, the original mother hen, would be there daily to check on her grandson. "Okay?"

Jenny glared at him. "Okay."

Wait until she got out of this place. Just wait until she could raise her voice and yell at him. Nothing got through to him unless she screamed, that was the only time he seemed to hear her.

EIGHTEEN

Janet felt happy in her new life, more content. Although she would never forget Jim Stevens, she discovered a new love with Richard. The days of guilt and depression over Jim's death were now a hazy memory, while her problems with Jenny receded to the back of her mind. Jenny's situation seemed to have improved since the baby's birth, and it helped that Esther was keeping an eye on things at the townhouse and called her every week to report how things were going.

While to Janet, Steve and Jenny's living in sin was not a satisfactory way of doing things, at least Steve appeared to have settled down and found a job. They did not seem to lack for money. Janet offered to buy any baby things they needed, but Jenny proudly said Steve was making lots of money, and they had even started saving to buy their own home. Janet accepted this statement with a touch of scepticism knowing Jenny would consider a few hundred dollars a lot. Janet hoped it was in an account in Steve's name for if Jenny managed to get her hands on it she would fritter it away.

Richard, working on a case in Montreal, commuted daily by train. Janet, wisely deciding to stay on at the office, was kept busy although he was away from home a lot. Right now they were living at the house, but she knew Richard preferred them to have a new residence. Her house held too many memories for his liking, memories in which he held no place. The real estate agent brought over selected listings but as yet they had not found anything suitable.

When Richard was home, they often entertained and Janet liked her new friends. Things had changed so much in her life that even entertaining became effortless. All she needed do was call the caterer and the florist and they took everything care of everything. Long gone the days when she spent hours in the kitchen and missed most of the party because she was making sauce or finishing the dessert. Now Janet relaxed and thoroughly enjoyed having company.

Of course she and Richard were still in the first stages of passionate love. They were founding members of a private club to which only they two could belong and keeping her hands off him was sometimes difficult. She knew that people of their age didn't go around welded at the hip like young lovers, but she felt so much love for Richard. Yes, she'd made a wise decision, she told herself again, as she called the florist to order an arrangement for their Saturday evening dinner party. She smiled with satisfaction as she hung up, thinking it wonderful to be able charge everything. No longer did she have to count pennies, no longer did she have to agonize over every purchase, now unlimited funds were at her disposal.

Her wardrobe had changed considerably. She wore good label or designer clothes and shoes. The salon styled her hair once a week and she had a regular appointment Friday afternoons for a manicure, pedicure, massage and facial. That alone made Janet feel like a completely different person. She became confident and sure of herself. The change in Janet amazed even Jenny.

It surprised Janet how little time it had taken for her to get used to her present affluent life, how comfortable she was with it. For once, no guilt pervaded her pleasure.

Jenny and her problems faded significantly since Janet's visit with Dr. Ross. The visit was very cathartic and he advised her not to mention the adoption until Jenny settled down and the baby was older. Even so, both knew she must tell her daughter, and the sooner the better. She didn't wish to think about that one blot on her happiness.

Jenny continued her twice weekly sessions with Dr. Ross who told Janet that Jenny was becoming more stable. Her hysterical outbursts were tapering off, she was calmer and took time to think things through. Dr. Ross also said Jenny blamed both her parents for trying to make her into something she was not. Jenny had not wanted to go to college or have a career, all she wanted was to marry and have children. J e n n y had felt threatened by her parent's ambitions for her. Dr. Ross was very polite when he told her, but Janet felt his words keenly. Apparently as parents they had done everything wrong. Their love for Jenny, especially Janet's, had not made her feel wanted. On the contrary, it made her feel restrained, confined, unable to measure up to their expectations. None of this revelation made Janet feel very good, even when Dr. Ross explained to her that most teenagers went through these stages, which was why so many of them rebelled. He was a kind man, Janet thought, as he patiently explained to her why she shouldn't feel any guilt and repeated that Jenny was adult enough to make her own decisions.

Dr. Ross, writing his notes later, was also concerned that Jenny's problems were deeper than he had told her mother, but until he had dug deeper into the young woman's psyche, he held his peace. Many things could have affected her mentally, so many that it was dangerous to hazard a guess, although he had his suspicions.

FAS (fetal alcohol syndrome) and FAE (fetal alcohol effect) came to mind. FAS manifested itself physically in that children so affected were obvious. Their eyes had short openings, their eyelids sometimes drooped. In one way Jenny showed this in her eyes, which were almond shaped although the lids were normal. FAS also manifested itself in other facial characteristics. A snub nose that was slow to develop as it was in Jenny's case, although now her nose had grown enough to match her features and looked normal. FAS children often lacked the philtrum - the two grooves under the nose to the lip - but Jenny was normal in that respect. Of course, one could not diagnose FAS or FAE from simply talking to a person. Diagnosis involved physical, psychological and behavioural testing.

A child with FAE was the most difficult to diagnose as many of them were extremely intelligent, as in Jenny's case where her IQ was considerable, but all were mentally challenged in some area. He dare not jump to conclusions as her problems could possibly be attributable to other causes. It would be many months before he could be sure and, after talking to Janet in depth, he now knew Jenny's home life had been stable and loving.

As he finished his notes, he made a note to see her medical records and ask Janet for the name of her doctor. He must research everything.

It was the week after Christmas and Janet gazed around her with delight. They were sitting on their fourth floor Paradise Island balcony having breakfast. Although it was not yet eight, the sun blazed down from the pale blue sky. Sea birds wheeled and screamed as a beach boy tossed food out to a school of fish. The birds dived as the fish leapt over the azure blue waves. Watching this daily early morning show was wonderful.

They had been on the island three days and the surroundings alone completely relaxed Janet, though it was taking Richard longer to unwind. Days were spent strolling the white sand beaches or lazing under palm leafed shade.

On their first evening, they went into the Casino but Janet felt uncomfortable as it brought back painful memories of Las Vegas. Richard, sensing this, took her to supper at one of the gourmet restaurants and then to the main club to see the lavish show.

As the days passed, Janet came to realize that she loved Richard deeply. It was not, as she had previously thought, anything to do with his financial stability or standing in the community that made him seem so very attractive. That helped, of course, she couldn't deny that. Her love for him was much stronger than that she'd had for Jim Stevens.

That made her feel uncomfortably guilty, as though the years they had spent together were as nothing compared to this all encompassing feeling she now experienced. Each day she thanked God for this second chance at happiness.

'Unless we receive payment within ten days, this account will be placed in collection.' The red flagged form letter from the finance company stated in large black letters. Jenny stared at it, unable to comprehend the problem. Why were they so worried about a measly fiftydollar payment? After, all she was an heiress. For heaven's sake they had seen the will copy and had a copy of it in her file. What a lot of fuss. They would get their money if they let her miss again this month. It was Christmas and she wanted to buy toys for Christian, and she must buy Steve a gift.

Screwing up the letter, she tossed it into the garbage can. This reminder was nothing new as they sent one every month. Usually she took the payment money out of her welfare cheque, but sometimes she couldn't afford to do that. Once or twice she had managed to con Steve out of the money. However, he was not going to fall for that again. Now her welfare payment did not go far, so she had to rely on his handouts or the credit company.

As she played with Christian, her mind niggled about the debt. She and Steve had one humongous yelling match when he found out how much she had taken from the credit company. He wanted to know exactly what she had spent the money on and, naturally, she was unable to show him anything but the car, and that was now uninsured because she forgot to make the payment.

"...and I bought the microwave," she said, pointing at the counter.

"How much was that? Two hundred bucks?"

"Well, it all adds up, I bought trays and dishes and stuff as well."

"It doesn't add up to more than five thousand, no matter what you say. What on earth did you do with the money?"

Jenny couldn't figure it out where it had gone, now she thought about it. She glanced around the kitchen.

"Oh! I got this dining room set."

"Another hundred and fifty?" He looked at the already shabby Arborite and chrome set.

Jenny wrinkled her brow. What *had* she done with the money? She could recall buying comics, chocolates and soft drinks, going to movie matinees a lot, but nowhere could she see any major purchase. A few hundred she spent on tricky little outfits for Christian who had grown out of most of them before he even wore them, and she bought herself new Reboks, new blouses and some very expensive makeup.

She blew out a breath. "Oh, I don't know. I spent it, I guess."

Steve was angry but he kept his temper. "What about this Hydro bill? Why didn't you pay that if you had money? They'll cut us off if you don't clear it," he warned.

"*You* pay it. I don't have any money. You know that. You won't let me have access to the bank account."

"Too bloody true, Jen. You'd spend every cent we had if you had access."

"No, I wouldn't. It's not fair! You keep treating me like kid. I know how to handle money, I want . . ."

"You want?" Steve bellowed. "What about this lot?" He waved the dunning letters at her. Jenny had tossed them in the rubbish bin, but he'd spotted them. Now she was in deep trouble. "Is this your idea of good money management? What were you going to do when they came and repossessed the car? Tell me somebody had stolen it?"

"Do leave off, Steve, you'll wake the baby." She didn't appear to be much concerned and that angered him immensely. "Anyway, they wouldn't take the car. Welfare wouldn't let them."

"Huh! Is that what you think? I have news for you, missy, welfare doesn't condone living beyond your means, and you live way over your means. You can't afford a car!" She opened her mouth to speak but he waved her down, "Never mind about you telling them it belongs to your mother, and you were borrowing it. Look what happened when it broke down, they told you to pay the repairs and send them the bill.

Then because you hadn't enough money, it sat there like a pile of junk for at least two months. If I hadn't got Ernie to work on it, it'd still be rotting at the curb."

"They would have paid me, though, the money for the repairs," Jenny said petulantly.

"What has that got to do with the money you've been borrowing against your trust fund? Where does it say you're entitled to collect welfare and draw money out of the fund as well? I'm sure the welfare people would love to know about your little fiddle."

Jenny shrugged, her shoulders were very eloquent. "Oh, but you won't be the one who tells them, will you now? You live here with me and the welfare pays the rent. Is that legal?" Jenny didn't like being in the wrong, but this time she considered Steve was juat as wrong.

Steve suddenly tired of everything. It was like talking to a statue, she never heard anything he said. "I don't have to stay here, Jenny, you know that. I can go back home and my mother will look after me a lot better than you ever could. You only want me around as a dogsbody, somebody to shove around, someone to babysit while you go out, someone at your beck and call. You're the most selfish bitch I've ever met."

"I thought you loved me. You said you did," Jenny wailed, "I adore you, Steve, I've shown you how much. I gave you a son, didn't I? Don't you love me any more? I love you."

Steve growled his annoyance. "Oh, for heaven's sake! I know you do, but that isn't going to make me love you. I won't marry you, Jenny, and I know you're warming up to that again. I can't afford you and I can't stand all this emotional blackmail."

"Blackmail? What blackmail?" Jenny looked puzzled, what *was* he talking about?

Steve waved his hands around, his exasperation showing in his tone of voice. "Oh, all this business about not letting me see Chris, about him being a bastard, about what your mother and Wyatt said, what my mother said. It's like the Chinese water torture, Jenny, day by day, drip by drip. You keep on at me all the time, but I can tell you now that it's not going to work. I don't have to stay here and take it any longer."

Jenny picked up the letters he had tossed on the kitchen table. She glanced through them. Same old stuff, they could all wait.

"Can you pay this one, Stevey?" she asked, passing the Hydro bill to him as if she hadn't heard a word he'd said. "Poor little Christian is going to be really cold if they shut off the Hydro. We won't have any heat."

"Oh, all right!" Snatching the paper out of her hand, he picked up his windcheater. "Try and have supper ready when I get back. I'm off to Niagara at seven."

Jenny smiled as she watched him start his pick up truck. He would pay the Hydro and she could keep the money her mother had given her for that purpose and pay half the credit agency demand.

When Christian started to cry, she went upstairs to get him, and after changing him she played with him on the carpet in the front room. Steve surprised her when she suddenly found him standing over her, glaring. "So where's my supper?"

"Oh, you're back already," She glanced through the archway at the kitchen clock.

"Jenny! I've been gone over an hour and a half. I went to the bank and paid the bill through the banking machine. Then I went to the office and picked up the truck and the papers. Where's my supper? God damn it, woman, how can you expect me to drive for eight hours on an empty stomach?"

Jenny slowly stood and put Christian in his arms. "I thought you went to transport cafes. Surely truck stops make better food that I do. I seem to recall . .,"

"I seem to recall that I told you that truck stop food is not that good. It's greasy and stodgy, and they can't cook vegetables properly. No point in me working out if I'm going to eat stodge, is there? Come on, make me some supper."

"Oh, Steve, look at him," she smiled at Christian who was blowing spit bubbles and chuckling merrily, his arms and legs working like choppers. "Isn't he gorgeous?"

Steve looked down at his son. He was a big boy, solid. Definitely took after his father, he thought. "Yeah, gorgeous. Supper?"

Jenny poked around the fridge looking for something to cook. She must become more organized, she thought, make a list of meals and stick to it, like her mother had told her, so she didn't go through this constant scramble each day when Steve was at home.

Finally she made scrambled eggs and McCain oven french fries. A tin of peas and a couple of slices of toast would help fill him up, and she could have a chocolate bar and a Coke.

"Any dessert?" Steve asked hopefully, still hungry.

"Pudding? No."

"Then make me some sandwiches to take with me, I'm still hungry. You're going to have to learn to cook properly, Jenny. I can't survive on the starvation rations you dish out."

"Why should I bother?" Jenny said, picking up Christian and hugging him as she walked around the kitchen table. "I mean it's not as if you're going to marry me, now is it? Why should I waste my time?"

"All right, that's it. Enough said." Steve, grim faced and weary, picked up his jacket. He rubbed at his leg. He had hurt it getting down from the cab a couple of days earlier and it was gradually becoming more painful.

"What time will you be back?"

"Who cares?"

"I care," she shot back. "I care a lot, Steve. When will you be back?"

"Maybe tomorrow, maybe not," he said, shrugging nonchalantly and walking to the door.

"You know, I've had it with you, Steve Rigby," she spat vituperatively, "You're not a fit father for this child. I'm going to find someone else to live with. I don't need this constant aggravation."

Steve shrugged again. "Suits me."

Jenny put Christian down on the sofa, and grabbed at his jacket as he opened the door.

"Come on, Steve, when will you be back?"

"Do you care?"

"Of course I care. I care a lot. I love you, Steve. Don't you love me? Please tell me what time you'll be back, please?"

"So you can get your other fellow out the way before I get here?"

Steve said, joking. Any other time they would have laughed together at that remark as Steve knew Jenny had eyes for nobody but him. Today his words did not amuse her.

"I resent that, Steve," she blazed. "I don't mess around, not like you with all those women. I bet you've got at least three of them sniffing around you right now. Don't tar me with the same brush. I'm decent."

He heaved a sigh. "All right, Jenny, it was a joke. Lost your sense of humour altogether, have you?"

"It's not a joking matter. I know you go out with other women while I've never even looked at another man. It's time *you* grew up."

"They should give you a medal for fidelity. Mother Teresa has nothing on you, eh? Come on, let go of my jacket. I have to leave."

Jenny grumpily stood back and let him out the door. He was such a sod, was Steve Rigby, such a playboy and yet she loved him. She loved him so much that she would do anything for him. Not that her love went as far as scrubbing floors or washing sheets.

So here she was with the finance company after her again. She had missed two payments and she knew from experience the third letter would be a final notice. What would Steve say then?

"Not to worry, baby boy," she said as she cuddled Christian who pulled painfully on her hair. Time would come when Steve would pay the bill and she'd be free of hassle for a month or so. So why worry?

She decided to change the baby into one of his new outfits and go over to her mother's. Maybe she could borrow some money from her mother or Richard. Borrow, that was a funny word, she thought, she never ever paid it back, but still called it borrowing. Never mind, once she got her trust fund they could have every penny back . . . but not unless they asked for it.

When Steve arrived home the next afternoon, he found the house empty. Jenny and the baby were out and the kitchen looked like the third world war had blasted through. With a snort of disgust, he filled the sink and started to wash the dishes.

Last night's pan held congealed scrambled eggs. Lazy and slip shod, she had not thought to soak the egg encrusted pan. He saw stacked plates from at least four meals in the sink, with mugs and cups, glasses and cutlery all tossed in together.

It took over an hour to clean the kitchen and that didn't include the sticky floor and counter tops. Steve grew angrier by the minute. The only thing Jenny did these days was feed the baby, play with him and take him out for walks. She considered nothing else worth doing.

Today, he suddenly remembered, was Jenny's appointment with Dr. Ross and knew his mother would come back to the house with them. Well, it simply had to stop, he was not equipped to handle things domestic, and it made him less of a man in his own mind. While he had promised his parents he would stay with Jenny, it was simply not working out and he had to get from under, son or no son.

When Jenny arrived home with Esther, she smiled to see how clean and tidy the kitchen was, especially since Esther had eagle eyes. Not that a messy house bothered her. Jenny liked clutter, it was homey and comfortable. And if it were messy, Esther usually cleaned it. Esther's house was spotless, so model-home looking to Jenny that she felt uncomfortable. Today they had been outside on the front when Esther arrived and she thought that Esther would probably start cleaning when they got back.

Esther hugged Steve. She had not seen him for more than two weeks.

"How are you, son?" she asked, smiling up at him.

"Okay, Mum," he said, shrugging off her hands and taking Christian from Jenny. "I hurt my leg. It doesn't half give me pain when I drive a long stretch."

Esther's eyes flashed around the kitchen. "My word, this place is a regular little palace. See, didn't I tell you that if you did something each day, it would stay clean?" she said to Jenny, who was filling the kettle for tea.

"Yes," Jenny said, glancing at Steve with raised eyebrows.

He said nothing but continued to bounce Christian on his knee. So that was the way it was, he thought, his mother was giving lessons on housekeeping and Jenny was ignoring them. However, that went without saying. Steve knew she already figured she knew enough about everything, without going in for full time house cleaning.

Esther took Christian from Steve and rocked him in her arms. Christian liked his Gran, much to her delight, and put his arms up to her whenever he saw her. Esther was a warm, loving person who loved children and they sensed it. "How's my great big grandson doing?" she chortled as he chuckled up at her, waving his arms like windmills.

"Come along then, we'll play on the couch, eh?" She took the baby into the other room.

"So?" Jenny said as she waited for the kettle to boil. How nice to open a cupboard and take out clean mugs for a change, she thought. "How was your trip?"

"Okay. Had a lineup a mile long at the border. Not that I crossed over this time but the Burlington skyway was packed."

"Did you manage to bring me anything?" she asked, hopefully.

"Nope. I was delivering bottles to the winery, came back empty."

"Oh," she felt disappointed. It was usually like Christmas at the house when he got home. He brought her things he smuggled over the border, things he picked up from other truckers that had conveniently fallen off a tailboard, or items he got as a perk.

"I was with your Mum most of the afternoon," she said, "She took me over to see Dr. Ross and looked after the baby while I saw him. Then we went to the mall."

Steve felt a sense of annoyance and decided to let it all out. It was giving him ulcers, all this pussy footing around.

"Tell me something, Jen, why didn't you wash the dishes last night? I mean why don't you wash the dishes after we've finished eating?" He kept his voice low so Esther could not hear.

"What is this? So you washed a couple of dishes. Cut it out, Steve. I'm not maid of all work, you know."

"I do know, you keep telling me so, but I'm getting tired of working day and night and coming home to a garbage tip. Try to keep the place tidy at least, Jenny. What would my mother have said if she had found the kitchen in the state I found it?"

"I don't know and I don't care," Jenny said snippily. "I don't work for your mother and she has no control over me or this house. Anyway, she usually does it for me and I don't stop her. She likes cleaning and stuff."

"How are we doing here?" Esther said brightly as she popped her head around the door. "Have you any rusks for the baby, Jenny? I think he's starting to teethe. He keeps gnawing on my finger."

"Will a cookie do? I don't have rusks. Steve, go to Beckers and get some," she ordered.

Steve glared at her, but since it was for the baby and his mother had asked, he went. Now he noticeably limped and his leg hurt badly, all the way up to his groin.

Esther and Jenny sat drinking tea, watching Christian as he tried to put his entire fist in his mouth.

"He's growing so quickly, bless him," Esther said, wiping the drool off his chin with the bib.

"Soon be chasing the girls, I expect, like his daddy," Jenny said sarcastically.

Esther looked at her sharply. "What's going on, Jenny? Has Steve been seeing that other woman again?"

"Oh, I don't know!" God, why had she opened her mouth? Esther would go on and on now. "It's only that I never know when he's going to be home with this horrible job he's got. He tells me he'll be back in one day, or two days and then doesn't turn up for a week. He usually says he did an extra trip."

Esther shook her head. "I'm going to have to sit that boy down for a long talk. He can't go on like this. He's got a son to think about now. By the way, when is the christening?"

Christening? Jenny felt a jolt of shock, what on earth for and why should they bother? Neither she nor Steve was religious and considered church going a complete waste of time. They had registered the baby with the government when he was born and named him so why would they want also to go through some archaic religious ceremony?

"We aren't having one," Jenny said firmly, knowing an argument loomed since Esther was very old fashioned.

Esther gasped. "Not having him christened? That's deplorable! Don't you know what a christening signifies? Don't you want the child to have godparents who would look after him if anything happened to you two?"

"That's not what it's about at all. It's about religion and we don't have one. Christian can decide what he wants to be when he grows up. He can get christened then."

"Oh, Jenny," Esther said, her voice cracking, tears springing to her eyes, "The poor little innocent child, he's not got any guardian angel. He's got no angel to watch over him and keep him safe. Religion has nothing to do with christening, not if you don't want it to. It's about having godparents."

"What a lot of old claptrap," Jenny said scornfully. Honestly these old people were weird. "You think this is still the middle ages."

"At least I'd know how to address his birthday card. Is his name Rigby or Stevens? You say it's Rigby and Steve says it's Stevens. What are you going to tell him when he starts asking questions? That you didn't love him enough to have him christened like all the other children?"

"Right!" Jenny slapped the table with the flat of her hand, making Esther jump and Christian screech. She grabbed the baby. "That's it, Esther. You go home now and don't come back unless we invite you."

Esther stood grim faced, and picked up her purse. "I'll wait here until Steve gets back," she said very coldly. "I need to talk to my son."

"Wait in the hall, then," Jenny said rudely, "I want to feed the baby."

Esther stood in the hall for fifteen minutes and then sat on the stairs. She checked her watch. It was taking Steve an awful long time to bring a packet of rusks.

After half an hour she knew he wasn't coming back. That bloody minded son of hers was a law to himself, she fumed, slamming out of the house without wishing Jenny goodbye.

Jenny heard her go and smiled. "Goody, the wicked witch has flown away, Chrissy. Let's play pattycake," Jenny said as she laid Christian down on the carpet and tickled his tummy. Having her very own baby was so lovely. A person who depended on her for everything, a person whom she loved almost as much as he loved her. To heck with Steve. This was more her speed.

NINETEEN

By the time Steve got back, Jenny was sizzling with anger. The fact he came in smiling like a sozzled fool, made it no easier.

"Where the hell have you been? The baby needed those rusks," she yelled angrily. "Where are they?"

Steve smiled foolishly, patting his empty pockets. "Oops!"

"You are a moron. You know that? Can't even do one little thing to help your child. You've been in the bar drinking away our grocery money by the look of you. This is going to have to stop, Steve. I can't let . . ."

In his inebriated state, Steve felt masterful and decided to speak up. "Shut your big mouth, Jenny. I've had enough of your nagging. I know I told you I would stay with you, but I've changed my mind. I can't even walk in the house without you listing all my faults. Nag, nag, nag. You should listen to yourself. Obviously you don't want me here, so I'm leaving."

"Steve!" Jenny gaped and pulled at his sleeve. "Don't leave me, Steve, don't leave us. I love you. We need you." As Steve gazed at the ceiling, ignoring her, she became panic stricken. "I'm sorry, honestly I am. I'm sorry!"

The baby started to make sounds, wanting attention, and she picked him up. "You see? He needs those rusks and you didn't even think about him." She cuddled the now mewling child who chewed on his fist, rocking him in her arms.

Steve looked at them. Jenny was still so juvenile, if everything didn't go her way she acted like child. He knew if he stayed she would revert to her usual sloppy ways and he would suffer even more since he'd let her get away with it yet again. No, he steeled himself to it, he had to leave, no matter how much she begged, no matter how much his mother chastised him. He had to get out from under.

Pulling up his windcheater zip, he hobbled to the door.

"Don't go, Steve. Oh my God, don't go," Jenny screamed at the top of her voice. Christian joined her in a loud shriek.

Steve looked back. Although he felt as guilty as sin, he knew that leaving was necessary. This relationship, child or no child, was going nowhere. He couldn't live this way any longer.

"I'll call you," he said, and limped down the path.

Jenny put the baby on the chesterfield and rushed after him. "Steve, Steve," she yelled.

Steve got into his pick up and started the engine as she threw herself inside the cab. He did not look at her. "Get out, Jenny. Get out now." His voice was steely.

"No, Steve," she grabbed his arm and held it close to her chest. "Please don't go. Don't you love me anymore? Please?" Tears streamed down her face, but they didn't impress him. He'd seen too many of Jenny's crocodile tears.

"Let go, Jenny!" he said firmly and tried to pull his arm away but she clutched him even tighter. "Come on, Jen, get out. We'll sit here all night if you don't. I'm going. I mean it. Let go and get back in the house."

"Please don't leave me, Steve. Pleeeeease." Her voice was like a skill saw, cutting into his brain.

With a strong wrench he pulled his arm from her grasp and opened the door. Going around to the passenger side, he pulled her out of the cab.

"Go back in the house, Jenny, and stay there." He pushed her to the path.

Quickly he got into the cab and restarted the engine. Jenny, unwilling to be put off, quickly jumped into the back of the pick up. Throwing herself to the floor, she crawled forward so she lay directly behind the cab. At least she would find out where he was going and woe betide him if he were going to that woman again.

"You poor little thing," Mrs. Green exclaimed as she hugged the baby closely. "Jenny, Jenny!" she yelled up the stairs, then down the basement stairs. Where would Jenny have gone, and why would she have left the baby untended?

For nearly an hour she heard the baby screaming through the thin wall and eventually came to investigate. All babies cried, that was the way they were, but the constant screeching as if in pain had worried her.

Christian was on the floor when she found him and she wondered if he had fallen off the chesterfield. What should she do? If the child had fallen, he might have concussion or other injuries, and he was now screaming so loudly that she was afraid he was mortally hurt.

Marguerite Green, a warm hearted Jamaican woman, had tried to befriend Jenny, but Jenny would not even talk to her. Marg supposed it was her colour, it was always her colour. Although they shared the fenced-in area behind their houses, they each stayed out of the yard if the other was using it. Of course the Green children were always playing outside and Jenny did not seem to mind them, giving them candy or cookies.

Cuddling the baby, Marg called her doctor. He advised her to call social services and get the child admitted to hospital for observation. It could well be that the mother had walked out on her baby, he said. While Marg somehow doubted that, she couldn't afford to let the baby continue its hysterical crying. Something was dreadfully wrong.

A distraught Marg Green watched as the ambulance took Christian away. Poor little mite and not a sign of Jenny anywhere.

Janet smiled as she opened a letter from Brenda Thompson. They still corresponded. Ernie, as good as new, was back at work where they had recently promoted him to vicepresident of sales. While this correspondence often brought back those nightmare days in Las Vegas, Janet felt so happy with Richard that it didn't bother her so much.

Brenda and Ernie were coming over for a holiday and would be staying at the Wyatt's for two days during their twoweek stay in Ottawa. Janet so looked forward to their visit.

"Two weeks to go," she said happily as she waved the letter at Richard.

Richard took a bite of toast thinking Janet looked even more beautiful than when he first met her. He supposed it was the pampered life she now experienced. She worked at the office, insisting she needed to get away from the house, but her job made her more interesting. She would, however, be taking the two weeks off to entertain her friends.

"You're looking forward to this visit, aren't you?"

"Yes. I am. You'll like Ernie and Brenda, Richard, when you know them better. They're salt of the earth type of people, like most Lancastrians. Never an unkind word and always pleasant."

"I look forward to joining you on some of your jaunts. I deserve a couple of days off after the Mulholland case."

"I should think so, too. Eighteen hours a day for three weeks is a lot of work."

"Yes, but look at the verdict! We won far more in damages than expected, so you and I can probably have a long holiday this year."

"Good. You need a holiday," Janet kissed him as she refilled his coffee cup. "Will you be home for supper?"

"Not tonight. I have a law society meeting."

Janet smiled as she handed him his briefcase. Although she was also going to the office, she used her own small car as Richard usually worked much later than she. Now she quickly glanced at the clock. If she didn't get a move on, she'd be late for work. Smiling she wondered why she needed to be on time, she was the boss's wife for heaven's sake. Who could say anything to her?

As she was leaving, the phone rang. Torn between letting it ring and stopping to answer it, she answered.

A hysterical Jenny yelled in her ear. "Why didn't you answer the phone all night? They've got my baby, Mum. Get Richard to get him back," Janet gasped. Jenny cried frantically, gasping and sobbing, "Get him back, Mum."

Janet knew the reason Jenny could not get through was Richard's insistence that they unplug the phone after six in the evening. It was only plugged back in when they got up in the morning when they turned on the answering machine.

Jenny had stayed in the back of the pick-up until Steve went into the apartment building and then running over to the lobby, read through the names of the tenants. Shit, that blasted Rita Spencer, he had gone to her again. Pushing the buzzer she kept her finger on it until Steve's voice answered.

"Who is this? Stop it at once."

"Steve? You get down here and take me home. At least now I know where you are," Jenny screamed, banging her fist against the wall.

The superintendent, who was emptying the lobby ashtrays, stood inside the lobby watching her. He didn't want any trouble on the premises and the girl looked like big trouble. As the elevator door opened and a strange man got out, he glanced at him.

"She belong to you, son?" he asked gesturing to Jenny with his head. "Get her out of here, and now."

Steve went into the vestibule. "What are you doing here, Jen? How did you get here?"

"You brought me here, I got in the back of the truck. I had to know where you were going."

He took her arm. "Come on, I'll take you home. Whether you know where I am or not makes no difference. I'm not coming back to you, ever." Jenny pulled away from him and sat on the lobby steps crying. She looked a mess, her hair in rats' nests, her makeup smeared. Wiping her nose on the back on her hand, she rubbed it on her jeans. Steve looked at her with distaste. The way she looked right now anyone could take her for a homeless street person.

When they got to the house, he dropped her off and sped away as quickly as he could. Jenny went inside, suddenly realizing she had gone out and left all the doors unlocked. Not that she had anything worth stealing and on the housing estate everyone was in the same situation as herself, on welfare. Still, some residents were not above stealing the other's possessions.

Going into the kitchen she opened a can of Coke. Goddamned man, she thought, he'd better settle down and marry her. His mother would be furious. She picked up the phone and called Esther.

It was only when Esther asked about Christian that she realized her child was missing.

TWENTY

"I'm not having her coming around here making trouble, Steve," Rita said grumpily. She didn't want Steve either come to think of it, having had enough of his blarney the last time he stayed with her.

Rita never really forgave him for hitting her and walking out. The man thought she was a convenience. She glared at him. Recently she had met a nice guy who was becoming serious about their relationship. She didn't want Steve Rigby messing things up.

"She won't come around. I can guarantee that," Steve said as he pulled her into his arms. "I missed you, Rita, I missed you a lot."

"Well, I didn't miss you, Stevey boy," she said stonily, pulling away. "I've got another guy now and you'll have to find somewhere else to stay. I don't want you here. Go home to your mother, if she'll have you."

"Rita!" Steve said, shocked. Rita had always been such a good friend and here she was throwing him out. Last time they parted because he lost his job, but *he* was the one who left so she had no reason to complain about him overstaying his welcome.

"Where can I go? Let me stay tonight at least, 'Ree. I'll find a place tomorrow." He figured by the time he had finished with her in the sack, she would be only too grateful to have him stay permanently.

"All right, but you sleep on the couch," Rita said firmly, already deciding to lock the bedroom door against his advances. She picked up the telephone. She must warn Harry that she had company.

Janet called the office and asked that Richard call her when he arrived. Meanwhile, she would call Jenny back and try to make some sense of what she was saying. How could anyone take the child? Where was Jenny when they had taken him?

When Richard and Janet went over to Jenny's they soon discovered that Christian was in the custody of the Children's Aid Society. Jenny was completely hysterical so Janet sent for the doctor, who sedated her. At the moment she was sound asleep.

"What can we do about this, Richard?" Janet felt worried. Too late now, she realized they should never have expected Jenny to fend for herself.

Richard remained calm and she thanked God for that. "First we have to find out *why* it happened. Too bad Jenny isn't lucid."

Someone knocked at the back door and Janet went to answer it. Marguerite Green stood on the step awash with tears.

When she saw Janet, she smiled through her sobs. "I'm Marg Green, I live next door. I'm so sorry about all this carry on. I had no idea they would take the baby away from Jenny."

"Please come in, Mrs. Green," Janet said as she led the weeping woman into the front room.

Richard listened as Mrs. Green related the events of the previous evening. "Was Jenny in the habit of leaving the baby alone?" he asked.

"Oh, no sir, she was always with the baby. She loves him so much, you see. But when it was nearly an hour and the baby was so upset, I didn't know what to do. I called my doctor who told me to call an ambulance to take him to the hospital."

"You did right, Mrs. Green," Richard said, "Don't feel guilty, you simply did what anyone else would have done."

Mrs. Green wiped her eyes on the Kleenex Janet took from her purse. She stared at Jenny who lay on the chesterfield, out to the world. "Poor child, she's hardly out of diapers herself."

"Yes," Janet agreed, wondering what would happen next.

Richard spent the morning on the phone and eventually went down to the CAS and spoke to the director. Christian would stay under observation for two days and they would release him to Jenny on the understanding that she had an adult in the house with her. Esther, who turned up unexpectedly, immediately volunteered.

With a sigh of relief, Janet sent Richard back to the office, then she and Esther waited for Jenny to wake.

Steve had gone over to pick up his things, thinking Jenny would be at the park with Christian. He was shocked to find both Janet and his mother at the house.

"Come on in, son," Esther said. "You should see a doctor about that leg of yours." His limp had gotten worse.

He didn't like her tone of voice. Then he noticed Jenny asleep on the chesterfield.

"Where's the baby?" he asked, noting that neither of them was holding Christian. His mother normally never let him out of her arms when she came over.

"In the hospital," she said.

"What?" His jaw dropped, what was going on? "What's the matter? Has there been an accident?" He glared at Jenny.

Esther gave a grim smile. "The Children's Aid took him away. Jenny had left him and the neighbour sent for an ambulance when she found him on the floor screaming. That's as much as we know. Jenny was too hysterical to tell us much. The trouble was that the neighbour didn't know where Jenny had gone, but she should never have left the baby alone like that."

Steve swallowed. It was all his fault. Because of him, Jenny had left the child, because of him she had lost their baby.

"Oh, my God," he mumbled as he sat with his face in his hands.

"You'll stay for supper?" Esther asked and Steve nodded miserably. It was not a question, it was a command.

Janet, sitting on the couch, tried to read a magazine, glancing at Jenny occasionally. Unable to concentrate, she picked up her purse and went into the kitchen to talk to Esther.

"I'm going over to the hospital to see about Christian," she said, "Maybe I can find out how he is and when he can come home."

Esther also wanted to go, but knew somebody had to be around when Jenny woke. Too, she wanted to talk to Steve.

"Good idea, Janet," she said, "Call back here before you go home and let me know what happened."

Janet drove over to the hospital. Christian was perfectly fine and lay in a play pen with another baby, both were on their backs, but were looking at each other and gurgling happily.

"He's a very sweet tempered child, your grandson," the nurse told Janet, who felt thrilled.

"When will you release him?" she asked.

"When the CAS gives permission," The nurse looked very hard at Janet, who noticed her appraising her expensive clothes and probably wondering why the baby's mother was on welfare.

"I'd better call them," Janet said, giving Christian a last tummy rub.

"Why can't we have the baby here with us, Richard?" Janet asked when she got home. She had thought about it a lot on the way home. Jenny was not a fit mother, not that she would ever hurt the child, but she simply didn't have enough common sense to look after him properly.

"Do you want a small child here?" Richard asked, his eyes glancing at the pale colours of the carpet and furniture, the white sheers, the polished surfaces.

Janet knew he would never refuse her, and it was her grandson after all, but she knew what his look meant. Yes, it would be a strain on both their relationship, and the furnishings, if she were to take Christian and Jenny into the house. She sighed with exasperation knowing he was right.

"You're right, Richard. I'd be foolish to take Christian on full time. What *are* we going to do about Jenny and the baby?"

"Janet, I mean this in the nicest possible way," Janet felt her heart sink. "Jenny isn't a child. She is now an adult, no matter what you think. She isn't mentally unbalanced, nor is she incapable of working for a living. Jenny must make her own way. She chose to have this child, and it is up to her to provide for him. Now, don't look at me like that, Janet. I'm not an ogre. We're interfering in her life. You can't take the child away from her, and you certainly wouldn't want both of them living here. We'd have no marriage within a month."

Janet nodded miserably. "Yes. She'd drive a wedge between us. I know Jenny all too well. Yet it's the baby, and I do worry about that child. Oh, how I wish Jenny would grow up. Mind you, I've been saying that since she turned sixteen, but she's still as childish as ever. Jenny can't see any further ahead than five minutes from now and thinks only of herself."

"All right, Janet, stop torturing yourself," Richard said as he took her hands. "We've had this talk before. You brought her up the right way, you tried to instill proper moral values into her, you gave her a good home, every creature comfort and a good education. Didn't you?" She nodded. "Why should you now start castigating yourself because she isn't perfect? Even natural born daughters are a trial to their mothers. I should know, I've seen enough of them."

"You never showed me the last report from your contact," Janet said as it popped into her mind. Richard, annoyed with the snail's pace progress of Parent Finders, had hired a detective who specialized in tracing families. He discovered Jenny's natural mother was still working as a prostitute in Montreal and probably suffered from syphilis or VD.

He sighed. "I'm reluctant to tell you, actually, but here goes. Jenny's birth mother is still living in Montreal. She's a prostitute. She's had a hard life and lives in poverty. I didn't learn much else."

Janet gasped. "Oh my God! No wonder you didn't tell me. To think my Jenny came from such a family. How will we ever tell her? You know that I do have to tell her soon, don't you? Do you wonder why I keep putting it off?"

"It's not going to be easy, is why. I think perhaps I should tell her or get Dr. Ross to give her the news."

Janet picked at the skin on her thumb, her mind whirling. "She's going to be so upset, Richard, and I can't blame her. However, it's not your job and she probably wouldn't believe it if it came from you, don't you think? I mean, who would want to know their real mother is living on the streets?"

"I've thought about it a lot. Dr. Ross must decide who should tell her."

Esther pushed at Jenny who was beginning to move around on the couch as she woke.

"Come on now, Jenny, here's a nice cup of tea."

Jenny groggily opened her eyes to find Esther standing over her with a mug in her hand. Rubbing at her eyes, she sat up.

"Where's the baby?" she asked, taking the mug.

Esther looked through the doorway at Steve who was sitting at the kitchen table. "He's in the hospital," she said quietly, gesturing to Steve to come into the front room.

Jenny threw the mug down, tea splashing all over the place, and jumped to her feet. "What hospital, what happened?" she cried, frantic. "Come on, take to me to him, take me to him, take me to him, TAKE ME TO HIM!" she screamed frantically.

Dashing into the kitchen, she bumped into Steve who was limping from the table. It all came back to her.

"What the hell are you doing here?" she screeched. Her nerves were jangling and she bobbed from foot to foot, uncontrollably wringing her hands.

Steve looked over her head to his mother who looked away.

"Well?" Jenny's voice was harsh and shrill. "Why are *you* here? Have you and your mother come to take my baby away?"

"No, Jenny," He put his hands on her shoulders, but she twisted away from him. "Calm down. Mrs. Green from next door found him on the floor and you were gone such a long time that she . . .,"

Jenny's voice was strident and her lips were twitching. "Now you listen to me, both of you." Quickly she scrambled around in her mind. She wanted to get her child back, and they would keep him if she said she'd left him on the couch. "I *put* the baby on the floor. What do you think I am? I would never put him on the chair or the couch unless I was there with him. Honestly, you both try to make out that I'm a few bricks short of a load. You two, of all people, who have hardly one active brain cell between you. Come on, take me to get my baby. Now!"

She rounded on Esther who was standing, arms crossed, red faced with anger. "Come on, Missus, let's get the show on the road," she ordered.

Steve drove them to the hospital. Esther wouldn't speak, scared of what she might say if she did. Steve was monosyllabic, but Jenny nervously chattered on and on about nothing. It was obvious she was afraid they would refuse to return Christian to her care.

Where were her mother and Richard? she wondered. They had been at the house this morning, hadn't they? Had they deserted her again?

Jenny's brain couldn't assimilate everything. Why was this happening to her?

TWENTY-ONE

Janet called on Jenny the next day. By this time Christian was home under Children's Aid supervision. A CAS visitor was to call at an unspecified time each day during the week, and they warned Jenny never to leave the child unattended, and said Esther must stay at the house with her.

Esther was in her glory, cuddling the baby at every opportunity and cooking up a storm. At least, Janet thought, Jenny would eat properly for a change. Steve had gone and Janet diplomatically decided not to ask his whereabouts.

When Janet finished her tea and cake, Jenny asked her to go for a walk with her, they would take the baby to the park, she said. Janet went, realizing Jenny probably wanted to talk to her alone. Esther was all set to put her coat on also, but Janet gave her a steely look.

"What's the matter, Jenny?" Janet asked as they strolled along the street.

"Nothing," she muttered, looking away.

"I see." Janet said, glancing at her daughter's stubbornly set face. Jenny, she knew, would get around to spilling it when she was ready, but not before.

They sat on a bench and let the baby play on the grass at their feet. He was such a happy child, laughing constantly. When Janet picked him up and he chuckled with joy, pulled at her pearls and spitting bubbles at her.

"Looks like he's going to be a lady's man," Janet said laughing as he tangled his fingers in her hair. "I think he likes me."

"Don't get carried away, Mum, he's like that with everybody," Jenny said sharply. "He takes after me, not that bastard Steve Rigby."

Janet, hurt and angry, knew Christian was the spitting image of his father, however, she said nothing. Something was wrong and starting an argument would accomplish little.

After they sat for half an hour, Janet picked up her purse. It was a waste of time. Jenny wasn't going to say a word.

"I'll be going now, Jenny," she said, stroking the fair down on Christian's head. "Give me a call if you want to talk. I have to get to the office."

"Hey, wait a minute! I need to talk to you now," Jenny said, putting her hand on Janet's sleeve.

Janet sat on the bench. "I was under the impression that was what you wanted, but you've been quiet for the last hour. I don't have all day, Jenny, tell me what the problem is."

"Well, pardon me," Jenny said sarcastically. Janet could have kicked herself. To start antagonizing Jenny was useless as she would rebel immediately. "I don't want to take any of your precious time, mother. It's not something I want to talk about, but I have to sort it out and I thought you'd help me."

"Of course I'll help you. Tell me." Jenny calling her mother was a bad sign. Usually she called her Mum.

"Well, it's Steve again. He's gone back to that woman. I left the baby because I had to find out where he was going, but I did put him on the floor, *honestly*," she hastened to add.

When she said that, Janet knew Jenny had left him on the couch. She took in a shaky breath. Jenny always lied her way out of things.

"So what do you want *me* to do?" she asked. As for her, Steve's defection was all to the good.

"Go over there and tell Steve he has to come back to me. The wedding is all arranged. Esther and I decided we would only tell him at the last minute so he wouldn't weasel out of it again."

Janet felt her blood pressure rise. Again Jenny had planned a wedding and not told her about it. Esther was as bad, at the very least she would have thought Esther could have called her. Jenny was her daughter, for heaven's sake. She blew out a breath of annoyance.

"Jenny, I'm your mother. Why am I never told about your arrangements? Why are you and Esther planning the wedding? It's up to your parents to pay for certain things. Were you going to send us a bill?"

"I suppose," Jenny said sulkily. "Anyway you and Richard are still honeymooning, climbing all over each other and kissing all the time." She laughed mirthlessly, "I mean, why would I want to take you away from romance?"

Janet's lips compressed. "I find that a feeble excuse at best, Jenny. Richard is always a perfect gentleman, and we do *not* climb all over each other."

Jenny waved her hand irritably. "Well, what does it matter? You know if I marry Steve, you won't have to worry about me anymore. You can concentrate on your spiffy new husband," her lip curled, "the man who took my father's place."

"Do you have to be so cruel and thoughtless, Jenny? He isn't taking your father's place. Nobody can do that. Nevertheless, your father is dead and I am still young enough to want a life."

"You never loved my Dad did you?" she said scathingly, "I bet you're glad that he's dead. Now you've got a sugar daddy and can live in luxury. Poor Dad could never support you like that, and look at all the money you got from the insurance. Dad's worth more dead than alive, isn't he?"

"I'm going now, Jenny, before I say something that I'll regret. How could you talk to me this way?"

"I can talk to you any way I like," Jenny shouted. "There you are living high off the hog, driving around in a flash car, wining and dining with the bigwigs, while I live on welfare. You should be ashamed of yourself. Why can't you go over to see Steve and tell him to come back to me? I want to get married and live in a proper house. I hate the estate, all those poor people and blacks."

Her eyes narrowed as another thought occurred to her. Janet stared at her, wondering what went on in her mind.

"Huh! You've got lots of money, haven't you? So have I, but I'm not allowed to touch it, am I? What do you think is going to happen to me? I'll probably starve to death at this rate and then you can keep all the blasted money for yourself. I hope it chokes you, Mum. My Dad wouldn't have let this happen."

"Jenny!" Janet was shocked to the core. Squaring her shoulders, she stood and faced Jenny. "How could you say these terrible things? I know you've got it hard right now, but you've got to admit that you brought it all on yourself. It's beginning to wear thin, all this passing of blame. For a long time I spent hours feeling guilty about you. However, Richard and Dr. Ross have both convinced me that you have to live your own life. If you choose to travel a path that I or another adult has warned you about, then you must learn the hard way."

She gazed at Jenny whose face was set into the harsh lines of discontent and lowered her voice. "I would never want to deprive you of anything, Jenny. Your father and I spent a lot of time with you when you were growing up, and gave you everything we could afford. For what? You paid us back with insolence and disobedience, you walked out of your home and went to live with Steve claiming you were an adult. Well, so far you're doing a great job of proving your maturity. It hurts me to see you living this way, but I thought you would learn from it."

Jenny smirked and shrugged. Janet knew she was not getting through to her daughter, nothing she said seem to bother her.

"I'm not staying here to listen to a lecture on my faults, Jenny. I will not see Steve, and I won't have anything to do with the sham of a wedding you are planning."

"You miserable old cow!" Jenny spat. "It's just like you to walk away and leave me here with nothing."

"Stop it, Jenny," Janet flared. "Find yourself a decent job and make a life for yourself. Try to forget Steve for a start. When you're ready to talk sensibly, you know where I am. For now, I have no further wish to continue this argument."

Janet walked quickly away so Jenny would not see the tears. She held her up head until she was behind a grouping of flowering bushes, then wiped her eyes. What a stupid young woman. Janet realized those angry words against her marriage were not what Jenny thought, Jenny was simply lashing out because she felt so frustrated and alone.

Yet how could she walk away and leave the girl to her own devices? Jenny hated any interference, though now the CAS were taking an interest, that helped ease Janet's conscience. Knowing that Esther was going to stay at the house for another week also helped.

What mother would leave her daughter stranded like this? Jenny thought vituperatively, as she watched her mother leave the park. What was she going to do if nobody fetched Steve back from that woman? She couldn't go herself and Esther refused point blank. Now the CAS were having her followed, at least she thought they were. When out walking the baby she had spotted a brown Ford twice. Of course it might be someone who lived on the estate, although she would put nothing past the CAS. They were probably trying to take her baby away again so they could give him to some old couple who wanted a child.

Jenny hated her parents right then. She hated her father for getting himself shot and not leaving her a lot of money she could get at immediately. She hated her mother. What mother would watch her child live in poverty? Jenny felt wrathful. Surely it would have been the decent thing for Richard Wyatt to advance her inheritance, and then she could live in a pleasant neighbourhood, among decent people.

With distaste she watched two tall black boys playing basketball against the wall of the community centre building. She felt afraid of them. They were so tall, so gangly and so smiley. Those smiles, she thought, didn't denote friendship or cheerfulness; to Jenny the smiles meant they were plotting to either rob or rape her.

Blast Richard Wyatt. What man would stand aside while his

stepdaughter lived in poverty? He was rich enough that he could have bought her a house, even given her his condo. It was his fault, and she blamed him for turning her own mother against her. Surely her mother wasn't acting the way a mother should: Richard Wyatt had brainwashed her.

Glumly she tucked happy little Christian into his pram, and made her way back to the house. Esther would be there, preaching and teaching, making her life a misery. It wasn't fair. If only she hadn't left the baby, if only Steve had not run out on her, if only . . .

Jenny's appearance depressed Janet. She looked ever more like a hardship case, with her unkempt hair and dirty, soiled, creased and torn clothing. For a young child who was prissy about the slightest wrinkle in an apron, she had apparently simply given up, didn't want to try.

Janet had no idea what Jenny was doing. Jenny had not given up, this was the way she was working her way back into her mother's good graces. The more down at heel she looked, the more it would worry Janet, and that was as it should be. She stopped washing clothes other than those for Christian, let her hair hang greasily around her shoulders, rarely bathed, and wore ragged clothes simply because they were ragged. Now every time her mother came over to the house she knew she looked awful and was glad of it. She could tell it bothered her Mum, bothered her a lot.

Richard got home early that night, and over supper they talked about the situation.

"She's not trying to help herself, Janet," he said. "You can see that for yourself. She has no reason to walk around looking like a bag lady."

"I know that, Richard," Janet said sadly. "Esther is keeping the house clean and Jenny treats her like a housekeeper. If I were Esther I'd tell her where to get off, but Esther, bless her soul, is a good sort and tries to keep the peace. Jenny is suffering from depression, that's what Esther said Jenny said Dr. Ross told her."

"More fool Esther for believing it. Jenny is suffering from lazy-itis,"

Richard snorted. "If either of you tries to sway her, she'll simply dig in her heels and laugh at your efforts. You know that well enough, Janet."

"Yes, I do," Janet sighed, nodding. She knew Jenny only too well. "We're going to have to tell her about her adoption soon, though. Time is passing and it's not going to make it easier if we keep putting it off."

"True. I do think, though, that we shouldn't tell her where her mother is, that would be too much for her to accept. You do realize that she's going to blame every bad thing in her life on you once she knows?"

"I know," Janet sighed miserably. "Dr. Ross said as much. Still, we have to tell her, then it's up to her to what she wants to do with the information."

"She's also going to think you told her now because you don't want her anymore. Did you consider that aspect?"

"She wouldn't!" Janet said, not having thought along those lines. "Gosh, I think you might be right. She'll interpret it as my wanting to get rid of her for good. Oh, Richard, what <u>am</u> I going to do?"

"Leave it to Dr. Ross. He's a good man and he'll use his professional experience to tell her. You needn't worry about Jenny if we let him tell her. I'm sure he'll help her with her sense of lost identity."

Janet sighed quietly as she poured more coffee. If only they had told Jenny when she was younger, maybe none of this would have happened.

Steve snored loudly and Rita punched him in the stomach. "Shut up, you fat pig," she shouted, waking him with a start.

"Wha . . . ?" he said, rubbing his eyes.

"Stop snoring, you pig. I can't sleep with all that racket. Thank God you won't be here tomorrow." Going back into the bedroom, she slammed the door.

Steve lay for a moment, wondering where he was and why and then it all came back to him. He had left Jenny, the childish, selfcentred, self-indulgent Jenny. He was well out of it, he knew that, but his child, what about Christian? His son Christian who was his spitting image, everyone said so. Yet Christian was with her so when would he ever see him?

His mother was making wedding plans again. Oh, he knew what she was up to, he saw a notebook with a list of things to do and things already done. Now his father constantly talked to him about settling down and raising a family. They were all in on it and Jenny was the instigator. Wearily he sighed and winced as a spike of pain shot through his leg muscles.

What was he going to do? Where was he going to live until he found himself another decent job and could afford an apartment?

The truck driving lark was okay to a certain point and then it became one great big bore. While he was his own boss away from the office, he was also tired of talking to himself. When he made good time, he could sit in the transport cafes chatting to other drivers and maybe playing cards for money at the back of the restaurant. In reality, it was a boring life. It was even worse to have to come back to nagging Jenny, nag, nag, nag, gimme, gimme, gimme Jenny.

After he had pulled the tendon climbing down from the cab, he went to the doctor who told him he should not push himself too much for a few weeks. That was all right he supposed, but how was he supposed to support himself? After reporting the accident to his current employer they sent him to the doctor at the industrial accident clinic. Tomorrow he had an appointment at an occupational management clinic to which the Worker's Compensation Board had referred him.

TWENTY-TWO

Esther took the casserole out of the oven and placed it on a trivet on the counter.

"Hmm. What's that?" Jenny asked as she sniffed the air. "Smells good."

"Tuna casserole," Esther said, checking the crisp cheesy surface with satisfaction.

Jenny pulled a face. "Ugh! I don't like fish. I never eat fish. I'll have toasted cheese, thank you very much."

"You'll eat your supper," Esther said, good naturedly. Jenny was a mass of 'don't likes' and 'never ates.' "This is good for you, Jenny. I don't suppose you've ever eaten anything like this before."

"I don't suppose I ever will, either," Jenny said as she crossed to the bread box and opened the bread wrapper. "You eat that crap and I'll eat something I know I won't throw up again."

Esther set the salad on the table and dished out two helpings of tuna casserole. She put salad in the bowls knowing Jenny never took salad if she did not give it to her.

Jenny seated Christian in his high chair and began feeding him.

"What's this doing here?" she asked when she saw the meal at her place.

"It's supper, Jenny. You have to eat properly. Now eat up and don't let's have another argument," Esther said as she chewed her salad.

"I'm not eating that muck," Jenny said her face pulled in disgust. "That looks like something someone sicked up, and you know I never eat rabbit food. I'll eat my cheese sandwich. Clear this away." Petulantly she pushed the plate and bowl to the other side of the table. The plate slid off the edge and crashed to the floor.

"Jenny!" Esther shot to her feet, her face red with anger. "You are without a doubt the most ungrateful and stubborn person I've ever known. Look at all that good food wasted! Well, you can clean it up, I won't." She took her own plate to the sink and stood eating the remains of her meal. All the time she glared, Jenny munched her sandwich while making goo-goo noises at Christian, who was wearing most of his supper.

"I'll be calling the Children's Aid when I get home," Esther said as she rinsed her plate. "I'm not staying here to listen to insults. I'll also call your mother." she warned as she put on her coat. "Stew in your own juice. Why should I give up my clean comfortable home and my husband's company to stay here looking after an ungrateful and extremely infuriating young woman?"

Wearing smirk of satisfaction, Jenny watched her go. Upsetting adults was so easy, they were such morons and so easily bated. She knew which of Esther's buttons to push now and made use of the knowledge. They, her parents and Esther for example, had little education, certainly not as much as she.

Let stupid old Esther call the CAS and her mother, she didn't care. She was all right here with her baby and her house. The welfare people wouldn't let them starve, and if she could find some cash to pay off some of her bills, she'd manage all right. Eventually one of them, Esther or her mother, would come over and start in on the cleaning and meanwhile she could do her own thing.

"Come on, baby, let's play patty cake," Jenny chortled after she wiped the baby food off his hands and face.

Steve slowly wandered the streets after his appointment, his limp more noticeable. The nurse at the clinic informed him that he required therapy four times a week. He would receive Worker's Compensation until they deemed him fit to drive.

How could a jump from a step have caused so much damage to his tendon, he kept asking? They used high faluting words to explain, but it was shattering that they considered him unfit. What else could he do? His only other job was that of a security guard and since they blacklisted him in that field, his future looked bleak.

Morosely he contemplated his next move. Now he couldn't stay with Rita. She had given him an ultimatum and shoved his stuff into green garbage bags, telling him to take it out of the apartment or she would toss everything down the garbage chute. He couldn't go home to his mother's house as Esther would insist he go back to Jenny, and he wouldn't go back to Jenny. No way, he'd had enough of her childish behaviour.

So what *was* he going to do? Popping into the gym, he talked to one of the trainers about his tendon. Not much wiser and a great deal sadder, he limped around the park. Where could he stay?

Then he spotted a mate of his, Mark. Mark had been one of his best high school buddies and worked as a telephone line man.

"Yoh, Mark!" he called as he approached.

"Hi there, Stevey boy. How the hell are you?"

"Not bad," Steve said, no use going into a tale of woe straight off. "How's by you?"

"Can't complain. They cut so much staff that we're all working overtime. Brings in big bucks, though. Mind you, I could do with a Saturday off occasionally."

"Sounds good to me, Mark. I'm off work right now. A bad tendon in my left leg. Can't drive, can't do anything. I've got to have therapy four times a week."

After they talked for nearly half an hour, catching up on each other's lives, Mark took Steve to the coffee shop. Soon Steve had a place to hang his hat, albeit temporary.

During the weeks of his therapy, Steve took to stopping in at the coffee shop across from the industrial clinic where he often talked to Joyce, a friendly waitress. Joyce admired the well built young man who, although limping from an accident, was muscular and tall. She sure liked his bedroom eyes.

Each morning and afternoon he dropped in and sat at her station. Before too long he made a date with her. She seemed thrilled to bits and his self esteem soared.

Steve liked Joyce. She was tall and slim with ash blonde hair and an air of sophistication. Divorced twice and widowed once, she lived alone in a new town house on a residential street in the old part of town. Before too long Steve moved into her home.

Unfortunately Jenny saw them together in a mall coffee area one Saturday afternoon. When she saw Steve kiss the woman, she felt a rage such as she had never experienced in her life.

White faced, she stood with the pram inside the entrance to Zellers, oblivious of the customers pushing past with their shopping carts, staring at them and becoming angrier by the second.

He was happy, God damn him. Look at him laughing at something the woman said and look at the way she put her head on his shoulder and kissed his cheek. Steve had an arm around her and was rubbing his hand up and down her back. How could he?

Blind with rage, she moved toward them. Christian woke and started to chunner, but she didn't even hear him. All her attention was fixed on her socalled common law husband, the father of her child, the two-timing bastard who had walked away and left her. It was as if someone had pushed her and she began to move faster toward their table. Christian immediately started to gurgle, content with the pram's movement.

Jenny stopped in front of them. They were gazing longingly into each other's eyes and didn't see her until she threw a cold cup of coffee at Steve, who jumped up, startled.

"What the . . . ?"

Joyce gasped, pulling herself to her feet, ready to move away. What was happening? Was this woman mad?

"Jenny!" Steve gasped.

"Do you know her, Steve?"

"Know me?" Jenny shouted. "This is his child, that's how much he knows me." Her voice rose shrilly, People started to stare. "You two-timing son-of-a-bitch, walking off and leaving us to starve to death. What sort of man would . . ."

Steve took her arm and started leading her to the mall doors, pushing the pram with his free hand. Everyone stared curiously and the security guard moved closer, uneasy.

Jenny shook off his arm. "Oh, no you don't!" she screamed, "You can't get rid of me that easily."

All movement in the area stopped, everybody was staring as her voice echoed through the open space. "This cheap bastard is going to be so ashamed of himself that he'll not be able to hold his head up in public again. Who the hell do you think you are?" she shrieked. "God? You can't walk out on me and your child like that. Who is that peroxide tart? Another one of your prostitutes, is she? I think you'd better get a medical soon, God only knows what diseases you've picked up since you took up with a tart like her."

Joyce, standing statue-like at the table, felt like crawling under the floor tiles. Who was this angry young woman? Steve had told her nothing about a baby. Moving back, she let the crowd surge ahead of her. She would go home and wait for Steve, let him sort things out for himself. Nevertheless, he would have a lot of talking to do once he got home.

"Please, people, move back now," The security guard ordered, "Nothing to worry about, only an argument. Move along now." People had begun to cluster around the couple, avidly waiting for someone to say something. Women muttered to each other and men looked embarrassed.

"Come on now, folks," The guard said quietly, putting a hand on each of their shoulders. "Take this outside. Take it home. A public place is . . ."

"Yah, yah, yah," Jenny said nastily. "Push off, Marshall Dillon. Come on, Steve, I need to talk to you."

Steve looked around for Joyce but couldn't see her. Maybe she had gone home. He walked with Jenny to the mall door and they stood outside on the pavement.

"Who is that tart?" Jenny asked as she wiped Christian's nose and slavery chin.

"She isn't a tart." He stood with his hands pushed into his bomber jacket pockets.

Jenny glared at him. "Pardon me, maybe I should have asked how much she charged. She's no lady, you can tell that by her black roots."

"That's enough, Jenny," Steve said, his voice very even. He wanted to get away from her and knew that making her angrier would not help.

"Who is she?" She glared at him, Christian in her arms now, cheerily waving his hands at his father.

"She's a friend," he said, "A very good friend."

"I could see that without you telling me, Casanova. Talk about soppy, kissing and cuddling in public."

Yet, she recalled when she and Steve were so wrapped up in each other that they couldn't keep their hands off each other, no matter where they were. Where had those halcyon days gone? she wondered disconsolately. What had changed them into these miserable, indignant people? Even so she still loved Steve, even though he was a two-timing bastard. She loved him, so much so that she would have done anything to get him back. Not that she could let him know it, because she had to hold the balance of power, not him.

"Why don't you come home, Steve? We need you. Please come back to us."

"Jen, I won't come back, I can't and I've told you why already. I'm not working anyway and I can't be of any help to you."

She grabbed at his arm, glaring with wide eyes. "Who is that woman? You didn't say."

"She's only a friend. I live at her house."

"Do you sleep with her, Steve?"

Two perfect tears slowly trickled down Jenny's cheeks. In spite of himself Steve watched, intrigued. She had done that trick often but it still held a certain fascination for him.

"Yes, I sleep with her. Happy now?" he asked as he turned away.

Jenny caught hold of the back of his jacket and tugged. "Please don't leave us, Steve. Your mother wants to know where you are and my mother is furious that you skipped out on us and . . . and . . . I miss you. Look at Christian, he misses you." She pushed the baby at him and Christian held out his arms and chuckled.

Steve could not look at the baby and stared stoically over Jenny's shoulder knowing if he looked at the child, he would be lost. He loved Chris, loved him like he'd never loved any other human being, but he couldn't allow her to use him as a form of blackmail.

Jenny stared at him, eyes narrowed. God, how she despised this man, the father of her child. Yet she would have cheerfully jumped into bed with him at that very moment. Steve was her whole life and would always be. His very touch set her tingling and his voice made her tremble with desire. How could he not love her after he had taken her virginity, made love to her in countless ways? Surely he felt more than friendship for her, although looking at his face now, he didn't even seem friendly. No, he would sooner sleep with that tramp. He was so ignorant, but then she had always known his mental limitations.

"Please Steve, come back. Is she better in bed than I am?" Jenny had to ask, she had to know. Tears streamed down her face, "Please look at Christian. Look how he needs you, his daddy. Look how I need you."

Steve turned on his heel and said over his shoulder. "Goodbye, Jenny."

Jenny screamed with anger and rushed after him. A man caught her by the arm and asked if she were in trouble, but she shook him off, determined to follow Steve. Passers by stopped and gawped, the security guard watched closely and followed.

Steve ran through the parking lot and jumped into his truck. He took off with squealing tires and a puff of blue exhaust smoke. She stood with Christian in her arms watching him race away. The tears stopped and her face wore a look of outrage. She would teach him, she would sue him for support, she would set her stepfather on him, she would . . .

TWENTY-THREE

Janet listened to Jenny's tale of woe. While she was justifiably angry that Steve would walk out on his own son, she considered they were all well rid of him. It was a never-ending soap opera with Jenny. Repeatedly Steve left, then Jenny persuaded him to come back, only for him to leave again. If Jenny could only see the light and realize she could make a better life for herself without him.

Richard sat reading the paper as Janet spoke on the phone and when she hung up, put the paper down.

He looked at Janet's grim expression. "Am I right in assuming that lover boy has skipped out again?"

"Yes, he's living with another woman and Jenny saw them at the mall. Apparently she made a terrible scene and he took off like a jack rabbit, now she doesn't know where he is. She wants you to sue him for child support."

Richard laughed mirthlessly. "If I can find him! The man is a loser so she'll never get a penny. Is he working? No. Does he have prospects? No. There's an old saying 'you can't get blood out of a stone' and that applies here, I'm afraid."

"I agree. Apparently he hurt his leg and is drawing Worker's

Compensation. Jenny told me he spends his time at the gym or going for therapy."

"What is it with these young women that they take up with worthless men like Steve Rigby?" Richard mused. "He's tall, dark and handsome, I suppose, and has a great body, but there's nothing at all between his ears. He lacks any ambition. What *do* they see in him? He leaves a trail of mentally abused women behind him. I think Jenny is better off without him. She should get herself a job and make a life for herself, instead of chasing after a moron like Steve."

"I agree. She's asking to come and live with us again, Richard. I told her I'd have to speak to you. Well you heard what I said."

"Yes, and I won't have it, Janet. I don't want Jenny here upsetting our life. I don't want the child here, cute as he may be. We're past being baby sitters and it goes without saying that Jenny will expect you to constantly look after him. I hate to say this, Janet, but your daughter is selfish."

"You don't have to tell me that. I know only too well. I always thought she would change as she grew up, but she hasn't grown up at all, she's as childish as ever, always wanting someone to bail her out. Unfortunately Jim and I did that too often, it seems." She sighed bitterly.

"What do *you* want to do about Jenny?" Richard asked, worried that he might have been too harsh on the girl.

"I don't know, Richard, I only know that I don't want her here. Can we rent her a nice apartment and get her out of the welfare housing?"

"Yet what good would that do? If we subsidize her, they'll cut her welfare payments. You are aware that they expect ablebodied welfare recipients to work now?"

"Yes, but I want to get her off welfare. It's so demeaning."

"Jenny doesn't seem to think so as she makes absolutely no effort to help herself. She constantly holds out her hand to other people. It is a case of her having to learn the hard way, Janet. Hard hearted as it may seem, she has to learn for herself."

"Are you going to see Dr. Ross about her birth mother?" Janet asked.

"I'd planned to. As far as I can see, it's better for her to learn the bad news while she's still trying to handle Steve's defection. Not that I know anything about psychiatry, but to my way of thinking it might help take her mind off Steve. Mind you, that's for Dr. Ross to decide."

"It might also send her over the edge," Janet said worriedly, biting her lip.

Richard smiled. "Over the edge? Come on now, Janet, Jenny has the constitution of a Sherman tank. If it's in her own best interests, nothing fazes her. All she wants is what she wants and that, at the moment, is Steve. She wanted him so much that she got herself pregnant. Surely that alone tells you she could handle anything. Another young woman would never have tried to force a man to marry her by such means. Please don't take this the wrong way, Janet, but I must say that all your attempts to teach her the right things seemed to have made little impression, and you did all the right things, Janet, don't ever think you didn't."

"I know," Janet said miserably as the statement didn't help. All the words in the world would not change the way she felt about Jenny. How much it distressed her when all her grand plans for the child went awry. She often wondered what Jim would have thought of the current situation.

Richard stood and felt in his pocket for his small appointment diary. "I'll make an appointment with Dr. Ross tomorrow. Don't worry, Janet. Jenny will come to no harm. Come here, darling," he held out his arms. "Come and have a cuddle."

Janet snuggled close. He was such a wonderful man. Richard was a good provider, a fabulous lover and she wanted nothing to spoil their happiness. Unfortunately, Jenny was trying to do that, even from a distance.

Smiling up at him, she kissed him and murmured: "Sorry, Richard. Let's not think about her tonight, let's talk about our vacation."

They did, although Jenny and the baby occupied her mind.

Esther was livid when Jenny told her about Steve. Her stupid son had done it again! She sympathized and clucked as Jenny spilled out her story.

"Do you know where he's living, Jenny?"

"No. He roared off in the truck and headed west. Maybe he lives out that direction."

"Don't you worry, lovey, I'll find him. We know he goes to therapy four times a week and Worker's Comp. must his address to send his cheque. I'll find him for you. You sit back and look after my lovely little grandson. How is he?"

They talked about Christian's progress and Jenny felt elated when she hung up. Esther would fetch Steve back because she was a good sort. While she still didn't like Esther, she could be very useful at times. Look at the wedding plans the two of them made behind Steve's back. They were not going to waste that planning and she would marry Steve Rigby whether he wanted it or not. His mother would see to it.

That night she lay in bed making plans. It was as if Steve was simply away on a driving trip and she was waiting for his return. The woman he was living with vanished from Jenny's mind completely.

If it were not for the nosy social worker who kept popping in unannounced, her life might have been better. It was a nuisance that she had to keep the place neat and tidy and not leave Christian untended for second. Still, that would soon be over.

Yet Dr. Ross and all the therapy she was taking: what good was that doing? They had talked about all kinds of things but she didn't feel any different, she still loved Steve as much as she had when she tried to kill herself. Not that she would admit she was only putting on an act, not even to Dr. Ross, that would never do. If she could only get out of going to his office, but Esther never missed. She was always at the door an hour before they had to leave so that she could play with the baby.

When Dr. Ross gave Jenny the news about her adoption, it overwhelmed her. He talked for ages and was very compassionate, but it all boiled down to an adoption. In that split second her thoughts were that her mother was probably a socialite, her father a wealthy businessman. How dare Janet and Jim not tell her this? How dare they pretend they were her real parents?

Jenny gaped at him, her mind in chaos. What was she going to do? Dr. Ross calmly sat back and watched. She was outwardly taking it very well, but he knew what she was feeling.

"Where are they? My real parents?" she snapped.

"Your father is unknown, and . . .," he started to tell her.

"You mean that I am a bastard?" she shouted as she struggled to her feet. Trembling, she stared down at him. This was not what she wanted to hear: she wanted a nice father, a rich father, a film star maybe.

"Jenny, please sit down and listen. You have to hear this out whether you want to or not. It is very important that you know who you are."

She slumped in the chair, hearing Christian chortling in the outer waiting room and Esther laughing at something he was doing. Yet this horrible man was telling her she didn't have a father.

"As to your mother . . . " This was going to be difficult, how could he tell her that her mother was a prostitute?

Jenny perked up, maybe her mother was wealthy.

"Your birth mother lives in Montreal."

Wow! Montreal, she had always liked the vibrant city when they had been on visits. Now she could go to Montreal and live with her mother. Yes.

Dr. Ross watched the expressions on her face and knew exactly what she was thinking.

"Have you got her address?" She asked, digging in her purse for a pen.

"Unfortunately, no," Dr. Ross said, deciding it unwise to that divulge any further information.

"So how do I get in touch with her?"

"I have no idea, but leave it with me and I'll see what I can do." Stalling her would only work for while, but at least he could talk to Mr. and Mrs. Wyatt to see how they felt about this development.

"Let me know as soon as you find out. I want to see my mother, I *have* to see her," Jenny said standing and picking up her purse. Wait until she told Esther. Wouldn't she be surprised.

Dr. Ross reviewed his notes after Jenny left. He had been right about one thing, Jenny's psychosis was the result of something that happened before she was born. He doubly researched Foetal Alcohol Effect and spoke to many experts on the subject. Now he knew it was a fact with Jenny. Her birth mother, working as a prostitute probably drank heavily throughout the pregnancy.

Poor Jenny, she would never be normal as people knew the meaning of the word. Although not mentally incapacitated, and, in fact, intelligent, she lacked certain basic social skills that most people learn easily. She would always be a problem to Janet who would not understand that Jenny saw nothing wrong in the way she acted. Jenny could not distinguish between good and bad judgement, would never learn from her mistakes.

FAE had shown up early in Jenny although no one had seen it as such. It revealed itself in her bad scholastic record, her inability to concentrate, her periods of hyperactivity. The school records revealed a great deal, although back then most educators had known nothing about FAE, and lumped all aberrant behaviour as ADD or hyperactivity.

If only Janet and her husband had sought professional help when Jenny was young, she might have stood a chance of a normal life, but it was too late now. He closed the file and placed in the filing cabinet. He could foresee a long period of counselling ahead. Better tell Janet Wyatt.

TWENTY-FOUR

For days Jenny thought about her real mother. A French-Canadian no less. How she wished that she had paid more attention to French at school. French had been a dead boring subject to her back then, as were any subjects that required study, but now it could be very handy if her mother spoke no English.

How upset Janet was when she informed her that she knew all about her lies, how very distressed. Jenny found that very satisfying. They argued about trust and denial. She wanted to make Janet pay for not telling her sooner, so was not subtle when making her announcement.

"How dare you deceive me like this? You're a rotten mother and I'm glad I'm not your child. I've found my real mother now and you can go to hell. I'm furious, and I blame my so-called Dad for this as well. The pair of you, laughing at me behind my back, knowing you didn't need to worry about me, because I didn't belong to you. You kept my birthright a secret."

Janet tried to speak but Jenny continued with her diatribe. "Jenny, please . . ."

"Shut up! You deceived me, you pretended you were my real mother. You didn't care about me, I can see that now. All the times you refused to let me do things or buy me stuff. Everything bad that has happened in my life is your fault."

Janet stood, white faced and sick to her stomach. She had expected some recrimination but not this monologue of hate and abuse.

Janet seemed devastated and Jenny felt pleased at her ability to wound. She grabbed her coat and left her mother standing in the middle of the kitchen, immobile with shock.

Richard Wyatt called her the following week. "Jenny, your mother is in the hospital."

"Huh! My *mother?*"

Richard ignored her words. "She's suffering from nervous exhaustion, not doubt caused by your temper tantrum. You said some very hateful things." He seemed abrupt and cold.

"It's only what she deserves," Jenny snapped, "As far as I'm concerned she's only getting what was coming to her. I hate her for deceiving me all these years. Pretending she was my mother, when she wasn't."

Richard sighed. Jenny would never learn to think before she spoke. Janet seemed heart broken after Jenny's outburst. "Well, Jenny, If I were you, I would take some time to think about what you said. Janet has always loved you, cared for you, and thinks only of your best interests. I can't understand why you're turning against her."

"Oh, she'll get over it. She always does. Anyway, don't tell her then, leave it to me, I'll tell her face to face."

"I hardly think that's advisable. Why don't you do as I said and think about it first?"

"All right, but she shouldn't have kept it secret. She should've told me years ago."

"What good would that have done? Jenny, take time to think this out. If she *had* told you, it would have made no difference. You were still her daughter, she was still your mother. She raised you from a tiny baby and she's the only mother you ever had. I don't want you making her even sicker and suggest you wait before going to see her. She needs to build up her strength before you knock her down again."

"Oh, I see! It's all my fault now, is it? I didn't make her sick. She picked up a germ from someone, so don't start blaming me."

"Jenny, I'm trying to be reasonable. Your mother is now my wife and I will do everything in my power to ensure to protect and care for her. Please do me and your mother a favour, and don't visit her."

He hung up on her before she could win the argument. She fumed about it for ages and then realized she wasn't being very nice to Janet, and of course snubbing Janet meant snubbing Richard. Yes. She must think before she spoke next time, better not burn any bridges, as they say.

Meanwhile, she contacted Parent Finders, who were tracing her birth mother. Dr. Ross had told her the adoption had taken place when she was only five days old. Now she knew the date of her birth although Janet had refused to let her have her birth certificate; scared she would run to her real mother, she supposed. Well, Janet should well be scared because that was the first thing she must do. Jenny wondered what would have happened if she'd had to provide her birth certificate? She was unaware the certificate would not have helped.

Parent Finders worked wonders. Her mother's name was Monique Lalande. What a lovely name Jenny thought, Jennifer Lalande, yes, it was attractive. Mentally she visualized her mother. She would be fair haired as Jenny was, she would be tall and slim, have a lovely smile and be such a French personality, all gestures and shrugs. Armed with the address, she planned to go to Montreal. She told nobody. It would not do to let people know. They might try to prevent the trip.

When Esther arrived to pick up Jenny for her doctor's appointment, she discovered nobody home. Christian's stroller was missing so she figured they were out somewhere. She drove around the subdivision and looked in the park but did not see them. Worried, she drove over to Janet's in case Jenny had gone there, but, as it was a workday, nobody was home. Strange, she thought, as she stopped at the drug store to telephone Dr. Ross. She thought it a slight chance Jenny had gone to the appointment on her own.

No, he told her, Jenny was not with him. After he hung up, he wondered what Jenny was doing, knowing she had always a purpose behind any of her actions. When he told her about the adoption, she had been justifiably angry, as would be anyone in her place. Her Thursday appointment hadn't shown much change in her attitude: she was still upset but seemed to have accepted it well enough so they had talked about her present situation.

Steve smiled at Joyce. She had just told him, she was pregnant, and strangely, this time he felt pleased. Joyce wanted to get married before the child arrived and, again faced with the prospect of marriage, this time he was all for it. What the difference was, he didn't know. Maybe it was because she hadn't asked him to marry her. In fact, he made the suggestion.

Steve didn't much like women, but knew that in his heart they were a necessary evil. If they looked after his physical needs and supplied creature comforts, they were all right. Other than that he could do without them, any man could. If his mother hadn't been such an interfering old busybody, he would have preferred to stay at home. At least there she fed and housed him without any hassle.

Yet what differences existed between Joyce and the ultra childish Jenny. Joyce was two years older than he, had already been married and divorced. She also received support from her ex-husband which allowed them to live comfortably, although Steve still was not working. His Worker's Compensation cheques added enough to their income that they could afford to eat out a couple of nights a week, and Joyce loved eating out. In Steve's mind a woman who had an income was preferable to one who didn't, because it meant less responsibility for him.

"What shall we call her?" she asked from the circle of his arms. Joyce hoped the baby was a girl, she didn't like little boys. Steve was a man, muscled and strong from the time he spent at the gym and while she liked men, she didn't particularly like small boys, they were messy and cruel. No, it had to be a girl so she would concentrate on that as hard as possible and her dream would come true.

"Suppose it's a boy? I do have a history of making boys," Steve said smugly.

"Don't remind me." Drat him, why did he have to mention his son by that girl. The childish female he constantly told her was nothing to him, saying neither was the child. Joyce knew, though, that he still thought about the baby as she often saw him looking at little boys when they were out together, but she couldn't blame him for that. A man wanted a boy to carry on his name. Well, as for her, she wanted only girls. "What shall we call her?"

"Don't you think it's early to start thinking of names?" he asked, hugging her. "Think about it for now, we'll decide closer to the time."

It was going to be another boy, he knew it and felt thrilled. What a difference this was to the last time when Jenny announced her pregnancy. No, this was much different, he loved Joyce and she loved him. She was an adult and acted like one. Full of pride, he considered the wedding. His mother would have to know, of course. Oh lord . . . his mother!

Joyce felt his arms stiffen and looked up at him. "What's the matter?"

"My mother," he said glumly. "She's always wanted me to marry Jenny. She even tried to arrange a wedding behind my back, twice yet. She likes Jenny, says she's posh and all that."

"Your mother will have to accept that we are going to be married, and if she doesn't like it, she doesn't have to be there. We're only going to City Hall, anyway."

"I don't think I'll tell her," he said, kissing her softly. "I mean, why look for trouble?" He thought they would be very happy because he felt happy now.

Joyce wondered when she should tell him about her children. She already had two small girls who presently lived with her mother. Her mother advised her not to tell a man that she was a mother until the ring was practically on her finger, pointing out that no man wanted a ready-made family. At first Joyce made it a point to tell a date about her two children then realized they lost interest in her immediately. That was when she kept it a secret and look . . . she had almost had a husband already. She wondered how Steve would take the news.

TWENTY-FIVE

Jenny reached Montreal early in the afternoon. Christian slept most of the way, but after such a long period of inactivity, became decidedly cranky. Sitting in the bus station, she fed him a bottle of formula. He didn't take much of it, being at the stage where solid food interested him more. Unfortunately she only had the one formula bottle. She realized she had not planned properly, having decided on the spur of the moment. At the time she had only the one thought in her mind, seeing her real mother. She felt around the small bag, she found one other bottle, so he had one of formula, one of juice, and three diapers. Still, when she got to her mother's house, she figured her mother would send out for baby food, in fact she was sure of it.

Now she became suddenly very nervous. Would her mother want her? Surely she would, for what woman could turn away her very own child? Look at the way she herself loved Christian. She could never turn him away, no matter what, but then again her mother had given her away at birth. What monster of a woman did that?

Fears began to crowd in on her. Was she doing the right thing in seeking out this woman? Was her mother a kind person? Would she even like her or love her, her very own child? Surely her mother couldn't have felt about her the way she felt about Christian, but she was here in Montreal, and would discover what her birth mother was like.

"4278 Rue Dupuis in Lachine," she told the red cap who booked taxis.

Looking at the child in the stroller and realizing she could not afford such a fare, the redcap advised her to take the subway. She could then catch a bus to Rue Cooper, he told her, Rue Dupuis was a short walk from the bus stop.

The journey took more than two hours, and by this time the overtired Christian was cantankerous. He whined continually until she felt like leaving him on the bus. What a nuisance he was, so fidgety and heavy.

The area her mother lived in looked run down, in fact seedy. This was not what she had expected, having ridden past streets of well kept, large homes, she expected her mother's house to be similar. It was not.

4278 was a run down, tar papered shack with unpainted window frames that looked lopsided. Cardboard patched the panes in places. Was this her mother's house? Surely not.

Involuntarily she shuddered and rocked the stroller for Christian who set up a thin whine because they had stopped moving.

Apprehensively she knocked at the paint chipped door, wondering who would answer. An old man peeped around the edge, not opening the door further than the chain would allow.

"Oui?"

"I'm Jennifer and I'm looking for my mother. Does she live here?" she said, hoping he spoke English.

With a Gallic shrug, he shut the door in her face.

This turn of events stunned Jenny. What was she going to do now? She looked up and down the short street. Maybe she could ask a neighbour. After trying four doors and getting no reply, she was at a loss and went back to her mother's house where she knocked again. The grim old man peeped around and slammed the door before she said a word. Was that her grandfather? Jenny sincerely hoped not.

As she slowly walked along the street, a woman came out of one of the duplexes. She waited until the woman reached her.

"Excuse moi," So she still remembered some French. She felt proud of herself, but what to say next?

"Oui?" The woman said, stooping to look at Christian who was now blissfully asleep and caressed his soft cheek with a finger.

"The people who live at fortytwo seventyeight," she said, pointing to the house, "Do you know them?"

"Yes, I know. They bad people, lady is very bad." Her English wasn't good but at least Jenny could understand her.

"Does Monique Lalande live there?"

"Ah, oui," the woman nodded, "Very bad lady, prostitute. She's been in jail lotsa times. We not want her on our street. Her father he charged with murder, her brother he sell drugs. They bad peoples."

This news turned Jenny to stone. Was this her ancestry? Oh my God! This was something for which she had not bargained.

"You not go to that bad house, lady," The woman said shaking her head. "You go away from here and take baby home." She started to leave.

Jenny watched her walk away, her eyes full of tears. How she longed to see her mother, but from what the woman had said she was a prostitute and that her grandfather was a murderer. Even so, she was dying of curiosity. It was too much for her to assimilate so she sat on the grassy bank in front of a house and rocked Christian's stroller.

The woman must be wrong, she told herself, she was jealous or something and was repeating gossip, or maybe she had the wrong house. Jenny decided to try again, she had to prove the woman wrong. It was all lies, her mother wasn't a prostitute!

As she again approached the front door, it opened and a raddled female came out digging for something in a large purse. Jenny took her in at a glance. She was tall and had bleached blonde hair, dry and straw like. Her clothes were cheap and on her feet she wore five inch heels, so high that she tottered on their spikes. As she looked up, she saw Jenny standing in her path.

"What?" she asked, eyeing Jenny suspiciously. Was this someone else from the authorities?

"Do you know Monique Lalande?" Jenny asked, dreading the answer.

"Sure, c'est moi."

No! A sense of horror descended on her, and the hair on her arms stood on end. This couldn't be her real mother. She wouldn't have it. Look at her! A common prostitute, her face plastered with makeup, those too long beaded false eyelashes, her clothes shouting her profession. She looked so old, much older than Janet. Dear God, what *had* she done?

"So? Who are you?" Monique asked, still suspicious. What would this young mother, so well dressed and refined be doing in the neighbourhood?

Jenny felt torn with indecision. Should she tell her who she was or should she make up some excuse? Not thinking clearly, she decided to tell her straight out. After all, Monique was her real mother and should see how well she had turned out, if nothing else. It suddenly occurred to her to wonder if Monique had not given her away, would she now be living in this squalor, or would her being with her mother have sent Monique in an entirely different direction?

"I'm your daughter," Jenny said, unbidden tears coming to her eyes.

Monique's eyes widened with surprise. Her daughter? Which daughter? She had given birth to four and had given them all away, and the two boys. Recently Parent Finders contacted her to advise her that one of her children wanted to know about her. She categorically told them she didn't care about her children, if they wanted to know who she was, so be it. Still, she never expected any of them to show up!

"When were you born?" she asked and listened to the answer. Was this her first child? The one she had when she was fourteen, or the one she had when she was fifteen, or the one she had the following year? The the last one she'd had when she was seventeen. Her memory was not so good these days, what with the drugs she used so often, and her drinking problem. No matter which child this was, she had given birth to her when she was a child herself, only seventeen at the most.

Was this child also a prostitute? Monique's quick eyes spotted that although she had a child she wore no wedding ring. Had she come to live with her mother to continue her profession?

Jenny waited. Monique outwardly showed no interest in her grandchild, though Jenny edged closer so that Monique could see him better. A tiny part of her ego wanted her mother to be proud of her, though she thought her horrible.

"Well, I had four girls, all of them I gave away for adoption, and two boys. Why would I want to see you? What do you want?" Monique asked. She did not want this child, or its child. The baby was lovely, she glanced at him from time to time, but felt nothing at all for him.

Jenny felt suddenly exhausted. This was not what she had expected. It was like Janet always told her, she lived too much in fairyland where everything was wonderful. Well, now the reality of life faced her and she didn't like it one bit.

"I live in Ottawa, the west end, and I wanted to see you," Jenny said, sorry now she had admitted to anything. "I wanted to see my mother."

"So? You've seen me, now go away. I don't want to see you," Monique said, hitching up her shoulder bag and pulling down her neckline. Pushing past Jenny, she walked quickly away, her hips wobbling because of the high heels.

God, Monique thought, a real live daughter had found her. Talk about your chickens coming home to roost! She was such a lovely girl too, and that baby, that baby was her grandchild.

Monique mentally thought of herself as twentytwo or so and it shocked her to realize she was old, much older than she would ever admit. The years had not been kind to her, she knew that, her skin was like an old parchment, dry and lifeless, caused by her lifestyle. The bags under her eyes were now permanent.

Jennifer's unexpected appearance started her thinking. She had borne six children, all of them scattered to the winds, had lived with at least twenty or more different men, all of whom had been pimps. What had she achieved? Nothing. She was old, old and worn out and still on the game. It shook her only a month ago when some John asked if he got her cheaper because she was a senior. How insulted she had felt, but he had been right, goddamn him. She was old.

Her mood of dejection was all that girl's fault, all her fault that she now felt older than her years, washed out and washed up. Putting back her shoulders, she pushed out her sagging chest and pasted a smile on her face. Forget that girl, forget her, she told herself, the visit means nothing. It was unlikely that she would ever see them again. Yet even as she strutted down the street she felt her age creeping up on her. Her a grandmother!

Jenny watched her go, wobbling her way on stick-like legs with too-high plastic shoes. How dreadful to discover her mother was a slut, and how deplorable that she lived in such poverty. She looked again at the decrepit house. No wonder Dr. Ross had not wanted her to come here. Glumly she realized he must have known about Monique.

As she rode home with a rambunctious Christian, she mused on her discovery, rationalizing it to suit herself. The people at Parent Finders must be wrong, that woman could never have been her real, real mother. It had to be some huge mistake. Why, she hadn't seen any resemblance in Monique to herself. She had been old, ugly and horrid. Yet even as she considered it, Jenny knew in her heart that Monique was her birth mother. Now she felt humiliated because of what she had said to Janet. All those terrible accusations and to think she had been so pleased to see Janet so upset.

Too, she thought with a sinking heart, she had bragged to Esther how one day she was going to find the real mother who would be so beautiful and rich. How could she have talked that way? What was she going to do now?

"You what?" Esther roared.

"We're married, Mum," Steve said, smug and complacent, his arm around Joyce. Let the old woman roar all she wanted, he thought, it wasn't going to change anything. It was a good job he had not told her before the event.

Esther looked sharply at Joyce. In the family way, she saw, glaring at Steve, who stood with a stupid grin in his face. The look he used to wear as a boy when he did something mischievous.

"Thank you for inviting your father and me, I don't think," she said caustically, plopping down in her chair. She didn't invite them to sit, but picking up her knitting, ignored them.

"Does Jenny know about this?" she asked, eyes down, knowing he would never have told Jenny. For all his size, Steve was sometimes such a coward.

Steve moved over to the chesterfield and sat, pulling Joyce down beside him. This was not a comfortable situation, realizing how Joyce must feel it more than he.

"Joyce is expecting, Mum," he said, his face glowing with the proof of his virility, for the sake of starting a conversation.

"I know," Esther said, counting stitches.

Silence reigned. Steve didn't know what to say and Joyce was scared of opening her mouth. The very air was fraught with things unsaid. Esther placidly knitted and none looked up or spoke.

They sat like statues until Frank came home.

"Hello son, who's this, then?" he asked, bright and cheerful, apparently not feeling the tension.

"Dad, this is my wife, Joyce," Steve said, voice full of pride, stressing wife.

"Hello, Joyce," Frank said, nodding at her, wondering what to say next. He glanced at Esther, but her head was down, counting stitches. "Wife did you say? So when did this all happen?" he asked, mystified. Steve noticed he kept casting anxious glances at Esther who stalwartly kept her eyes on her knitting.

"Last week," Steve said, grinning, "We didn't invite anybody. It was a City Hall ceremony."

"You needed witnesses, didn't you?" Esther snapped. Hurt to the quick, she felt extremely angry.

"A couple getting married after us stood up for us," Steve said, smiling at Joyce, trying to make it all right.

Esther's head shot up as she gasped: "Well, I never did! Complete strangers stood up for you? You have a cheek, Steve, you really do. What person would sneak behind their parent's back and marry on the sly?" Standing and dropping her knitting on the chair, she bustled off to the kitchen, flaming red with rage and trembling with anger.

She turned it over in her mind. To hell with Steve and his pregnant wife. What about Jenny and his son? Had he forgotten them? Washed his hands of the problem? That would be typical of Steve. He never had many smarts.

Frank cleared his throat, he felt ill at ease but thought somebody should make the young woman feel welcome.

"Nice to meet you, Joyce," he said, sticking out his hand. "Welcome to the family. Don't mind Esther, she'll come around."

Gingerly she shook his hand and smiled, feeling better.

Steve went to the kitchen where his mother was cleaning out a cupboard. It didn't need cleaning out, but she had to do something.

"Mum?" he said quietly.

"What?"

"Please don't be like this. Joyce is a nice person and you'll like her a lot if you give her a chance."

"She can be as nice as she wants," she said in a flat voice. "I want to know what you're going to do about Jenny and your son? How *could* you, Steve?"

"Look Mum, I've always said I would never marry Jenny, you know that. I love Joyce and I married her. So can we start with a clean slate?"

Esther shrugged but said nothing as Steve wandered back to the family room. She was not a cruel person and sensed the agonies Joyce was probably going through, knew how she must feel on being treated this way on their first meeting. Shutting the cupboard door, she switched on the kettle. She would make some tea.

Jenny got home at ten-thirty and Marg immediately rushed out to speak to her. She had been watching the road for hours.

"Jenny, child, where on earth have you been? Esther was here looking for you for your doctor's appointment, and the lady from the social was here to check on you, and your mother called me to find out if I knew where you were. Where on earth had you been all this time?"

"Come on in, Marg, I'll tell you all about it,"

This invitation surprised Marg because Jenny usually treated her like a leper. Jenny handed her the sleeping Christian and took off her coat. Gee, it was nice to be home. She smiled.

They sat in the kitchen and drank tea as Jenny told her tale. The story of the adoption amazed Marg, and yet, incredibly, Jenny had found her birth mother. Of course she didn't say what her birth mother did for a living.

When Marg went back to her own house, she immediately called Esther and told her about Jenny. Esther, shocked, said she would visit Jenny the next day. Esther realized that under the circumstances, Steve was not liable to see Jenny so someone had to tell her about his marriage. Esther then called Janet and gave her the news that Jenny was back, but said nothing more.

Janet was not at all pleased at being woken from a sound sleep. Her nerves were ragged with worry and Richard was still at the office, working on a criminal case that would take up most of his time for the coming year.

The following day, Esther, busybody that she was, called Richard at the office and told him about Jenny. She didn't deem it wise to tell Janet where Jenny had been, knowing she was only now recovering from her illness.

Richard sat thinking about Esther's news. So Jenny had found her mother, though Dr. Ross had not given her much information. Jenny was crafty, but also very intelligent. Parent Finders was doing a superlative job, he thought, wondering if they knew what horrors they had unleashed in this case.

TWENTY-SIX

Esther sat on the couch watching Christian play on the carpet. She had brought him a wooden toy train and he pushed it back and forth."

"What a happy child he is," she said. "So?" she said, to Jenny who sat picking nail polish off her nails.

"So what?"

"So tell me about your trip yesterday."

Jenny eyed her suspiciously. Old Marg must have been opening her big mouth, or how else would Esther know she had been anywhere?

"What trip?"

Esther sighed. "Come on now, Jenny. I'm not stupid. What about this bus ticket to Montreal?" Esther brandished the envelope Jenny left on the chesterfield. Jenny could have kicked herself. What a stupid thing to leave lying around, but she hadn't known that eagle-eyed Esther was coming.

"What about it?"

"Tell me, Jenny, tell me why you went to Montreal," Esther said quietly.

"No," Jenny said picking up Christian and hugging him. He immediately started struggling to get back to his new toy.

"Jenny, stop being so secretive. Tell me what you were doing there."

"No. It's none of your business."

"Did you tell your mother?"

"My mother isn't exactly a friend to me at the moment, I know you're well aware of that." Her face was set in sour lines as she nursed her umbrage. "You know everything, don't you? Always poking and prying into everybody's business."

Esther sat back, her lips a thin line. Should she tell Jenny she knew about the birth mother? Better not.

"Dr. Ross wasn't pleased you didn't call him before you cancelled your appointment. He asked me to tell you to call him today."

"Sure."

"Will you do that, Jenny?"

"Sure."

Esther realized that Jenny wouldn't.

"I'll get him on the phone and you can talk to him," she said, pulling the phone toward her. As she dialled the number, Jenny walked into the kitchen.

To hell with Dr. Ross, Jenny thought, to hell with Esther, to hell with Janet, to hell with the whole lot of them! All of them trying to run her life, all interfering, all nosy, all bossy. To hell with everybody.

"Dr. Ross, I have Jenny here, but I don't think she will talk to you."

"That's all right, Mrs. Rigby. Bring her over to the office as soon as you can. I think the trip to see her birth mother most ill advised, especially since she went alone."

"All right, Dr. Ross. Leave it with me. We'll come now." She replaced the receiver and called to Jenny. "Jenny, get your coat and get Christian's outer clothes, we have to go see Dr. Ross"

"Sod off! I'm not going anywhere."

"Yes, you are, my dear, oh yes you are." Esther almost shouted as Jenny came back into the living room drinking a Coke.

"Come on, get ready. Where's the baby's things?"

"Shoot, who died and put you in charge? I don't feel like going out."

Esther bundled up Christian and got Jenny's coat. "We're going even if I have to drag you."

Jenny sat in the car resentful and sullen and spoke not a word. She cuddled Christian and made goo-goo noises. Not a wod did she say until they got there and then complained about the long trip Esther said nothing but held her arm as they went to the office.

"Come in, Jenny, please sit," Dr. Ross said.

Jenny recognized his patient voice, the one that dragged things out of her, the one that was so caring and warm. She wouldn't sit in the usual arm chair, but sat on one of the hard side chairs.

"I understand you went to Montreal yesterday," His voice was very quiet. The voice of a confidante.

"Who told you that? Esther the ferret?" Jenny snarled. Stupid old fool, who did he think he was?

"Among other people, yes," he said calmly.

"Nobody else knew. Nobody!"

"Your neighbour knew. You told her when you got back."

"Huh! I should have known that Marg would spread the news. Like a bloody jungle drum, she is. No wonder they call them jungle bunnies," Jenny stared at his diplomas, counting the seals.

"Did you see your birth mother, Jenny?"

Jenny whipped her head around and stared at him. Her features became feral. "What if I did?" she challenged.

"I asked you if you saw her."

"Yes, I did."

"How was she? Was she nice?" he asked quietly, watching her expression.

Jenny burst into tears, hot scalding tears, tears that came from her very soul. Dr. Ross took a box of tissues from his drawer and placed them close to her. He let her cry and when she became quieter, turned on a relaxation tape. The office was filled with calming music and eventually Jenny sat up to wipe her nose and eyes.

"Was it hard to see her, Jenny? Tell me about it."

"It was awful. *She* was awful," Jenny said, mentally picturing the woman who gave birth to her. She shuddered involuntarily.

Dr. Ross smiled. "I didn't want you to see her, Jenny. I told you that when I gave you the news. You should never have gone there alone, you know, someone should have been with you. I knew what she was and tried to protect you."

"Sure," Jenny said scathingly, now she felt more secure. "She's a common street walker, a horrible, ugly woman who didn't want to know me." This rejection felt worse to Jenny than the fact her mother had given her away. "She had other daughters that she'd given away and sons, too. She had to figure out which one I was. Can you imagine that? Imagine my roots, Dr. Ross, I'm the bastard child of a prostitute and some unknown man."

"No, Jenny, you are not" he said quietly, "You are the product of a very good home where you had the best possible care. You had caring and loving parents who gave you everything."

"You mean Janet and Jim?" Her voice rose, "But they aren't my real parents, you told me that, and I just told you."

"Oh yes, Jenny, they *are* your real parents. You were very special and they chose you over all the others. Imagine if you had stayed with your birth mother, do you think you would have enjoyed all the advantages Janet and Jim gave you? Would you have gone to good schools, lived in a nice home?"

Jenny thought about that for a minute or two. Dr. Ross could see her mind working. He knew she would soon come to realize the truth in his words, come to accept that Janet was more her mother than Monique would ever be. Patiently he waited.

"Still, they should have told me," Jenny whined, always everyone else was wrong and she must make them pay for their perfidy. He empathized with the perpetually dissatisfied Jenny. "They shouldn't have kept it a secret. Of course, the minute I knew about her, I wanted to know what she was like. Who wouldn't? I mean, it's human nature, isn't it? I wanted to see my real mother, but it was appalling."

Dr. Ross nodded. "Yes, I can see that. However, some good will come of this. You shouldn't have gone and yet maybe you should. You had to know, I understand that."

Jenny nodded sadly. "Yes, I had to know but now I'm sorry that I do."

"What you went through is not so unusual, Jenny. Every adopted person pictures their birth parents as beautiful or handsome and infinitely rich. Your mind usually goes back to some fairy story, but fairy stories aren't real life. You know that. Think about it for a moment and realize rich people never give up children for adoption. Only poor people, unable to support a child, would give it away. Anyway, this is the time to start thinking ahead, Jenny. Put this behind you, put it out of your mind." He put up his hand to prevent her interrupting. "I know you can never forget, but soon it will be a bad memory. Only there at the back of your mind. You can't let it rule your life," He paused, she was listening attentively, waiting for him to make it right. "First you must put your relationship right with Janet."

Jenny stared at him. How could she talk to her mother now? She had said horrible things to her. "She'll never forgive me for what I said to her," Jenny started to cry again and took a tissue.

"Now Jenny, Janet is a very caring person. She still loves you. She will always love you. You're her daughter, no matter what a piece of paper says. Do you need help to talk to her?"

"Yes, I do."

Dr. Ross felt pleased. This was the first time he had ever known Jenny to admit she was at a loss. Maybe the shock of seeing her birth mother had straightened out her thought process. Time would tell.

"I'm always here for you, as you know, and if you prefer to meet with your mother here at the office, I'd be pleased to arrange it."

"Yes," Jenny nodded her head. Dr. Ross would help heal the rift. Already she began to feel better. He talked to her for more than an hour, an hour where she actually listened to him for once.

Esther was quiet as they drove back. She still had to tell Jenny about Steve's marriage.

Jenny chattered on about her adoptive mother, she called Janet that now. They were going to have a session with Dr. Ross, she told Esther, suddenly sounding so cheerful that Esther eyed her warily.

Then Esther realized that when she talked to Janet about the session and about Steve's marriage, Janet could tell Dr. Ross. The problem was no longer hers.

"Shit!" Steve exploded. The stupid woman already had two kids. What mess he had gotten himself into this time?

Already he was becoming weary of Joyce's morning sickness, her constant mood swings, her continual harping about him getting a job and staying away from the gym now that he had a family. Joyce had become a nagging wife, no longer a lover, and a definite killjoy in all senses of the word.

"We'll have to get a larger place," Joyce said, looking around the cramped room. "We need at least three bedrooms now."

Steve glared at her. That was it, he decided, he was leaving. Nobody was going to saddle him with someone else's children. Going to the closet, he took out his windcheater.

"I might be back, but don't count on it," he said coldly as he left, slamming the door behind him.

Joyce stared at the door and shrugged. He'd be back: she knew it. She hadn't yet told him that her husband had stopped support payments after he discovered she had remarried. Darn her friend Trudy. She always did have a big mouth.

Esther sat knitting a layette for the new baby. White, as she didn't believe in the blue and pink custom. White was always safe. To think she was going to be a grandmother again. How enjoyable to have little ones that lived elsewhere, that parents took home once they started to get fractious, and who loved seeing their granny. Esther very much liked being a grandparent.

Idly she wondered about Jenny's birth mother. What was she like? If she had been wealthy or beautiful, she had no doubt Jenny would have bragged and boasted. The fact that she had not told Esther anything about her meant that something was not right. Eventually she would discover the whole truth, she always did.

Steve worried her, his defection and marriage to Joyce had upset both her and Frank. Joyce wasn't a bad sort, she supposed, but she wasn't the type of woman who would be of any use to Steve as she didn't possess the intestinal fortitude to keep him in his place. No, Jenny would have been perfect for Steve, she would have kept him in line. Well, maybe she would, once she had gotten herself sorted out with Dr. Ross.

She turned the row and admired her work. Nice, a nice little jacket for the new baby. Christian had outgrown most of his clothes before he even wore them. Esther was angry when Jenny gave them away to another woman for her new baby.

One day when she had gone to pick up Jenny for her appointment, she saw a baby dressed in the crocheted jacket and bonnet. Recognizing her own handiwork, she felt indignant, but said nothing until the woman pointed out the baby's attire and said, "Isn't Jenny clever to have made such lovely things?"

That had caused a huge argument that took place while she was driving Jenny home. Jenny shrugged, quite unrepentant.

"Look, you gave them to me and they were mine to do with as I wished."

"I suppose that's true, but why did you tell her that you had knit them? That was a huge lie, Jenny. All the hours I worked on that jacket, all the love that I put into it, yet you blithely claimed it as your own work."

"So what? I did it and that's that."

"You shouldn't tell lies, Jenny, you'll always get caught," she said firmly, determined to have the last word.

"Butt out, Mrs. Rigby, what I do and what I say is no concern of yours."

It was left like that, but it left a bad taste in Esther's mouth. Still, Joyce would never do a thing like that. She wasn't the type.

"Not you again!" Rita said as she looked at Steve. Rita was currently living with a very attractive man and they were planning to get married. She didn't need Mr. Steve 'Feathers for Brains' on her doorstep.

"Can I come in?"

"May," Rita snapped. "It's may I come in, not can."

"All right, can I?" he said, smiling hopefully.

"I suppose," she opened the door to let him pass. "As long as it's a short visit," she warned, "I want you out of here in less than half an hour. Okay?"

"Okay," he said, glad she let him in.

"What's up?" she asked as she lit a cigarette and waved away the smoke.

He glanced around the small apartment. It looked as cosy as he remembered and she had bought new carpeting. It made the place seem very plush.

"You know I got married?"

"Yup."

"She's pregnant," Steve said, with a touch of pride. He was virile, hadn't he proven it?

"Good for you, Mr. Spermbank," Rita said caustically. Thank God he had never gotten her pregnant. She wasn't stupid enough to allow such a thing to happen outside marriage.

"But she's just announced that she's got two other children and wants them to move in with us," he added miserably.

"Good grief!" Rita laughed uproariously. His face blackened, it wasn't that funny. "You got yourself into a real mess this time," she sputtered. "It was bad enough with that little girl you got pregnant, but now you have . . ."

"All right!" he snapped. "I wanted to talk to somebody, not get a lecture on morals."

Rita felt sorry that she had laughed. She felt sorry for him if it came to that. Poor sod, saddled with two kids, and newly married with one on the way. Steve was a moron and she was glad to be shut of him.

"All right, Steve. I'm sorry I said anything. You can talk to me."

Steve talked and talked. The words came tumbling out . . . all his fears, all his dreams. By the time he had finished, he seemed close to tears. Rita listened and said not a word. What could she say to help him? What could she do to make things better? Nothing.

Steve felt better now he had told somebody. Saying it aloud was cathartic. Feeling better, he left to go to the pub where he planned to get drunk. They were pleased to see him at his old haunt and he didn't lack for drinks. Soon he was well on his way to being plastered and had accepted a bed for the night with a friend of his.

TWENTY-SEVEN

Janet, while pleased Dr. Ross had invited her and Jenny to talk it out at his office, dreaded her next meeting with Jenny, but she knew it essential to have a professional referee.

Richard thought Janet almost back to her old self physically. The doctor said she was well over her illness and would continue to recover. He knew Dr. Ross had helped her accept Jenny for what she was, and, from their conversations, she'd begun to accept that whatever Jenny had done to herself did not reflect on her as a mother. Too, to help her span the chasm between herself and Jenny, Richard now spent more time at home so Janet would not feel so alone until she got back to work full time. As for Jenny he could care less, but he cared very much about his wife's mental health.

They arrived at Dr. Ross's office within minutes of each other. Janet looking nervous and wearing navy blue, was sitting in the waiting room and jumped to her feet as Jenny walked in alone. Jenny looked at her mother warily. but said nothing.

In his large panelled office Dr. Ross asked them to sit facing each other while he placed his chair at the end facing them both.

"Why don't we start by saying hello?" he suggested.

Jenny took a deep breath. "Hello," she said. She felt unnerved by this meeting, frightened in case Janet rejected her.

Janet said 'Hello' in a very tiny voice. She also felt panicked in case Jenny didn't accept her, still hurt at the terrible things Jenny had said. The only person who was visibly at ease was Dr. Ross. An hour later they were still talking and practically reconciled, much to Dr. Ross's satisfaction.

"Before we adjourn, I have something to tell you, Jenny," Dr. Ross said, his voice very even. "Steve is married."

"What?" Jenny shrieked, her face blanching. It couldn't be. He couldn't do this to her. Married? No!

She flung herself into Janet's arms, and Janet smiled at Dr. Ross over her head.

"Oh Mum, say it isn't true. He has to marry me. He has to give our son a name."

Upset as she felt, Janet felt elated that Jenny had called her Mum. It was a major victory.

Dr. Ross gave Jenny a mild tranquillizer to calm her and sent them home together. Jenny had come by bus since Esther knew nothing of the appointment day or time, and Marg had agreed to look after Christian.

It took a month or so but Jenny finally began to accept Steve's marriage. First it hurt like a raw wound, then she became angry. The anger helped her accept the situation, and too, her mother and Esther both pointed out that if she had married him, he would probably have left her for this woman anyway.

Face to face, Esther seemed all concern, was very sympathetic, but when all was said and done, Jenny realized her son Steve was her main interest. Esther pointed out often that now Steve was married, they could not undo it. Slowly Jenny accepted it and Esther promised she would continue to take Jenny to the doctor and would always visit her grandson, no matter what Steve did.

Janet visited Jenny's house once a week. Jenny and the baby went over to Janet's place each Sunday afternoon and stayed for supper. Richard, not as forgiving as Janet, sometimes found it hard to keep his temper. Jenny was still so selfcentred that she was completely uninterested in anything which did not revolve around herself. She seemed discontent with everything in her life and the only joy she found was in Christian.

One Sunday unexpected guests arrived. That was when things came to a head.

"Well, hello!" Janet said as she opened the door to find Ernie and Brenda on the doorstep.

"Wow!" Brenda said, glancing over Janet's shoulder as she kissed her hello. "What a lovely place you have, Jan. Isn't it grand, Ernie? Much grander than when we visited you last time."

While the Stevens had often been abroad for holidays, they had never been inside anyone's home other than Janet's Alta Vista house, and, being used to their small terraced house back home, the size of the new place awed them. Janet and Richard had sold the other house and moved into a new custom home in the same neighbourhood.

Making the move was not difficult for Janet because when she came back from Vegas she felt like the house was dead. Its owner had died. It was as though Jim had taken the soul of it with him. She did not miss the old place at all these days.

"Yes, this is much larger and much nicer. I love it." She took them to the family room where Jenny was playing with Christian and Richard was watching a golf game on television.

"Richard, look who's here, Ernie and Brenda from England." Janet felt vaguely uncomfortable. She didn't want to start talking about Las Vegas or Jim again. It had taken her many months to stop mentioning his name, but Richard was understanding when she sometimes called him Jim. Thank goodness she'd never said Jim's name in bed. That would have been awful.

Richard immediately switched off the TV and stood extending his hand. "Welcome to our new home," he said graciously. He shook hands with Brenda who gazed at him with delight. Richard was a very handsome man.

"Nice to see you again, Brenda. Ernie, you're looking great."

"This is my daughter Jenny, and her son Christian," Janet said, trying to suggest with her eyebrows that Jenny should stand up and be introduced properly.

Jenny remained on the floor and scornfully looked the couple up and down before saying, "Hi." They weren't very well dressed and they didn't wear good jewelry that she could see. The man wore a Timex watch. They were nobody important.

"Nice to meet you, Jenny," Brenda said.

"Yeah." She glared at them balefully.

"Jenny!" Richard said.

Janet glanced at Richard. He was red in the face, detesting bad manners. She laughed to defuse the situation.

"Jenny, please stand up and greet our guests properly," she said, hoping for once her daughter would cooperate.

Thankfully, Jenny stood and bent over to pick up Christian. "Say hello, Chrissy, say hello."

Christian gurgled and Brenda smiled and took his little hand in hers.

"Isn't he lovely? May I hold him?"

"Sure," Jenny said, pleased Christian was getting such attention. The attention reflected well on her, of course, as he was such a lovely baby and he was hers.

Janet offered Ernie a drink. He glanced at Richard who was drinking a scotch.

"Whatever Richard is having," he said in broad Lancashire.

"Hey, where are you from?" Jenny asked hearing his accent.

"England, same place as your Mam," Ernie said, taking the glass from Janet.

"She doesn't talk like you, though," Jenny said, looking puzzled.

"That's because we still live there and your Mam's been in Canada a long time now."

Jenny was curious. How peculiar the way they talked. Her Mam? Mam, like Mammy, brought a mental picture of a black woman wearing a cloth on her head. "Did you live near each other?" she asked.

"Once't, aye," he said, smiling at Janet. "We all went to the same school."

Richard excused himself as the phone rang and went to take the call in the kitchen.

"How long are you over for this time?" Janet asked, wondering why the visit.

"We came to visit Montreal with friends. They came to see people here, so we decided to make a short side trip to see how you were getting on. I do hope we aren't imposing," Brenda said worriedly.

"Not at all," Janet said wondering whether she should invite them for supper, or if she had enough to serve five.

"We'll only stay a while. We've got to catch a train at five thirty," Ernie said, looking around the room at the furnishings and smiling. "This is a smashing house, Jan. Lots of room and very nicely furnished. You've got a real touch, you have."

"Not enough room for me and the baby, though," Jenny said peevishly.

Brenda noticed Jenny didn't wear a wedding ring and kept her mouth shut, but Ernie ploughed in with both feet. "Where's the lad's Dad?" he asked, "Why isn't he here?"

Jenny glared at him. "I don't talk to his father, he married another woman," she said spitefully, "What's it to you, anyway?"

"Sorry, lass," Ernie said, glancing at Brenda who was looking daggers.

"My Mum should let me come home," Jenny said, glaring at Janet who was visibly ashamed of Jenny's behaviour. "I have to live on welfare in a subsidized house, you know."

"Jenny!" Janet said. If looks could have killed, this one would have mortally wounded her.

Brenda felt the animosity in the air and nudged Ernie who looked at her surprised. The nudge meant 'let's leave'.

Richard came back into the room as Ernie was finishing his scotch.

"Same again?" he asked, taking the glass and heading for the buffet. "How about you, Brenda? A sweet sherry maybe?"

"Yes, I'll have one," Jenny said.

Richard stared at her. Jenny rarely drank.

Brenda knew they should leave, but Richard was being hospitable and maybe the quarrel was only between Jenny and her mother.

They sat talking about the weather in Canada and economics in

England for a while as Jenny played with Christian who was at the trying to walk stage and falling down.

"How old is he?" Brenda asked.

"He's nearly a year now," Jenny said proudly, "He's very advanced for his age."

"Maybe he takes after his father," Ernie said.

"No, he takes after me," Jenny snapped. "There's nothing of his father in him."

Janet and Richard both knew not to pursue the subject although Christian was the spitting image of Steve.

"Are you working now, Jan?" Brenda asked changing the subject.

"Yes, I work for Richard at his office," Janet said smiling, glad things had worked out so well for her.

"That's another thing," Jenny said loudly, "My stepfather should give me a job in his office, but he won't. He'd sooner have me on welfare. He and my mother are very much alike. They like to live in ease while their only child lives like a pauper."

Janet glanced at Richard and saw the look on his face. He was furious. Jenny had done it now. Typically, she had opened her big mouth in front of others and embarrassed him.

"Jenny," Richard warned. "This is not the time or the place to bring up family problems."

"My real Dad would have let me work in his office," she said scornfully. "I can do anything my Mum can and better than her. If she can work for you, so can I."

"I doubt it," Richard said scathingly. "Her attitude is better and she gets along with people."

"I get along with everybody," Jenny said smugly. "I just don't get along with you, step-daddy darling."

Richard recognized she was out to put him down and didn't rise to the bait. If she succeeded in making him angrier, then he would become the loser.

Janet smiled at Brenda. "Is it possible that it's been almost a year since we last met?" Deftly she changed the subject. "I so look forward to your letters."

"Same here," Brenda said, "It's nice to know that you're doing so well now. When I think about the time we met up in the states I go all goose pimply. What a horrible time that was."

"What happened?" Jenny asked, her usual nosy self.

"That was when your Dad got shot. Ernie too," Brenda said.

"You mean that these are the people that you were with in Las Vegas?" Jenny asked Janet, her voice loud and excited as she jumped to her feet.

"Yes," Ernie said, eyeing her with caution.

Jenny was furious. "You mean you're the idiot that got my Dad shot and now I'm stuck with *him*?" she shouted, pointing at Richard.

"Jenny!" Janet said, mortified at Jenny's rudeness.

She tossed her head. "I don't care. If they hadn't gone for supper with you, my Dad would still be alive." She turned to face Richard, "And *he* wouldn't have let me live on welfare! My dad would have let me live at *home. He* would have given me a job."

"Jenny, stop it, please," Richard said, his voice very low.

"No, I won't! If it wasn't true, you wouldn't be trying to stop me talking about it. I bet you were fooling around with my mother for years before my Dad got shot. I bet that . . ."

"Jenny, that will do," Janet said, as angry as she had ever been. "Get your coat. I'm taking you home."

"Shit! Throwing me out again?" Jenny picked up Christian. "I know where I'm not wanted. I knew all this Sunday stuff was to ease your conscience. I know that's true now." She started collecting Christian's toys. "But don't you worry, Mr. God Almighty Wyatt. I won't be coming back, I get the message loud and clear. It's really something, isn't it? Talk about the wicked stepfather! You sure take the gold medal for that."

Brenda and Ernie didn't know where to look and stared at the blank television screen, wondering how to leave without making too much fuss and embarrassing Janet further. Janet was almost in tears, Richard stonily stared at the ceiling and Jenny glared at everyone. What a mistake this had been, Brenda thought, arriving like this, unannounced. They should have called first.

Jenny, face set in a pout, flounced to the hall closet and got out her coat. She picked up the baby bag and Christian and stood waiting. She had to have the last word.

"Goodbye and good riddance," she said to the Thompsons, who gasped, astounded at her rudeness. "So? Come on then, mother dear, let's hit the road," she said to Janet who picked up her purse and took out her car keys. "Time to go back to the slums, as they say."

Ernie cleared his throat as the front door shut. "Seems like you've inherited a right handful there, Richard, lad. Rather you than me."

Richard nodded. His blood pressure settled back. "I'm afraid Jenny has a lot of problems. She's still having therapy but it doesn't seem to help. I feel sorry for Janet, she's the one who suffers."

"Yes, poor soul," Brenda said, "Jenny's not a very nice person considering how lovely Janet is, and Jim was a very nice man. It's strange that their child turned out like that. Very strange."

"Not at all," Richard said, deciding to break a confidence. "They adopted Jenny. I don't suppose Janet will mind you knowing."

Brenda nodded. "Poor Janet. She loves that girl and now look at her, all very big mouth and very bad manners. I'm sure Jim and Jan brought her up with the right values. Too bad that nothing stuck, isn't it?"

"Does she know that? The girl I mean, that she's adopted?" Ernie asked, puzzled.

"Yes. The psychiatrist told her. She's in therapy. Better that a professional gave her the news."

"I'm surprised Janet and Jim didn't tell her when she was younger," Brenda said.

"So am I, but there it is. Now she knows and now she is pricklier than ever." Richard sighed and finished his drink.

"Has she ever seen her birth mother?" Brenda asked, wondering if Jenny had ever seen her.

"Yes, unfortunately. Janet went to Dr. Ross with Jenny to talk about it."

"Poor thing," Brenda said, "It's horrible that she found out that her Dad wasn't her Dad. She seems to have been very fond of him."

Richard nodded, saying nothing, though he knew Jenny had never liked her father. She certainly held no love for him when he was alive.

"Anyroad, we wanted to thank you in person for all the work you did when I got shot," Ernie said. "We're set for life now."

Richard bowed his head in acknowledgment. He had combined their case with Janet's.

"Well, we'd better be getting along. We have the hire car to return and a plane to catch," Ernie said standing and putting his glass on the coffee table. "We enjoyed seeing you again, Richard."

"Yes, nice to see you under happier circumstances. I'm sorry Jenny made such a scene."

"Don't worry about that, Richard. You worry about the young lass, she's needing a lot of support from people who care, I should think," Brenda said.

Richard saw them out and waved them off. He went back inside and poured himself another drink. Darn Jenny, why did she have to be such a problem?

Jenny sat in the kitchen, half listening as Esther's tinny voice yakked in her ear. Why she had called Esther she didn't know, only knowing that she wanted human contact and who else would listen when she called?

She wondered why, when she had the chance, she had not told her mother the details about her visit to Montreal. She was sure Dr. Ross must have told her, or Esther. Still, Janet said nothing about it. Her antics of this afternoon weighed heavily on her, knowing that taking it all out on Richard and her mother was stupid, but she wanted to hurt Janet. Angry, she wanted her to suffer like she was suffering.

Those English people, they had done all right out of it, hadn't they? Pots of money they got, while she lost her father. Oh, not that she missed him, he'd been another person in the house, someone who talked at her now and then. The stupid idiot had left her money she couldn't even touch and what father would do that to a child?

She decided to talk to Dr. Ross about it. Dr. Ross was never judgmental, he always listened. More than her mother did: her mother never listened, she gave orders or told her what to do. The same as old

Esther, she was busy telling her what to do and how to do it. The older generation thought they knew everything.

"Sorry, got to go," she said as she rudely slammed the phone down on Esther.

Sod Esther, sod her stupid son, Steve. Esther still thought Steve was wonderful, Jenny knew that. Still, somewhere she had read that if the devil had had a mother, she also thought her son was marvellous. Not that it made it better, but knowing how she loved Christian, she recognized maternal love.

If anyone had ever told her that she could love another human in such a way, she would have laughed. Christian was her entire world and she would walk through fire for him. The faded love, once passionate and all encompassing, she once felt for Steve was nothing compared to this aching love for her son.

Steve, that stupid son of a bitch, look at what he'd done to her. He'd made her pregnant, left her and married another woman. Brooding on this slight made her angry again. It was time to get him out of her system, time to start afresh. It was time to find another man. She would ask Marg to babysit one evening and go to the new nightclub, Ruby's, that had recently opened. She might find a nice guy who had money.

Steve felt wretched. How could he have done it? How could he have married this nagging shrew? Why hadn't he seen what she was like?

To think he now had a ready-made family, two girls, each as belligerent as the other. They thought he was made of money, always sticking out their hands and calling him Daddy. God, that made him mad. He was not their blasted father, he was only their mother's husband.

The eldest girl, Colleen, a crafty little thing, was all smiles and dimples and stealing from his pockets, and an expert shoplifter. The corner Mac's milk had sent for Steve and Joyce when they found Colleen with a pocket full of stolen chocolate bars.

The youngest girl, Wilhelmina, known as Billy, was plain nasty. She was a cruel girl who liked to torment smaller girls and animals just to see them suffer. A neighbour had called the police when he had caught Billy tying up his cat and trying to hang it from a tree.

He thought about Christian. A lovely little boy, a boy worthy of being his son. He was happy and good natured, the spitting image of himself at that age, and didn't he have a photograph to prove it? Yes, Christian was a proper son, a son he loved. He dearly wanted to see him grow up and become an athlete.

Yet now he had botched things up by marrying Joyce, the stupid cow. How was he going to get out of this? How was he going to get his real son back? His mother would know. Putting on his coat, he yelled up the stairs: "Going out," and left.

"What is it with you, son?" Esther asked. "Why do you do things like this?"

Steve said nothing, he sat head down, his gaze fixed firmly on his shoes. Esther had to have her say before she would help him so he was not going to make her angry by interrupting.

"You walk in and out of the lives of these young women with absolutely no concern for their feelings. It's all for yourself, isn't it? You consider yourself God's gift to women. Now you want me to help you get out of this marriage?" As her voice rose alarmingly, Steve's hopes sank as low.

Esther put the coffee mugs on the table and, opening the fridge, brought out an apple pie.

"Want it warmed up?"

Steve's heart rose, she was okay with it. If she wanted to feed him, she had forgiven him.

"Yes, please, Mum," he said, grateful it was all over, bar the shouting.

Esther cut the pie and popped it into the microwave on low for ten seconds. Steve was such a problem because he never thought about the results of his actions. All this bed hopping couldn't be good, the continual changing of partners. Was it that they threw him out, or did he leave? She didn't know and he never said, although strangely he kept going back to them time and time again. It was like once the newness wore off, he didn't want to know anymore. Esther knew that when he saw a woman he wanted, he pursued her lustfully, but once he had what he wanted he didn't want it. How very childish. If he kept on this way, he was going to finish up a lonely old man.

TWENTY-EIGHT

oyce looked around the living room. Toys lay scattered everywhere and she couldn't be bothered picking them up because the kids would only scatter them again. They wrought havoc on the small townhouse. Why had she brought them here? She should have left them with her mother, or at least waited until they had found a larger place.

Both children were accustomed to her mother's, a large detached house with a big back garden with swings and a teeter-totter. The townhouse had a small paved area outside the back door and a strip of weedy grass that the landlord cut once a year, whether it needed it or not. Not that the neighbourhood kids cared about its condition.

Sighing, she began to tidy the room. Unfortunately, after she left her kids with her mother until she got herself sorted, she grew accustomed to having a neat house. It hadn't taken her long to become used to peace and quiet, the ability to do anything she wanted, anytime she wanted. Now she was nothing but a mother, a frazzled mother who wanted out of this mess.

Why couldn't things be as they were? She knew why, it had seemed like such a good idea to bring the kids here. It had, however, turned into a disaster. Naively she had thought they would all grow to like each other and Steve would soon love her children. What a delusion, and now what a predicament because Steve couldn't stand them and was already withdrawing his love, spending more time at the gym and the pub than at home.

If he had a job it might be different. Surely, she had thought, someone would soon employ him, but they hadn't. She noticed all kinds of jobs advertised in the paper, but he wasn't interested, even when she cut them out and gave them to him. Oh, no, she thought bitterly, Steve was only interested in collecting his Worker's Comp. and going to his beloved gym. He had muscles on his muscles now and was a fine figure of a man, but what good was that doing them financially?

Joyce presently worked in a factory office as a filing clerk and her money supported them. Her salary paid the rent and bought food, but since she fetched the kids over, they were having a hard time to make ends meet. The kids needed so many things and were always hungry. She was tired of making do, of going to the food bank, of buying second hand clothes from Goodwill.

No matter how hard she tried, she couldn't make Steve find a job. He kept saying the doctor wouldn't allow him to work until his tendon was fixed. As far as she could see it was perfectly fine. Each morning he ran a mile and had a steady date to go jogging with his pals in the evening. How hurt could it be?

Weary, she put the last of the toys in the large old trunk against the wall and surveyed the room as she rubbed her aching back. It was too small for two adults, never mind two adults and three children. The furniture was ancient castoffs from relatives and soon they would need a new couch. Billy had pulled the stuffing out of one arm, ripped one of the seat cushions, then Colleen had been sick all over it. It smelled horrible though she had scrubbed it twice with Lysol.

No, they were going to have to move. They needed new furniture so Stevey boy was going to have to shape up and get himself a job. Yet how to get him to do something? It was her own fault that Steve was bent out of shape over the children and he wasn't exactly over the moon that she was having another, although it was his.

Quickly she ran a duster over the table and coffee table. It seemed as if she were forever moving heaps of dirt around. The children made such a mess, bringing in clods of mud in on their feet which got trodden onto the parquet and rose as dust onto every surface. When they moved, maybe they would have carpeted floors: though that might be worse, knowing the kids. After she finished the living room, she went into the kitchen where a stack of dirty dishes waited.

"Mummeeee! Mum!" Colleen screamed from outside. Pushing the curtain aside with a soapy hand, Joyce looked to see what was happening.

Billy had caught a dog and was holding it by its collar. The dog struggled to break free but Billy stepped over its body so she was straddling it as she held onto its neck hair. Then she put her body weight on the animal and it collapsed shrieking in agony.

As Joyce rushed outside, she noticed Billy smiling with glee and knew she had enjoyed hurting the dog. A small crowd of neighbours assembled, tutting and shaking their heads. That girl was a holy terror, they said, listing her sins and glaring at her mother who was now carrying the dog to its owner, a smirking Billy running alongside.

Jenny allowed Esther to visit her grandson and not only when they went to see Dr. Ross. Each time she saw him he had grown and was now walking sturdily. His delight in seeing her filled her eyes with tears.

As Esther cuddled him, he put his little arms around her neck and gave her sloppy open-mouthed kisses.

"You're a good boy," she said, kissing his forehead as she picked him up. "What a good boy you are."

Christian chuckled and kicked at her stomach with his feet, windmilling his hands through her hair.

"Don't get carried away now, Esther, he treats everybody like that," Jenny snapped. "Even the mailman gets the same treatment."

Esther felt piqued. Jenny needn't have said that. So what if the child was outgoing with everyone? Jenny should have said nothing and let her enjoy her moment with Chris.

Putting the child down, she watched as he toddled over to the toy he had forsaken to greet her.

"How is your loving son?" Jenny's tone was sarcastic, "Still with his *latest* wife?"

"What do you mean by that?" Esther asked unperturbed. Jenny rarely said anything nice about Steve so Esther didn't expect her to say anything complimentary.

Jenny smiled malevolently. "He was here, you know, wants to come back to me and his son."

"He was?" Esther looked up, shocked.

"Yup," Jenny was smug. She was not going to make it easy, let Esther dig for the information.

"When?"

"Last night, as a matter of fact."

Esther wondered if Jenny were lying, she wouldn't put it past her. Last night Steve had stayed with them, arriving at ten-thirty saying he'd come from the gym. Why would he have lied? It was more likely that Jenny lied.

"He was at the gym last night," Esther said looking everywhere but at Jenny.

"I know," Jenny said, a cat smile on her face.

Esther was determined that Jenny would tell her but that she wouldn't ask. If she had to sit here for hours she would sit and wait; Jenny, she knew, was unable to keep her mouth shut for long.

The evening had gone swimmingly and Richard felt gratified with the results. For a long time he had courted a VP from System House and was now assured of gaining a retainer and contract as their legal advisor.

What a nice life it was, Janet thought. They entertained often and of course somebody else did all the work, caterers, florists, music, cleaning, even ordered wine and liquor. What a lovely way to throw a party. Of course she had to be a gracious hostess, but that was a very small task compared to the gargantuan efforts necessary to bring a dinner party for twenty people together without a hitch.

"It went wonderfully well, darling," Richard said as he unzipped her gown. "Have I told you lately that I love you?"

Turning, she melted into his arms.

"It went well because of you, Richard," she laughed. "I didn't do anything. Your secretary made all the arrangements. All I had to do was attend."

"You were the hostess par excellence, darling. You have a way with you that makes people feel at ease and, let's face it, tonight we had a very diversified group. I noticed how you got old Nunn talking to Munroe and that was a master stroke." He kissed her. "I adore you, Janet, I don't know how I ever managed without you."

Janet felt ecstatic. Richard loved her. She had a life of glamour to the extent that he mixed with such an eclectic group and she wanted for nothing. Blissfully she sighed as he picked her up and carried her to their king size bed.

Then the phone rang stridently. They had forgotten to switch it off after the guests had left.

Richard sighed as he caressed her but made no move to answer it. The answering machine would pick up, but it somehow spoiled the mood. Janet knew he was wondering who was calling at this late hour and why.

Pushing him away, she smiled. "Go on. Go and find out who it is and what they want. I'll keep your place warm for you."

Richard kissed her and padded off to the den to play the tape and assuage his curiosity.

"Janet," he called abruptly, "It's Jenny, something has happened."

"Oh my God. What is it now?" Janet felt a tingle of alarm.

"She was so hysterical on the tape that I couldn't understand her. Maybe you'd better call her."

Janet pulled herself up on the bed and picked up the phone. Richard sat beside her and held her free hand. As the phone rang, she smiled at him tremulously, glad of his support.

"Hello," an unfamiliar voice said.

"Who is this, please?" Janet asked. It was not Jenny.

"No! Who is this calling?" The voice asked.

"I'm Jenny's mother. She called here."

The phone changed hands and she heard the woman say: "It's all right, it's your mother."

"Mum!" Jenny cried, her voice full of tears. "Please come here and bring me home. Please, you've got to. I can't stay here now." She started sobbing and talking so wildly that Janet couldn't understand her.

"Jenny, please let me talk to the lady there. You're hysterical and I can't understand you."

"Yes?" The woman said.

"Who are you?" Janet asked.

"Marg Green, you know, Jenny's neighbour. You'd better come and fetch her. She's going to have a breakdown if she has to stay here much longer."

"What's happened?"

"You come here and she'll tell you. It's not for me to say. You come here and soon."

Janet stared at Richard. "I've got to go over there and find out what has happened."

"Come on then. I'll drive you. It's almost two-thirty."

His coolness impressed Janet. The way he accepted this late night journey, the way he wasn't judging Jenny, although she had spoiled a lovely evening.

When they arrived at the house, it was lit up like a Christmas tree. Janet wondered why Jenny had switched on all the lights.

Janet knocked and turned the handle. The door was open.

The living room looked a mess, toys and clothing tossed everywhere. Paper cups that once held juice or pop were on the coffee table with glasses, cups, cans, bottles and mugs. Old magazines were strewn around, dust and lint lay under the dining table. Janet caught Richard looking around with disgust.

"Jenny," she said, holding out her arms. Jenny threw herself at her mother.

Marg wavered, unsure of whether to stay or go. She decided to say in case the baby starting crying, but went into the kitchen.

"What is it, Jenny, what has happened?"

Jenny raised her tearstained face, mouth open to start whining, when she saw Richard standing in the doorway.

"What's *he* doing here?" she snapped angrily.

"Now, Jenny, I see no need for that," Janet said quietly, "Richard drove me over. It's three in the morning. Now what is the problem?"

Jenny heard the warning tone in her mother's voice. She obviously was perturbed about this call for help. Her mother looked annoyed and that would never do.

"There's a man trying to get into the house," she said, looking around as if he would suddenly appear.

She did seem frightened, Janet thought, and looked over Jenny's head at Richard with raised eyebrows. He shrugged, saying nothing. "Who is he? Do you know this man?" Janet asked, pulling Jenny down onto the littered couch and putting an arm around her shoulders.

"Yes, I know him all right," Jenny said bitterly, "He's out to get me."

"What makes you think that?" Janet asked, mystified by this turn of events.

Jenny used her little girl voice, which made Janet immediately suspicious, and tears rolled down her cheeks. She looked a picture of misery and wronged womanhood. An act Janet had seen often before.

"I went out with him for a drink and now he thinks he can knock at the door any time he likes," she lied.

A drink? More like a roll in the hay, Janet thought, ashamed of herself for thinking it. Looking at Richard, she could see that he had the same thought.

"Why does he think that, Jenny?" Janet sighed. "Come on now, let's have the full story."

"Take me home, Mum. I'll tell you when we get there."

"So this is what it's all about," Richard said, making a moue of distaste. Since their wedding Jenny had been trying to wheedle her way back home. This was only the latest in a long line of ploys. He shook his head firmly as Janet glanced at him, no way was Jenny going to spoil his life. She nodded.

"I'm sorry, Jenny, it isn't possible. We can't take you back. This is your home and here you must stay," she said stoically, though her heart was breaking.

"You'd let me come home, Mum, I know that. It's *him*, isn't it?" Jenny pointed an accusing finger at Richard, her face contorted with rage.

"No, it isn't," Janet said firmly. "You're not going to spoil everyone's life because of some whim."

"It isn't a whim," she whined. "The man is trying to rape me, he keeps trying to get in. Marg?" She called to the kitchen, "Come and tell my mother about the man."

Marg sidled into the room. She knew Jenny had been shacking up with an older man, but had thrown him out when he wouldn't cater to her. He brought over all his clothes and possessions, moving in completely. Then Jenny had packed his things and tossed them onto the lawn. Now he wanted his stereo system back and Jenny wouldn't let him enter the house. No wonder he was mad.

"This man, he wants his stereo back," she said, opting for telling the truth, "That one." She pointed at the black and silver unit on a room divider. "Jenny wants to keep it and won't let him in." She glared at Jenny, who stared back with dagger-like eyes.

"Shut up, Marg, just shut up!" Jenny shouted.

"All right, why won't you let him have his property back?" Janet asked looking at Richard who tossed his eyes heavenward.

"He *gave* it to me," she said pouting, "You know that, Marg, you were here when he gave it to me. Why won't you tell the truth?"

"I am telling the truth, Jenny girl. Norman, he brought the stereo over when you said you liked music. He said as long as he lived here, it would stay. It cost him nearly two thousand dollars, so why would he give it to you?"

"He was sleeping with me, that's why," Jenny spat and regretted it immediately. Her mother's face was a picture of horror and she knew what was going through Janet's mind. Her darling daughter living with another man, and already the mother of an illegitimate child by Steve. Darn it, her trouble was that when she got angry, she found it difficult to hold her tongue. Then it struck her she was taking after her birth mother after all. The thought chilled her.

Richard moved into the room. "Shall we go, Janet?" he asked quietly and Janet stood.

Jenny looked up at her. She had blown her chances of going home now. Wait until her mother found out that she was pregnant. If she could get her hands on money, she must have an abortion. Then again, maybe she should take Steve back and let him think it was his child. Her thoughts ran around like caged mice, twisting and turning to find the way out of a maze.

Janet waited for a second, then picked up her purse.

"We're leaving now, Jenny," she said. "I do think you could have more consideration for other people, calling us out in the middle of the night. If this man bothers you again, I suggest you give him back his property or, failing that, call the police."

"Gee, thanks a lot, Mum, and you too, step-daddy!" She always called Richard that because he didn't like it, emphasizing it as sarcastically as she could. "Yeah, thanks a lot for your support. Where would I be without a loving family, eh?" She almost spat this at Richard, who stood watching, his face expressionless.

Janet knew Richard was justifiably angry. "Jenny, talk this over with Dr. Ross. I'm sure he can help you resolve your inner conflict," she said, reluctant to leave Jenny, but unwilling to accept her into her own home.

"Sure," Jenny scoffed, "Sure, he'll help, I don't think! He'll take me into his house or find me a condo. He'll get me off welfare and back home where I belong. Sure, Dr. Ross can cure anything."

Janet clamped her mouth shut. She was unwilling to get further involved in the situation. The best thing they could do was leave.

Tomorrow she would call Dr. Ross and inform him of this development. Jenny was her own worst enemy, but Janet felt unwilling to do anything to help because Richard meant the world to her and she didn't want to jeopardize their relationship. While she knew she was being selfish, she also knew that no matter what they did, it would not be enough for Jenny.

TWENTY-NINE

t startled Steve to see Jenny outside the gym. "Hello," he said, smiling at Christian in his stroller and stooping to take his small hand. "Hello, my big boy."

"Dada," Christian said, "Dada dada dada."

Steve beamed with joy. "He said dada, did you hear that?"

Jenny stared at him, grim faced. "He says that to every man he sees," she said spitefully. "Don't get carried away with it."

Christian had called Norm dada because Norm had taught him. It was his only word.

"How is he?"

"Same as he looks, fit and well."

"How come you're here?"

"I came to see you."

"That's obvious."

It was not going well, Jenny knew. She had to change her tack.

"How are you, Stevey?"

She smiled her little girl smile and his heart thumped. Jenny still had that certain something.

"Okay, I guess. Not back at work yet."

"You've obviously spent a lot of time here," she gestured at the gym. "Got a great bod, Stevey boy, great pecs."

Steve posed and pulled in his stomach. He knew he looked great, often basked in the admiring glances he received from both sexes when he wore shorts and a tee shirt.

Jenny put out a hand and squeezed his upper arm. "God, it's like iron."

Steve smiled, liking her compliments.

"Shall we go for a coffee? I want to talk to you, Steve."

At the food court Christian sat in a high chair and played noisily with a spoon as they chatted.

Steve looked at her quizzically, he never knew what went on in her mind.

"Why do you want me back with you all of a sudden when you said you'd never speak to me again only a short time ago?"

"I was mad at you, that's all. I need you, Steve. Your son needs you. Look at him. He's the spitting image of you."

"Yeah, he is, isn't he?" Steve felt inordinately pleased and grinned widely. Chris was his son, his very own son. To hell with what Joyce was going to have, he already had a son, a fantastic son.

"Look, Steve, you came over and asked if you could come home and I said no. Well, I've changed my mind. Please come back and live with us. We need you."

He looked at her. Jenny was as dressed up as she ever got. Her blouse of pink and white made her face look peachy. She wore new jeans and clean sneakers and a beauty salon had cut her hair properly so it fluffed out around her head. She looked very attractive, almost as she was the first time he had seen her.

Against his better judgement, he agreed. He could always leave again, for heaven's sake, and meanwhile his mother would be pleased. Anyway, he didn't want to live in a house with another man's kids and a nagging shrew of a wife.

Huh! Some good his mother had been, when he thought about it. She hadn't come up with a way to get him out of his stupid marriage and had, in fact, told him he had to stay with Joyce. Mind you, she loved Christian and that meant she still liked Jenny - no matter what she said.

Marg and Jenny had a flaming row over Marg's opening her mouth and telling Janet about the stereo. They were no longer speaking. Jenny treated her now with frigid glares, even knowing it made getting a baby sitter difficult. Steve had promised to move back in at the weekend and Jenny wanted to go down to Ruby's one evening to pick up a man while she still had some freedom.

Jenny liked sex. She'd picked up many men in her trips to Ruby's and discovered that sex was as good with another man as it had been with Steve. To think she had not wanted to lose Steve because of how he made love to her. In fact, Norm was as good if not better and she'd had two others before him. One had been a complete dud, but the other had been more than adequate. Sex was power. Sex was a way of getting her own back on the world. She laughed when she thought about her old mother doing it with Richard Wyatt. What she wouldn't give to be a fly on the wall in that bedroom.

When she first slept with Norm, she had thought she had found the right man until he started getting too serious and wanted to marry her. That had turned her right off him. She didn't want to become tied down to an older man, an older man with a dead end job. Norman was only a bus driver for heaven's sake!

As for Steve, he was not exactly setting the world afire with his ambition, was he? He would do well enough for the time being. He was young, good looking and well built, and also Chris's father. Once Steve moved in, Norm would get the message and stay away from her.

After phoning around for nearly an hour she got a teenage girl from the next street to baby sit and happily went off to pick herself up a stud for the night.

Joyce wondered where Steve was. She'd been watching the clock for ages because they were going over to his mother's in half an hour, and somehow he had managed to sneak out of the house without her knowledge. Stuck until he got back, she decided to call Esther to tell her they would be late.

"Where's he gone?" Esther asked. This was most peculiar. Steve always came home on Sundays to see them and surely would not have made other arrangements without letting her, his mother, know.

"No idea," Joyce mumbled, "He'll turn up in a minute, I expect. Maybe he went to Becker's." Esther thought she sounded strange.

Two hours later it dawned on Joyce that he had gone for good. The kids were loudly fighting over a game and, because she was angry, she smacked them both. After checking the closet, she discovered that Steve's clothes were missing, the bathroom cabinet was empty of his shaving cream and toothpaste. The rotten bastard had left her!

She immediately called Esther who was most upset, although she didn't offer suggestions about where he may have gone. Joyce's first thought was that he had gone home.

"Shut up, you little pests!" She yelled at the kids who fell silent and watchful. Goddamned man, he had deserted her and she was almost due. What was she going to do with the kids while she was in the hospital? She had a million things to worry about. Putting her head on her arms, she sobbed uncontrollably.

The children looked at each other, their faces frightened. What was the matter with Momma?

For a while she stayed at the table, thinking and sobbing, then felt sorry for the girls who were whispering and anxiously casting glances at her.

"Come on, we'll go for ice cream," she said, wearily pushing back her untidy hair. The poor little things were paying for something they hadn't done. Quickly they laughed, all forgiven, and ran to get their outdoor shoes.

Janet felt like she was drowning in guilt: guilt that she had left

Jenny in her hour of need; guilt that she had called Dr. Ross and told him about that night; guilt that she was living a life of luxury while her daughter and grandson were living in poverty.

Jenny made her feel inept, uneducated. Richard recognized that she was troubled and did his best to help. Nevertheless, Janet grew thin and pale, her hands trembled and she had trouble sleeping.

When he suggested she visit Dr. Ross, she readily agreed, realizing someone had to help her shoulder the load. The whole situation was harming her well being and affecting her relationship with Richard. Dr. Ross was very helpful. He helped her understand that she couldn't take the worries of the world onto herself. Jenny was as she was and would never change, so she must stop letting her child influence her life to such an extent. Talking was easy, he admitted that, but she was not doing herself any good, nor was she helping Jenny.

They discussed FAE, fetal alcohol effect, and Janet came to realize all the childish temper tantrums, all the uncommunicative silence, all the mood changes were a result of FAE. Scholastic examinations could not possibly suggest the presence of FAE, not in a case like Jenny's where few physical signs were evident. The fact that she and Jim had provided a stable and loving home environment was probably the reason Jenny came through her school life with any results at all. Janet shuddered to think of how it could have been if they had simply thought of her as mentally retarded. She voiced this.

"Jenny is not mentally retarded," Dr. Ross said, "She is, however, brain damaged in some areas. Her teachers could easily mistake her behavioural characteristics for Attention Deficit Disorder, yet when she was at school that disorder was not common knowledge. They considered her unmanageable, a problem child. It is only today that we know it as ADD. Your pediatrician's notes show he considered Jenny as hyperactive, although she was a very healthy child in every other way. She's a very intelligent young woman when she tries, though I'm sure you've heard that many times. In some areas she's deficit and in others above average so that the school's overall picture was of an intelligent child. All you can do is accept her as she is, make allowances for her, try to steer her in the right direction. Do not, for one moment, think that she will ever thank you for it, though. Her mind does not work that way and what you take as selfishness is not that at all. She knows no better and never will."

"It's all so hopeless. Will she be like that all her life? Can we expect to see any changes in her behaviour?"

Dr. Ross shook his head. "Some, but that will take time, then again I can't make any prediction. She needs positive reinforcement, a routine, a constant home environment. This isn't to say you should take her back into your home. I don't think that will help her. She has survived now for a long time out in the real world, and from time to time she displays a sense of conscience, of knowing she has made mistakes. Whether or not that will turn to positive action on her part, I cannot say. Suffice it to say, you've done everything you could for her and shouldn't feel the slightest guilt for any of her actions."

"Are there any pills you can give her, any medication that might help?"

"No, and if there were, do you think she would take it?"

"You're right. It would need someone constantly monitoring her."

"Jenny will manage all right once she comes to accept that her actions rule her life."

Janet drove home thinking over what he'd told her. No matter what she did or tried to do it wouldn't change Jenny one bit. Of course it never had, she realized that now. All the hours of worry, days of trying to make her see sense, to see things from an adult point of view, they were a waste of time. Jenny was capable of living her own life, but she had to learn that picking up the telephone to demand help or money was not going to work any longer. In some way she had to wean her daughter from a ready supply of assistance unless, of course, it was an emergency.

As she lay in the hospital bed, Monique decided to get out of the business, wanting now to see her daughter. The police had found her unconscious in a dark dockside alley after a sailor had attacked her and stolen her evening's takings. Now she wanted to get away from this rotten life, to make a new start.

This was the fourth time she had been beaten up and left for dead. Her chosen career was not exactly a safe one, everyone knew that, so why had she gone back on the game each time? Monique did not know the answer, only recognizing that she was fit for nothing else. Who would employ her? What job could she ever hold down? She had no training in anything, no other means of making money than by using her body, or stealing.

Then it came to her, her daughter Jenny was a well educated, sensible young woman and could help her, and suddenly she wanted to see her grandson.

When they released her, she went home to pack her things. Her father would look after the house, such as it was. After his release from jail he had come back to live. Nowadays he never ventured on the streets until it was dark.

After the cleanliness of the hospital ward, the poverty of the small house shocked her. Seeing it, after being in an antiseptic whiteness and after a prolonged absence, only pointed out what a dump it was. Look how the roof sagged, see how ill-fit the windows were. She stood on the sidewalk and looked up at the rotting net curtains in the upstairs window, suddenly realizing that this was destitution. All those men she had let use her body, and look what she had achieved. Nothing, nothing around her but impoverishment.

The envelope that had fallen out of the girl's pocket would help her find her daughter's house. Too bad that the girl was in big trouble with a collection agency. However, the way Monique figured it, if she owed them so much money it must mean that she had enough collateral to cover the loan and couldn't be exactly poor.

She smiled as she caught the bus. While she didn't have much money, she had enough for the bus fare and about twenty more dollars. Her daughter would look after her. Too bad she had sent her away when they had met that first time, but she could always plead pressure of work or something.

THIRTY

"**J**enny, how long has this been going on?" Steve asked testily as he read the letter. Jenny had left the envelope on the table, the flap was unstuck so she must have already read it.

"What?" She turned from the stove where she was stirring something in a pan.

"This," He waved the page at her.

She glanced at the letterhead and knew it was from the collection agency. Normally she tossed them in the garbage, having no money to pay them anyway.

"A long time," she said, stirring the spaghetti sauce.

"They can put you in jail for this, Jenny," Steve said worriedly.

"Nah," she said positively. "My old daddy Warbucks Wyatt would make sure that I got off."

Steve raised his eyes to heaven. Jenny was such a child in so many ways. She treated Richard Wyatt like dirt, and yet expected him to bail her out. "You think so? What did you do with this money, this loan they gave you?"

"I told you that ages ago. I don't know now. Anyway, it was a lot of little amounts, you know, like when I needed money."

"This lot of little amounts comes to more than five thousand dollars. How are you planning to pay it back?"

"Oh, Steve, don't be so serious," She waved the spoon in the air. What a worrywart he was. "I have the money. It's in trust for me as you know. That's how I got the loan. When I get my money, they'll get theirs."

"When is that?"

"When I'm twenty-five," Jenny started laying the table.

"They aren't going to wait that long, you know," he said, his brow rucked with concern.

She shrugged. "If I have to wait, they have to wait," she said firmly. "Old Wyatt will sort it all out. Nothing to worry about, Steverino."

He was not so sure. Jenny was not exactly Richard's favourite relative at the best of times and knowing how she often mocked and belittled him would not make him willing to leap to her defence. She was right, though, he thought, if she had the money coming to her, she had the funds to pay them back.

"Look, you have to pay something back every month. I keep telling you how the interest mounts up and every month you don't pay they add more interest. If you don't do it, you'll have nothing left of your inheritance when it comes time to collect. It'll all belong to these people."

"Yeah, yeah, yeah. I've heard that a hundred times already. Do leave off, Steve, you give me a headache."

Steve tossed the letter aside and watched as she tipped the spaghetti into the colander to drain. Jenny had put on weight, he noticed, and put it down to the fact that she was learning to cook and they now ate a substantial meal each evening.

Or was it food? Hadn't she been off for the last few mornings? Was she pregnant again? If she were, it wasn't his child, that was for sure. He'd only slept with her once without protection since he arrived two weeks ago and, while Steve knew he was not a genius, he was not completely stupid. Narrowing his eyes, he took careful notice.

Christian crawled across the kitchen, the knees of his overalls greasy from the dirty floor. He pulled himself by the table leg and started to wave his arms at Steve. "Dadadadada" he chortled, drool running down his chin. The poor kid, Steve thought, he was always dirty, always wearing a sodden diaper and yet Jenny loved the child, doted on him and yet didn't see his condition.

"Come on, sonny boy, let's change you and clean you up for supper," he said, scooping up a chuckling Chris.

"Don't put clean overalls on him, Steve," Jenny said as he was leaving the kitchen, "He'll only get them filthy the way he spits out his food."

That was true enough. Usually more food spread itself on his clothes and the high chair, than in his stomach, but still he thrived. He gained weight weekly and was hefty and solid with it. A real boy, a boy who would make him proud.

Monique soon found the street. Nice houses, she thought, looking at the long rows of welfare town houses, nice compared to her own home, and lots of young families here.

Walking down the street, she looked at the house numbers. Here it was, needed paint maybe. Screwing up her courage, she rang the doorbell. A tall, well developed young man answered the door.

"Jenny lives here, please?"

"Yes," Steve said, eyeing the woman.

To Steve she looked old, ragged and not very clean. Her face was free of makeup. Deep lines ran from her nose to her chin and she had a scar where a deep cut ran from the corner of her eye to her cheek. A woolly hat partly covered her straw-like hair.

"Can I tell her who is calling?"

Monique smiled, revealing a gap toothed mouth. "But of course, her mother from Montreal."

"Her mother?" Steve gasped as Jenny came into the hall.

"Who is it, Steve?"

She glanced at the woman standing on the step and did not recognize her.

"Say's she's your mother from Montreal," he said, his face incredulous.

"My mother? What do you mean?" She challenged Monique, standing with her fists on her hips.

"Monique Lalande, mon nom, you came to see me with your son."

Jenny stared at Monique. Her hands flew to her mouth. It was her mother! Oh my God, what had she done?

"You'd better come in, I suppose," she said churlishly as she stood back to allow Monique to enter. Steve glared at Jenny, wondering what the hell was going on.

Monique looked around the cramped living room.

"What a nice place you have," she said as she went over to the playpen where Christian sat bashing a teddy bear against the bars and chuckling.

"Ah, mon petit," she said as she stooped to talk to him. Christian chuckled louder and put his arms out to her, wanting her to pick him up.

"Dada, dada, dada," he said.

Steve pulled at Jenny's arm and towed her into the hall.

"What the hell is going on here?" he hissed, "Who is that woman and why did she say she was your mother?"

Jenny pulled free. "Later, Steve, I'll tell you about it later."

"Damned right you will." Pulling his coat off the hook, he started to put it on. "I'm off to the gym. Make sure she's gone before I get back."

Jenny went into the living room where Monique had Christian on her lap. He was sucking on her beads and crowing with delight at having a new fan.

"So, Zchenifare," Monique said in her strongly accented English, "that is this baby's father, yes?"

"Yes, that's Steve." Why had Monique sought her out? What did she want and how had she found her?

"Zis a very nice house. You have lotsa room, non?"

A pang of fear ran through Jenny's heart. "No, we don't have lots of room. We have only two bedrooms, ours and the baby's."

"S'allright," Monique said, smiling widely, "I share with baby."

"No. Steve won't have it. You can't stay here, we don't have the room," Jenny became alarmed. She didn't want this woman in her house, God only knew what germs she carried on her person.

"But Jennifer, I am your mamma, you came to see me. I need to live with you now."

Jenny panicked, she could hardly get her breath. What was she going to do? This was her birth mother and a prostitute. How could she explain that to everyone? She burst into tears.

Monique took the tears a sign that Jennifer was upset that she couldn't have her stay with them.

"Non, non," she said putting Christian back in the playpen and putting her arm around Jenny. "I need not stay with you, you can get me nice apartment, yes?"

Jenny almost had a heart attack. Get her an apartment?

She stopped crying. Her tear stained face set and hard. "Look here," she sobbed, "I'm on welfare, I have no money, not even money to pay for this place. The province pays the rent."

"But your man . . ."

"Steve is on Worker's Compensation. He can't work," Jenny said through her tears.

"Look at this," Monique said, passing Jenny the old envelope. "You got a lot of money, it says so here."

"I *had* a lot of money, I don't have a penny now. Not even enough to make a payment on this loan. So you can't stay here, you can't," she moaned. Oh God, what *had* she done?

"So I stay until I find something," she shrugged, smiling. "I will help with baby and cooking. I'm very good cook."

"You can't! You can't stay here at all," Jenny shouted making her jump. Running to the kitchen, Jenny snatched up the phone. She would call Dr. Ross, her mother, Richard Wyatt, everyone to get the horrible woman out of her house.

Why had she gone to Montreal? Why had she sought out her birth mother? Why, oh, why was she so stupid? Dr, Ross was right, she was her own worse enemy.

Richard smiled wryly as he related Jenny's frantic call to Janet, who was all for going over to the house. He called Dr. Ross about this latest catastrophe. After a great deal of reasoning from Richard, Janet decided not to go to the house. This was Jenny's fault, he said firmly, a situation of her own making and if she were ever to grow up she had to learn to solve her own problems. She could come to no harm, the woman was her mother, and what mother would hurt her child?

Janet was also upset that Steve had apparently moved back in with Jenny. What had happened to his new wife? Steve was a loose cannon, and it seemed like Jenny was always in more trouble when he was around.

"The trouble is, Janet, that you and Jim always bailed her out of hot water," Richard said patiently, "You were someone to run to, someone who would get her out of any mess she made. She relied on you for that, and she's still trying to have you solve her problems. It's constant, you know that, it's one thing after another. You, like the good mother you are, you're always there with a safety net."

Janet smiled sadly. "I know that, Richard, I know that only too well. Dr. Ross explained that it isn't all her fault, nor is it mine. She's suffering from Fetal Alcohol Effect, but I can't walk away from things this way. She's my daughter."

"Adopted daughter."

Janet's head shot up and she glared at him.

Richard knew he should not have said that. "All right, all right, don't look at me like that. However, it's a fact, and one you must face since she has found her birth mother. The fact that she doesn't much like what she found is not your problem."

"I know you're right," Janet sighed wearily, "But, Richard, this behaviour of hers is not her fault. There's something missing in her brain, a gene that affects common sense. That's as near as I can figure out all the medical jargon. It's still so hard for me not to jump in and help, though."

Richard put his arm around her. "Let Dr. Ross take care of it. He's the expert and we know she listens to him."

"What did he say when you told him she's taken Steve back?"

"He sounded very surprised."

"I expect he would be. Jenny was so upset about the marriage when

I was there with her at Dr. Ross's. Apart from getting Jenny to accept my life as it is now and my relatively minor role in her life, it was about getting her to accept that Steve is now married, and wasn't the man for her anyway."

"As I say, let Dr. Ross take care of it. Stop worrying about it, Janet, she won't thank you for it, you know."

"I know that well enough." Janet kissed his cheek. What would she do without Richard? No way was she going to jeopardize what she had with him by allowing Jenny to run her life, no matter how much she loved her.

THIRTY-ONE

Esther gasped. "You did what?" Steve told her he'd gone back to live with Jenny, though not that she was pregnant. "What's the matter with you, boy? Has all that weight lifting scrambled the few brains you have?"

Steve looked glum. While he had not expected her to relish the idea of his leaving Joyce to go back to Jenny, he hadn't expected this reaction.

Esther stood and glowered at him, her arms crossed over her formidable bosom. "You listen to me, feathers for brains, get back to your wife. Pack your bags and go back home where you belong. Joyce is due any minute and who's going to look after the kids if you move back in with Jenny? Don't you have anything in your head but Scotch mist?"

Steve shook his head, this time he was going to dig in his heels. "I'll not go back to Joyce and those screaming kids, no matter who asks me. Anyway, I think Jenny is expecting again."

"What? Oh, my God!" Esther felt like she was living in a soap opera. What next? "You take the prize for stupidity. Do you mean you've been carrying on with Jenny all this time?" Esther glared at her son, wishing him on another planet.

"No," he said stonily. "I have not been carrying on with her."

How stupid he was, this son of hers, did he only think with his groin? "Think about it then, how can this latest be your child? If you only went back to her two weeks ago, you must have rocks in your head to think that this baby is yours. She's having you on."

Steve nodded. "That's exactly what I think, and I'm more than angry. Yes, Mum, you are right, as usual. Jenny took me back to make a patsy out of me."

For a couple of minutes he seemed deep in thought. Esther said nothing. Let him work it out for himself, she thought.

"Right!" he said as he stood, his face set in grim lines. "I'm going back to tell her and then going home to Joyce."

"Good lad," Esther said with a great deal of satisfaction. About time young Jenny learned a hard lesson the hard way.

"Thanks, Mum. Good job I talked to you, eh?" Steve said as he shrugged into his jacket.

"A very good job, and don't go making any other hasty moves until you talk to me, you hear?"

"Yes, Mum."

Esther worked in her kitchen for the rest of the afternoon. Baking soothed her and she made cakes and pies and casseroles until she knew she wouldn't have any more room in the freezer. Feeling better, she made herself a cup of tea and sat reading The Enquirer.

Dr. Ross was not very helpful this time. He diplomatically pointed out that she was the one who had sought her birth mother, after he'd advised her against such a thing. The fact her mother had sought her out now and wanted to live with her was further proof that Jenny had not thought things out before she had acted.

"You'll have to tell her to leave. I can do nothing, Jenny." Dr. Ross wanted her to assume some responsibility for her actions.

"I can't," she whined. "She won't go. She said she'd sleep on the floor when I told her we had no room. She says she'll look after the baby and she'll do the cooking. I told her I didn't want that, but she won't leave."

"Call the police, call Social Services, look after it, Jenny."

"I can't," she wailed.

"Yes, you can," he insisted, "You can do anything you want. It's about time you took on responsibility, Jenny. It might seem difficult at first, but you have to grow up. Fortunately you always had your parents looking out for you and you were content to let them do so. You were so complacent that you rarely made a decision for yourself."

"I suppose," Jenny said sulkily. "I don't know what Steve is going to say about this."

Dr. Ross sighed. She was a walking disaster, this young woman. "Ah yes, Steve. I was under the impression that Steve was now married and his wife was expecting a baby and has two other children. Am I right?" Hadn't she realized that the man had other commitments?

"He was, and she is," Jenny said smugly. "Steve wanted to come back to me. He wants to live with me and I want him back." She smiled, happy at the thought. "He's getting a divorce. We're going to be married."

"You are?" Dr. Ross seemed surprised, she thought. He rarely showed any emotion when talking with her.

Maybe Jenny was what they called a textbook case, he'd often thought, maybe she would be famous in psychiatric books. If she kept going the way she was, she'd probably be in therapy until she was sixty.

"Steve loves me and he loves Christian." She smirked, proud of herself.

"When did he come back?"

"Oh, about two weeks ago," she said, pushing her fingers through her hair, puffing it up. Dr. Ross noticed she'd had it cut and styled.

Esther was playing with Christian outside in the waiting room and they could hear him laughing. Dr. Ross thought Christian was mongoloid, although he hadn't voiced his opinion as the child looked to be normal. It was that he was too happy, always laughing even if he had fallen and hurt himself. Of course, Jenny's condition must have contributed something to his development. It was all down to the same gene source, of course. Whatever brain damage Jenny suffered would be passed to a degree to her children and from what he had heard about the wonderful Steve he wasn't exactly a rocket scientist.

"So what are you going to do about your mother?" he asked.

"I don't know."

"What do you think you should do?"

"I don't know."

"You must have some feelings about it. What does your heart tell you to do?"

Sometimes getting Jenny to talk was impossible, getting her to state her fears or her concerns: while at other times it was impossible to stop the spate of words. At those times he had to make sense of her babble.

"I don't know, but I don't want her living with me."

"In that case you must tell her so. Don't listen to any excuses, don't allow her to stay in your house."

She put out her hand, beseeching him. "Can't you talk to her, please?"

"No. I already told you this is a problem you caused by your inability to think things out properly. You have to resolve it on your own. Take charge of your destiny."

She looked very uncertain.

"How old are you, Jenny? Are you an adult?"

"You know how old I am and, yes, I'm an adult," she said hotly. Stupid old fool.

"Then naturally you are responsible for your own welfare, your own life. Do you agree?"

"Y..e.e.s.s.s, I suppose," she said slowly. Dr. Ross could tell she was beginning to get the picture.

"Why, then, do you expect me to sort out your life? Is it not true that this is the life you chose for yourself when you left home?"

"Yes," Now stronger in her agreement.

"Why do you expect other people to solve your problems? Do you know?"

She shrugged and looked at him under her brows. "Well, they know more than I do. They're older and have more experience."

Wonderful, he thought, she was at long last beginning to recognize that age had some qualities. To date she had always been down on her elders, thinking they were all out to spoil her fun.

"Did you speak to your mother Janet, about this?"

"Yes."

"What did she advise?"

"That I tell Monique to get out," words started to rush out. ". . but *she* should do it, she's my mother, or Richard should do it. He's a lawyer, he should . . ."

"Why should they do anything?"

"Because."

"Do you think that's a good answer, Jenny? Because? Because what? Because why?"

"Because."

"Small children use that expression, Jenny. I thought you were an adult."

"Oh, all right!" she snapped. "They should do it because they're my family. I don't even know this woman so why should she park herself on my doorstep?"

"Oh, do they know her?"

"Well, no, but . . ."

"You admit you're the one who sought her. She would naturally come to you."

"I don't want her," she sobbed, "Someone has to get rid of her. It wasn't my fault that I was adopted, was it?"

"I prefer it if you stopped thinking that way, Jenny. We've talked about this before, have we not? You must start to take charge of your life, Jenny, tell this woman to leave. You admit you sought her out and brought her into your life, so it is up to you to send her away."

Dr. Ross was right and she knew it. She'd been so stupid, so block headed, so always right about everything and all she'd done was ruin everything for herself. It was not going to be easy, it was going to be the hardest thing she had ever done, but she *was* going to do it. Suddenly it came home to her that she brought these things on herself. It was like someone had opened a door in her brain, someone had let light penetrate a dark corner and she saw her faults, but even as she saw, the door shut again.

Yes, time to take charge. Nobody had said that being an adult was so difficult. She had naively thought that automatically she would know what to do and when and how to do it. However, it wasn't that way at all.

Joyce knew she was soon going to be in labour. It was like when the other two had been due, she was very hungry like the previous times, and had been stuffing food into her mouth since she got out of bed.

Thankfully Steve had come home two days ago. Looking out the window, she could see him working on the old swing set. A neighbour had put it up twice already, but somehow the kids managed to free the legs enough that it became unsafe. This time Steve was setting the legs in concrete.

"Steve," she called through the kitchen window, "Come here, please." Time to tell him how to feed the kids and look after them for the few days they would hospitalize her.

As she took her already packed bag from the closet and placed it in the hall, she wondered how he would cope. The kids didn't much like Steve, no matter how much he tried to bribe them. They were a lot smarter than he in many ways, their minds were sharper, and they always managed to get the better of him.

Steve clattered into the kitchen and started washing his hands at the sink. "Well? What do you want?" he asked belligerently.

"I think it's going to be today, Steve," Joyce said lifting her huge stomach in both hands. "I recognize the signs. You'd better not go to the gym this afternoon. Stay here in case."

He sighed, a miserable sigh as if already dreading his upcoming ordeal with the kids. "If I have to, I have to. So can I get back to what I was doing now?"

"We need to talk. I have to give you a list of what to do and when to do it."

"Why would I need a list?" He counted off on his fingers. "I get them up for school and send them off with a sandwich and an apple. They come home after school and I feed them. They can play outside for an hour and then it's time for a bath and bed. What's so difficult about that?"

"Yeah," she was sceptical. "Sounds like you've got it sorted all right, but those kids aren't going to cooperate with you for one minute."

He stuck out his chest. "I'm the adult around here. What can two small kids do?"

She laughed. "Oh, you'd be surprised. Sit down and let's get this sorted out." Pulling the writing pad and pen toward her, she said: "If I make a list you won't have to worry about anything, follow the instructions."

The kids started screaming in the yard as if they were killing each other, but that was normal and neither bothered checking.

Steve sat at the table, unwilling to waste time on such trivialities, but he'd better let her think he was interested. Joyce had a tongue like a sword when the mood took her.

How would he manage with those two little savages? How could he get them to cooperate? First chance he got he would buy ice cream and chocolate bars, earn himself some brownie points.

THIRTY-TWO

t didn't take long for Jenny to realize that Steve had left her again. He hadn't come home from the gym at supper time, not that that was unusual, but when he stayed out all night, she knew.

Monique was sleeping on the couch, much to Jenny's annoyance as she could not make her understand that she had to leave: or Monique knew it and didn't want to understand. They had a screaming row, to which Christian added a penetrating screech of glee. Monique remained in the house and had no intention of ever leaving it as far as Jenny could see.

She lay in bed and thought about things. Now Steve had gone, she had no reason to throw Monique out. Her prime reason she used about him not wanting Monique there had apparently left her. What was she going to do? Dr. Ross had told her that she had to do it herself, so had her mother, and Richard Wyatt would never help.

That only left Esther. The day after tomorrow Esther would come to take her to the doctor and Esther had a sharp tongue and a way with her. If she could last out that long. The woman was getting on her nerves.

Esther's nerves were worn to a frazzle. Things were getting worse instead of better. Now Steve had left Jenny and gone back to Joyce. Joyce was in the hospital, having given birth to a girl. Jenny was at her wit's end and couldn't get her birth mother out of her house and demanded that Esther oust her.

She felt exhausted, what with rushing over to help Steve look after the other children, and arguing with Steve about his parenting skills. Esther had many arguments with Frank about her constantly leaving him to fend for himself. Now she was trying to keep her sanity when all about her was chaos.

Not that anyone who did not know her well would recognize her inner turmoil, as outwardly she was all calm efficiency. Because of the stress, she was watching her temper and was being soft spoken and agreeable. Frank recognized it as a bad sign.

Jenny called Easther as she was getting into bed. It had been a long hard day and she pulled a face as Frank handed her the phone.

"Yes, Jenny," she said, her free hand forming into a fist.

"Esther, please come to my house and move this woman out. She's been in the bathroom now for nearly an hour and I'm busting."

Esther's carefully controlled temper let go.

"What? Listen to me, that is your house and you heave her out of it. Don't call me and expect me to come over to do the dirty work for you. It's bedtime and I'm tired. Why the hell should I get out of bed because you can't get into your bathroom? Go next door and use theirs. Then tell the woman to get out."

"They've gone to bed next door. Marg next door won't speak to me any more," Jenny whined. "Please come and move her out of here, please help me."

"Go and pee behind a bush, then. Stop calling me, Jenny. Call your mother, call Dr. Ross, but stop calling me! I'm liable to say something I'll be sorry for if you keep this up. Goodnight!" Slamming the phone down, she glared at Frank as if it were all his fault.

She settled under the covers. "That girl is driving me bananas. Why do I put up with her whining?"

"Maybe because it was Steve who got her in trouble. She's a nice young girl," Frank said his voice calm, trying to smooth things out. When Esther was annoyed, it was usually he who paid the price.

"Nice young girl? Nice?" Esther sounded incredulous. She sat up, pulling the covers off him. "That nice young girl chased after our Steve until she caught him, Frank, and she got pregnant on purpose so he would marry her. Mind you, I thought she could be the making of him at one time."

"Can we switch off the light, Esther? Time for sleep, not talk."

"Oh, go to sleep, you old fool. Time was when we shared our problems. I've got them all calling me and you sit back and watch me wear myself to a shadow."

"That's because you will insist on shoving your oar in, Esther. Stay away from them, tell them to get lost. They're all adults now, not children. Let them get on with it and make your life peaceful."

"Easier said than done, lad, easier said than done," she said as she wearily snuggled down under the covers.

Nevertheless, she had to take his advice, what with Steve and Jenny she'd no time for herself or Frank. Frank was a good husband, he loved her and she loved him, but she was pushing things these days. Yesterday she had forgotten to make his lunch. That annoyed him.

Janet felt pleased that Steve had again done his disappearing act, as she thought Jenny's taking him back had been a bad mistake. It hadn't particularly eased the problem because now Jenny felt deserted and was constantly calling her, asking her to come over and evict Monique.

Richard refused to have anything to do with the situation. He forbade Janet to get involved. This hurt, although she felt pleased he had put his foot down. She wasn't willing to face the mother of her daughter, she never wanted to see the woman, never mind evict her. Poor Jenny, she was always so sure everything she did was right and it usually resulted in her making a complete mess of things.

When was her daughter going to grow up? Janet still felt a real sense of guilt about leaving Jenny to fend for herself, though Dr. Ross advised her not to interfere. That, along with Richard's forbidding it, relieved some of the blame she placed on herself, but didn't make her feel much better. Somehow, though, she felt like she was letting Jenny down and while her heart went out to Jenny, they were all correct.

If she were a victim of Fetal Alcohol Effect, and she agreed with Dr. Ross's diagnosis, it explained so much. They could have lavished everything on Jenny, and they essentially had, and still it wouldn't have made her into anything other than what she was now. All their work was for naught, all their love wasted. She was glad Jim had never seen Jenny as she was today. It would have devastated him.

Strange, she thought, how much influence Jenny had on so many lives, though God forbid she would ever know it. Apart from herself who suffered from Jenny's sharp tongue and selfishness, look at Esther who out of the goodness of her heart still took Jenny to see Dr. Ross. Esther who baby sat from time to time at a few hour's notice. Esther who was right in the middle of the feud between Jenny and Steve. It must be harder for Esther than it was for herself, since she lived so far out of town.

Then Steve. The poor young fool still was on compensation and unable to work. According to Esther, his marriage with Joyce was already on the skids, and Janet knew his limited capabilities offered him no escape from a life of near poverty. The fact that Jenny was constantly calling him and trying to see him, would make his life even more difficult.

And Richard, concerning Jenny annoyed him because she made Janet miserable and he hated to see Janet upset. Then Dr. Ross who must be at his wit's end when it came to making Jenny see sense.

Christian, poor defenceless little Christian. He was a lovely child, Janet thought, Dr. Ross diplomatically suggested that she have Jenny take him to be checked. So far Janet hadn't mentioned it, having decided to watch the child carefully. So he was happy? Was that so unusual? On the other hand Janet had never seen him crying for more than a second or two for the past six months; if he bumped himself or fell he laughed as if it were a huge joke. He still could only say 'dada'.

She sighed, how difficult life was sometimes. Look at Jenny, she was the one with real problems and yet they were all sitting back expecting her to solve them without help. Surely a girl could not suddenly become a mature adult overnight? Not one with Jenny's behavioural problems. Maybe she should call at the house, ostensibly to see Christian, but also to size up the situation. To put her mind at rest.

Richard wouldn't like it, that was for sure, and she didn't want to go behind his back, but she had no other recourse. Talking to Jenny on the telephone was not the same thing at all.

"Where are you?" Guy asked, wondering why she had called him.

"I'm with my daughter in Ottawa," Monique said, hoping he didn't suggest a visit. Guy Bonsoleil had been her pimp for the past three years. Today she had to talk to a friend, no matter what. This daughter of hers was very moody, she never talked unless it was to tell her to get out.

"I am not doing so well without you, Monique, when are you coming back? The other girl is stupid and keeps pocketing the money, and I miss you.

"I don't know. I need a break, after my accident and all . . ."

Monique could not say it aloud - that she had been beaten up by a drunken customer.

At least he wanted her back. Someone wanted her.

Janet, dressed in a power outfit of a tailored navy blue suit and white blouse, simply told the woman to pack her bag and get out. Monique, recognizing authority, meekly picked up her purse and coat and went out the door.

Jenny looked at her mother through new eyes.

"Oh, thank you, Mum," she said as she hugged Janet. "I don't know what I would have done about her. She wouldn't leave, no matter how much I begged her. Yet you told her to go and she went."

"Well," Janet smiled, glad it was over so quickly and painlessly. "I suppose it's not what you say, it's the way that you say it."

Janet felt pleased with herself now she had one less problem. Richard would be furious if he found out she had been here, but she made Jenny promise never to mention it. The formal suit had been her suit of armour, something to hide behind. It worked and she needn't worry about Jenny for some time. Though by the look of her, she was again pregnant.

While she had been at the house, Jenny had said something strange. "All I can say is that I hope I'm more like you than her."

"Do you think so?" Janet felt greatly pleased.

"Oh, you know . . .," Jenny said, not elaborating further.

Janet thought about it as she drove home. Did this mean that Jenny hadn't liked what she had seen of her birth mother? Maybe through this close contact Jenny discovered her birth mother was not a very nice person. To Janet, Monique looked like an old lady, older than she and yet she knew that the woman was at least fifteen years younger. She must have had a hard life, but then Dr. Ross had said that she had been, and still was, a prostitute.

If only they could talk about it, she and Jenny. If she'd only been open with Jenny from the first instead of keeping the secret all these years. Thinking about it made her very sad and tears flooded her eyes. She didn't see the intersection, or the gravel truck.

Two days later Janet gained consciousness in a hospital bed. Richard sat at the bedside holding her hand.

"Richard," Her voice sounded growly and dry.

"Janet," He smiled at her. "Thank God. You're going to be all right."

Janet had been unconscious since they had brought her in and they were watching her vital signs carefully. He pushed the bed button to summon the nurse.

"Lie still darling, everything is going to be all right. Relax, I'm here with you."

Janet sighed shallowly, her chest hurt. She tried to smile but her face felt stiff. Moving, her arm hurt and the back of her hand hurt where they had inserted an intravenous drip.

Memory slowly returned. Something had happened when she was

driving home. She had been in an accident. She dozed off even as the doctor came to see her.

Richard spent many hours at Janet's side. He'd not told Jenny about the accident yet, but now Janet had regained consciousness he must let her know, although Janet was still in intensive care and could have no visitors other than himself.

THIRTY-THREE

Steve felt hungry and cold. He strolled along the street after working out at the gym for hours. The days were drawing in now the clocks had been set back. At the house, things were at sixes and sevens as Joyce had not cleaned up or cooked him a meal since her return from the hospital. The squalling new baby had her entire attention. Well, he'd had enough of being nagged at or ignored. His life had been miserable since he went back to Joyce.

Childbirth obviously agreed with her, he thought. She was in fine fettle now and forever nagging. His mother, the interfering old bat, was always at the door, coming to see his latest child, her lovely grand-daughter. Ashley, Joyce had named her, Ashley Waterton-Rigby. Sounded like an upper class British twit name to Steve who would have preferred something like Rosie or Daisy.

His mother, oohing and aahing over Ashley as though she were a princess, ignored him, spending her time either cuddling the baby or talking to Joyce like they were the greatest of friends. Women! He was at his wit's end. He went to see Jenny, but she refused to open the door. Sitting in his pickup in front of the house, he saw her when she ran to the house next door but one. She was visibly pregnant. That was enough for him. He left.

Rita wouldn't even talk to him, hung up when he called her. What the hell was he going to do? What else could he do but run? Run like hell to somewhere else, somewhere where they would never find him.

Yet where? He had little money, no prospects and his Workers Comp. cheque for the month was already spent. Miserable and upset he walked slower, reluctant to enter the house.

Jenny suffered terribly with morning sickness and nausea that became so intense and lasted so long that in desperation she went to see the doctor. He immediately admitted her to the hospital. Marg, unable to turn away someone in need, took in Christian and promised to look after him.

When she called home to tell her mother, Richard answered the phone.

"Oh, it's you," she said, her tone not exactly diplomatic.

"I could say the same thing, I suppose," Richard said snippily, "And what is your latest problem?"

"I'm in the hospital. Will you tell my Mum?"

"Is it serious?"

She looked at the phone in her hand. What was it with him?

"Not very, only observation."

"Your mother is in intensive care in the Queensway-Carleton," he said in an icy voice. "She was involved a bad car accident. She can have no visitors apart from myself."

"What?" Jenny was aghast. "Weren't you going to tell me about it?"

"If I had, what would you have done for her?" Richard asked sarcastically. He had not wanted to sound so nasty, but he was worried sick about Janet. He had called Jenny but nobody answered and had been going to try again later. "I thought it best that I told you once we knew she would be all right."

"Will you tell her I'm in the Grace Hospital?"

"I don't think your mother is in any condition to hear anything at the moment. Keep me informed, though." He hung up.

Richard felt bad about his abruptness, but Jenny had to learn that the whole world did not revolve around her. It irked him that she had not uttered one word of concern, had not asked how Janet was, had thought only of herself. Oh well, if her illness was not serious, why should he worry an already weakened Janet?

Jenny slumped against the wall in the telephone booth. Round and round went her thoughts. She couldn't make sense of things anymore. Tears of self pity ran down her face. Right now she needed her mother, now more than ever, but her mother had been in an accident and that stupid old sod Richard Wyatt hadn't told her. Suppose Janet had died? Would he have told her then?

Hysteria at her own condition, worry about Christian and the news about Janet combined to cause her to faint. A passing nurse called a doctor. She miscarried.

Esther was upset. She cried and cried when Richard called about Janet. To Esther, whose world was very insular, Janet represented affluence, sophistication, high moral standards and good manners. To think she had nearly died in a car crash. How terrible.

After hanging up, she immediately called Jenny, nobody answered. She must be out at the mall, she thought. After her fifth attempt she called Marg to ask Jenny to call her.

"She's in the hospital, Esther. Went in yesterday. I don't know when she'll be out."

Esther slapped her forehead with annoyance and worry. "What about the baby?"

"He's here with me and mine. Good little boy, no trouble."

"I'm coming over, Marge, I'll pick him up and fetch him back with me. I'll call Jenny." She grabbed the pencil and pad. "What hospital and room is she in?"

Esther called the Grace Hospital and learned Jenny didn't have a phone in the room. They told her, however, that Jenny's condition had improved. She would be up in a day or two. Esther left a message with the nurse about Christian.

She went to Marg's house to get her grandson. He was such a lovely cuddly boy, hugging her tightly around the neck when she picked him up.

"He's gone, I tell you, vamoosed," Joyce said tearfully.

Esther sighed irritably. Another problem: one got resolved, and another immediately arrived on its heels.

"Have you any idea where he could have gone?" she asked, racking her brain.

"Maybe he went back to the girl and his son," Joyce said wearily, not much interested at this stage. She had enough problems. "I don't know where he went."

"No. She's in the hospital and I have Christian here with me," Esther said. Esther felt the burden of everything on her back. Why did everyone call her? "Have you checked with the gym?" she asked lethargically. "Has he been there?"

"First place I checked. No, he's not been there since last week."

Esther rubbed at her forehead. "Well, I do know one other place he might be, leave it with me and I'll call you back."

Rita knew nothing, not that she would have told Esther even if she did, Esther knew, but she sounded sincere enough, Esther thought. That young fool, Steve, always causing bother and fuss. She fed Christian and played with him until he got sleepy. What a lovely boy he was.

Frank came home to discover Esther and Christian asleep on the sofa and his dinner drying out in the oven. What now? Why was the baby here? He crept into the kitchen and ate.

When Joyce telephoned at eight, Frank answered the phone.

"Any news yet?" she asked.

"News about what? What's going on now?"

"About Steve."

"What about Steve?"

"Who is it?" Esther asked, coming into the kitchen rubbing her eyes. "Give it here, Frank."

She grabbed the phone from his hand and spoke. "Is that you, Joyce? No, nothing to report. Call the police. I would. They'll find him for you."

"I can't report him as missing for another day, Esther. Fortyeight hours, they say."

"So, call as soon as you can," Esther said impatiently. "I don't know what I can do for you, Joyce. I have no idea where he is."

As Esther hung up, Frank cleared his throat. "Sounds like young Steve has done another runner."

She took out a cup and saucer and her chamomile tea. "He sure has. I'm getting tired of being on call night and day with this family, Frank." She checked the coffee pot, poured Frank a cup and set the kettle on to boil.

"It's your own fault, Esther. I've told you time and time again to let them get on with it. It's because you interfere that you now have to take the flack. That baby, how long's he going to be here?"

She glared at him. "That baby is your grandson, Frank and he'll be here until they send his mother home from the hospital."

"How long will he be here?" he insisted.

"I don't know. I'm going to the hospital tomorrow and I'll find out then."

Frank heaved a big sigh. "I like the child well enough, but surely at my age I am entitled to a quiet life. Surely I could come home to a decent meal and an attentive wife. I only want to relax, but you've stopped that. You're such a busybody, you always have been."

She listened and knew he was right. Too bad that he was getting long in the tooth for her shenanigans because she sincerely meant well.

Jenny felt relieved when the doctor finally agreed to tie her tubes. She didn't want the responsibility of more children, wanted to have a full sex life, have some fun while she was young. The nutritionist gave her a lecture and a book. The stay in the hospital, however, had given her a chance to think.

Even as the doctor had tried to talk her out of tubal ligation, she pointed out that it was her body. She didn't want more children, no matter what he said. Now, she thought, smiling, she was free to sleep with whom she chose, with no worries.

Dr. Ross visited to talk to her. She figured he was worried about her therapy sessions being in jeopardy, and as long as the province was paying him, so he should. If she had her way, she'd never go near him again. Still and all, he had helped her a great deal. Not a bad old stick, she thought, deciding she might as well continue seeing him. It didn't cost her anything. He seemed upset about her being ill, so she cried to please him.

After reading her file, her decision to have tubal ligation surprised him, she was so young, he said. When she pointed out that it didn't seem like she would ever marry and already had a child, he still expressed amazement that she would take such a drastic step. It was as though he hadn't thought she had the sense to realize unwanted pregnancies were not only dangerous, they were costly. He'd taught her a great deal without knowing it, had Dr. Ross.

After seeing him for months, she had become expert in knowing where his questions were leading and answering as she thought he wanted. What she didn't know was that he knew what she was doing and slanted his questions in a way that brought him the right answers.

Richard Wyatt sent a potted plant from himself and her mother. Esther came down and visited, fetching Christian who was overjoyed to see her.

"Steve's gone again," Esther said bluntly.

"I know, I told you," Jenny said, smiling as she played with Christian.

"No, no. I know you told me that he'd left *you*, I mean now he's left Joyce and the kids."

That was such good news that Jenny laughed and laughed. Esther found it so infectious that she had to join in and Christian chortled happily, looking from one laughing face to the other.

"Sorry, Esther, I know he's your son and all, but he is such an idiot,"

Jenny said, wiping her eyes. "I'll be darned if I know what I ever saw in him." She noticed as Esther stopped laughing, and pulled her face. "Sorry, Esther, but you know what I mean."

"Yes, I do, Jenny. Trouble is that all his faults come bouncing back to me, as if I could do anything to make things right. Last night Joyce must have called me seven times. And when he left you, you were always calling me." Although she would never have admitted it, Esther liked always being on call - it made her feel wanted.

"Never mind, maybe he'll sort himself out and be a better person for it," Jenny said, personally of the opinion Steve would never change now. He was too old to change. It didn't occur to her that she should change her own attitude.

Esther nodded. "One has to hope. Look at his brother Shawn. Such a good lad, got a good job and sticks with it. Steady girl he's got, single, intelligent and good looking. I think they're living together, although Shawn would never tell me if they were. Still, he's no bother at all, never a cause for worry with him. I don't know where we went wrong with Steve, I really don't."

Later, after Esther had gone, Jenny considered this statement. Did your parents make you what you were? Maybe they did, they certainly browbeat you enough. Look at her Mum and Dad, they were always nagging her about stuff.

Maybe Dr. Ross was right, Monique had nothing to do with the way she turned out, she was as she was because of Janet and Jim. Yet her mother, Janet, didn't see that or like it. Still, she must have inherited something from Monique, her love of sex maybe, or her stubborn streak. Look at the way Monique refused to leave when asked, look how she refused to listen when Jenny argued with her. Yes, she supposed she had a lot of Monique in her after all. Horrified, she shuddered, recalling the raddled face and worn out body. Janet, sophisticated and well dressed, was probably older than her birth mother. Yes, she would have to work hard to change herself into being more like Janet: think before she acted

Why was Steve so stupid and Shawn so clever? Esther was very sharp and Frank she didn't know about, although he seemed nice and talked a lot of sense. She guessed Steve's problem simply was that he *was* stupid.

As for herself, look at all the years when she rebelled against everything her parents wanted for her, that was her power, power to make their lives miserable, power that became a habit. She had thought that she knew best, that she what to do and how to do it. Yet when it came down to it, she'd spoiled everything she'd ever touched. Yes, she suddenly saw how she had ruined her own youth, spoiled her relationship with Janet, spoiled it with Steve.

She sighed, thinking she had been too young and inexperienced to see the result of her actions. Maybe that was what growing up was all about, maybe you had to listen to your elders, learn from their mistakes instead of making yourself miserable. What worried her was, if your mother had rotten genes and was destined to become a prostitute, did it follow that you would follow in her footsteps? She would hate to be such a person, but hadn't she gone chasing after men and slept with them? Lying back, she stared at the ceiling and thought about her life, what did she want? All she wanted was to find a nice man who loved her, who she could love back, marry him and have a quiet life with lots of kids. Though now, after her operation, kids were out of the equation. If he were wealthy, so much the better and they could adopt.

Thinking about her life as it had been when she lived at home, it slowly dawned on her that she owed a lot to Janet. Poor Janet, she had called her names, even said she hated her. Right now her mother was in intensive care and maybe would die, and the only memory she had probably retained was of Jenny saying she was glad that she wasn't her mother.

Tears sprang to her eyes. How stupid she had been, how selfish, thinking about herself, as usual. This soul searching brought home to her how rotten she'd always been and yet she had no idea of how to fix it. It was like Janet had always told her, no matter how much you apologize or atone, you could never take back a single word of what you had said. She sighed. Trouble was that words spouted out of her, like she had no control over her thoughts or her mouth.

When they discharged her, she decided, she would go over to the Queensway-Carleton to see her mother. It was imperative she saw her quickly, to tell her how much she loved her. Somehow she had to make up for all the bad things she had done and said, if it were at all possible.

Steve cadged a lift from Ernie, a trucker friend of his and accompanied him to Toronto. Ernie, on his way to the Oshawa Wholesale food terminal, dropped him off on Lakeshore Boulevard near the downtown core. Steve still limped but now he could walk a long distance without pain. Feeling carefree for once, he strolled up to Yonge Street. This was the place, he thought, a bustling city with lots of jobs going.

After walking around for an hour, he realized he was cold as his only outer wear was a bomber jacket that did little to retain heat. Wandering around Simpson's and Eaton's to get warm, he realized that apart from forty dollars and the clothes on his back, he was destitute. Where could he find shelter?

When he wandered through to the subway, he stopped to chat to a wino slumped on the stairs getting in everyone's way. If anyone knew where one could get a warm spot for the night, he would. After rambling around downtown streets, he discovered winos and street people filled the mission houses. Distressed at the state and smell of them, he decided to head to the food terminal to cadge a lift back home. He had not yet sunk that low.

Going into Woolworth's cafeteria, he read the Star newspaper someone lad left, and looked at the Situations Vacant. With a sinking heart, he realized most jobs were for professional people, people with computer skills, people who had degrees. The other jobs were minimum wage jobs that would hardly pay for a room over his head. He could get lots of those back home.

Stupid, he was, stupid! What had he thought he would find elsewhere? He had no university degree, no higher education, no training, no experience. His heart sank. He was a loser, a born loser. Why had he run? What had he expected to find? At least back in Ottawa he could possibly find a place to stay until he found work. As he got off the subway and started walking to the terminal, he grimly faced his future.

Did he want to live with Joyce and her two kids by somebody else, plus one of his own? What future was there in that? Not much as far as he could see. If Joyce had stayed as she was when they first met, maybe things would look different. Yet disenchanted with him and her life - something that never have occurred to him - she had turned into a shrew. He found nothing to look forward to with her but a life providing for two kids whom he didn't even like, and one of his own, while Joyce turned into a junior version of his mother.

On the other hand, did he want to stay with the childish Jenny and Christian? He considered that as he slogged along. Jenny had prospects, that much was in her favour. She would inherit a tidy sum when she was twenty-five, at least if she didn't keep borrowing against it, and when her mother passed on she would inherit more, he was sure. Then, too, Richard Wyatt, Jenny's stepfather, had no other children, so maybe she would inherit his estate. Of the two, Jenny seemed the better prospect.

Feeling better about things, he whistled as he walked the road. So getting away had accomplished something, it had cleared his mind. He could talk about it with Ernie on the way back.

THIRTY-FOUR

Esther was happy as a clam with Christian at the house. She watched as he played with the pan lids he had pulled from under the sink. One lid hit the other with a satisfying clatter of metal and he chortled.

"Can we have some quiet, do you think?" Frank asked irritably from behind his newspaper. They were sitting in the kitchen waiting for the roast to finish cooking.

"He's enjoying himself," Esther said, "Aren't you, lovey?"

Clashing the lids against each other, he crowed with delight.

"Gawd! A man wants peace and quiet when he gets home. Take them lids off him, Esther."

"Go in the other room if you want quiet. He's playing," Esther watched fondly as Christian tossed two of the lids against the stove where they made the most satisfying racket.

"I don't know what's come over you, woman," Frank said, tossing the paper down and standing. "You'd never let our kids make a din. Why do you let him? If he does that again he'll chip the enamel off the stove and then what will you do?"

Esther smiled at Christian. "Oh, do leave off, Frank, let him play. He reminds me of our Steve when he was that age."

"Oh, yeah," Frank said sullenly, picking up his paper again and turning it to the sports page. "The way he's acting he's going to be as puddled as Steve is. Not a brain in his tiny head."

"How can you say that?" Esther turned on Frank with a glare.

"Anyone with half an eye can see he's not right. Look at him, drooling all the time, can't say nothing but 'dadada' and he's not even walking properly yet, ten steps and he falls over."

Esther picked Christian up; he laughed joyfully and pulled at her hair.

"How can you say a thing like that? There's nothing wrong with the boy. He's a late developer."

"Oh, yes," Frank was cynical, "It'll be about forty years before he learns to speak at the rate he's going right now. Take him to the doctor and get him checked out if you don't believe me." Frank went into the lounge and collapsed into in an easy chair.

Esther followed him. "Do you think he's backward?" she asked worriedly. Now Frank had mentioned it, surely it was not right that Christian was perpetually laughing and jolly.

"When was the last time you heard him crying?" Frank asked, "I'm not talking about a few tears when you take something off him that he wants. I mean crying because he's hungry or wet or hurt?"

Esther sat on the couch and set Christian down at her side, he laughed up at her, drool running out of his open mouth. She wiped it with the cloth diaper she always had on her shoulder, Frank snorted at the child's dribble.

Frank was right, she decided, Christian was abnormal. Wiping his chin, she picked him up again. He was such a lovely child, though, he didn't look mentally deficient or anything, it had to be that he was a late starter. Nevertheless, he had a certain look in his eyes, something that pointed out that things were not right with him.

Worried, the following day she took him to the free clinic. They were very helpful and a doctor did some simple tests. Of course, he told her, the child's mother should take him for proper testing, voicing concern that the child's doctor had not already suggested it. Esther knew Jenny had not taken Christian for a check up since a month after she'd come home from the hospital with him. Then he was a small baby, so who knew how he would develop? She did some very fast talking.

The doctor told her that Christian could be mentally disabled, that he may have developmental trouble, suggesting again that the child's mother take him to the Children's Hospital for a proper diagnosis. He was a healthy child, he said, that much was obvious, but someone should diagnose his condition before he grew much older.

With a heavy heart Esther drove home. Poor little tot, he was backwards all right. Frank would be only too happy to say 'I told you so!' Why hadn't she noticed it herself? Maybe it was because the child was her first grandson, and she didn't want to acknowledge his failings. Suddenly she recalled Janet mentioning something a while back, something about his always laughing, so maybe Janet also suspected.

What was Jenny going to say, and why hadn't she taken him to the doctor? Had she also known his condition and decided to ignore it? Exactly what Jenny would do, Esther thought grimly. Well, now she had to tell her face-to-face that Christian was mentally retarded, whether Jenny wanted to hear it or not.

Frank said nothing when he heard, except, "So?"

"Will you come with me to tell Jenny?"

Frank looked at her. His wife was a strong woman, little she shirked, even the delivering of bad news. He nodded and smiled, Esther needed him.

When Steve got back to Ottawa he headed straight to Rita's, knowing it was possible that her latest had dumped her, or she had dumped him. In either case, he would have a place to stay.

His luck was in. Rita's lover had become engaged to another and Rita was at a low point. She was very glad to see him.

It was not long before they moved to the bedroom where Steve rid himself of a great deal of frustration and Rita of a great deal of anger.

"I want to see my son grow up, though," he said as later they talked about his situation.

"So?"

"I don't want to go back to Jenny. She's such a spoiled child."

"Sounds like you're between a rock and a hard place." Rita said, wondering why it took him so long to figure things out. "Why don't you take the baby and bring him up yourself?"

"That's not on, 'Ree. How could I do that? Even if Jenny would let him go, and I very much doubt that. I have no job and no home."

Rita narrowed her eyes. She was running out of time as far as having her own children was concerned. Look at her, she didn't even have a man and the years were rushing past far too quickly.

Rita looked at him for a second and decided to take a chance. She couldn't be too choosy anymore, she decided, she needed a man in her life.

"We could get married, you and I. You could get a divorce and then we'd get married. We have a home here and I have a job to support us and you can keep looking for one. When you get one we could move to a town house so then we'd have a small garden. Children need a garden."

Steve looked at her with admiration. Good old Rita. He had always liked Rita, she had a good head on her shoulders and used it well. It might work, it might. A load shifted from his shoulders.

They talked about it for hours and had made all their plans by the time they went to bed.

Janet was relieved to hear they were moving her out of intensive care. Although Richard visited each day and kept her company for as long as they would allow, she looked forward to moving out of the quiet, hushed and sometimes hectic ICU.

"I'm getting you a private room," he informed her.

"Why?" Janet asked. She was looking forward to having a room mate, another woman with whom she could talk. While she loved Richard very much, sometimes a woman was better as a confidante.

With Richard she was careful not to let him know how very worried she was about things, about the way she would look once they removed the facial bandages. Would he still love her if she were ugly? Would he feel repulsed?

Richard squeezed her hand. "I want you to have some space around you, a nice room with television and radio, a private nurse to tend to your needs, a bathroom. It is a shame the way they rush the nurses on the wards off their feet. They've cut staff back so badly that you could burst waiting for a bedpan."

"Lots of people are on the wards, what about them?"

He kissed her hand. "Indulge me, Janet, let me do this for you. I want you to have a private room. Once you're mobile you can visit the other wards as often as you like. You're going to be here for a while, so it might as well be in comfort."

"Thanks, darling," Janet said, she loved him so very much and, of course, they could well afford it.

Janet thought about the coming few weeks. The doctor said she would be taking physical therapy for at least a month. A niggling worry was that she would be permanently lame, but had been assured that the bones were knitting well. Yet it was not her leg that concerned her, it was her face and neck. She'd already had minor surgery twice on her face and knew it must look horrible if the look on the nurse's face was anything to go by when they changed the dressings. If only she could look in a mirror, she thought. Intensive care had no mirrors.

Richard was also worried about her reaction once they removed the dressings. After seeing her terribly scarred face he was arranging for her to go to California where the best plastic surgeon practised. The doctor would restore her looks, and maybe even improve on them.

It was to prevent anyone showing disgust or alarm when looking at her face, he'd ordered the private room and a private nurse. The sooner he could get her booked into California the better and until such time he would move heaven and earth to protect her.

Steve thought about it long and hard. On visiting Jenny's house, Marge the next door neighbour, told him Jenny was in the hospital and Christian was with his grandmother.

"What happened, she have a accident?"

"She got sick and lost the baby," Marge said watching his face.

"Oh," was all he said.

"Guess it wasn't your baby, eh?"

He shrugged as he said a mental prayer.

"Got to go." He walked away.

At least he would not get stuck with another child. In fact this was perfect. He would visit his mother and pick up his son. His mother would let him take him out for a treat, he was sure. That way he would pick up his son and simply wouldn't take him back. It was all working out wonderfully well.

"Yet will she let you take him out?" Rita asked when Steve told her.

They were in the small kitchen where she was making an apple pie, Steve's favourite. She paused, her hands covered in flour.

"Of course. I'm her son and he's my son. Why shouldn't she?"

"What about your wife?" Rita asked worriedly, "Won't your mother want you to go back to her?" She started to roll out the pastry.

"Of course she will, what do you think? Mum's always sticking her nose into everybody's business. Anyway, I'll do what I want. I don't answer to her," Steve spoke with a conviction he didn't feel. His mother would attempt to have her own way, she usually did, but in this case she couldn't force him to go back to Joyce, no matter how many children were involved.

"What about the other baby, your daughter? Don't you want her as well?" Rita stared at Steve. "I sometimes wonder what goes on in your head." In this instance his thinking had her flummoxed. She put the pie on the counter ready for baking later. Steve liked hot pie.

"Nah. Who wants a girl?"

"Well, you for one," Rita laughed, pointing at herself.

He put his arms around her. "You're a woman and that's different. A man wants a son, not a daughter. Let Joyce keep her. She's used to girls."

"Are you sure we can keep Chris? Won't Jenny have the police on you?" Rita felt worried now. She had wanted the child, but only by legal means, not through kidnapping. She thought about it as she cleaned up the table and counter.

Sighing, she turned to him. "Is this going to work? I mean I know he's your son, but he's hers too."

Steve grinned. "Don't worry so much, 'Ree. Like you say, he's my son. You and I are a couple. She's a single mother with not much between her ears, so who do you think will get custody in the long run?"

"Her stepfather is a big time lawyer," Rita said shrewdly, knowing that Richard Wyatt was one of the city's top legal minds. "Won't he have something to say about it?"

Steve didn't think so. "Nah. He doesn't have much time for Jenny. She's so childish and selfish that she doesn't brownnose. He doesn't like that, I expect."

Rita considered other stumbling blocks. "So what about her mother? Won't she make trouble for you? You told me she doesn't like you."

Steve decided to tell Rita the truth. "Janet's her stepmother. Jenny was adopted. Her birth mother lives in Montreal. I met her twice and I didn't like her. A tart, she is, not a very nice person. Everybody says so."

Rita gasped. "Jenny adopted? Who would have thought? Still, no matter what you say, Steve, this isn't going to work unless it's done legally. Even if he is your son, you can't walk in and kidnap him. They have laws against that."

Steve threw out his hands, Why was she making waves? He had it all figured out. "Come off it, Rita. It'll be okay. You and me will have a son and you'll be a proper mother. Won't it be great?" He looked around the apartment. "Just think, we'll have to buy some furniture, a crib and stuff. I'll fetch his stroller with me when we come home."

Rita gazed into a very murky future. Somehow getting Steve and his son was not giving her a good feeling. Not this way. If they legally granted him custody, that might be different.

As for Steve he felt pleased with the way things were going. He would get his son and Rita to boot. They would be very happy and now luck was back on his side he'd soon find a job. They would get married, buy a house and be a real family. Steve had not considered the consequences of his actions.

Putting on his jacket, he headed for the door.

"Going to get our son now," he said, his face happy. "Get some baby food in, some diapers. You know what to do."

Rita nodded, her face grim. Somehow this was wrong, terribly wrong. Whatever had possessed her to suggest he get his son? Steve had a one track mind at times and it was her fault that he was all charged up and determined to get Christian. Fretfully she sighed and went to change. She would buy the baby food and diapers in case he did bring the child home, although she was praying his mother wouldn't permit Steve to take him out.

It was definite, Jenny could go home. After the doctor gave his permission for her release, the first thing she did was call Esther and tell her to come get her.

Esther felt annoyed. How come she suddenly was the family chauffeur and general dogsbody? Jenny wasn't even a relative, come to that. Grumpily she agreed, thinking she would have the bother of taking Christian as well and he was a right nuisance when she was driving.

Jenny sat in the day room and thought about going home. Soon she would be back with her son. Good. Of course she had the worry about the bills that would be waiting for her. The darned credit agency would be dunning her again and threatening legal action like they did every month. If Janet would only help her out financially. She had pots of money and so did Richard Wyatt.

Still, if her mother was in the hospital maybe it wouldn't be a good time to start asking for assistance. If she hadn't been so stupid with the money, maybe that would have helped. She could hardly recall enjoying the thousands she had borrowed, apart from the small car that was now a heap of rusting metal at the curb, completely vandalized.

Yet what could they do to her? Nothing, as she was on welfare and had no collateral. Yes, they would have to go whistle for their money, she thought, shrugging off the problem. If Steve had stayed with her, he could have sorted things out properly.

Richard smiled at Janet as they took off the dressings, determined not to let any indication of concern show when they revealed her face. It was bad, the bruising was terrible and her cheeks and chin were badly swollen.

"Not bad at all," The doctor said with a certain amount of satisfaction. "It looks better than I had hoped. Soon have you back to normal, Mrs. Wyatt."

"May I see it?" Janet asked before they put on another dressing.

"Not today, it would only upset you. However, I assure you things will be much better in another few days. The bruising from the last operation looks bad right now but is quite normal."

"Will I have scars?" Janet asked worriedly, putting up a tentative hand, afraid to touch her face.

"Some, but we can take care of those later. Meanwhile, don't worry so much. I've seen far worse. I can assure you that I'm exceptionally pleased with your progress."

Janet sighed and looked to Richard for assurance. He nodded and smiled, trying to reassure her.

"The doctor is right, Janet. If you had only seen what you looked like right after the accident, you'd know that you look 100 percent better today."

Janet wondered because Richard had kept his face so very still. No flicker of any emotion crossed it when they had taken off the bandages. That meant it must be absolutely horrible.

After they had dressed her face and gone she looked at Richard.

"Tell me the truth, Richard. I know it's bad. I could tell by your lack of expression."

"How do you know?" So he hadn't pulled it off. "My lack of expression was because I was trying hard not to upset you, yes, but also because you know what a softy I am about things like this."

Janet considered that. Richard was a big baby in many ways. Even a thing as tiny as a paper cut was to him a major accident. Maybe he was right and it wasn't as bad as she thought. She smiled.

"I'm arranging for us to go to California when you get out of here," he said.

"California? You mean I finally get to go to Disneyland?" She laughed. A holiday would be what she needed when they released her.

"I've made an appointment at a private clinic for you. Doctor Weinstein is the foremost plastic surgeon in the states." Janet's blood ran cold, she was horribly disfigured: he thought she was ugly now. "He does work for most of the movie stars."

Janet burst into tears. "Oh, my God! I'm ugly," she sobbed as Richard sat on the bed and put his arms around her.

"No, no, no," he laughed. "This is simply to attend to the small scars that remain, and a holiday too, remember. Disneyland?"

"Okay, if you say so," Janet said tearfully. She so wanted to believe him.

"Believe me, darling, would I lie?"

Actually, yes, you would, she thought, knowing he would do anything to make her happy.

THIRTY-FIVE

Esther went to Jenny's room.

"Where's Christian?" she asked as Esther walked into the room empty armed.

"He's with Steve," Esther said, expecting fireworks.

Steve had so surprised Esther when he walked into the garden, that she almost dropped the washing she was hanging out to dry.

Not for Esther the disposable diapers, she used cloth ones. Fortunately she still had a whole drawer full she had not disposed of after the boys were toilet trained. Over the years she used a lot of them as dusters, they were so soft. Now she had a whole line of diapers drying.

"Hello, Mum," he said, as if he were paying a daily call instead of returning from God knew where.

"Hello, stranger," Esther said, not very pleased with his actions in leaving Joyce. "Where've you been?"

"Toronto. Where's Chris?"

"Asleep. What did Joyce have to say when you got back?"

"Not much."

Esther looked at her son. He was lying, she knew. "When did you get back?"

"Last week," Steve said, realizing he had put his foot in it. He prayed that Joyce had not spoken to his mother since then.

"I wonder why didn't Joyce call me," Esther said, looking at him closely as she took some dry diapers off the other line and folded them.

"Oh, she's been too busy, what with the new baby and the kids," Steve said airily. Too airily.

Esther glanced at him sharply. "Strange she didn't call. She called me often enough when you took off. You been to see Jenny?"

He didn't look at her. "No. I thought it best not to."

"She'd like to see you. She lost the baby, you know."

"Uh-uh," He shook his head, though Marg had told him. He felt released somehow at that news, although he was not the father. One less thing for Jenny to hold over him.

Esther started up the path. Time for elevenses. Over a cup of coffee she would find out what her stupid lout of a son had been up to this time.

It was with some reticence that she allowed Steve to take Christian out for the afternoon as it would save her nerves while she was driving to the hospital. He had wanted to walk the baby so badly, to spend time with him.

"You let Steve have the baby?" Jenny was livid. "How could you?"

Esther kept her voice even. "He *is* the child's father, Jenny, and you know how Christian is when I'm trying to drive. Anyway, you're coming back with me to the house, I'll look after you for a few days."

Jenny sighed with frustration. She wanted to go home, to be on her own with her son, not stay with nosy old Esther and her nerdy husband. Probably Steve would keep popping in to play with Christian.

Jenny had thought long and hard about Steve over the past few days. It finally sank in that he was a loser. She realized he was a nothing and would never amount to anything. Her life would be better without him in it. Look at the way he kept popping in and out as if she were just a convenience. Look how he had two-timed her, slept with other women while they were living together. Enough was enough. She didn't want to see him again. Her mother would be so pleased, she thought. That news would cheer her up no end.

"Do you think we could stop at the Queensway-Carleton so I could see my Mum?" she asked, trying to be nice since Esther had the wheels.

"Your mother's still in intensive care and you won't be able to see her." Esther said firmly. "Why don't you phone Richard first? He'll probably pick you up and take you to see her when she can have visitors."

"Darn it all," Jenny said hotly, "My mother is ill and I *want* to see her."

"I'm sure she wants to see you too," Esther couldn't resist getting a dig in, "Though I don't know why she should, after the way you treated her."

"Yes, I've thought about that a lot, actually," Jenny said quietly, surprising Esther who'd never noticed her caring about anything but herself. "She's put up with a lot from me over the years, I know that now. That's why I have to see her, I have to tell her how sorry I am that I said all those horrible things."

"She was going home from your house when she had the accident, you know. I do hope that you parted amicably," Esther said waspishly as she navigated her way out of the full parking lot.

Jenny glanced at her. Esther was trying to blame the accident on her, she could tell. And come to think of it, it probably was her fault that her mother was so upset. "Yes, we did as a matter of fact. She threw that woman out of my house, you know," Jenny switched to her old peevish tone. "That's more than you would do, wasn't it?"

"No, and why should I? I wasn't the one who fetched her from Montreal." Esther refused to take blame or castigation. "I know Janet was very upset when you went to Montreal to see her, and personally I think it was a terrible imposition for you to ask Janet to get rid of her."

Jenny smiled smugly. She usually got her own way in the end and this was no exception. "My mother loves me," she said, "She'd do anything for me."

Esther glanced at her. What a selfcentred individual Jenny was, completely oblivious to anyone else's feelings. She clamped her mouth shut, wishing now that she had not offered to have her at the house for a couple of days.

By seven that evening, Jenny was frantic with worry. Steve hadn't come back with the baby, and even Esther became concerned. For hours she'd been making excuses and offering explanations as to Steve's tardiness. As time passed it was obvious, even to her, that Steve had kidnapped Christian.

Jenny, ignoring Esther's pleas, called the police who swung into action. Esther sat shredding a Kleenex, thinking about the big trouble Steve was in, while Frank sat reading his paper, completely unconcerned at the hysteria around him.

Steve felt ambivalent about the baby now. Within half an hour of taking him home, Rita pointed out Chris was not right. He was mentally defective, practically a mongoloid, she said. They had a terrific row, and all the while Christian laughed at their loud voices and played with the wheels of the stroller.

"Take him back, Steve," Rita said, "Jenny must know about his condition and is probably frantic with worry. Take him back to your mother's *now*."

"Come with me?" Steve asked, ever the coward.

"No way. Hurry up, Steve, take him back."

As he drove back to his mother's, Steve kept glancing at Christian who was sleeping, lulled by the movement of the truck. His son was retarded? *His* son? It made him feel sick to his stomach and he suddenly found Chris repulsive. Rita was right. The child's place was with his mother.

When he arrived back in Carleton Place, his mother yanked opened the door. "Where on earth have you been, son? Jenny's here and she's already called the police to report him being kidnapped." Esther got a great deal of satisfaction out of Steve's alarmed expression.

Jenny rushed out of the kitchen.

"Christian, Christian. Come here, my little love. How could you, Steve? How could you take my baby and not bring him back?" She kissed the baby who woke up and gurgled happily. "I called the police on you. They're probably looking for you right now. I hope they arrest you and throw you in jail."

Steve watched as she cuddled the baby. Christian smiled up at her laughing, glad to be back in his mother's arms.

"I'll be going then," Steve said, opening the door. "All this carry on is silly. You'll call the police, Mum, and tell them it was a mistake, eh?"

"I suppose," Esther said, not very pleased with the upset he had caused. "Another thing, you haven't been home. The first place I called was there and Joyce said she's not seen anything of you since you left."

"Yeah," Steve hung his head, unable to look her in the eye."I was going to go home, but then I couldn't, Mum."

"Well? What about Joyce and your other child? Are you going to desert them completely?"

"I suppose I am," he said shortly. How could she know how trapped he felt? How could she know what it was like to have two other kids dumped on you like that?

"This isn't good enough, Steve. We didn't bring you up to be like this. What's happened to your good sense, your morals, your compassion? You can't waltz in and out of women's lives, leaving a trail of broken hearts and fatherless children. You need professional help, Steve. See a doctor, get yourself sorted out."

"Yes, Mum," he murmured as he went out the door. It would be a snowy day in hell before he let his Mum run his life again. To think how hard he had worked to get out of this house, how hard he had tried to get out from under his mother's thumb.

"By the way that kid is a mongoloid," he said to them with a great deal of pleasure, quietly shutting the door behind him.

As he started the truck, he began to think about the baby. Was it because of him that his son was retarded? Did his genes carry a defective link that had turned Christian into what he was? It hardly bore thinking about if he wanted more children. He turned the truck around to go to Joyce's, to look at the new baby, needing to set his mind at ease.

Jenny laughed as she tickled Christian who lay naked and freshly bathed on the big bed. He was so lovely, he loved her and she loved him. Tenderly she wiped the drool from his chin.

"Jenny," Esther said as she stood in the doorway. "When you've put him down for the night, please come to the kitchen. We need to talk."

Jenny glanced back at her. What was the old bat nosing into now?

"Would you like some hot chocolate?" Esther asked when she came into the room.

"Please."

"Christian is not normal, Jenny," Esther said, as Jenny sat at the table. "You must know it yourself. You aren't stupid. It's like Steve said, even he can see it, and that's saying something. No use being an ostrich, putting your head in the sand and hoping it will go away. It won't."

Jenny sat sullen and mute. Esther was always poking her damn nose in everybody's business. Christian was fine, he was a slow developer, hadn't Esther herself said that many times?

Tomorrow she would make Esther take her to see her mother. To heck with calling Richard again. He hadn't wanted her to go to the hospital and bluntly told her so. Whom did he think he was? Janet was her mother and he hadn't known her as long as she had.

Suddenly her adoption had come to mean a great deal to Jenny. Dr. Ross's explanation when he first told her about it, suddenly clicked in. To think her mother had chosen her from all the other children she might have taken. Lately the thought that she might have grown up with Monique made her feel nauseated. Her mother would tell her the truth, she always had now that she came to think about it. Esther was annoyed because Steve had turned out so badly; it was all spite on her part.

"Will you take me to see my mother tomorrow?"

"If you like, but you probably can't see her," Esther warned. "She's not allowed visitors."

Jenny thought that a conspiracy. They were all preventing her from seeing Janet, which meant that something was terribly wrong. Was her mother dying? Was she disfigured? What was the reason?

That night she couldn't sleep. Lying awake, she thought about the baby. If he were indeed retarded, what did that mean? Could she look after him as he grew older? Would he grow out of it? Maybe they could give him drugs to cure it.

Again her mind flipped back to her mother. Why wasn't she allowed to see her? Had Janet asked that she must be turned away from the ward? Everyone was against her, Esther, Steve, Dr. Ross, Richard Wyatt, maybe even her mother. Jenny tossed and turned; her life was rotten. Never had she felt so unsettled and unhappy.

Miserably she thought back to her big romance with Steve. Once he was the man of her dreams and now she could hardly stand the sight of him. How could he have changed that much? Or was it that she had changed? Though it seemed hardly credible, that must be the case. She was more intelligent than he, everyone knew that, so it had to be his fault.

If only her mother had allowed her to go back home. If she were home, everything would be different. Things wouldn't be in this huge mess. She wouldn't owe all that money for a start, she would live in a nice house, a comfortable house. Why, oh, why had she ever left home?

As she tossed, she realized she was again thinking only of herself. Not once had she given much thought to Christian, only how his condition would affect her life. Surely that was very selfish? Her current problem with the finance company was her own fault. Why should she expect someone to bail her out?

What was it her grandmother Holme had once said? "If we hate it, we probably created it." Well, that was true enough, wasn't it? She had put herself into debt. As for Steve, Steve was a moron, and she had only herself to blame for staying involved with him. Look at the trouble he had caused her, and hadn't her mother and father tried to warn her? Yet had she listened? No.

All those hours in the hospital when she had thought about things were coming back to her. She had to change. She had to think about other people before herself, surely she could put more effort into that. It was easier said than done, of course, she realized it, but knew she had to try.

If she remained as she was, selfcentred and stubborn, she wasn't going to be very popular in the future. Dr. Ross had tried to tell her that ages ago, but she hadn't listened then as it hadn't made much sense. Now she felt she had to make a change in herself, had to become more caring, warmer as a person. Was it possible to change so drastically she wondered? Could she remake herself?

THIRTY-SIX

Richard didn't want to argue with Janet, but she was trying his patience.

"All right," he sighed, "I call her and tell her to come tomorrow evening."

"Thank you, darling. You do see that I can't go to California without seeing her? You said yourself that she's called every day."

"Yes," he said, thinking selfish Jenny was on the take again. Surely she would come with open hands, begging for something.

"I'll be very relieved to see her," Janet said, "She must have been worried."

"Yes."

Somehow he didn't think Jenny was worried. If she ran true to form, there had to be something more to her visit.

Dr. Ross had asked Richard to come to his office when they first hospitalized Jenny. They talked about her problems and he pointed out that her condition was not curable. Fetal Alcohol Effect manifested itself in many ways, and unfortunately with Jenny it was not obvious until he had taken time to dig into her psyche, to psychoanalyse her. He was positive now her condition was as he had diagnosed earlier. She would never be totally in control of herself or her emotions, he said, would never have the sense to know that she put herself in jeopardy because of her actions. However, the baby was everything to her and Christian's condition was probably a result of the defective gene Jenny carried.

Richard listened to him with something akin to horror. Janet probably could not accept this diagnosis, never see Jenny's mental impairment. He would not mention this conversation until she was much better, more able to handle it. It was with a sense of relief he heard Dr. Ross say Janet already knew about it, that they'd had a long talk.

They would always have the worry that Jenny might do something foolish, and yet he knew he could never have her under the same roof as themselves. It would ruin their marriage. He would support Janet, though. He loved her and his heart bled for her, knowing how she'd lavished love and affection on a child who could not return that love.

Now Jenny was coming to visit and he prayed it went better than he anticipated.

For a second Jenny stood in the doorway looking at her mother, thinking she looked awful and all those bandages.

"Mum!" Jenny said moving to the bedside. "Gosh, it's good to see you. I was so worried and *he* wouldn't let me talk to you."

Richard frowned.

Janet put out her arms and hugged Jenny to her. No matter that she was a problem child, no matter what she had said in anger, Jenny was her child and she loved her.

"Now, tell me what's been going on," Janet said, settling back for a chat.

"Well. . . euew, your face is a mess isn't it? You look awful."

"Thank you. I needed that, Jenny." She had to smile.

Jenny didn't hear, she was all wrapped up in herself, Janet noted, as she listened to the stories. All about Steve running away, first from her and then from his wife: about him trying to kidnap Christian, about the baby being mentally deficient, about everything. Strangely though, through it all, she noticed Jenny did not whine, although she mentioned how hard things were with her, how she was suffering and how Janet had to help her because she was her mother. She spoke in a normal conversational tone of voice and that was a first for her.

Richard sat at the window and listened to her tale of woe. He didn't interrupt.

"I want to thank you, Mum, for adopting me," Jenny said suddenly, looking at her shoes, unable to look at Janet directly. "I want to thank you for throwing my birth mother out of the house. I want to thank you for everything. I haven't been a good daughter, I know that now and I want to say I'm sorry for anything I did to upset you. I want you to forgive me."

The tears sprang to Janet's eyes. Jenny was sorry? "Oh my dear, of course I forgive you," she held out her arms and Jenny sank into them, half-lying on the bed.

Richard watched with barely concealed amusement and impatience. What was the girl up to now? Not for one second could he bring himself to believe any of it, although it sounded genuine enough.

"I am sorry, Mum. When you got hurt, it was my fault. I upset you, didn't I?"

"Let's not talk of that now. The past is over, time to look forward," Janet said firmly. If it were only that easy, she thought. For all her apologies it was going to take a long time for them to become close again. "What are your plans?"

"Guess what? I've got a job, in an office too!" Jenny said with a great deal of pride. She was going to work for a small factory in their office and while it was only an entry level position, it could lead to better things. "Marg is going to look after Christian while I'm at work."

"What about the baby?"

"They tell me he has to have some tests, Mum," she said worriedly, "He's going to need special care and special schooling. Why did it happen, Mum? Was it because of my mother in Montreal? Was it because of her that he's defective?" She looked close to tears.

"Don't worry about it too much now, Jenny, he's still so young, but he's a special child. You'll need to pay him a lot of attention."

"I know. I worry about that a lot, Mum. You know me," she laughed mirthlessly, "All big mouth and not much thought behind it. I have a lot to learn, don't I?"

Janet smiled. How often she had heard this over the years. Jenny saw it in her attitude and knew what she was thinking.

"Oh, I know you don't believe me now, but you wait and see." She stood and hugged herself. " I'm growing up fast of all a sudden. I can see now how stupid I've been, running off to live with Steve, having the baby, borrowing money. You were right all the time." She laughed, though she seemed close to tears. "You know, I think you *do* know more than I do! Dr. Ross opened my eyes to many things and although he says I'll never be very smart, I have to think before I open my mouth, or do something stupid."

Janet glanced at Richard.

"Do we have your promise that you'll listen to Dr. Ross and your mother?" he asked quietly. "Or is this another spurt of hot air?"

"Oh Richard, I'm sorry. I've done a lot of stupid things and said terrible things to my mother . . . and to you. I have learned something, though, and I honestly am going to try." Her face was serious and she sounded as though she meant it. Richard wondered whether it was another of her empty promises, another of her ploys to get her own way. Still, he was willing to listen.

He nodded. "Yes, you're certainly renowned for putting your foot in it. I don't want you upsetting your mother again. If I could for one minute believe what you say . . ."

"Give her a chance, Richard," Janet said holding out her hand to him. "She should have a chance to prove herself. It's the least we can do."

Richard sighed as he crossed the room and sat on the edge of the bed. He held her hand and patted it.

"All right, Janet, only because you want it." He looked at Jenny who now sat on the chair at the other side of the bed. "All right, Jenny, we'll see how it goes. Don't start making demands of your mother, and if ever again you embarrass us in front of other people . . ."

"I won't, honest. Thanks Richard. I will try. Dr. Ross is sending Mum a letter. I expect you'll read it too. He explained it all to me. It's all the fault of my birth mother. She drank alcohol when she was pregnant.

Dr. Ross told me all about it although I can't imagine what that has to do with what I think or feel. So you see it wasn't my fault." She saw the way they were looking at her. "Oh, it's all right, I'm not making excuses. It's a fact. Apparently I'm a case in the journal of psychiatry. Isn't that something? Anyway, I feel better about myself now that Dr. Ross has really talked to me. I'm sorry that I went after that woman, she's not my mother, she was never my mother. I'll make it up to you Mum, honest I will."

Janet smiled sceptically.